Bedear
Rica

The Messiahs
of Princep Street

moshe elias

moshe elias

 **WRITERSWORLD**

THE MESSIAHS OF PRINCEP STREET

By

Moshe Elias

ISBN: 978-1-9041816-1-3

This book is published by WRITERSWORLD, and is produced entirely in the UK. It is available to order from most bookshops in the United Kingdom, and is also globally available via UK based Internet book retailers.

Copy Edited by Ian Large

Cover Design by Marian Hill

WRITERSWORLD
2 Bear Close Flats, Bear Close, Woodstock
Oxfordshire, OX20 1JX, England
☎ 01993 812500
☎ +44 1993 812500

www.writersworld.co.uk

The text pages of this book are produced via an independent certification process that ensures the trees from which the paper is produced come from well managed sources that exclude the risk of using illegally logged timber while leaving options to use post-consumer recycled paper as well.

Behold, I will make thee fruitful, and multiply thee,
and I will make thee a people separate unto me.

GENESIS 48 iv

This book has no dedication except, perhaps,
to the hope of diminishing mistaken belief.

1

My mother, God bless her, conceived me on a Saturday, in September 1933, at night. My father, God rest his soul, was a pious man who spent the Sabbath in synagogue praying, mostly. After life itself and freewill, he said, God's most generous gift to mankind was the Sabbath and in gratitude he shut his shop early on Friday, went upstairs for his weekly shave, slapped Bay Rum, his only extravagance, over his prickling face and massaged what remained on his fingers into his thinning hair. Dressed in the fresh drill trousers and white cotton shirt my ma had starched and ironed, he went down again where she was waiting at the bottom of the stairs to slip a clean handkerchief into his pocket, wish him *Allah wi'ak*, God go with you, and set him on his way.

He walked slowly in his only pair of leather shoes she made it her business to polish for him to look the best among his friends on that day when the spirit of God came down to fortify him. Then, at the end of the service when he raised his voice and said, The Lord shall be One and His name be One, sang the final Amen, kissed and folded his prayer shawl and slid it into its bag, he became buoyant, light on his feet, filled with new energy to take him home after sunset. On that Saturday, probably the second in the month, God must have recharged my father's batteries so full they spilled over and caused me.

We were good friends and in the seventeen years I spent with him I heard every word he said to me. But now, thirty years after he died, I wonder if I had really listened. He was a simple man and nothing he said was beyond me. So what went wrong? Will I hear it differently if I look back? Then what? I can't change anything. Suppose I stitch together a few stories of my life in a kind of order that makes sense, somehow, what then? Well, I could ask myself the questions everyone asks, What if? What if not? That sort of thing and maybe separate dream and hope from reality. Would that help? What have I to lose?

I was their third child. By then my father had well and truly settled into a weekly rota of six ordinary days and one extra-ordinary night, never going any other time in unto my ma as the Good Book describes the coming together of Israelites, that is to say men going in unto women, not in unto each other which it calls an abomination in the sight of the Lord, side by side with going in unto offspring, brothers' wives, beasts of burden and suchlike.

The Torah, by which I mean the five books of Moses, the testament that shaped and stamped my father's life, does not specify when, where, how or under what circumstances a man can go in unto his wife. Except that it is forbidden to uncover her nakedness as long as she is impure by her uncleanness he was free to seek guidance elsewhere and that's what he must've done. Everything a Jew needs to live his life, he'd say holding up the only two books he ever read, is in here, totally. The rest is just words. So, when in doubt, not often, or wanting to prove himself right, he consulted the Shulchan Aruch, a manual to guide those who marvel at God's greatness, are grateful for all He has done for them and want to follow the path that keeps them in His good books.

Under **MODESTY** it advises men not to be too frequent with their wives: well-to-do idle men who pay no taxes may go in once every day, donkey drivers should keep it down to once a week, camel drivers thirty days and seamen six months, in other words don't meddle with other sailors, hold off till you get ashore. With shopkeepers getting no mention, I guess he decided, trades aside, once a week would fulfil his obligations to his creator in the matter of going forth to multiply. A sage said so, what more did he need to sleep secure?

Each night, before shutting his eyes, he wound and put under his bed the Smiths clock, alarm set permanently at 5.45 and woke at 5.30 to turn it off not to wake my ma. Then he got out of bed so rapt in routine I doubt he ever wondered how it might feel to surprise his wife first thing in the morning. Even on holy days – twenty per cent of the Jewish year give or take – when his shop was shut and he could have hoisted his sarong before going off to commune with God in Waterloo Street synagogue just around the corner, he didn't. What chance a sudden flanking manoeuvre in broad daylight?

It may have been the way he was – an average, ordinary man with ordinary needs, content with no more than average due, more ordinary and less than average in the pleasure sector with no real passion except for God whom he, more than anyone I knew, loved and trusted. Or it may have been living in Singapore that made him so.

Stand on the roof of Fullerton Building – the old General Post Office, grand whichever way you looked at it especially if you lived in an attap hut out in the *ulus* – shade your eyes and 135 kilometres to the south, you just about see the equator where nothing changes much. The sun takes a few minutes to rise without ceremony from the South China Sea and twelve hours later plunges head first into the Indian Ocean as quickly and at much the same time each day. In between, for an hour at noon, your shadow squats obediently beneath your feet when you're still and you trample over it when you walk. Now add the two seasons – hot and humid, hot and wet – and it cannot be a wonder that the force of habit holds you down more than gravity. And when the island, all of it, is 42 kilometres east to west, 22 north to south, the numbers less impressive in miles, you also walk slowly.

My father walked slowly and never did anything he hadn't done before and, to be even surer, pulled around him like a security blanket the dozen or so streets he slowly walked. To venture beyond the *mahallah* where Jews lived, he needed friends, best route, bus numbers, how many changes and would anyone accompany him if he chipped in with the fare? All he wanted was to feel at home because, where Jews were, he knew where he was and that gave him a good feeling.

We lived in Princep Street, one of the earliest in the old town Stamford Raffles built after signing a treaty in 1819 with one Malay Sultan of Johore, Hussein, playing him off against his brother Rahman, the other Sultan, in the tried and tested style of divide and rule. Princep Street was away from the sea and behind what was then called European Town, all part of Raffles' plan to build a great trading centre around the natural harbour, encourage free trade, bring in Chinese and Indians by the boatload and build the city.

Jackson, his engineer, laid out the town keeping communities segregated and giving the best parts by the sea to Europeans. No one really minded. There was lots of work, enough food, and natives who could afford it got to live in brick houses that didn't leak in the monsoons. Whites used to call non-whites natives but seeing as how the natives were as much immigrants as the whites, the word got to mean what it didn't.

By the time I arrived more than a hundred years later, we'd become a flourishing Crown Colony bustling with roads and cars, schools and hospitals, amusements parks, cinemas and a race course. The Europeans had taken off into sprawling bungalows on higher ground and cleaner air away from swamps and rivers that stank as the population grew to half a million and, for most people, broadly speaking, life was just fine.

Slantwise from our street ran Selegie Road, *orang selegie* being the Bugis pirates who used to live up the hill behind.

In time Selegie stretched to become Serangoon Road which in turn got its name when people, riding bullock carts along the track through the jungle, hammered gongs to scare off tigers. The other way was Dhoby Ghaut where dhobis used to wash and hang clothes to dry, all of which gives an idea of our part of town. No. 47 was, approximately, in the middle of a block of narrow shop houses, shop-down house-up, and narrow houses up-and-down, the kind of place most of us lived in, in those days, not counting Europeans.

My father sold stationery in a shop without a name or signboard which would've been nice across the front, like other shops, just to invite people in like

---

Welcome we sell paper, all kinds, ink, pencils & rubbers.

Large Stock   Best Prices   Friendly Service

47 Princep Street

---

but he didn't think so. People need names or how will they know to answer when you call them? Shops? Since when? Do I need to pay a Chinaman to climb a ladder and paint a signboard when any fool with one eye can see what I'm selling? Paper. I'm selling paper. All kinds, very thick, thick, not so thick. Cardboard also if you want, minimum order twelve pieces. Pencils, rubbers, anything you need. Ink, all colours, Quink, Pelikan, Waterman, your wish. If you come to buy, ask; if not, pass along please, thank you.

Every morning, not Saturday or a Jewish holiday, he slid out the red meranti planks at the front and stacked them ready to close up at night. The shop then joined the 5-foot way giving a kind of common veranda where people could walk in the shade, browse, buy or wait for a sudden downpour to stop or, more often, sit on stools and eat all manner of food. *Ah pong* and *buboh* and *kutu maniam* men arrived early and sang to tell us it was time for breakfast. When they'd gone, rice and noodle hawkers, Malay, Chinese and Indian brought lunch and so on like a passing parade that came and went and changed the smells to suit the time of day.

The *ayer batu* man, on the other hand, stationed his cart further up toward Middle Road where I'd go with my two brothers when we had one cent to toss to see who got first suck of an ice-ball with all the syrup flavours and colours. When my sister showed up my father gave us two cents for two ice-balls, same colours and flavours. With only two per ice-ball we soon learned how to suck together.

Our shop ended at a bamboo bead curtain after which was the dining room then the open-air kitchen under a zinc roof as if kitchens don't deserve a place inside the house, my ma said, to show proper respect for food, not to mention cockroaches inviting themselves over. The wooden lavatory by the back lane also had a zinc roof and stood two steps up. I called it the Squatter's Palace – squatter for obvious reasons, palace for none. Squatting wasn't the problem but not having a flush was. To look at someone else's, especially my father's, might destroy my respect for him.

Upstairs we slept in two and a half rooms and showered in a cubicle at the end. This was how shop houses were and if you visited one at the other end of town you wouldn't get lost. One more thing. We had a cement patch beside the kitchen up to the back door and open to the sky which my ma said was a blessing to hang washing on proper lines with proper pegs like respectable people and not show our dirty linen from windows like Chinese flags on bamboo poles as if we arrived from Canton in a *tongkang*.

2

Perhaps my father should have opted for Friday. Jewish days start at sundown when the first stars appear in the sky. *In the beginning all was darkness*, then God said, *Let there be light*. If you still don't get it, the Bible gives another clue: *And there was evening and there was morning, the first day.* Each day God stood back to admire what He had created and *saw it was good* until on the sixth day He stopped what He was doing and *blessed the seventh day, and hallowed it, because in it He rested from all His work which in His creating He had done.* There was something magical about the way my father's eyes shone when he read the Bible as if he was in a private place sitting with the angels.

Friday night, beginning the seventh day with God's blessings intact and ongoing, would have been better for conceiving than Saturday night when they'd lapsed with all His hallowing. On that day too, the Sabbath I mean, restful enjoyment of conjugal bliss is especially blessed, proper partners of course, taking time to relish God's strange gift that drives even the likes of beetles crazy. But since nothing can be all good that night was our all-sitting-together-at-the-table family dinner and if there was one thing my father loved about my ma it was her cooking.

Dishes, plates, cutlery may have lost their way and come together in our house from different sets at different times by different routes and the Friday-nights-only faded blue check tablecloth was too small whichever way it lay on the table. But the food was good and my ma always served him the best bits first because she saw her mother give them to her father and, as she said, following suit is the best way to keep peace in the house. So when she put his full plate in front of him and he thanked her, she said his smile was worth all the sweat never mind what the sun on the zinc roof did to her until she was ready to go frantic. That night of all nights was the night my father left the table as full as his plate was empty, praising my ma's hands which did such wonders.

Friday night therefore was out of the question seeing as how his belly would have come into conflict in the manner in which I was conceived.

It had to be Saturday and knowing her husband would soon come in, silent and serious and promptly switch off the naked 40-watt ceiling light, my ma lay down, pulled her nightgown over her feet and put her arms by her side.

Here's a thought. Why do we spend more time and effort preparing for departure than arrival? That one moment decides your life, start to finish, places you go, things you do, people you love, stories you tell, songs you sing, all there, no getting away from it. And it never happens by accident. If you don't wind the clock the bells won't ring.

Shouldn't I wonder what happened that particular Saturday night? My father, much refreshed by the Sabbath, would have been switched on – himself, not the 40-watt light he switched off – wound his clock, not the Smiths. Then? Did my ma's bells ring? Would that have made a difference to how I was put together? Suppose it had been Friday night instead with God's blessings still on hand. Or a different month with planets in a different arrangement. Venus and Pluto, let's say, in friendly orbits. Love and money. What else does a fellow need for a good life? Would my palms have creased differently? I have no girdle of Venus. Her mount at the base of my thumb is flat. My heart line is snapped, long gap, both hands, left more than right. On the other hand Pluto's mount between my heart and head lines is fat and fleshy.

I don't think either of my parents considered for a moment how much depended on what they were doing or that they even gave me, the end product, a single thought. With the quota of a donkey driver my father was following the calendar no passion added. My ma was no more willing nor wanting, just doing her marital duty. Jewish women like her didn't have sex anyway. They received the overflow from their husbands' sperm banks as if fitted with overnight deposit boxes. Did they enjoy being at the performance is not even a question. A six-year-old pays more attention doing homework than his parents did making him. Yet everything, from how your parents were feeling at the time to engagements of stars millions of miles away, affects your making. Otherwise why are siblings so different? Using the same tools, one would think, would produce similar goods, so how come saints and sinners find their way into the same family?

They slept in narrow single beds. Metal frame, loose bolts, cranky nuts, squeaky wire mesh with a kapok mattress, inch-and-three-quarters thick in the unslept parts. She lay in the middle, still, not a word in case God forbid something happened she didn't want to think about. Only after he'd uncoupled, wound the alarm clock, put it under his bed and started snoring would she move.

What's more God made us lopsided, crowding all Adam's tantalisations into a single station while blessing Eve with a pleasure map all over her body. It was she the serpent cosied up to. My father may have been Adam but my ma was no Eve. When she got pregnant with my brother Jonah, her mother said, Fine. Every woman must, once in her life at least or how will her womb know what it's for? But don't make a habit of it, she said, and don't wear hugging dresses. When a woman walks everything shakes and men are men. Wear a rappa like me and soon they forget if your body bumps like a *qar'a yabisa* or goes straight down like a *labu*. So don't come crying and say I didn't warn you.

It worked. Even when brimming over with God's spirit, my father would kiss us children then walk right past his wife in her white Friday night rappa, closed slippers to hide her bunions, hair loose and curly, smelling of Eau de Cologne and go directly to the table. He blessed the wine and the bread, blessed us one by one, blessed the house and anything needing special mention then settled down to eat.

They were man and wife, not lovers. If already they hadn't combined to ensure that any long-term result of their short-term attachment would be well formed and blessed with a long happy healthy life, my ma should have stuck to routine.

Would you like a nice piece of fried fish tomorrow?

He grunted.

In that case I'll need a dollar twenty from your **KLIM** tin first thing to get the fish fresh before the sun kills everything.

My ma was frying fish, my father lost track and I rushed out. What was God thinking about anyway? The way He designed us must have been an afterthought or why would the same body parts have two unrelated functions?

What's more, in no time at all I was ringing the bell and crossing the threshold into my abode for the next nine months. Now it seems I may have been too much in a hurry to get in ahead of the crowd. I should have hung around three, four, five days, asking myself, Should I? Shouldn't I? much as I do these days but then I wouldn't have been who I am and that's a situation I cannot imagine so I'll leave it.

When my ma told my father she was vomiting in the morning, he said it must be something she'd eaten. She should take more care. How many times did he have to tell her not to eat from hawkers? So she told her friends and they said it was time to pay more attention to herself. Housework was one thing but health came first. It was her duty to stay well or who would take care of her if anything went wrong, God forbid? First of all don't eat heaty foods like ginger and chillies and for goodness sake not jackfruit. Durian? Oh God no. A mile away, at least. On the other hand she needed lots of cooling things like barley water and cucumber and banana and the white of hens' eggs and try to rest in the afternoon even half an hour would do her a world of good. Most important, they said, make your husband do the heavy lifting or only God knows what will happen.

As the months went by they noticed she was carrying low, backside spreading, face puffy, clear signs of a girl and wasn't that what she wanted after two boys?

3

An orderly wheeled my ma out of the Labour Ward into the Delivery Room where we didn't stay long, seeing as how I was out in less time than it takes to spice a Calcutta curry, as an old English doctor said under his handlebar moustache, red and black striped necktie peeping over his white hospital jacket, even although tiffin wasn't for a couple of hours.

A young Indian intern, also wearing a striped red and black necktie sticking out halfway down his white hospital jacket to show he was every bit ready for his call in life, laughed louder than it was funny to make a good impression if not as a budding doctor then at least as someone who'd got the joke and enjoyed wry British humour which might come in handy one day.

I made my exit by myself, more or less without urging, fuss or delay, this being the second of the two things I did fastest in my life, going in and coming out, like as though I was in such a bloody hurry to get made and even more to find out what life had in store. The place was blazing with light off white-washed walls, white sheets, white uniforms, the white doctor's white jacket not to mention the sucking-up Indian's even whiter seeing as how he had something to prove. Everything white as if nobody gave a hoot what that does to a baby's eyes that have never seen light.

People were speaking in low voices and someone shouted over my ma's cries, Remove the cord, quickly, round his neck when a kindly nurse said, See, see, Mrs Messiah, a baby boy and I was hanging by my legs between the fingers of the young Indian doctor who whacked my bum harder than necessary to impress the old English doctor that he knew how to open my lungs and start me breathing.

Steady on young man, the English doctor's moustache twitched. You don't want the little fellow to think this is a cruel world which got the young doctor laughing again at such wryness coming so unexpectedly, but not so loud because his hands were shaking. I guess I was the first slippery body he held upside down and what would his career prospects be if he dropped me on my head?

A quick wipe followed by wrapping in a square cloth, also white, like a French loaf with its head showing and I was put in my ma's arms, wheeled out of one door, baby beside mother not to get mixed up, as the next lady was wheeled in. Seeing as how all the others were Chinese with small eyes or Indians with brown skin, fat chance I, with round eyes and skin a shade of beige, would end up with the wrong mother. But this was 1934 and though we had paved streets with gaslights and houses with electricity and running water, the hospital was overcrowded, short of trained staff and with a name like Kandang Kerbau – cowshed – would have you wondering what might walk in from the surrounding fields.

It was fine. Nurses in starched uniforms and caps explained in Cantonese, which my ma could speak, how to slip a hand in behind the nappy before fixing a safety pin and not stab the baby and how to clean him without bathing the first seven days and so on. All good intentions accompanied by a smile as they showed how to make up a bottle of **KLIM** milk from healthy European cows if they could afford it. It may have been okay feeding babies with rice water or soya milk once upon a time but these were modern days and natives should raise their standards, also said with a smile.

My ma said she knew what to do, I was her third and the nurse asked if she boiled the water which got a lady laughing two beds away. Chinese were boiling water two thousand years ago, she said still laughing. Do we need *ang moh kui* to come and tell us? Friendly of course, especially her smile.

19

Well, maybe not *ang moh kui*. Red-haired devil isn't a nice way to describe white folk, but when you use it often it kind of loses its sting.

I settled nicely into our ground floor ward, doors open for maximum cross ventilation, seeing as how only 1st and 2nd class had electric fans. It was spick and span and wherever you looked Indian ayahs were cleaning this showpiece of colonial care. I wasn't coughing, wheezing or making unhealthy sounds. There were no complications, post-natal irritations or staff having to bother with me, though junior nurses did, coming every hour to tell my ma what a beautiful baby boy she had and so much curly hair it was a wonder.

My ma was also doing fine.

Next day the Ward Sister – Chinese in 3rd Class, Senior Ward Sister, Eurasian, in 2nd, Matron, European, in 1st, that's to say segregation by class, colour and height above ground – doing her morning round, told my ma to wrap me and take me home. She wasn't gruff, a little short maybe with so much going on, women groaning, babies crying, nurses smiling, trolleys and wheelchairs rattling in and out and ayahs cleaning everywhere.

My ma, polite by nature, asked nicely if she could wait for her husband to take us home when he came at visiting time.

Don't wait, the Chinese Ward Sister said. Take a *beh chah*.

Okay, that was a bit gruff. She could've said: Why not take a rickshaw, Mrs Messiah, you'll be home so much the sooner. I'm sure your family and friends can't wait to see your boy. He's so handsome, we're all crazy about him, don't I have to stop my nurses picking him up and spoiling him for you? That sort of thing. But she had a point. The hospital was full and beds never empty long enough for mattresses to cool.

No need, my ma said to herself. No need was her way of solving problems. Rules are rules, she mumbled, others have needs, as she could well see, sitting ready to burst on benches along the corridors. She parcelled me head to foot, slung her bag of dirty linen across a shoulder, took me in her arms, said goodbye to the ladies either side who wished her *Hao yun* and out I went in the blistering sun wearing a knitted cap. If anything could've killed me even before reaching the gate it was the sun chasing my pink woollen cap seeing as how my ma took note of what her friends had to say about my gender.

Chah, she shouted to a line of rickshaws across the road which wasn't necessary as one had already come to get us. The man dropped the shafts, raised the accordion sunshade and smiled with a single gold tooth in an empty mouth.

Do you run fast, she asked in Cantonese.

I'm fastest.

I don't like fast. I like slow without bumps and holes.

I'm slowest.

I have a new baby.

No worry. Twenty years best rickshaw in Singapore for baby boys.

Who said boy, my ma asked as she climbed in and sat with me in her lap. My cap hadn't fooled him. I don't suppose Chinese colour-code babies.

Boy baby, mother face happy. Where?

Princep Street.

He tied the strings of his coolie hat under his chin, got between the shafts and we were off.

Too fast, my ma shouted.

Son coming, father waiting, he said without slowing.

Hah, Sabiha, here so soon? My father came out from his shop which brought Jonah and Joshua jumping up and down on the 5-foot way, one with a thumb in his mouth, the other a finger. People came out of shops and houses along the row, asking, Boy or girl? Boy, my ma said stepping down from the rickshaw. Wah, so lucky. Altogether how many? Three, my father beamed. *Allamah*, perfect number, heaven, earth, man, three times lucky, bringing their faces so close I got no more than a patchy look at the down-in-the-mouth part of town I'd be spending my first 25 years.

My father lowered the large yellow corrugated **KLIM** tin hanging from a pulley in the ceiling, took out a 5-cent coin for the fare, breathed on it, shined it on his singlet and gave it to the man. *Terima Kasih*, he said. You brought my son safe and sound.

The gold tooth grinned. Three boys, wah, his crooked finger said as it counted, *yat, yi, saam*. Rich man.

My father went back to his **KLIM** tin and picked out three coppers. *Makan nasi*, he said pressing the coins into the man's hand.

That was a 60% tip. I felt proud to have such a father, especially as I'd been asleep when he visited and even now couldn't take a proper look at him in the crowd.

The rickshaw puller spread the coins on his palm. Give money, get money, he said.

Insh'Allah, my father said and looked up at heaven.

The man dropped the coins into the pouch on his string belt, reached in under the rickshaw seat, pulled out a rag and wiped the sweat streaming down his bony face and sunken chest. He looked like a skeleton bundled in shrinking canvas.

Nanti. My ma told him to wait, put me in my father's arms and went in with Jonah holding onto her rappa and sucking his thumb. He was 5 and Joshua, who was 3, sucked his middle finger and hung on to Jonah's shirt. My father walked through the crowd, head up, big smile telling everybody 3 was his lucky number and No. 3 had arrived.

A man in the crowd said, 3 is *saam* sounds like *saang*. New life coming to our street brings good luck. A couple behind asked for three more digits for the 4-Numbers lottery.

7, my father said.

A woman with a child on her hip said, 7 lucky, 8 more lucky. 3-7-8, one more.

An Indian peanut vendor off to the Capitol Cinema for the matinee stopped to see what was going on. Jero, he called out, whole universe.

3-7-8-0 ran back and forward through the growing crowd.

My father took off my woollen cap, thank God, and blew to cool my head. Leave them with their numbers and their lotteries, he said to me. Never bother with such things. When God wants to give He finds His own way in His own time. Come, I want you to see the shop and learn from me. Slow items, he said pointing at the shelves, you put high up at the back, understand? Fast selling, low in front. That's your first lesson, so remember. I will teach, you will learn. Totally. Your brothers, he shrugged, who knows? With fingers in the mouth how will they learn to do bizz-i-nezz? That's how he said it – two long zeds.

If that was what it took, I wouldn't suck my thumb. It was a good day for both of us.

My ma came out again with a tin mug of water and a thick, homemade tomato jam sandwich. Jonah, thumb in mouth carried a star fruit, Joshua who'd switched to his little finger held a banana. The rickshaw puller said *Doh chay* a hundred times, squatted by the roadside, ate his lunch and the crowd went home.

I have no idea how they fared in the lottery. When you are two days old and your father says God will provide, you take his word for it.

Five days at home and I was getting used to the starch in my cot sheet and the smell of citronella oil mingling with the rubber under me. I also knew I had ended up in a dump of a neighbourhood, inside the house no better than the street. The 3rd class ward and a don't-wait-just-wrap-up-your-baby-and-take-him-home-we-need-your-bed Chinese Ward Sister should have made that plain enough. But, with a father who knew how God thought and what He did, why should I worry?

Instead I went over what I'd learned. The young Indian doctor sucking up to the old English doctor taught me my first: play the game. My father telling me to leave things in the hands of God, my second, and now a couple of *chichak* living on the beams above my cot were teaching me my third.

Motionless with a dead stare, once in a while licking to clean their lidless eyes, the lizards waited for careless flies to come within reach of their long sticky tongues. That was a trick worth remembering.

My ma never kept me waiting, spoke sweetly and I repaid her kindness by putting on weight which she checked by bouncing me gently in her arms. *M'sh'Allah*, she said. She said that a lot to keep away the evil eye, looking up for God to hear and protect me from all the things that come silently in the dark to take away little children and please God, make him like a tree planted by the rivers of water that whatever he does shall he prosper. Soon, she said, you'll be so heavy, *m'sh'Allah*, I'll not be able to carry you, *m'sh'Allah*.

My father came up from his shop now and again, smiled when I took his little finger and put his hand on my head to say a blessing and my brothers tried to teach me to suck my thumb. All in all I was comfortable, well fed and convinced humans were decent, never suspecting what my parents had in store. Had I forgotten the lizards so soon?

4

On Wednesday, eighth day of my life, my father didn't open for business. He removed five or six planks for people to squeeze through and enter the house via the shop. The other way meant passing the squatter's palace where, if luck ran out, you heard the *toti* truck clanking and men shouting *Paow! Paow!* running along the back lane, an empty bucket swinging each end of a bamboo pole. When they stopped outside your wall, done or not, you pulled up your pants before the full honey bucket slid out and you never knew if a *toti* man might take it into his head to poke you in the bum as he pushed in the empty one.

Every Monday the *toti* foreman in khaki canvas shoes, khaki shorts, khaki shirt, khaki *topi* with a white chicken feather poked into the sweatband, came round to our shop chased by a squadron of bluebottle flies, yelling in high-pitched Hylam, You're taking food from my children's mouths.

Farmers paid two cents per full honey bucket, solids and liquids and Jeyes Fluid made it worthless. My father promised to tell my ma not to do it again, pulled down the **KLIM** tin and gave him two cents.

Two cents? The foreman shrieked, yanked the notebook out of his shirt pocket, rolled the pages to 47 Princep Street, took the pencil off his ear and sucked the point. Two cents, shit once a week. Shit every day, 14 cents. Also now one person more. That was me, my portion lost to Jeyes. He changed 4 to 5 at our address.

From this point on fingers negotiated, a thumb being 10.

3.	/	13.
4.	/	12.

5 wrinkled my father's face into a half smile. His open

palm lingered in front of the man's face like a *hamsa*. Polite, it wards off evil eye, but with *a'bwail* in heavy Iraqi accompanied by a sneer, as my father said it and did it, means five fingers in your eye.

6.	/	11.
7.	/	10.
8.		

The man crossed his arms. The crowd was disrupting business. My father took back the 2 cents, gave him 10 with a three-quarter smile, did a double *hamsa* close to his face and said, *Kus'umuk*, which I prefer not to translate. The *toti* man took his money, spat in the drain and hurried off to the waiting truck with his bluebottle escort.

Today's downstairs sounds weren't Monday sounds or any other day sounds. They were new sounds of pushing and pulling, someone asking, Where? My father saying, There. Here? No, not there, there. Where? *In'zule*, which isn't a curse, just impatience. There, put it where my finger is pointing? And shouts from the street, *Y'Allah*, Yehudah, hurry up.

Then a freshly-baked smell curled up the stairs after which came my father's coffee smell but stronger, like pots and pots, a whole bucket of it and when my ma came back into the room she brought more smells, fried eggs, cheese, coconut, almonds, rose syrup. She lit the mosquito coil which she did only if she pulled aside the net around my cot and I knew she was going to talk to me so I opened my eyes.

So sorry, she said brushing her hand down my face to close my eyes. I told them to keep quiet. Would they listen? No more noise now, I promise. Your father did a grand job. Ordered more than enough of everything. Nobody dare say we skimped.

My brothers came in bringing their own smells.

What's his name? That was Joshua.

Secret, Pa said. That was Jonah.

Hello, Secret, Joshua said, digging a finger into my side. Wake up.

Pa says Fuli's coming. Jonah said to my ma. Is it true?

Whatever your father says is true.

Is he bringing his knife?

My ma looked down at him and lowered her eyebrows.

See. I told you. Jonah put an arm around Joshua and whispered in my ear, Poor ting.

Go down and don't touch the food, my ma said, chased them out and was about to shut the door when my father slipped in with a happy sounding, Hah.

There's nobody downstairs, my ma said. Anyone can walk in.

Silman and Shooli came. One watching the shop, one the food.

Did you cover it from the flies?

Are you saying I'm a fool?

All over?

Are you saying I don't know what to do? Now let me talk to my third son, he said, came close and I got my first really good look at him. I want to explain to you, he said with a smile that grew by quarters as he spoke, same as I told your brothers, this day of all days, that to be a Jew you must suffer without complaining. My father, that's to say your grandfather, may he rest in peace, used to tell me the same thing every day of my life when I lived among those who took our forefathers as their forefathers, then started to kill us without saying why until I had to run away to save my life which as it turned out, was not all bad because it brought me to this day with a party for you, my third son, in my own house without fear.

Thank God, my ma said opening her almirah. But must you tell him the whole story now I'm trying to get ready? Tell him tomorrow.

Maybe tomorrow, he said, his smile shrinking a quarter, when he finds out what it really means for a boy to be a Jew, he won't be so happy to hear what I have to say, follow what I'm saying? To put me at my ease he beamed the full smile that opened his eyes, raised his forehead and pushed back his ears and I felt fine.

So be quick, she said, I need to change.

Who's stopping you? I won't look, he said turning his back to her. The first thing I want to tell you, he said to me, is that we belong to God, whose name is blessed, you, me, your brothers, your mother, all. God chose the Jews from all other people in the world and that's why they get so mad with us. We lived, me and my family, in a house made of mud which we couldn't whitewash to look better than Arab houses, understand what I'm saying? From day to day we never knew what would happen. Would a basha or a mullah make another new law for Jews? That's how it was and when they said we were not allowed to wear matching shoes, left must be different from right, I said to myself, enough is enough. If they caught you with same shoes, they made you take them off in the street, tied your legs and beat your soles till you couldn't walk for a month. That's when I said I cannot live like this and left. As you grow I will tell you stories to know how to live your life. For now this is enough so if your mother has finished I'll open the door and go down to my friends.

Go, my ma said and out he went without looking behind.

When he'd gone she undressed, got into her special-occasions rappa, white with pink flowers, extra yard for frills, square lace collar and sang her dressing-up song,

> *He stood in a beautiful mansion*
> *surrounded by riches untold.*
> *He gazed at a beautiful picture*
> *that hung in a frame of gold,*

about a man who, for all his great powers and riches, knew he could never replace one thing in the mansion that was absent, his wife's tender, smiling face because she was dead and he'd give up everything to have her back. It was a sad song but she made it happy that day by missing out those bits.

I followed her with my eyes as she moved from bed to almirah to tallboy, all one-of-a-kind, second-hand, picked up at auctions and watched her hands working round each other behind her head, twisting her long, thick, wavy, black hair, where I got mine, into a tight bun. That was nice especially the bit when she stuck in a fake tortoiseshell comb which made her grand. She angled the tallboy mirror to catch her face, stuck a finger into a Chinese teacup of squashed leftover lipstick from her sister and friends, smeared her lips, and rubbed her finger clean on her cheeks for rouge. Short-sighted and without specs, she usually ended up with jagged multi-coloured lips. Today she got it right, somehow.

Her neck, forehead and rappa sleeves got a quick dab of 4711 Eau de Cologne, then two drops on a handkerchief she fanned in front of my nose which is why to this day that smell reminds me of what was about to happen. Dressed, lipstick, rouge, fake tortoiseshell comb, handkerchief tucked in like a single shoulder pad, my ma was quite good looking in a Jewish sort of way with a girlish voice that hovered just below the ceiling.

She changed my nappy talking, clucking and smiling to make me feel safe. Then she pulled my arms through the sleeves of a long white satin robe my brothers also wore on the eighth day of their lives and was straightening the line of dummy pearl buttons down the front when her younger sister Flora who couldn't understand how anybody would live in a house without a flushing toilet, barged in with a new smell.

Nice Shabby, she said to my ma's back, but for God's sake take off that ribbon. It makes you look like you're still pregnant. How's Jujube?

Auntie Flora called my ma Shabby and me Jujube. I can't say I liked either but right this minute she was bending over my cot, clicking her tongue and giving me a blast of Evening in Paris at 9 in the morning. Side by side, one, a million dollars in silk draping her well-moulded body, hair short, waved and teased at the tips, a string of fine pink cultured pearls swinging from her neck, the other – well, she was my ma – and the two sisters looked like a dove posing with a pigeon.

He's fine, my ma said and Auntie Flora went to the mirror to check her teeth for lipstick, sucked them just in case and said, How d'you see in this light? If I had a husband like yours, she turned to face my ma to finish the sentence, changed her mind, put her hands on her hips and said, you're still wearing that ribbon? How many times must I tell you? Ribbons don't suit if your waist is more than 24, 26. You're what, 42, 44, 46?

My ma flicked her who's-worried fingers whereupon Auntie Flora pulled a tail of the bow, bunched the ribbon, threw it into the open almirah and banged the door shut. I don't think she liked the look of my ma's four rappas hanging in a row.

No Shabby, you *should* be worried. Look at me, she said sideways, pulling in her belly and stroking it which I will say was pretty flat under an outstanding bust. Who'd believe four children? You should take care like me. What's tomorrow?

Thursday.

Not possible. Friam's clients for dinner and Friday's always busy. Sunday. I'll send Fatimah to knead and push your *kishkish* back in place. In the afternoon when she finishes at my place. Be ready. Twice a week, five, six weeks and you'll be fine.

No need, my ma said, opening the almirah, taking out the ribbon and rolling it round two fingers. I'm fine already. She put the ribbon with the others on the small corner shelf and closed the door. I don't go to parties like your husband drags you to.

Drags? Drags you say? Why drags? her voice rising with each drags. Let me tell you, here and now, her eyes sharpening, I go by my own free will. Nobody, but nobody, drags Flora Ezra nowhere. Now her eyes were pointed. I love parties, especially the women. Remember what happened first time I wore my diamond?

My ma's face blanked.

Sure you do. Six months ago. The very next day I came and told you. You must remember, she said as my ma turned away. How I walked in, ring turned round, platinum band showing, diamond inside? No?

My ma left her sister talking to the almirah. Auntie Flora followed her, twinkling her fingers in my ma's face. They were drinking cocktails, she said, comparing diamonds. 1¼, maybe 1½, let's say 2 carats to be generous. Colour, clarity, cut, how many flaws when I twisted my 4½ and they died? Sure I didn't tell you?

My ma picked me up in the flowing white gown, held me against her and rubbed my back. It's not that she had anything against her sister's diamond story. More like Auntie Flora had more than one diamond and more than one diamond story. By now she was beginning to understand my ma's silence so she said, Don't worry. I'll pay Fatimah. Three hours including going and coming plus bus fare. Just roll out your mat, wear your petticoat and leave the rest to her.

No need, my ma said again. I don't have to show myself.

What d'you mean, show myself? Fatimah is a woman.

I wasn't talking about her. No one needs to see if I'm slim or not?

To hoot with no one. It's what's-his-name, your husband. He's cares more how my *mahashas* look on his plate.

And at night? When you're alone. When you take off everything. Petticoat included. My ma walked me around the room, rubbing and patting my back. You're not telling me … no … Shabby? Clothes on? Can't be. In the dark? My ma didn't answer. Missionary? Auntie Flora eased her face into a sly I-can-believe-it smile.

Missionary?

Don't you know anything? Man on top.

Chih. Do you need to talk like that? We were brought up in the same house. Same mother, same father, *Allah ir hamu*, may they both rest in peace. What happened to you?

Auntie Flora's hands went onto her hips, her head tilted and the sly I-can-believe-it smile reappeared. What happened to *you*, she said. Did you never learn anything?

Same school also, you and me, my ma said.

School? School you're talking about? School? Her voice again rose with each school. Convent of the Holy Infant Jesus you call school because nowhere else was there place for us? Two Jewish girls and a thousand Roman Catholics. Auntie Flora was getting fiery as she often did. That you call learning? From nuns with faces and fingers only? When do they take off their clothes to know why God gave women bodies?

My ma went out to the landing, poked her head over the banister, came back and said very quietly, Come Flora, the house is filling. We should get ready.

Auntie Flora tossed her head, straightened her dress, returned to the mirror, took a brush from her handbag, flicked the tips of her hair, licked a finger to tidy her eyebrows, ran her tongue over her teeth and smiled to see she was as lovely as when she came in.

In that case, she said, no need for Fatimah. Why waste her time and my money?

My Eau de Cologne ma handed me to Auntie Flora, my godmother. She held me in her Evening in Paris arms, gave me a joyous smile and said, Don't worry Jujube, everything will be alright, the one thing guaranteed to get me worrying, but six steps down at the landing where the stairs turned, she passed me to her husband, my godfather Uncle Friam who smelled of Red Hackle. He gave me a different kind of smile as if one of his horses had won and I was the Gold Cup. This is my lucky day, he said, a baby boy in my arms.

Downstairs people were singing a hymn to welcome me into the congregation and as I passed, a woman with a squint, fizzy hair and bent smile, stroked my head and said, God bless you, darling. Auntie Sally was my father's sister who came to dinner Friday night when I was asleep so I smiled to say pleased to meet you just as Uncle Friam murmured under his whisky breath, Your father doesn't need three sons. One day I'll come at night and steal you.

Try and try again, he never could draw a son from his wife's lucky dip. I thought I'd sigh in sympathy but the smells of food and smoke and perfume and noise of out-of-tune singing and clapping were getting to me. Was this how people behaved when a boy was eight days old? Then, without warning, he held me a moment in Elijah's chair, always empty at Jewish gatherings in case the prophet who rode a whirlwind into heaven should suddenly show up and put me in my father's lap and he turned me to face the *mohel* who gave me a broken smile.

Okay I thought, enough with passing the parcel, I'd like to sleep if nobody minds when this man lifted my robe, unpinned my nappy and had a go at my little man. He had a short beard, bad breath and started tugging my foreskin to full stretch, so I peed on him. People laughed and he swore worse than my father though I doubt anyone understood. A name like Fuli Shtambuli meant he was Raphael from

Istanbul and I could add Turkish to the English, Cantonese, Malay, Hylam, Hokkien, if I'm not mistaken a snatch of Japanese, Arabic, Tamil and Hindustani more or less in that order, of my first seven days.

Fuli told nobody in particular to hurry and wipe the floor or God forbid he'd slip and give me a crinkle cut. I could see he was a little edgy and belched a lot, not the sort to put a person at ease especially when he's got designs on your dingdong.

Firm, he said to my father, I want no kicking. I don't think he trusted me. He slipped a shield over my foreskin to protect the glans, said a blessing and, in one clean sweep, I lost my prepuce. As if that wasn't enough he took the edge of what remained between thumb and index finger of each hand and tore down the centre, back to the corona.

I lay there stunned, wondering why I'd rushed out of the safety of my ma's womb when I felt he'd got me in his mouth sucking away and I was only eight days old. What did he want with me? To remove blood and apply an antiseptic was one thing, but what he was doing must have a name. I yelled, more shock than pain. He sprinkled dusting powder, tied a bandage with a double reef knot and my father said the benediction:

> Who hast hallowed us by Thy commandments
> and commanded us to make our sons
> enter into the covenant of Abraham our father,

and the whole body of men replied,

> even as this child has entered into the covenant
> so may he enter into the Torah,
> the nuptial canopy, and good deeds.

So that's what it was. To join the club you need to have your penis peeled and God gets your foreskin to seal the deal. Everyone wished me good omens, good luck, good life, clapped as they sang when Auntie Flora, without so much as a word to my father, took me off his lap and upstairs to my ma who said how sorry she was, she should've stood by me, but what could she do, women don't count, please forgive her.

I cried even louder so she cleared out the ladies who'd been sitting with her while I, without consent, was making my covenant, closed the door, struggled out of her rappa and gave me her breast. What the hell, I thought, better than nothing.

Hold on. As Auntie Flora carried me upstairs she said, It's okay, Jujube, two, three days, you'll not know a thing. You'll be a Jew without an extra piece getting in the way. Jujube? She must have heard Fuli asking my father, *Ma esmouku?* what's his name? and my father say, Yosef Adam, so I'd better get the matter of my name out of the way.

One of the guards at the tomb of Daniel who spent a night in a den with lions and came to no harm, was called Judah. This was in Shushan in Persia in the days people robbed graves. Then the guard moved to Iraq where people called him Yehuda MiShushan – Judah from Shushan. Jews hang on to names and down the line, centuries later as the story goes, it became my father's. When he showed up at the Registry of Aliens in Singapore he spoke little English. Saying Yehuda MiShushan three times in his cloudy Iraqi accent didn't help. The clerk managed Judah from Yehuda, but MiShushan was too much so he introduced the Messiah into our lives.

The day he married, as the other story goes, my father made a deal with God whose unutterable name is spelled, *yod, hey, waw hey* – Yahweh, approximately Jehovah in

English. Give me healthy children, he said to God, right number of parts in good working order and I promise their names will start with *yod* like yours and mine. In short, my birth certificate says I am Joseph Adam Messiah but I prefer to call myself,

J Adam Messiah

which is kind of suave.

5

In the next months I became the apple of my ma's eye in a manner of speaking, lifted my head, stretched my neck and followed her around the room with my eyes, enough for her to understand I wanted a better view of what was going on in my world. It was fine without a pillow when I slept, but awake, would she please put a couple under my head and prop me up so I could look over the top of my cot, take stock of what I came into and wonder where I was going while she tidied the room?

She moved fast about her chores, singing her version of The Prisoner's Song

> *Oh please, meet me tonight in the moonlight,*
> *please meet me tonight all alone,*
> *for I have a sad story to tell you,*
> *it's a story that's never been told*

at which point she stopped and I never got to know the story that's never been told. When I asked years later she said, What makes you think I know? Did we learn anything start to finish? That was life in those days. We got what we got and thanked our lucky stars.

She dusted, made beds, pulled sheets tight tucking them in under the mattresses with sharp envelope edges, not easy seeing as how the kapok had wandered over the years and quit the corners. She beat the hell out of the pillows, aired them at the window and when she'd done the room, plumped health back into their tired bodies lining them with the wall, all of which came from Convent Girls' School in Victoria Street where nuns taught the women of tomorrow the three R's and how to deal with life's necessities, besides.

She learned little of the first, Reading slowly, Riting okay and as much Rithmetic as she needed not to be cheated in the market. The other stuff they taught made her proud of her home and happy with her family, good children with everything in the right place, healthy, thank God, maybe because our names began with *Yod* including Yehudit, my sister Judith, who arrived two years later. What more could she ask?

Fridays she changed sheets, towels and everything else putting them in the basket for Sunday. She wasn't a machine. She had only one pair of hands and one pair of legs to go up and down those stairs, the more you climbed the higher they got, till she was sure she'd fall one day if God wasn't with her and there was enough to do, cooking, cleaning and getting the house ready for Shabbat all by herself to let the laundry wait.

It was early afternoon. She'd finished and come up to catch her breath and talk to me a few minutes before bathing and seeing to herself and what else a woman has to do that men don't need to know about. House quiet, brothers playing in the street, the time I loved most having her to myself going about her business and telling me how it was in school where nuns didn't smile because the world was so full of wickedness and it was their job to make sure no girl went through their hands and came out a sinner. I liked her stories. My father's too, but his ended with questions to answer or he'd say, How much d'you have to carry in your head? I told you only two days ago, hah, and I'd feel I'd let him down.

There was this girl Mary, sitting next to her who said, When all Jews accept the one true faith the Messiah will come and save the world so why don't you hurry up and become a true believer, don't you want to go to heaven? Little did she know, my ma said as she did another wipe under my father's alarm clock on the table between their beds just to be sure, that one day her name would be Messiah or she'd have put Mary, Mary, Quite Contrary in her place, where she belonged in the wastepaper basket behind Sister Solace's desk. And while on the subject of remembering, she may as well tell me it wasn't right, a mother treating two daughters so differently. She was a bit of a sourpuss anyway, she said, without going into detail because her mother was dead and it's not nice to talk bad about those gone to rest. Unless you've something good to say about people, say nothing especially a mother who went through hell to bring you into the world as any woman who's been through hell will tell you.

So fine, she said coming to my cot, I know for a fact I'm not pretty or clever like Flora, but all the same it wasn't right to say my wedding was more than I deserved. All I got was a family-only dinner which she made me help to cook and Flora got bridesmaids, flower girls in rainbow colours and a page boy in white as if to say we are Europeans. That's your Uncle Friam for you. If you're not lucky to be born European, he says, pretend. Seaview Hotel if you please, two hundred guests not including your father who wasn't invited and grand, don't ask. Wedding cake, seven tiers, MC in suit with tails if you can believe it in this heat. Pray, Ladies and Gentlemen your attention please, the bride and groom will now cut the cake and out flew pigeons from the bottom layers to everyone's surprise. Then the band played and he taught us how to do the Lambeth Walk which everyone was doing in London in those days.

My ma held me with one hand, lifted her rappa with the other, kicked her legs, moved forward and back, side to side, singing along as we went,

> *Ev'rything's free and easy,*
> *Do as you darn well pleasey,*

Why don't you make your way there,
Go there, stay there?
Once you get down Lambeth way,
Ev'ry evening, ev'ry day,
You'll find us all doin' the Lambeth walk, Oy!

laughing with the Oy! cuddling me and it wasn't even her wedding.

Why she was telling me this after all these years, she'd never know, except that now and again she needed to get things off her chest with nobody listening and have a little dance which a woman needs once in a while she said and put me back in my cot.

With the dancing and cuddling I must've fallen asleep because I woke to see a ring of faces around my cot, had a fright and wet my nappy. *Sm'Allah*, my ma said with a smile and rubbed my cheek with the back of a bent finger. My friends are here to say hello, she said removing the pin, raising my legs, slipping away the nappy and giving me a wipe. She went for another from the rattan basket and the three faces came in for a closer look.

Two were edged with wet hair in slides, mascara shadows, rouge dabs, red lips and a lingering smell of chicken, onions, garlic and Lifebuoy soap, unmistakable Friday afternoon smells. They'd bathed, styled their hair with waving clips, dressed and come over and my ma was still in her house clothes which means she was running late.

The third face was new. Instead of make-up it had the smile of a woman who gladly spent her time alone, the rest of the world could go to pot for all she cared. They were all clucking, making kissing noises, looking at each other to see if everyone was having as much fun, turning back to look at me because joy grows into happiness as my ma liked to say, laugh and the world laughs with you, weep and you sit in the corner and tears make wrinkles in your cheeks and you get old before your time.

They were friends the way people were when nobody called before visiting, asking my father as they entered where my ma was, knowing full well. Where else if not running, doing last minute jobs before the Sabbath caught her at sunset which would be bad enough if he didn't add that men were always ready why couldn't women?

Friendship was easy-going, standing on ceremony the worst kind of rudeness, so my father waved them in with his fly swatter, not because he lacked manners, but because he had nothing to say to them. To talk about God and the ways of the world you have to talk to men, know what I'm saying? So he said, Hah, and they said, Yoo-hoo, pushing aside the bamboo curtain and calling out, Sabiha, where are you Sabiha? Yoo-hoo.

The two with washed hair were done for the day. The third didn't care, or putting it another way, the Sabbath, she said, was made for man not man for the Sabbath and if you really wanted to know she didn't give a fig or a fart about either, pardon her Dutch.

I was nine months old, chubby, hair thick enough for a curl along the top of my head not the only thing that drove the ladies crazy because I'd peeled perfectly which prompted one of them to say, What jewels he has. He's going to make some lucky girl so happy.

That was Sophie Sitting Right because her clothes hugged her body down to her waist, took a dive over her womanly hips and hung neatly around her thighs. She'd either push her elbows into her sides or wriggle her shoulders to keep things sitting right or as now, run her hands from below her breasts down to her hips and thighs.

She said she'd set her hair to look like Gloria Swanson in *Sadie Thompson*, so when it dried it would hang in cascading waves, patted and pushed it up behind her head when she said cascading waves and stepped back to look at the almirah.

Sabiha, don't you have a full-length mirror?

No need, my ma said, she knew how she looked and how many times had Sophie been in this room saying the same thing? Sophie said it was beyond her how any woman could live without a mirror to check her clothes were sitting right and started to say she'd rather die … but Myrtle the Turtle was pointing at my bungaloos which my ma was powdering and said, God loves him. When he grows they'll be big and firm and he'll be such a man, and she reached out to touch them but my ma moved sideways, folded the nappy corners, one-two-three and fixed the pin, blocking Myrtle's hand mid air. She pulled down my vest and puffed up my pillow, at which point I sat up for the first time in my life which got her saying, God bless him, see what he just did. Sophie and Myrtle were tickled pink and Bicycle Becky said, He wants to join in, cheeky bugger, without excusing her Dutch.

She had a deep voice and people said behind her back they weren't sure. Why did she ride a man's bicycle with a bar she had to throw her leg over? Such a scandal, you had every right to say something. Always in black trousers and a white more-shirt-than-blouse, over fried-egg breasts. She said they were slacks, women's slacks if you didn't mind and her blouse had a bust line if you cared to look. You didn't have to be pigeon-chested to be a woman. So why did she bob her hair and wear a necktie and hat like Mickey Rooney? Were people wrong to come right out and say: It makes you wonder? So she took herself to live where nobody looked at her in that way or spoke behind her back in front of her face as if she couldn't hear what their eyes were saying.

She wasn't one of my ma's come-and-go, on-the-off-chance friends, coming and going like a blue moon so much so you'd think she'd emigrated only to see her riding up your street, coming over to hear the latest gossip. She was visiting now because the Pontianak tree behind her house told her my ma had laid another egg and seeing as how they were friends from the good old days, why not come over and see the little rascal? Also, by the way, my ma was the only one who'd spend time with her without fishing for information or tricking her into revealing herself, and, who would believe it, just as she was cycling along Selegie Road, Sophie and Myrtle were crossing. What more could she say?

To change the subject Myrtle asked Sophie, So how's it going? Six months married, is it still good? Sophie said, if she knew six months ago what she knew now, she wouldn't have bothered. Myrtle said, What do you mean, if you knew six months ago what you know now you wouldn't have bothered and Sophie went up to Myrtle's ear making her hand a screen and whispered when Becky shot round to the other side and leaned over.

Myrtle giggled and said, No, you're not saying that, no, I don't believe you, no, is that what he wants, did he say so himself? No, Sophie said, he sent me a postcard and Myrtle refused to believe it at which point Becky turned her head aside as if to say I'm looking down my nose at you while her face was saying, What else can you expect? Men are no better than dogs and she wanted them to know, she said it twice, I want you to know this is why, even as a girl, that too she said again, when I was a girl with pigtails I said, no thank you, that's not for me, I can do without, thank you very much. She'd rather spend the rest of her life in a single bed with a long pillow than share a double bed with a man whose balls are mashed in with his brains, excuse her Dutch.

My word, Sophie shook her head. Where d'you find such expressions? Becky gave Sophie one of her looks and to change the subject again, Sophie said, I blame my mother, fair and square. Kept me in the dark, not a word about what to expect. Fourteen when her parents married her off to a man double her age with no choice, so what could you expect? She turned to Myrtle who was still laughing about men's brains and said, I'm speaking the truth, no? What do you know that you can say in all honesty your mother told you?

Nothing, Myrtle said blowing her nose and tucking her handkerchief into her sleeve. It's true, not a thing did I learn from her about that.

Isn't that what I said? Sophie asked my ma who said, Fault or no fault, parents or no parents, choice or no choice, a woman knows. It's only natural, she has to bear it, it's the way we are made and have to take what life brings so get used to it.

I think my ma was saying more than usual so the conversation didn't go in a direction she didn't much like, but even so Myrtle didn't seem convinced. She wasn't married and her parents had made it clear she was well past her prime and well past her time. Twenty-six almost seven. Three years and she'd be on the shelf with the empty bottles and newspapers waiting for the *karang gunni* man to weigh her and take her away. They were looking for someone suitable before she passed the proper age to have children. As if. Did they think she'd be interested in any Tom, Dick or Harry who showed up with a smile and a good pair of leather shoes?

Leather shoes? Becky laughed. What he has on his feet isn't your worry. It's the leather invader in his pants. Have you seen one ready to do damage? Ruin your body? Surgeons remove the whole lot, piece by piece until you're no longer a woman. Damn them.

Both Sophie and Myrtle looked at her then at each other, their eyes saying, You first, I'll back you up, until at last

Sophie came right out and said to Becky in a testing kind of voice to settle the issue once and for all, Have you?

Are you asking if I've seen a prick on parade?

Oh God. Sophie, who'd gone and got herself married six months ago because she didn't know then what she knew now, had seen what Becky was talking about. A blush wouldn't pretend she hadn't and one from Myrtle could be taken either way, so when they didn't answer, Becky said, The whole world wants to know, which was when my ma went to the door to ask if anyone would like a cup of tea.

So Becky came right out and said, I've had enough.

Sophie thought she'd insulted Becky. She was going to drop her slacks right now and show them what she had or walk out and not be seen again until the Pontianak tree spoke to her. Sophie started running her elbows into her sides and Becky, with that look she did down her nose, said, I'm sick and tired of living in a community where men look for dowries *or*, now her voice rose, they are useless *or* they are useless *and* looking for dowries. I may as well tell you, she said rumpling her hair and pausing longer than it took to catch her breath, I'm thinking of going to America, Land of the Free, Home of the Brave, where everyone lives like in the movies. Jewish men are real men and handsome and know their way in the world with something to say, every word a pearl, like Douglas Fairbanks.

Douglas Fairbanks? Sophie's eyes opened wide. You're not saying? Douglas Fairbanks? Zorro is a Jew? Making eyes behind his mask till I was ready to wet myself?

Never mind about wetting yourself, Myrtle said, relieved things hadn't gone the wrong way with Becky. I want to hear it from your lips: Douglas Fairbanks, King of Hollywood, with a straight nose and two-million-dollar smile is a Jew. For such a man I'll cook and clean like I'm doing in a house with two useless brothers and nobody with a word to make me feel a woman with a heart to give. Just say when Becky and I'll carry your bags.

My ma, still at the door waiting for an answer, said, No point dreaming. We have what we have, make the best of it.

No, Myrtle said turning to Becky whom she now regarded as an expert on Jewish affairs in America. Is it true that Jews make all the movies in America?

Mostly, Becky said.

So, Myrtle said. I'll go to Hollywood, take lessons and tell them I'm a Jewish girl all the way from Singapore. They'll find me a part, no?

When no one answered and the silence seemed too long, Sophie changed the subject.

It's true, she said. Did I have a choice? Albert's a good man even though he did shock me while we were itching and scratching.

Itching and scratching, Becky said. Is that what you call it?

What should I call it? My ma was on edge but Sophie carried on saying, It's not as though you don't have three sons to prove you've done it. If I had a choice, Albert and what he wants from me or Douglas Fairbanks whatever he wants, I know who I'd choose.

By now they were having separate conversations and all I got was that our community was so small, if men couldn't find cousins they married nieces, if no nieces, Chinese girls, what would my ma do when my time came to which she said she wasn't worrying right now which got Myrtle saying to Sophie, Itch and scratch tonight. Give Albert what he wants, and who knows, Adam may have a girl ready for him, which got Becky looking at me and saying, I think he's heard every word we've said.

Let's go down, my ma said, and have a cup of tea before I lay the table for Shabbat.

Bicycle Becky took me from my ma so she could make tea when the bamboo curtain parted and Hannah Sefardi came in carrying her son Simon. She said it was nice to see them all, she wasn't staying, just wanted to know if my ma had bicarbonate of soda for Simon's nappy rash.

He was two months older and my ma was always telling me how special he was, already standing and trying to walk and don't even mention talking, sentences if you please. Not that she was putting the evil eye on him, God forbid, but a boy like that? She'd not say another word, but which mother wouldn't want a son like him?

My ma came back with the powder, spooned it into a packet from my father's shop and they left without having tea. It was good, in a way, because my father was agitating about being time to close the shop, go up for his shave and Bay Rum and so on, coming into the dining room three times saying things like, Nice to have people over but Friday is Friday, and Why not come tomorrow, and when eventually he said, Soon the sun will set, Sophie said, Just look at the time, I'd better be home before Albert gets back which got Myrtle saying, Remember what I said about tonight. Hannah said thank you and left with Simon and Becky gave me to my ma, saying, Toodle-oo, see you in apple blossom time.

Now I'm wondering why I stitched in this story. If, as my father used to say, every story has a lesson for life this may have one too.

6

He was born in Bir Haroon, Aaron's Well, a village outside Basra where our forefathers lived two thousand years from the time of Nebuchadnezzar, may his name be erased, in the year there was no rain, making his age approximate, and though he didn't live to be old he aged like an ancient Hebrew wrapped in God's blessings and commandments. His shop did well enough to feed us and keep the wolf from the door, as the saying goes, and a little besides if what he said when he fished my ma's marketing money from the **KLIM** tin was anything to go by. Here, he said, take 20 cents more and buy something nice for the children. That happened about once a month when we got *chikki*, both hard and sticky, and *kueh lapis* that's to say Indian peanut brittle and a Malay kind of cake with a dozen thin layers we'd peel off one by one. She cut everything four ways and each got a piece because fighting over food was the worst thing and the biggest sin especially when we had enough, thank God, and weren't starving. Sins come in one size.

Not once did he tell her to take a dollar and buy something from hawkers peddling tin toys from Japan, the kind you could wind up three times before the spring snapped. My father was careful with money for two reasons: One: God gave us money to use, not waste, and Two: if money grew like trees, wouldn't he dig up the cement patch at the back and plant a jungle? And, call it Number Three, he never had toys in Bir Haroon so why did we need them? In much the same way we didn't have a light in our house brighter than 40 watts and the reasons also had numbers.

One: he refused to give his money to the electricity

people for nothing you could eat or wear or keep in a cupboard.

Two: only Bashas had electricity in Al Basrah, the city he visited once a month with his father delivering plaited cheese to the *effendi* and his harem of thirty, forty, who knows? No one ever saw them although everyone knew they came from different lands with different colour hair and different colour eyes and different colour bodies that eventually drove the *effendi* so mad they had to lock him up in a cell with his two eunuchs. I asked what a eunuch was and why a man needed thirty, forty, who knows? wives, and he said, Later. My brothers didn't know either so I asked my ma and she said, Go ask your father. After that, with no cheese to deliver, my father went to Basra only once more to catch a steamer and leave the country to stay alive.

Three: his father was a *dhimmi* not a Basha. When I asked what a *dhimmi* was, he got mad just remembering. Anyone not a Muslim unlucky enough to be born in a Muslim land, he said. Turks and Arabs hate Jews and Christians, Jews more. Treated us worse than dogs, know what I'm saying, beat us with big sticks any time it entered their heads. We had to pay a special tax, *jizya* they called it, to make you feel you were not as good as them. If we didn't have the money we begged other Jews to pay for us. To stay alive, I had to leave. I asked why he couldn't stay alive by not getting into trouble? Trouble? That you call trouble? Trouble I can handle, he said, but not now. I said, When? and he said, There are things you need to know about my life in those days surrounded by people who wanted my blood until I said enough is enough, fight back or how will you hold your head high, understand? I said I didn't and he said, When you're older we'll sit, you and me. I will tell you and you will know how I stayed alive and came to be here today. I asked my ma what he was talking about and she said, Go ask your father.

Four: God, whose name is blessed, knew exactly what He was doing when He gave us the sun to shine half the day so we could sleep in peace at night.

This reasoning also led to the law that until we were at least three and a half feet tall we kids weren't allowed to use the squatter's palace except in daylight. Once a month my ma checked us against a drawing pin in the kitchen cupboard standing in four bowls of Jeyes Fluid to keep off the ants. Even then, we had to sing or whistle all the while for her to be sure we hadn't fallen down the hole, God forbid. Too dangerous in the dark, she said, and though she never said it right out, she thought the reason was One, and anyway 40-watts or 100-watts made no difference because there was nowhere to put a light near the palace and if the moon wasn't out and exactly in the right spot, how would we see the two steps? More than all the reasons put together was what she didn't want to think about, a foot going down the hole in the dark, God forbid, cutting a leg, God forbid, and falling into the bucket, God forbid. Infections were bad enough, but gangrene? Amputation? *Sm'Allah El Shaddai.* No. Please God, no. She put tin pots in our rooms for number one but, if we had to go, really, really, we should wake her even in the middle of the night, not to worry, the door wasn't locked.

Life was good but not all that exciting. One day seemed to spill into the next as if they were the same except that sunset brought the cool, sunrise the heat and that was just about it. My brothers went to school and took no notice of me or my sister. You're not experienced about true life, Jonah said which got Joshua laughing especially as they were taller than the drawing pin, didn't have to whistle in the squatter's palace and could do anything they wished. Only when I reached the pin would we be friends, so I could go find another crybaby to play with which wasn't fair because I wasn't one.

So I went up Wilkie Road to visit Simon. We were both five and I liked him more than my brothers who told me lies. I knew they were lies but didn't know which so I asked my father and he said to watch. If their eyes shifted a lot while they were speaking they were lying. My brothers must have practised because their eyes never moved.

Simon, on the other hand, said he'd teach me to read and write and how to do sums. Okay, I said, I'll pay you Rough Rider cigarette packets and he said it wasn't necessary. He had a way of saying things. Your success will be reward enough. Who'd believe we were the same age and he lived in the same *mahallah* up the road from us. What's more he didn't have a local sing-song accent. If people speak the way they hear, then I don't know who he was listening to. So I learned secretly and as soon I knew **The Ah Pong Seller** off by heart, I challenged my brothers to see who could read it without making a mistake.

That got them mad.

What's the bet, Joshua said.

Five Rough Riders.

Ten, Jonah said, and first show us you have twenty because we're going to beat you in four seconds flat. Nobody can read who hasn't been to school.

Jonah stumbled in the first paragraph, Joshua in the first line. When I read it through without a mistake, pausing at all the commas and full stops as Simon taught me, to give what you're reading the delivery it deserves, he said, they said it was a trick. I was using someone else's voice which was cheating. They weren't going to pay the bet or speak to me for a week and it served me right.

Time to time Simon came over and my father said I should listen and learn. A boy like him seldom pops up in streets like ours. You have to go where rich people live who have money to pay for teachers.

He doesn't have a teacher, I said, he teaches himself.

All the more reason, my father said. In Bir Haroon there were no clever people. Jews were horses, Turks were camels and Arabs were donkeys. When a rabbi or someone came with something to say, my father, that's to say your grandfather, brought him to the house, stopped making cheese and called his friends and family. On the floor, legs crossed, we sat in front of him two, three days, listening to every word until he got up, took his books and left. That's how we lived and learned and how I'm teaching you. So what am I saying? I'm saying stay by his side like a fish follows a shark picking what falls from its mouth.

When I wasn't with Simon I went up and down Princep Street alone and sometimes with my sister looking into shops and houses wondering why they were so narrow. You could stand against one wall and spit across to the other, all except the end one, the coffee shop, was twice as big. It had an icebox with Green Spot, 3 cents each, in glass bottles with cardboard tops you pushed in and drank straight from the bottle which we never got to taste. For 3 cents, my father said, you can get a full pail. Just mix a little orange syrup with tap water which is another thing I want to teach you. The cost of anything is nothing. It comes from the ground which God, whose name is blessed, gave us free of charge. It's what you put it in, a glass bottle or a tin or a wooden box that makes the price. From this you learn two things. One: only buy loose or wrapped in newspaper. Two: don't throw away the bottle or the tin – that's where your money went.

Of the fourteen houses in our row, eleven had shops, four selling food. Neighbours, my father said coming back into the shop from the 5-foot way as if he didn't want to look at them as he spoke, you cannot choose. Luck of the draw. So be sure you get on well and never pick a fight because you have to see their faces every time you pass for the rest of your life. Hawkers are different. If they come and sit in front and block your shop, you can tell them please move aside. Be polite. They also need to live. There are two rules. One: they mustn't sell what you are selling. Unfair competition, understand? You pay rent and they take your customers. Two: no food outside a shop selling paper. Oh yes, Three: if they are selling anything that comes from a pig, chase them off and no need to say please.

Twenty-two Lims lived next door at No. 49 if all were Lims, not impossible seeing as how Lim Ah Kow had two wives. Not being a Jew he knew nothing about not being too frequent in going in unto them. He sold dried Chinese foods piled high in baskets on the floor, heaped on shelves, festooned from ceiling hooks, with a narrow walkway through the shop and lived with his wives, children and children's children anywhere there was space to put a bunk or spread a camp-cot. They had spiky hair, spoke Hainanese and all their names began with Ah. The boys wore shirts and no pants until they were four-years old so they could make shishi in the drain and not mess themselves.

Lim's signboard ran across the front above the shop in red letters on gold:

I used to think Chinese for double happiness was two people with high hats holding hands and dancing to show they were happy. Dancing? Holding Hands? Happy? They may be happy, my father said. Do they care what they are doing to me? Each time the toe of his slipper shoved a basket of *bak kwa* or *rousong* or *gonbui* that had slipped onto his piece of 5-foot way, he swore vengeance, unspecified, if any part of his body became soiled.

Once upon a time, he said, Lim had four wives. First two died. Chinese, understand? Work all day, make babies all night, die young. So Lim salted, dried, and hung his dead wives, cuttlefish one side, sausages from animals Noah wouldn't take on his Ark other side, and sold them to customers, slice by slice. Living next door to Lim, smelling and seeing his merchandise every time he stepped out, tested my father's good neighbour rule to its limits. But he honoured it and forced a smile whenever he had to.

At No. 45, Mr P D Pillai, Senior Clerk, Public Works Department with Mahatma specs and Gandhi smile lived with a plump saried wife, two stringy sons, two plaited daughters with round lively eyes, shrivelled and lunghied father, bent and balding mother. They didn't have a shop. The house front was bricked with double doors and two barred windows giving them a narrow family room where they sat cross-legged on the floor speaking Tamil.

My father would have a word or two with Mr Pillai when both happened to be on the 5-foot way watching fireflies dancing around the gaslights at nightfall. How are you Mr P D Pillai? What good works did you do in your department today, Mr P D Pillai? Then he'd wring his hands behind his back as Mr Pillai went into detail about the good works they'd done. I too didn't understand half of what he said but I didn't care because I loved how his words sounded like when he delineated schemes afoot for public benefit, self-same progress Great Britain brought to Mother India, coincidentally tutoring his father who'd also come out to the

5-foot way to catch agreeable zephyrs at close of day and vouched for everything his son said, every word true as Coventry blue.

My father nodded and smiled and said, Yes, I see, Yes, I understand, Yes, yes, when Mr Pillai and his father stopped to check with each other in Madrasi Tamil what Britain had done for Mother India over and beyond what they would have expected from their own flesh-and-blood Indian government had there been one, but he neither nodded nor smiled nor said, Yes, I see, or Yes, I understand to Lim Ah Kow or any of the twenty-one other Lims, our left-side neighbours.

We were brought up to call older people Uncle and Auntie but didn't call Mr Pillai or Lim Uncle because they were neighbours. Lim didn't even get called Mister. Mrs Pillai and the two Mrs Lims didn't get called anything because I never spoke to them.

Two of the other three food shops in our row were no problem – **Happy Garden**, the coffee shop at the end and **Ong's Provisions and Canned Goods**. But five doors down, at No. 37, which my father had to pass on the way to synagogue, was Ng's

---

龙元　　**Long Yuan**　　龙元
Canton Restaurant

---

with large gold engraved letters on a silver board, Long Yuan having to do with dragons and money in the way Chinese put two squiggles together to say what needs a paragraph in English without meaning the same thing. His menu hung from hooks in their necks right beside the 5-foot way. Yellow dyed chickens, red lacquered ducks, a glossy pig head, a couple of varnished flattened piglets and ribbons of faded brown entrails dangled from a bamboo rail in the morning and disappeared before he closed at night. To walk that stretch my father had to look across the street or barricade his eyes from what Jews mustn't see.

The sound of Ng's chopper and fumes coming up the veranda every time he started frying drove my father crazy. He'd run and hide in the dining room until it was safe to come back into the shop and never turned left outside without listening and sniffing. Ng knew this and as soon as he saw my father step out, grabbed his chopper and banged away with nothing on the block. My father didn't see it as a game. To him Ng, with a full set of gold teeth and arms tattooed from shoulders to fingertips with dragons holding Kuo Ming Tang flags, was mocking Jews, plain and simple, no two ways, I could take his word for it. In the evening he prays with joss sticks to his *Tua Pek Kong* in a red house at the top of his pillar and leaves a bowl at the bottom with leftovers from his restaurant. Comes in the morning, sees the bowl empty and thinks his god came to sit by the drain and eat. Am I a fool to let such a fool make a fool of me?

One Friday evening, dressed in fresh clothes and smelling of Bay Rum, he set off for synagogue. Ng was smoking at his pillar, his back to my father, talking to someone. *Youtai lai*, Jew coming, the man told Ng and he went for his chopper. Enough was enough. My father stomped to within three yards and confronted him in Malay. Ng flashed a golden grin and that got my father going. He asked God, in Arabic, to strike the Chinaman dead. Ng, waving his chopper, cursed him in Hokkien and a crowd gathered. My father backed off but not Ng. He pulled down the pig head and chopped along the snout all the while hurling abuse at the top of his voice. People in the restaurant were laughing, others gathered in the street and my father bolted. From that day the two men exchanged neither nod nor grunt which told me something about my father and even more two years later.

7

There were mornings I'd hear him leave his room, *chappals* in one hand, grab the rail at the top of the narrow stairs with the other, say a quiet *Oyuma*, thump onto the first step which creaked and made him swear. He didn't switch on the light because electricity was gold and stumbling was the same in the dark. Another *Oyuma* turned the landing halfway down, another step creaked and another curse. It was time to leave my bed in *baju munyit* buttoned at the crotch and follow him out of sight and barefoot while the others were still sifting the dregs of sleep for a happy ending to their dreams.

I'd get to the landing as he unbolted the back door and stepped out into the morning air before it heated up last night's left-over smells brooding under our kitchen roof. On those days between monsoons when everything stank, even the fifteen or so feet of cement floor between our kitchen and the high wall separating us from the Lims didn't shield my father from the one thing he would've changed in his life – the smell of Chinese cooking. It troubled his bond with God and only urgency took him to the squatter's palace. God help my ma if he caught her cooking in an open pot.

Pigs! Can't you see? From the air straight to our food. How many times must I tell you? Cover, he said and made for the door.

Find me a pot that stirs by itself, she said rattling the cover on.

Don't stir.

Don't stir, you get burn. Stir, you get food. Which d'you prefer to eat tonight?

He walked off cursing pigs, open pots, Chinese food, what the Chinese were doing to his life, cursed the day he left Al Basrah to save his life only to live among pig-eaters. Taking his chances with Arabs would have been better seeing as how they knew not to live among pigs, totally, and slammed the door.

Pigs fly only in Basra, my ma muttered.

There are no pigs in Basra, I said.

In your father's head, she said looking at the top of the wall. Safe. She slid off the cover, threw in chopped tomatoes, baby bamya, two slit red chillies, pinch of salt, shake of pepper, splash of water, stirred like mad, covered, turned down the gas and checked again. No pigs, she said. In five minutes, lime juice, mint, teaspoon sugar. You watch for your father, I'll chuck them in. No stirring needed.

Flat-footed and dragging his *chappals* along the cement floor, he cocked his head to check if the traps by the door to the lane had received night visitors, cursed if they had because he had to get rid of their broken bodies before the sun brought flies, cursed if they hadn't because two were still living and breeding and why didn't Lim kill his own rats, salt and dry them and sell them to his Double Happiness customers?

Now it was time to attend to himself, God, himself, in that order. He stood at the sink and thanked God for the miracle of water running in iron pipes. As the oldest child he had to fetch it daily from the village well in leather skins until his shoulders bent out of shape which I could check for myself if I didn't believe.

With his piece of SUNLIGHT laundry soap – the yellow bricks with three grooves to cut into four bars he divided into eight so if one went missing it was only half – he worked a noisy lather into his praying parts. My ma said clothes are clothes and bodies are bodies so she cut the nicer smelling red LIFEBUOY into four bars, pressing the wet sliver of the last onto the raised letters of the next.

He wiped what he'd washed, pegged the towel on the line, fetched the KOLYNOS powder from behind my ma's pots and pans, brushed his teeth, turned on the tap, watched the sink water run in the shallow drain out to the back lane and prepared himself for his address to God. He rearranged his sarong higher up his belly, pulled down his singlet, exercised his toes in his *chappals*, brought his feet together, paused to listen for sounds next door and sniffed the air. Safe.

When Jews pray, go in and out of houses, drink a glass of water, eat a piece of bread or smell a sweet fragrance and any other time they have reason to rejoice or remember, they praise and thank God for His gifts and/or blessings and/or miracles. *Tefillin*, leather phylacteries, are worn when praising, thanking and blessing God for rescuing the Hebrews after 400 years of slavery under a Pharaoh whose name isn't known and therefore can't be cursed, but all the same may it be blotted out from the world of the living.

First of all, my father said, God hammered the Egyptians with plagues like no one can imagine. One would be enough for anyone to surrender. But Pharaoh? With a heart of stone? Harder. What's the hardest thing in the world?

Diamonds.

What's hard and rotten?

I didn't know.

Okay, he said, dried dog shit. Not only his heart. Head to foot, totally. Do you know how many Hebrew slaves he had? Fathers, sons, mothers, daughters. Worth millions in today's money. Why should he let them go? So, how do you deal with such a man?

Send ten plagues.

All at once? No. Try one, see what happens. So which did God send first?

Blood.

10 upon 10. Rivers of blood with dead fish floating.

You'd think that's enough, put up your hands, fly your grandmother's drawers from a pole. But some people live with stink. Like next door. Did Pharaoh care? Did he not live in a palace with incense day and night? Slaves fanning? So God sent the next.

Frogs.

Shabash. Not so terrible. Some people eat frogs. Like next door. In bunches with eyes still staring. They would thank God for free food. Understand what I'm saying? So He sent millions upon millions till they entered inside Pharaoh's palace, inside his bedroom, inside his drawers interfering with him until he could stand it no more. So he says to Moshe Rabbenu, Go tell your God, just like that, go tell your God, I'm ready to make a deal. He stops the frogs, I let his people go. God knew what would happen but He gives Pharaoh a second chance, understand? Always give two chances. Let that be a lesson for your life – everyone makes mistakes. So God stopped the frogs but did Pharaoh keep his word?

No.

Let that be another lesson for you. Trust nobody specially those with half a face.

Half a face?

Egyptians are painted from one side because the other side had no face.

Each plague grew in my father's head. Boils swelled into cabbages, lice had crocodile jaws and there wasn't a number in the whole world to count the locusts that blocked out the sun totally in the day, moon and stars, every last one, totally at night, until when the last plague wiped out the first born sons, Pharaoh could take no more. Even that wasn't enough for my father. He kneaded the story with his hands and every muscle in his face until the entire Egyptian army, men and chariots, drowned, swallowed forever when God closed the Red Sea to teach Pharaoh never again to fight with Jews.

Pharaoh was his name for anyone who persecuted Jews. He paraded them with animal heads until excitement and the heat got to him then grab his fan, work it close to his face and gasp for air and I'd rush to the kitchen.

Don't be so angry, Pa, I said giving him a glass of water, they're all dead.

Dead? He wiped the drip from his lips. Sure, but they rise from the grave. So long as there are Jews there will be a Pharaoh and since always there will be Jews, so always a Pharaoh. He calmed down, stopped fanning himself, looked up and mumbled a prayer so fast I didn't hear what he was thanking God for. It was many years before I knew.

By now I was at the door watching him pray with nothing between him and God but a narrow patch of blue sky brightening between the high walls at the back of our house, one tefillin on his upper left arm facing his heart, the other on his forehead, tallit draped over his head and shoulders. He paused to compose himself, lifted his head, closed his eyes and prayed silently even those passages he should have said aloud, lest the blessed words get tarnished by the vice next door. He had three-quarters of the prayer book and half the five books of Moses safe in his head and would have had them in mine had he lived longer.

Commandments fulfilled, he kissed his fingers and touched his eyelids, blessed the name of God, kissed his prayer book and packed everything into his tattered blue satin bag.

He put the kettle on to boil, took the aluminium *finjan* off the bent nail in the wall and dropped in two heaped spoons of his special coffee powder from

நல்வரவு	**Mysore Palace**	நன்றி
Welcome	**Best Quality Spices**	Thank You

in Middle Road, having taught the Hindu owner how he wanted his *katti* of beans roasted then ground with no more, no less, exactly seven cardamoms, fine as dust and do nothing until he turned up, 10 o'clock Sunday morning, rain or shine.

He added four half spoons of sugar, poured in the water before it came off the boil, stirred, returned the *finjan* to the fire, let the coffee rise three times and settle one minute. He counted to 54 either because Arabic numbers take longer to say or he reckoned an Arab minute was ten percent shorter. At this point I'd disappear into the shop and sit in my corner. Hah, you're here, he'd say, put his glass on the table by his chair, blow on his fingertips and go about opening up before our street filled with people.

Most times I kept him company even on those steamy afternoons when business was dead but not enough to bury while the others snoozed upstairs. When you're young you're like a towel, he said, and it's a father's duty to soak you with stories. And stories, I want to tell you, are nothing without a lesson for life which is to say: obey God's commandments and you'll be blessed. God gave us a perfect world, perfect in every way is what I'm saying, perfect totally. But all fathers have favourites, no? I didn't answer. We were four and I didn't want not to be his favourite. So, tell me, who are God's favourites?

Jews, I said. This was an easy question.

For sure. We got a little extra. No. God gave us with both His two hands and all His heart. He gave us Moshe Rabbenu – my father never called him Moses – and his five books, hear what I'm saying? Not one, not two, but five and included in those books are two things to make us special. First is Shabbat, day of rest, which God did Himself. Hear what I'm saying? God rested. He, who is tireless, rested that day. For whose benefit?

Ours.

Right. Second tells us what we can eat and cannot eat. So what am I saying?

God chose us to obey his commandments and I must do so all the days of my life.

He'd started when I was three and now I was five I'd heard his stories at least four times, changing them now and again to check I was listening. He was always there for me and I always knew where he was, what he was doing and where to find him when he wasn't home. When I started school he waited to smile when I came in, to tell me I should not say a word until I had washed my face and kissed my ma and had a drink and a piece of bread with something sweet and then, if I wanted, sit and tell him what I did that day. I was happy all the time I knew him and never had to compete with my siblings for his love.

When he had opened the shop he went into the street to catch early birds heading for the trolleybus stop at Ladies Green under the huge flame-of-the-forest that blazed between monsoons and turned the Green red with flowers.

Sure you don't need a pencil or exercise book from my shop? Better check before your teacher canes you. Most avoided him but enough came in to make it worth his while and again he thanked God as he dropped the first coins of the day into the yellow **KLIM** tin.

I asked him how much.

Count only when you give change or go to the Post Office. That way you won't put your own evil eye on what you have.

I guess he never knew how little he had.

8

One quiet Sunday morning I stood outside the shop, waiting for something to happen when I spotted the *tikam* man coming up the 5-foot way. Asking my father for two cents meant answering four questions – why d'you need two cents? didn't your mother feed you enough you need to eat from the street? don't you know money doesn't grow like trees? why aren't you with your brothers? I told him they wouldn't take me on adventures until I reached the drawing pin and showed, with my fingers, I was half an inch short when it was more like an inch and a half which wasn't telling a lie because I didn't say it.

So lower the pin.

Isn't that cheating?

Cheating is taking what isn't yours by rights. This is more like breaking rules that have no meaning for real life.

They hate me, I said. They say I'm your favourite like Joseph with a coat of many colours and if I don't watch out they'll throw me down a well and sell me as a slave.

Let them say what they like, he said with a full smile and gave me two cents by which time the *tikam* man had reached us.

I spun the wheel and the needle stopped over the 3. *Dapat!* I shouted. Most of the circle got you one piece of candy that took ten minutes to suck or broke a tooth. If the needle stopped over a thin wedge you got 2, over a tiny sliver, 3. When the hawker gave me one piece I told him he was cheating so he blew the needle over to 1.

Pa, I said, tell him he's cheating.

How many times have I said gambling leads to arguments?

It's only *tikam*, Pa. You can't lose, so it's not gambling.

Let this be a lesson, he said. Start nothing you cannot finish even an argument you didn't start. Isn't that what I said? Stand up for yourself. Either take what he gives with a smile or put the money back in the **KLIM** tin.

I took the candy and went to sulk in my corner, thinking the two pieces could have bribed my brothers to take me with them before I reached the pin just as a jade green Studebaker pulled up and Aunty Flora stepped out with her four daughters. Hello Jujube she said to me, Hello Judah, how are you, she said to my father.

Hah, he said then called up the stairs, Your sister Flora is here with her basket of flowers. 1 … Rosie, 2 … Lily, 3 … Poppy … and number 4 … Daisy.

The bamboo curtain snapped and crackled as Auntie Flora went through and I'm sure she called upon God as she pounded up the stairs. My cousins, in shades of pink with matching ribbons in their hair followed trying to look as if nothing was about to happen. Tell that husband of yours, my auntie said extra loud for my father's benefit, it's God's wish and no business of his if you have three sons and I have four daughters. He, of all people, should know better the way he's always telling the world about God's will.

I licked the sugar off my fingers, slid off the desk and went half way up the stairs to watch and learn how my father handled an argument he had started.

Auntie Flora was at the top of the stairs half covering her ears, half listening, half talking. He's at me again, she said and, seeing me on the landing, asked how old I was.

Five and a half.

Five and a half years and still he holds it against me. Whenever the *djinn* gets into him, he has another go. Now he's going to give me names for more daughters, wait and see.

Number 5 … Iris … floated up from the shop.

You know nothing about how I feel, Auntie Flora said to my ma, louder, trying to shout him down. What's going on inside, what hell I go through everyday …

… number 6 … Jasmine …

… because I smile and make out I'm happy-go-lucky you think all is fine and dandy …

… number 7 … Violet …

Auntie Flora's face was turning purple trying to get her daughters away from her as they went about asking my ma where Judith was they wanted to play with her.

… number 8 … Orchid. If you need more …

You hear him? Auntie Flora was fuming. And you stand there holding a stupid vase?

My ma looked at the vase in her hands as if seeing it for the first time. Judith's in her cot, she said to the girls, turned, muttered, asked one of them to please put the vase on the table between the beds, thank you, poked her head into the room, said, fine, right there, what? yes, sit on the bed, any one you wish, and turned to her sister, no, Flora, no.

It's your fault, Auntie Flora said throwing out her arms. Don't say no. He's never forgiven me for being Jujube's godmother and not Sally his cockeyed sister. How long does he hold a grudge, Arab-Jew that he is?

My ma held her sister's face in her hands and appealed to her eyes. I couldn't hear what she said but knowing how she hated wasting the oil she had to pour over troubled waters, she would've said, No need, Flora, I beg you, calm down.

Beg all you want. I'll *not* calm down. Why should I?

When you're angry, my ma said, you can't see straight.

That's just my point, Auntie Flora said. Sally can't see straight. You should've let your sister-in-law from Basra, where Arab-Jews live and learn nothing, be godmother.

No, my ma said, it's finished, it doesn't matter anymore, when my father's voice came out of the shop and up the stairs again.

If you're still short, there are names of jewels, like you wear morning, noon and night.

You hear how he's carrying on? You're going to stand there and not say a word?

My ma came down the stairs. Go find something to do, she said to me. This is not your business, and down she went into the shop where there was a lot of whispering. My father told her not to whisper. When someone has something to say he should say it for everyone to hear. She whispered some more, came out, walked past me up the stairs and told Auntie Flora, it was okay, my father wouldn't say another word, go into the bedroom and she'd bring something to drink.

I know him better, Auntie Flora said leaning over the banisters. It's clear to me, she bellowed as my ma tried to pull her into the room, that your husband learned nothing all the years he's been here. His head's clogged with the same shit as the day he left the boat in Telok Ayer. And what was he carrying in the baggage he didn't bring? Abracadabra he should've left with his broken shoes, if he wore any.

No Flora, my ma said. No more. There are children.

Good. Let them hear. Let them learn to stand up for themselves in life as I had to do every step of the way. Your husband thinks carrying a boy to be circumcised will find a man for his brainless sister. Huh. A hairless monkey won't look at her, huh, with eyes that see both ends of the street at the same time, huh.

Flora. Please Flora. No more. Why are you still here, she said to me. Go now before I lose my temper. I knew she wouldn't, but she glared so hard I went to my place in the shop, my father sat in his chair looking at his feet and five minutes later Auntie Flora marched through with her daughters and out of the shop saying she'd come to visit because that's what families are supposed to do. I ran after them and as they got into their car I said, Bye, bye, Auntie Flora, please come again soon. She put her hand through my hair and I could see her lips quivering and tears in her eyes.

9

Okay, a row was a row, not unusual and it didn't last. Everyone was speaking and friends again as if nothing happened which my father said was how the world must be or there'd be war and bad times we didn't want to think about.

Uncle Friam and Auntie Flora, my godparents, were rich, in our eyes, very rich. My father wasn't envious. Family are family, he said, everyone has faults but with family it's better not to notice otherwise how do you live seeing the same people till you can't stand the sight of them, know what I mean?

There must have been more to it and for sure it didn't start the day I was circumcised. More likely the late 1920s when my ma's father had given up hope for his son the likes of whom even a doting mother would hide in a cupboard as Auntie Flora used to say any time his name was mentioned. So the old man started hunting husbands for his two teenage daughters before they too became dead stock. Rich Jews imported friends or relatives from the old country for their daughters. Others made a list of local Jews not crippled in body or mind and let it be known there was a dowry. By then most men were wearing drill trousers and cotton shirts, some doing well enough for socks and leather shoes, but my father was still in *chappals* and blue *gelabieh* so he didn't get on the list.

In sunglasses Auntie Flora could pass off as a white with a tan so why would she give my father a second thought? Ephraim Ezra – that's Uncle Friam – was different. He got straight to the point. Keep your dowry, he said to my grandfather, pulled out his wallet, counted crisp hundred dollar notes slowly onto the table and stopped when the old man gasped, opened his eyes, stood up and said, *Hamdalalla. Furha, tal honi.* Come Flora you have a husband.

To give the devil his due, Uncle Friam was a mile and a half ahead of my father along the road of manliness. Tall, athletic, good looking, Clark Gable moustache, secretive eyes and Singapore Swimming Champion three years running. He grew his thick black hair long like Johnnie Weissmuller in *Tarzan the Ape Man* and Auntie Flora kept hers bushy to her shoulders like Maureen O'Sullivan in *Tarzan and his Mate.* People said they came from Hollywood to make a movie in our jungle and forgot to go back.

Uncle Friam, like my father, had come from the stagnant waters of Iraq, Kirkuk or some such place God never visited. But he put it behind and tried to imitate the Jews escaping Europe. Fair-skinned, educated and rich, they lived in sprawling bungalows with an army of servants among the Europeans on high ground or by the sea in acres of land fringed with coconut palms, where Streets were called Avenues, Gardens and Heights, with names like Cavanagh, Clemenceau and Braddell. Their children went to school in England to learn to speak through their noses without which they couldn't be members of Whites-Only clubs and clink glasses with the masters.

Poor and backward, we weren't worth a smile and, as the saying goes, they'd not be seen dead in our synagogue going to the one on the hill in Oxley Rise and, as the other saying goes, the twain never met. Even in Waterloo Street synagogue better off English-speaking local Jews sat on the brighter, breezier left, Arabic-speaking pedlars, small-timers and shopkeepers like my father and his friends on the right. Not even a thousand souls from everywhere on God's earth and one quarter of us looked down on the other three.

To disguise his skin, too dark to be a tan, Uncle Friam walked into Raab the Tailor in Amber Mansions. A Jew from Romania, he made suits for Europeans and wasn't going to lay his tape measure on the likes of Uncle Friam.

Suits, four, latest style, colours your choice, he said when at last Raab gave up trying to kick him out of the shop. Shirts: dozen, plain, stripes, dots, dashes up to you. Collars: detachable, gold studs. Cuffs: attached, folded. Links: **EE**, gold, 24-carat. Ties: half dozen, striped, different colours. Make it a dozen. Hats: two, narrow ribbon, no feathers. Shoes: Oxfords and anything else you think I need to make me look like you. Refuse and I'll take off my clothes, stand naked outside your shop and burn them. What do you say?

I'll need a deposit.

Uncle Friam peeled fifty dollar notes from his wallet onto the counter and stopped when Raab, the Jewish Tailor from Romania who made suits for Europeans and now, rich non-Europeans, put up his hand and smiled.

My father must have shredded her feelings that Sunday morning, poor woman. Each time she delivered a girl Uncle Friam disappeared for a week. When he reappeared he was as drunk as an empty whisky bottle and couldn't remember where he'd been. Jews need sons to carry on the family name and Uncle Friam was an only son with six sisters.

Not being on the first-choice list, my father had to make do with consolation prize getting the whole of my ma's dowry plus ten per cent of what Auntie Flora didn't need and I have to wonder if what I said about our lives being shaped the moment we are conceived includes a different mother.

Even so it took two more years before he could tell his family that his new wife came with a dowry enough to rent a house and take over a shop. Surely, they said, he could support one of them at a time until they all came from what was going on in Iraq. About the sea passage they'd scrape here and there, they said, all of which went back and forth by letter between him with an address in Singapore and them in a village somewhere outside Basra and if God didn't do His bit how did the letters arrive?

He wrote back that yes, he was doing well, of course, but not so well they should think he could support another person. He was flesh and blood, sure, but they shouldn't expect too much, life was still a struggle. As soon as he was ready he'd let them know and it would be best if his brother Suleiman came first. They could work together, he and his brother, maybe also send money, which he would like to do with God's help, amen.

The following year, a young woman in black *jilbab* walked into his shop screeching in Arabic. My father told her to please keep her voice down, he wasn't deaf, when she said, Yehuda? he said, Salha? and she started screaming again.

A week later a letter arrived to say how grateful his family were, may God bless him all his days. He should be pleased to know Salha was on her way. The steamer was *Glory* so please fetch her otherwise, who knows? Life in Basra was daily getting worse for Jews, the *Khalifah* going mad and making new laws every day. They wanted to send Suleiman, but two Jewish girls were raped in the street and they were living behind locked doors. The others would come every few months, one by one, and he, Yehuda, would always be blessed as the one who saved their lives, the whole family.

Auntie Sally wasn't as bad as Auntie Flora made out. Okay, her eyes did squint a little if you looked hard. My father, doing his bit, brought her to work in the shop, taught her English, told her things were different, there was law and order and not to hide when she saw a man. I did my best, he said. Her heart is good and being so happy here she gave customers more change than they paid in the first place. I told her these people are not the reason for your happiness, you owe them nothing, so for now, just come visiting, he said.

When she didn't show up for two weeks, he went to the Kasbah, that's to say the big old house at 60 Waterloo Street where poor and destitute Jews lived, pounded her door and warned her if she didn't come out of her room he'd send her back to Al Basrah. As if.

When I turned six my father thought it time to take me with him to synagogue. Some Jews, he said, are Jews only for festivals and you're old enough to learn what makes you a Jew all year round. This played right into my brothers' hands. They'd been going for years and knew everything by heart and anyway how could he teach all three of us at one and the same time which was how I got to meet my father's friends and hear their Arabic stories during the Saturday afternoon breaks.

They talked about God, the Bible and how difficult life had been in Iraq, Syria, Persia, Egypt and Turkey, and how their hearts were in their mouths whenever a sultan died. Would Suleiman be worse than Osman or better than Mehmet? Most of all they wanted to know why their fathers put up with it all those years and never thought to leave in those days when nobody knew where one country finished and another started and you didn't need passports.

Time to time when one had heard a rumour they talked about what was happening to Jews in Germany. Being at the edge of the British Empire newspapers reported only what Britain was doing and she wasn't doing much about Jews in Germany.

The women they talked about were either heroines or harlots who died centuries ago. One Saturday afternoon in

1939 when they were trying to work out what it was in Samson's hair that made him so strong, getting to where Delilah, the *gahbah*, got him drunk, shaved his head and went off to betray him to the Philistines, a group of strangers with blond hair and blue eyes walked into the porch.

No one understood a word they were saying until one said, *Redstu* Yiddish? waving his hands, then a little louder, Yiddish, still louder, Yiddish, Yiddish, Yiddish?

Hah, Yiddish. My father jumped up. Hah. He told his friends in Arabic maybe they were Jews, maybe refugees, maybe from Germany and a quick discussion followed. Two went off to the other synagogue to find European Jews and my father led the visitors into the synagogue, telling them in English to feel at home.

Before the evening service Mr Raab the Romanian Tailor arrived.

Listen carefully and let this be another lesson, my father said. Jews are never satisfied. They always want to make things better. German they took, added Hebrew, and made Yiddish. Now the world has another language. Follow what I'm saying?

The refugees were taken to homes and hotels and two weeks later boarded a steamer for the International Settlement in Shanghai. Meantime my father cornered a few who came to synagogue the following Saturday. Speaking English sprinkled with a few Hebrew words he hoped might sound like Yiddish, he asked what was happening in Germany.

They said they were Austrians, lucky to escape and told us about Kristallnacht, six months before. So we'd understand they ran around the synagogue shouting Pogrom, Pogrom, Pogrom, pretending to smash glass, throw Torah scrolls from the Ark, prayer books and shawls on the ground and stamp on them, then set the building on fire.

Did you hear? That was my father in Arabic.

Silman said, Not true.

Ezra said, Why not?

Shooli said, Even mad Turks didn't behave like that.

On the way home that evening my father said to me, I want you to know there is a new Pharaoh. He has a pig's face and a square moustache.

Only when our turn came five years later, did I understand what it was to be a Jew and a people separate unto God.

10

Of all boys Mun Chong whose hair stood up like coconut husk had to be beside me this of all days. I had my uniform over my arm as we were told, not sure why I was in a room full of naked boys and he was pointing. I wanted to say, Shut up Pigshit, but calling him a pig would have offended my father who said I wasn't to say that word until I was 13 and my ma who said not to use bad words without saying which because she couldn't bring herself to say them and knowing that God was everywhere and heard everything I said neither.

But did God know what I was thinking? Would it still be a sin if I just thought the words? Could I play safe by asking God to forgive me, for instance, if it accidentally popped into my head? Would He? I wasn't sure. Or if I said sorry first, like cancelling it before, could I say the word after? I asked my brothers.

Jonah said, No way. Being oldest he made a point of disagreeing with me to show he was in charge. He didn't have to do that with Joshua who always agreed with him, usually repeating most of what Jonah said like an echo in an empty room, which isn't saying my brothers were empty rooms. But right now Pigshit was getting me so mad I was thinking it and asking forgiveness so God didn't leave a mark on my forehead like He did to Cain and how would I face my father?

It all started five minutes after the bell on the first day of school, Monday January 13th 1941. Miss Beeston, Primary School Headmistress, stepped out of her office in white blouse and blue skirt to look like us and inspected the new boys two by two in the corridor. As she went by checking we were in proper uniform, Saint Andrew's blue and white, wearing good shoes, canvas was fine. What a beautiful head of hair, she said putting her fingers through my thick black curls so I gave her a big smile. Well I had to being the only one she bothered to talk to and she said, Dimples too. Heartbreaker!

When she left, Pigshit Mun Chong, the other half of my two-by-two, kicked my shins, called me a suck-up ball-carrier cissy, said I'd permed my hair and what's the use of a louse-house on your head? He was short and plump with beady eyes and had a loud, class-bully kind of voice.

But this was mid-morning on the third day. Half the class was naked in four neat rows of five like a field of tapioca, and he was telling the others to look at mine. I shifted my clothes to where my namesake planted his fig leaf hoping no one would see. What the hell. So what if theirs drooped like melting candles and mine looked like a young acorn?

What's going on at the back? That was the young English doctor in long white coat playing with the stethoscope hanging from his neck. Boys pointed at me. Come here, young man. His voice was friendly, I'll give him that.

I didn't budge, felt feverish and weak in my legs. The nurse took me by the hand and the doctor turned me to face 19 gaping boys, lifting their spouts to compare with mine.

Hands behind your backs, he said not so friendly this time, got down on one knee and put his arm around my shoulders. You must be Jewish. Are you?

Was it a trick question? Was he the Egyptian Pharaoh with no name who wanted to kill Jewish boys? He couldn't be because his face had two sides. If I said, No, would he know I was lying? I nodded and shook my head.

I'll take that as a Yes, he said then louder so the whole room could hear, this young man has been circumcised. He's just fine. You will be happy to learn that all the male members, he looked at the nurse, she looked away, by which I mean the men in our Royal Family, His Majesty the King, his brothers and the sons of those who have them, are also cir-cum-cised. If anyone has any questions about cir-cum-cis-ion, I will answer them. No one had so he said, In that case, thank you, Miss Langridge. We'll get on.

He still had his arm around me and to get things going, he smiled to ease me a little seeing as how it had all been too much and school was supposed to be a good place where boys should be happy and have fun or so Miss Beeston told us at our first assembly. I gave him back half his smile to let him know I wasn't holding anything against him.

You'll be fine, he said, gave me a twirl, pulled down my cheeks to check my eyes, made me look side to side, up and down, told me to stick out my tongue and say ahh, put a metal thing in my ears, took a long look each side, ran his stethoscope front and back and told Miss Langridge to check my temperature, height and weight.

You're hale, young man, she said with a little wink and a smile bigger than the doctor's. Get your clothes on and run along to your class.

It would've been okay if Simon had been there. Two cir-cum-cised dickybirds in one room would've dropped Pigshit's mouth enough not to say a word and if he had Simon would've shut it, but he was gone by half past ten on the first day.

We were seated in class according to surnames which was why I got stuck with Pigshit Mun Chong on my left and had to hold hands as two-by-two partners when we assembled. He didn't unless the teacher was looking and I didn't want to, being unsure if I could hold the hand of someone who ate pork. Simon Sefardi, S not M, shouldn't have been my right side neighbour but in a class of 35 Chinese, 3 Indians and 2 Jews, Miss Yong may have thought we'd like to be together.

After writing the alphabet on the blackboard and making us sing it together in tune, she gave out slates and slate pencils and small tins of long brown flame-of-the-forest seeds. She spoke slowly for those who didn't speak English at home. Take two seeds out of the tin, she said, her fingers showing what her mouth was saying, and put them on the table. Has everyone done it? Good. Now take another three seeds and put them side by side. Very good. Now I want you to count how many seeds you have, write the answer on your slate and put up you hand. Whoever writes the correct answer first will get a silver star to wear for the day. We call this ad-ding.

Simon didn't bother with the seeds. He wrote 5 on his slate and didn't raise his hand because he didn't want the silver star. When she'd got us adding seeds to get bigger and bigger numbers, she said, Clever boys, now I want to teach you how to sub-tract, which is the opposite of ad-ding. We had to lay out 7 seeds, put 4 back into the tin and write how many were left. By now Simon was bored and looking out of the window. He wrote on his slate: $7-4=3$ $7+4=11$ $7x4=28$ $7÷4=1¾$.

Miss Yong, walking between desks to see how we were doing stopped and opened her eyes large as lychees. Boys, I want you to be very, very quiet, she said and took Simon with his slate to see Miss Beeston. When they returned a few minutes later, he picked up his bag, said goodbye to me, went to Primary 2A, then upstairs to Standard 1A before the year was out. Even then we'd see each other during recess and I'd ask how he was doing, and he'd say he wished his teacher would hurry up and teach something he didn't know.

All the way home on the trolleybus with my brothers I told myself not to mention the medical check-up. They'd never understand how it felt being naked and having the unusual shape of your peepee explained to a crowd of goggle eyes. They'd only laugh. My sister didn't have one so she wouldn't know and I knew exactly what my ma would say. That's fine. They're just checking to see if your mother feeds you properly and keeps you clean and healthy and my father would say, You should be proud that you made your covenant with God.

You're not so happy, he said. Something went wrong today?

I sat in my corner at the back of the shop working my face into a pout.

Up to a week ago he was an unchanging father, the same in the morning, afternoon and evening. Now I was changing him into a morning father and when-I-get-back-from-school father and between times I had to learn lessons which were different from his stories with lessons for life and he wasn't there to tell me if they were right or wrong. Even worse was that I had to get ready for school and couldn't watch him pray and make coffee and open the shop and put the day's first coins into his **KLIM** tin without counting.

I didn't want to back away from him so I sat there telling myself I was only six and a half, my curly hair and what I had in my pants were mine and none of Mun Chong's pigshit business, God please forgive me for both words together, I'm sorry, they just slipped out.

I didn't answer.

I don't mind if you don't want to tell me, he said, but if it's okay with you, tell me what your teacher taught you today. To read a little maybe? A…B…C?

Until Zed, I said.

Very good. Now you can read Hebrew *Aleph* to *Tav and* English A to Zed. Which do you think is more important?

English.

Is that what your teacher said? I shrugged. First of all, he said, you should be proud. You can read Hebrew which few

81

in the world can do and second of all, I have a question. Your teacher makes you stand when you answer, no? I nodded. So stand up now, straight, head high, and be ready for the question.

I stood at attention.

Okay, here's the question so think carefully before you answer like you do in school. Why are Jews called People of the Book?

Because they wrote a book, I said. I'd forgotten.

Try again.

Because someone wrote a book about them.

7 upon 10, he said with an approximate smile. Not one book, but five. He held five fingers in an open hand facing away from me. Not someone or anyone, but God Himself, God bless His Name. Now I will tell you the whole story and how it happened. Are you listening? I nodded. God told Moshe Rabbenu to fetch paper and pens and come up the mountain. You know which one?

Mount Sinai.

Right. Covered with clouds, now and then thunder with a little lightning, know what I'm saying, a place where God would sit and look to see what we are doing and how to make life better for us. When Moshe Rabbenu arrived huffing and puffing, God told him, Sit and have a rest. He was old by then, tired from two million Jews bothering him every day for forty years in the desert. Also the mountain was very high and up in the clouds it's not easy to breathe. So he sat, and God said, Come, you and I, I say the words, you write them. Five books to make Jews more holy and, who knows, other people also will learn something useful. Now imagine. My father's hands spread to the width of a man. Here is Moshe Rabbenu, sitting, and here is, his hands moved to the right, spread, stopped when they could stretch no further, then came together in a quiet clasp. Never mind, just imagine, here is God, also sitting. So, what happened next?

God told Moses what to write and he wrote.

10 upon 10. But what I'm asking is: Which language did he write?

Hebrew.

You've forgotten? Those days nobody knew Hebrew.

Can I sit please, Pa?

Sit, sit. Did I not tell you how his mother Jochebed with his sister Miriam, sent him, eight, ten days old, not circumcised because Pharaoh, may his soul burn forever, would kill him for being a Jew, down the river in a baby basket ...

... to Pharaoh's daughter, I said. The story was coming back. She was bathing in the river and his mother hiding in the bulrushes. She sent Miriam to ask if she needed an *amah* and brought her mother who got the job.

10 upon 10. So. Now he's living in the palace what writing did he learn?

I wasn't sure. Did he tell me? I didn't answer.

Egyptians knew only how to build pyramids, one after another as if the world needs them. About letters they knew nothing. Words they made from birds, crocodiles, cats with big eyes and no tails. Remember? Good. Now God sees Moshe Rabbenu drawing snakes and ladders on good quality paper, so what does God do?

He tears the paper, throws it down the mountain and tells Moses to please move aside.

Clever boy! And He, God Himself I'm saying, started writing the first line to show how to write: *Bereshit barah elohim et ha'shamayim ve'et ha'aretz.*

In the beginning God created the heaven and the earth.

10 upon 10, he said with tears starting in his eyes. No line in the history of the whole world is greater than that one

line, and it is written in Hebrew, follow what I'm saying. God gave us a new language, he said, a lump working into his throat, the language God speaks. Right to left. I told you why, no?

Because God is left-handed.

You remember. The tears stopped and his smile brimmed over.

Was this a good time? I shifted on my perch. I'll get you water, I said, picked up the glass from his table, turned to move off and said, as if in passing, What's so special about right to left? Ah Fong says Chinese also goes right to left.

Ah Fong? From Double Happiness? One of those with black teeth and snot from his nose? From such people you want to learn? His neck veins swelled. Chinese you call writing? A fowl scratching for food writes better. Let's see who can read this rubbish, he said and marched to the 5-foot way. Hello, Mister, one minute, please, if you don't mind, and brought a young Chinese man by his arm into the shop. Sorry to disturb, he said handing him one of the small squares he cut from Chinese newspapers and punched a corner hole. Can you read this for me?

Sorry, the man said. This is Cantonese. I am Mandarin educated.

So you cannot read it?

I can, but it is difficult because there are differences which …

No need to explain, my father said releasing his arm. Thanks for your time. The man bolted and my father threw up his arms. What did I say? When God said, *Yehiye or …*

Let there be light, I said.

… 10 upon 10. What I'm asking is, when God said those words, was He speaking Chinese which is only good for this, he said, wiping behind his shorts.

I returned with his drink and he continued as if he'd been up the mountain. Now at last came the time for God to keep

His promise, he said. He would make us, Abraham's children, into a nation to be a light to shine for the rest of the world to see.

Where's the nation?

By and by, he said eyeing me over the rim of the glass. He whisked away the dribble on his chest and wiped his hand on his shorts. God knows what He is doing. At the right moment Jews from all over the world will live there and the Messiah will come and bring peace. He dropped into the rattan chair patched with sticking plaster and shaped to his body, and I returned to my place in the corner. Because, he tapped the *Chumash* on the table by his chair, of these five holy books.

How can books change the world? I was asking him one of his questions.

How? He widened his eyes and lifted one leg onto the knee of the other. Because they are the books God wrote. Follow me? God created the world. Why can't He change it? He already sent floods, fires and plagues, famine, now and again an earthquake. Did people learn? They became worse. Understand what I'm saying?

No, Pa.

Hah. I understand. How can books change the world? A flood comes, does a lot of damage and goes. Fire the same. People clear the mess, things go back to normal, they forget what happened, a new generation comes that didn't experience it and they start their tricks all over again. But books and what they say, last forever. That's my point. God said instead of floods and fires let me try something new and we still have those five books. Go now, hang these papers with Chinese writing on the wire hook for tomorrow morning and bring me a glass of water. Not so full this time.

That's how he taught me and made me believe we were special. Others had crept out of the ground, fallen from the air, crawled out from the sea, however, wherever, whenever, who knows, worshipping whoever, whichever, whatever. But God had taken us for Himself, totally. Could I ask him now? I'd blame it on one of the Lims again.

If Jews are so special, I said giving him his water, and God loves us so much, why are we so few and Chinese so many? Ah Chai says if all the Chinese pee at the same time they will drown all the Jews.

Again? One of the Ah people who eat what I wouldn't give the black dog in the street?

How about if I'm asking? If I'm God …

Never say that. NEVER, NEVER, NEVER. D'you know how big a sin that is?

Sorry, but I'd want millions and millions and millions of people.

Millions are only numbers, quantity not quality. I think his answer surprised him. He looked at the floor, at the ceiling, into the street, sifted his fingers as if working it out. Like … like, hah, for example in my village, when they brought olives from all over to grind and make oil. Do all olives give good oil? What do you think?

I took a fifty-fifty chance and he explained that if too green, they give bitter oil, too ripe, sour oil that quickly went bad. For the best oil they must be not just ripe but perfectly ripe, totally, ground with stones bigger than bullock cart wheels and heavy, don't ask and slowly, thirty, forty minutes. Too soon, less oil, less taste. Too long, flavour goes.

But what about Jews and Chinese?

Hah. Talking about olives took me back to Bir Haroon and my father, may his soul rest in peace, bringing oil straight from the stones, leaving it a week for us to sit and eat with *shtamboul* bread from his friend Mohammed who made them in his oven in the floor of his house. His eyes misted and his lower lip quivered.

The best oil needs the best olives which are few, I said. Is that what you mean?

His hands came together in front of his mouth, he nodded, let the tears run down his cheeks, swallowed hard, sniffed, wiped his face and said, You are my Joseph, like him in the Bible, who had a coat of many colours and became very rich. So you see, everywhere in life are examples. And this kind of quality oil is called virgin oil.

I asked what a virgin was. He looked at me, thought a moment and asked how old I was. Six and a half, I said and he said to let it wait.

11

Parts of my father's shop were neat and others a mess so I rearranged files in colour groups telling him they'd be easier to sell if people could see the colour they liked. He didn't need me to teach him how to sell, muttered in Arabic, slid on a kippah, walked out, looked up at heaven and said to God, What kind of sons did You give me? But only the right side of his face made out he was mad at me. The left had a wait-till-I-catch-you kind of grin and when he returned from telling God about sons who never listen and why weren't they how they used to be, what was the world coming to, both sides of his face were smiling.

Bad, but not the worst, he said dropping into his chair. Don't shuffle stock until you know what you're doing. I have a system. He fanned his face. Please. Glass of water.

Pa, I said giving him his drink, why don't you cut the shop front to back? Half, pencils and rubbers and exercise books and coloured files, same as now, half something different.

Like?

Something.

You're keeping it a secret?

Different.

Advice, he said, feeling it with his fingers, is no use unless it has stuff inside. Go to school, learn hard, think properly, then come and tell me.

I sat in my corner and closed my eyes. I wanted to say opium, guaranteed he'd be a millionaire selling to Chinese who smoke it and go mad, but I'd have to answer questions about how I knew and who told me and end up telling him about my brothers going to Sago Lane to see the Chinese death houses and brothels and they'd kill me so I said, Toys.

That's what you think? Who made you so clever, hah? First walk up and down the street, he pointed outside meaning there and then in the bleaching sun when even stray cats and mangy dogs were looking for a small triangle of shade. Soon as you see someone you think has left over money to buy toys, take his name and address.

I was sitting on the small desk he'd been given to advertise pencils, swinging my legs. A pretty Chinese secretary in a cut-out behind me held a spiral pad and a yellow Faber-Castell pencil, smiling at her European boss. My father couldn't see the point of it, shoved the desk into a corner and piled it with out-of-date diaries and calendars.

Okay, I said, like ... how about ...

He cut me off. Before opening your bizz-i-nezz first know who will buy. Customers I'm talking about. Not everyone can do bizz-i-nezz. Count how many work for others, coolie to chief clerk, then count how many do bizz-i-nezz. You need to know things, think them out, one by one, start to finish, no short cuts.

He counted, peeling fingers off his palm. First – brains, not plenty but enough. Second – courage, every problem is yours which you cannot pass to someone else. Third – hard work, early morning till late in the evening, rain or shine, sick or well. Fourth – honesty, with others so they will be honest with you. These are minimum. Then One – when to buy? Two – price, can you get cheaper? Three – quality. Can you get better quality, same price? Lower price, better quality? He looked at me, asking if I could do any of them.

And four?

Right. Four – credit, how many days? Thirty, sixty, ninety even one hundred twenty, if you know how to use your tongue. Be sure you can sell before you have to pay. That's Rule Number One before you even think to start a bizz-i-nezz. Start to finish, step by step, no short cuts. Totally.

I stopped swinging my legs, pulled them up onto the desk, hugged my knees and thought my father must be a tycoon as I leaned back against his dead stock. If truth be told, he paid cash not to be indebted and usually decided after the deed was done.

Cigarettes, I said. Everybody smokes. Matches. You use them only once.

Cigarettes? He thought a moment. Hah. Matches. Hah. He searched me with his eyes, opened them wide, narrowed them. No, he said fanning himself. You want to know why? His fan stopped. Because children don't buy cigarettes and children are my best customers. A good idea, all the same, from a boy your age. He counted on his fingers, *Wahid, ithnain, thalatha, arba'a, khamsa, sita, seba'a, thamania.* I'd just turned seven but he had a habit of adding a year until I was thirteen, a man in Jewish eyes, responsible for my own sins, which helped to remind him.

Right, he said, *seba'a.* 1934. So many came to your circumcision I had to close the shop. Wore trousers. Respect, you understand. Hah, respect for suppliers and customers. Understand what I'm saying? Add it to the list of how to do bizz-i-nezz.

Number 5.

Right. Like fingers. Easy to remember. We had a party, remember?

No, I said. I wasn't feeling so good.

He laughed, brought his hands together in a loud clap, called me to him and kissed my forehead. You are my number three, he said. Good number. *Aleph,* א, one, is arms and legs waving about doing nothing, I won't say like Yonah your brother but you know what I'm saying. Two is *Beh,* ב, which is a house. Good, but it stays in one place goes nowhere which also you understand I'm saying nothing about your brother Yehoshua. Now look at *Gimal*, ג. It's like a person running between *Beh* the house and *Dahl*, ד, number four, which is a door. What do you get? A man running from a standing still house looking for the door to take him to a better place. It will bring you luck. He put his hand on my head and said a blessing that would have been worthwhile if it turned out.

I sat with him in the afternoons when the sun had lost its pity and listened to stories Abdul Alim had told him in Bir Haroon. My grandmother sent him to fetch the beggar when food was left over and, while he ate, Alim told him stories about people being punished for what they hadn't done so I asked him why bad things happen to good people and why God allows such things in the first place.

For that you must hear what God said to Job. Were you there when I created the world? Do you know what was there before? Do you know what I had to do, just to find a good place for a world to be and for people to live? You weren't there and now you're telling me what I did was wrong? Answer me that.

Did Job have an answer?

What could he say? Only that he must be wicked to say such things. Better he shuts his mouth. Understand? How can we judge? We are nothing. Hah, I have the answer. Freewill. We share the world with others who also have freewill. If they choose to be bad, bad things happen to good people which is why I had to leave Al Basrah to save my life.

Why did you leave Pa? I thought going to school made me old enough and he'd tell me. All I got was what he saw the day he arrived, Chinese men with pigtails and women with feet so small they couldn't walk and why do people do these things when God created us in His own image after which he told me about how God made Adam and Eve and all the good things He gave them to eat in the Garden of

Eden. I had to wait until a few months before he died to know, start to finish, why he left Basra.

Things were going well. I was 7½, my first year had ended on Thursday, 4th December 1941 and I'd been promoted to Primary 2A. I thanked God for sending Pigshit to 2B. The word just slipped out and I promised I'd never say it again as long as he wasn't in my class ever. It was a half day to collect our report cards, listen to Miss Beeston tell us at assembly to enjoy our holidays and come back refreshed for another year of hard work. We sang the school song Up and On followed by There'll Always be an England and God Save the King then raced down the hill to the trolleybus. When we got off at Ladies Green Jonah ran ahead to show my father the last line of his report: Promoted to Standard 3B. My father took him back into the street, looked up and said to God, I have a son, 11 years old, and with your help he will be 12. I want to thank you for making his teacher feel pity on him after two years in Standard 2. Jonah said, Me too, and went to give my ma the good news.

Joshua who was 9 announced that his teacher told him it would be to his benefit and better all round if he stayed back a year in Standard 1. My father said he also thought so. That way he'd remember the answers from last year and, with God's help, pass his exams.

Judith, who was 5 and hadn't started school, asked why my report had only blue writing and my brothers' had some blue and some red.

Let me see, my father said. Hah. Two Goods, one Keep up the Hard Work. Hah. No need to read your brothers' red words.

I want to know, she said. Are red words cleverer?

Sure, my father said. Yonah's report has two red duck

eggs – Nature Study, History, and Yehoshua has three – English, Spelling, Arithmetic. Not everybody is so clever.

My ma came into the shop, looked at all three reports and said they were the best she'd ever seen. All her boys were very clever, thank God, and soon Judith would also be coming home with wonderful report cards with only blue writing, please God.

On Sunday, three days later as the sun was going down, I watched the man light the street gas lamp outside the shop. Judith had gone to sleep early and I was on the 5-foot way with my brothers playing *Tiga Kong*, 3-card poker with pictures, tens and aces, gambling for cigarette packets, mainly cheap Rough Riders and local brands like Glory, Yellow River and Heaven Gate. In the last few months, stunning blue, red, silver and gold ones appeared in our streets like Craven 'A', Senior Service, Player's Navy Cut, some 20-packs we'd never seen before, thrown by men with strange accents, khaki uniforms and leather boots.

We fought over who saw them first, followed the soldiers and nagged them until we got the empties. One said, Go fuck your sister, Sonny, and Jonah told him our sister wasn't called Sonny. Joshua said, sure thing, but none of us had heard the other word before.

Down along Bras Basah Road there was a shop,

My China Doll

144 Bras Basah Road   Open ALL Hours

where we found lots of the new packets but Chinese boys were also after them and we weren't looking for a fight. Anyway my father said we weren't to go there because soldiers got drunk, fought and smashed the place to pieces. Our policemen were half their size, quarter their strength and famous cowards. Worst of all were the girls, no need to say what kind, but we shouldn't go near them or bad things would happen to us.

It's a disgrace, my ma said. Would they behave like this in their own country?

In their own country, my father said, they don't see each other. Some are English, some Australians which is why they come here to fight in our streets.

When Auntie Sally came to dinner on Friday night she too had a story about soldiers drinking in the street, outside whatever it was, a café or a bar or what they wished to call it she didn't care to know. All she'd say was it was disgusting and the sooner they closed the better. The country was going to the dogs and she wanted to know what the government were doing about it. These are their type of people, she said, pink and white. It's their problem. Can you imagine, there were we, Tifa and me, just this morning, minding our business, walking along and they started whistling and one had the cheek to come close and say, fiddle-dee-dee and faddle-dee-dah, how about it, sweetie?

Half way through the year that was the talk of the town. Toward the end of the year Mr Pillai, our right-side neighbour, was using words like Outrageous, Scandalous and Offensive. Even the papers, he said, were reflecting grave public concern and banner headlines were calling for a HALT! This was not the example Europeans should set. Once or twice the papers went so far as to publish photos of soldiers with girls which my father covered with his fan so bad things didn't happen to us.

During the Saturday break in synagogue his friends talked, in fiery Arabic, about what was happening in our streets, all of a sudden, for no reason, each the size of a buffalo, red hairs are the worst which is when I heard Gahtan speak for the first time. He was one of my father's friends but not one who sat in the porch. He had a loud voice, big belly, walked with a stick and the only man I knew with one name including his surname.

The European war is boiling over, he said. Instead of fighting where they are needed, they come here to disturb our peace. Things are happening. He pointed his stick first at my father then at each of his friends in turn. Keep your ears and eyes wide open before you are overtaken by the Armageddon, he said then slid his stick under his arm and marched away talking to himself.

I didn't know what Armageddon was but knowing my father would say there was too much going on, all at one and the same time, Armageddon wasn't our biggest problem, leave it for now, I didn't ask him.

Late Sunday evening I shuffled the cards to play the next round of *Tiga Kong*, mumbling as if to put a spell on them, saying at the same time, Place your bets, and when my brothers did, raised them 5 before dealing. Let's see how brave you are, I said. They hated that and to show they weren't afraid, Jonah raised another 5 and Joshua 5 more on top.

Rough Riders were worth $1. The 10-pack new brands were $3, the 20-pack $5 and because I had the only Kensitas with a man holding a tray saying, Your Kensitas Cigarettes, Sir, I said it was $15. If they didn't agree I'd never bet it and they'd never get to hold it in their hands.

With Christmas close and Chinese New Year not far, the street was busy with lights and people and shops were open, ours too in case someone wanted to drop a few coins into my father's **KLIM** tin. He was on the pavement sitting with my ma enjoying the early monsoon cool. My Rough Riders were stacked, the others in separate piles and the Kensitas standing up like a challenge. I was winning as usual and they were threatening to cut me open till I screamed which got my father glaring and my ma saying brothers have a duty to love each other, never mind who was winning, that was life, get used to it, when the black dog that lay outside our shop got up, stretched and walked over to Ladies Green. He sat by the swings and howled and a couple more made their way slowly, got down beside him, stretched their necks and joined in which brought more strays from streets and lanes, one by one, baying one after another then in twos and threes.

What's going on, Pa?

Dogs are dogs, he said. One starts, others follow. Do they not remember when they were wolves? Did I not hear them in Mesopotamia howling in the hills? Maybe also the full moon drives them crazy.

I took my cards, picked up my bank and went into the street. The moon's not full, I said. About half. What's happening, Pa?

Nothing, he said. It's late. Go to sleep. All of you.

12

The first sounds were bangs far away. I sat up in bed, listened, ran out of my room and saw my parents' light on. The door was open and they were at the windows.

It's nothing, my ma said coming to stop me. Go back to sleep.

He's already awake, my father said and made a place for me at the window. I don't know what's going on, but it may be something for you to see and remember.

There was nothing unusual. Streets were lit and house lights were coming on as if one was turning on the next. A few people were in the street below, others coming out of houses, looking up, looking around, looking at each other. Then I saw other lights, long lights, high up, pointing into the sky. My father said they were searching and as soon as one had found an aeroplane guns went off.

Shoot it, I shouted knowing neither whose it was nor why it should be shot when the plane vanished and we heard a shattering noise, another and then another. I grabbed my father. *Shema Yisrael*, he said, Hear, O Israel, the Lord is our God, the Lord is One, and my ma shaded her eyes and continued reciting with him, Blessed be the Name of His glorious kingdom for ever and ever, when my brothers and sister came running in. She was crying and her pants were wet. My ma picked her up and hurried to the back.

What's the banging, Papa, Jonah and Joshua said together.

Have I heard such noises before? He was trembling. No one told us to expect noises in the middle of the night, he said, trying to keep his voice calm. There were rumours but nothing about what to do if rumours come true.

What should we do? My ma was at the stairs, towels in one arm my sister in the other.

I'm also asking, he said. Maybe the street is better if the house falls.

That got four kids crying.

No, Yehuda. God forbid. No, children. The house won't fall. God will protect us. She put a towel across each of our shoulders and my father urged us down saying nothing bad would happen, he was only saying, just in case.

The whole street seemed to be out in sarongs when we joined them, clutching towels, my ma in her night rappa, father in baggy drawers, singlet and cap, prayer book in his hand, finger between pages, muttering that there was no prayer about aeroplanes dropping bombs at half past four in the morning.

Two searchlights crossed beams, caught a plane, flashes popped and shouts went up along the street when the plane slipped into the darkness and we sighed.

Api, someone yelled, fire, pointing up Serangoon Road. Smoke billowed as a fire engine and an ambulance tore down Serangoon Road and raced passed. Wrong way, we shouted but they screeched round Ladies Green into Bras Basah Road and away.

Our left-side neighbours, all twenty-four Lims, high-pitched and noisy, were talking about Japs coming, wait and see.

I stayed close as my father went, group to group, listening, trying to pick up anything someone might say, work on it, make it tell him what to do. We reached the end of the street and were halfway back when our right-side neighbour Mr Pillai, now Deputy Chief Clerk (Planning), Public Works Department put out his hand. What do you think, Mr Messiah? What is your opinion? His whole family were out, dressed in street clothes.

I was coming to ask you, my father said. You are in the government. Maybe they tell you what they don't tell us.

First I must assure you, Mr. Messiah, we have no privileged information, certainly not within the ranks of locally employed officers. They tell us no more than they tell you, all of which is freely available in newspapers.

Newspapers, my father said. People are saying newspapers tell lies. Are they right?

Precisely for that reason have I been keeping my own records these past months when news and rumours have often been in conflict. Let me tell you what I have garnered from scraps picked up and what I have observed. Mind you, Mr Messiah, it has not been easy. Grade Two Locally Employed Civil Servants have access only to general files. But, where there is a will, if you catch my meaning.

Hah, my father said, I understand.

I have put together enough to reach conclusions I know with certainty. Rumours, I will convey separately.

A crowd was growing, a battle raging in the sky, explosions, fires and smoke and Mr Pillai was speaking slowly, checking grammar, choosing words most appropriate, practising to be chief clerk one day. My father knew this was just the introduction, it would take time, but right now Mr Pillai, his only hope, might say something to tell us what was going on.

All my Japanese co-workers have disappeared, he said. On a single day three weeks ago, not one reported for duty nor have any been seen since. My enquiries indicated that all Japanese labourers in my Department and all, I stress all, contractors had similarly dissolved into the ether.

Where? I don't think my father knew where ether was.

Further investigations revealed that other government departments were affected similarly. There are ways to do this, Mr Messiah, without making intentions too obvious.

So where did they go, Mr Pillai?

I must assume they had returned to Japan.

Hah, my father said. No wonder. No wonder the Japanese barbers in Middle Road where I buy coffee, you know where I'm saying, corner with Bencoolen Street? Closed. Locks top and bottom and iron bars. I want to tell you I never gave them my bizz-i-nezz. Never. The *bhai* comes, on the 5-foot way, me 40 cents, three sons 25 cents, four one shot, dollar fifteen wholesale price, fine for three months. Do I need Japanese barbers?

That may be so, Mr Messiah, but for all to have left, as if at a single moment, a sudden exodus, there must have been a call. That leads me to deduce that the aeroplanes we see and hear, bombing us without cause or provocation, are Japanese.

That was only half true. By now we could hear them, we could hear guns firing, we could hear explosions, but we couldn't see them. The planes were bombing the harbour and places I knew nothing about in those days. Then a shrill sound pierced the air, rising and falling, loud and close. People turned to look at where it came from.

What's that noise, I asked.

The air raid siren at the top of Cathay building, Mr Pillai said, which should have sounded before the raid to warn us. I fear someone will be in trouble later today.

Hah. Now I understand, my father said. I don't think he'd heard the siren. Hah. *Mumzerim*. All Japs are *mumzerim*.

I'm sorry Mr Messiah, I am not familiar with that word.

What word?

Mumzerim, did you say?

Kayfa takulu? my father said shoving me with his knee.

You want me to say the word? I asked and his knee said yes. People who don't know their fathers, I said to Mr Pillai.

Don't know their fathers … oh … I see. He smiled. Bastards, you mean?

That's the word, my father said, bar-stards. Japs are bar-stards.

Bastard is not a bad word, young man, Mr Pillai said to me. It is a perfectly legitimate definition of illegitimate birth.

Of course I knew the word, but my ma was close.

They live like friends with us. My father was getting angry. Do bizz-i-nezz, take our money. We treat them nice, then, all of a sudden, they come with aeroplanes and drop bombs. Such people I call *mumzerim*. Are you sure? These bombs are made in Japan?

That much I can say is certain. As for rumours, unconfirmed though persistent, they suggest that our Japanese residents, those you say we trusted and thought were friends, had been photographing our vital public installations, making them appear innocent by placing children and smiling family in the foreground. Moreover, some had recorded with moving pictures, comings and goings at the Naval Base and RAF installations.

Hah, you hear, my father said to me. Taking photos. What kind of people are these?

I can tell you, Mr Pillai said to me, it was only recently, inundated with exceptional paperwork with respect to improving road access to some of our sensitive installations, that I suspected something afoot. So why, I ask you young Adam, did the Authorities remain silent? I shrugged. The Japanese military now possesses information on every strategic aspect of our island which may be superior to our own.

Mr Pillai was going on and my father was listening, hands in front holding his prayer book, not wringing behind his back, saying the *mumzerim* took photos and woke us at half past four in the morning with bombs. It was like inviting people to sit in your house and eat your food and all the while they're looking for what to come back and steal in the middle of the night. Mr Pillai thought that was well put and went on to say that, fortunately, the Japanese had departed before our real strength arrived to reinforce Fortress

Singapore. By a lucky stroke he'd witnessed an event to confirm that whatever he'd earlier thought was afoot, was imminent and upon us.

My father looked at me. There are too many words he didn't know. I couldn't help. Please, he said, can you make me understand?

Mr Pillai came close as if to say what he shouldn't about how his duties took him last Tuesday to Canberra Road, the very gates of the Naval Base where, to great astonishment, he observed official cars entering, one bearing the crown and carrying Sir Shenton Thomas, Governor of the Straits Settlements. Unable to contain his curiosity, and without revealing his method, he stood at the waterfront and what did he see sailing up the Johore Strait? The pride of the Royal Navy, he lowered his voice, *Prince of Wales*, the largest British battleship, the very ship they called HMS *Unsinkable* with the battle cruiser *Repulse* and four destroyers following.

What are these, my father asked.

Great warships welcomed by the governor, military chiefs, lords and knights of the realm, many with their ladies. Mr Messiah, Britain is resolute, he said. She will not let us down. She may not, according to my researches, have been vigilant with regard to former Japanese residents ... though ... it may be ... now I reflect upon it ... yes, it was part of a plan. A potential fifth column. Masterly. Britain knows what she is doing. A nation cannot build a great empire until and unless it has complete control of every situation. Japanese are an Asian people. How will they challenge British organisation, technology and might? We have nothing to fear Mr Messiah, Britannia rules the waves. Those warships will send the Japanese into a funk.

So, will we be safe? My father looked at Mr Pillai hoping for a Yes, when there was an explosion so close everyone ran home and the street emptied.

13

When the late edition of **The Straits Times** arrived my father hooked the bamboo beads aside to mind the shop that hadn't seen a customer all day and sat at the dining table. My ma was clearing up in the kitchen, the others making up lost sleep. I'd been propped up in my corner of the shop all morning, taking short naps between wondering if war meant being woken by loud noises, people talking in the street, then everyone going home as if nothing happened. I followed and sat close to him, my head on my arms on the table.

He laid the newspaper flat and pressed out the creases.

JAPAN STRIKES AGAINST BRITAIN & U.S.

War Declaration After Attacks

LANDING ATTEMPT IN NORTH MALAYA

Japan declared war on Great Britain and the United States as from dawn today. Before the declaration Japanese air attacks were carried out on Singapore Island and Honolulu and elsewhere. Japanese troops attempted to land in North Malaya near Kota Bahru. They were repulsed by small arms fire and aircraft attacks. Some troops landed and were reported early to-day infiltrating towards Kota Bahru Aerodrome.

Air raid sirens sounded in Singapore shortly after 4 a.m. An air attack on the island developed immediately. Several bombs were dropped. Slight damage was done and there were a few casualties, it is officially reported.

Hah, he said, Mr Pillai was right. The bombs were made in Japan. You see what it says here, Japan strikes against Britain and us.

It's not us, Pa. It's capital U full stop, capital S full stop. What does that mean?

It means the typist made a mistake. Sleepy at four in the morning, in a hurry, printer chasing him, understand, to get the newspapers to the street. These things happen.

He read bits here and there, mumbled Singapore, Kota Bahru, Honolulu, shook his head, looked up at the ceiling and asked God to help him understand what was wrong with the world. Why was it so difficult to obey ten simple commandments and live in peace?

That was the noise, he said. They call it air raid siren. See where it's written: *Air raid sirens sounded in Singapore shortly after 4 a.m.*

That's what Mr Pillai said, I said. From the top of Cathay building.

Half of what he says I don't hear and three-quarters I don't understand.

Didn't you hear the siren, Pa? It was very loud.

Did we hear such sounds before? Did they tell us what to do when we hear them? We went into the streets. What do you do when you don't know what you're supposed to do? When we heard shouting in Bir Haroon we knew Turks and Arabs were looking for us. We didn't go to the streets. We hid. Please, he said massaging his throat, a glass of water and tell your mother don't clean too much. Who knows what they'll do to us tonight?

He put down the empty glass and wiped his lips with the back of his hand. While you were getting water, he said, I was remembering. How old are you?

Seven and a half.

Maybe, nine, ten, eleven who knows? That's how old I

was the year British soldiers came to Al Basrah to teach the Turks a lesson for joining Germany. Nur a-Din Basha was looking for Jews and Christians to put in the front lines then changed his mind. They are traitors, he said, helping the British and started killing us. But he needed food for his soldiers. Did we have sirens to tell us his men were coming? We saw dust rising and knew it was a messenger. My father, your grandfather, lost all. We were hiding. They took his cheese, his milk, his goats and looted from my mother's kitchen leaving nothing.

He sighed so I got up and put my arm on his shoulder. He'd always been so sure, knew the answer before I finished the question. Now he looked troubled.

Let's read some more, I said.

He turned pages reading bits in bold print and telling me that while we were roaming in the street the Japanese were landing their army at Pattani and Songkhla in Thailand and Kota Bahru in Malaya all together, one and the same time, can you believe it, are they crazy or are they mad? Mr Pillai says Japanese are Asians. Sure, they are barbers or fishermen or coolies. So how can barbers and fishermen and coolies do so many things all together, in different places? Thailand and Malaya are close but different. You fight your brothers one to one, no? You don't say, Come on, I'll take both one shot.

They do. They jump on me together.

Unfair. He smiled. Next time, call me and I'll join your side.

I'd changed his mood. He eased, shifted in his chair and turned back the pages.

Where is Honolulu? Do you know? I shrugged. They didn't tell you in school? I shrugged again. So is it true? We have nothing to fear?

What about the ships, Pa, I said without saying they'd send the Japanese into a word beginning with f the soldier said we should do to our sister and didn't know if I could use it.

Let's see if the paper has a picture to know if they frighten us.

Pictures showed *rubble in the streets, light damage, that sort of thing*, the paper said.

Mr Pillai is a good man, my father said, but he talks a lot. I'm not sure people who talk a lot know a lot. Let that be a lesson for you. If the ships are so frightening why don't they show them in the newspapers to frighten the Japs?

The Japs are gone, I said.

Hah. Right. Three weeks ago like the barbers in Middle Road. Maybe the British should invite them for a look, take them on the ships and frighten them. When you fight don't you show your enemies how strong you are? Didn't the Philistines bring out Goliath every day to frighten the Jews until David worked out how, with God's help, to kill him?

But Pa, Mr Pillai said he saw them himself, the pride of the British Navy.

Sometimes people see what they want to see.

He wouldn't tell a lie, would he?

I'm not saying lies. I'm saying seeing things and saying things we want to be true, understand what I'm saying? It's not telling lies, it's wishing. Read. See what you find to tell us he is right and we are safe.

I stood beside him looking at pictures, reading captions. This wasn't The Ah Pong Seller. It was a newspaper with small print. I read slowly, broke up long words, like **EDI-TORI-AL**. What's that, Pa?

Do I know? It's in a box. Must be important. Read and let's hear.

We have been wrong about Japan – and we are glad of it. That was easy. *We have felt all along that she would not go to war; at least not until she was forced into it.* Fine. *The idea that she would her-self throw down the chall-enge in such a blunt and irre-voc-able man-ner can have been pre-sent in the minds of very few people in-deed, even as late as yes-ter-day and her ac-ti-ons in-dic-ate stark mad-ness which can have only one result.*

Do you know what it means, Pa?

Hah. My father had been listening carefully to everything **EDITORIAL** said, trying to help with difficult words. He'd never been to school, and teaching himself to read made him a little better than me. Hah. Maybe it means what our Mr Pillai was saying. The British knew all along and now they're going to finish off the *mumzerim*, know what I'm saying, like a spider builds a web to catch a fly? Yes, maybe. Maybe. Is there more?

I continued where I left my finger. *Over-all it is clear that the lo-cal pop-ul-a-tion re-main-ed ab-sol-ute-ly cal-m. This is not an in-spi-red state-ment. It is the out-come of per-son-al ob-ser-va-ti-ons that ended less than an hour ago.*

Of course we were calm, he said. We were standing in the street like fools watching fireworks. Do we know what war is? Does a child know what fire is until he burns his fingers? In Europe they know. Have they not been killing each other since Noah saved them from the flood?

He tidied the pages and folded the newspaper.

Everybody is calm when he doesn't know what to worry about which is what I'm trying to find out. But who is there to tell us from one to two to three and make us understand up to ten? They are fighting in Europe like as though the Great War didn't kill enough. Great, you hear? They call their wars Great to make them sound grand as if war does good things for people, know what I'm saying? But Europe is far away. Now I'm asking, has it come to us? Noah built an ark. What will I do? Will we be the ones to drown?

He laid both hands on the newspaper, bit his lip, squeezed his eyes shut and started murmuring. In Bir Haroon we didn't see war but we saw trouble everyday if we didn't take care. They were going to kill me for what I did. Isn't that why I had to leave?

What did you do, Pa?

Do? Hah. I did a lot. You are too young to know these things and now we have other things to think about. Let it wait.

My ma was splashing water, chasing it with her *sapu lidi* all the way out to the back lane. She dropped the stick broom into the bucket and came in wiping her hands on the dish cloth over her shoulder. Good riddance, she said. I threw Jeyes all over and the stink is gone. They didn't empty the dustbins. Who knows what the bombing did to the *tong sampah* men last night. God protect them and let them come tomorrow. With heat and flies, you can't take chances. So? She looked at my father then at me. What did you read in the newspaper? Did they say anything we should know?

I'll close the shop early, he said. We'll go to synagogue and I'll ask God what to do.

They'd been gathering long before the service began, fifty or sixty of them, wanting a word with God ahead of the queue. They may say that wherever five Jews meet in one place there are at least six opinions but there were only two that evening.

One was sitting in the porch or standing on the stairs or crowding the lobby at the top. Uncle Friam, in rolled sleeves and crumpled trousers, nothing like himself, leaned against the wall between the two big doors leading this group. As it so happens, he was saying, I was at my club last night. Not being white his clubs were businessmen's clubs, not the Tanglin Club or the Swimming Club which you couldn't get into as a local unless you were a cleaner, a waiter or a cook.

And what did you hear? That was Rafuli the Mohel who circumcised me.

Don't worry, Uncle Friam said stepping back to avoid his bad breath.

They didn't say why not to worry? That was Shooli Deborah stroking his beard.

Everybody in your club said don't worry? Silman Pinhas slaughtered chickens, 5 cents each behind the synagogue, 10 at your house where he turned up in bloody trousers.

Did they say why not to worry? That was my father.

Are you saying I was drunk?

Did anyone hear me say Friam was drunk? No one? You see, nobody heard. So maybe the people in your club gave you a reason, which in any case, was five, six, maybe seven hours before we got bombed at half-past four in the morning. Don't worry was okay last night, but what would they say after half-past four?

Uncle Friam hadn't touched a drop from the time his wife woke him screaming until now. He'd tried to contact his bank to stop his letters of credit to Japan, but the exchange was jammed, lines came down in the raid and only when he barged into the manager's office did he know he didn't have to worry. Steps had been taken. The British knew what they were doing. Britain may have been sleeping but she slept like a lion sleeps.

Don't worry was enough, he said, which by the way were Reggie Sanderson's exact words, in broad daylight, in Raffles Place, as he walked me to the door, his hand on my shoulder. Don't worry Mr Ezra, the funny little Emperor of Japan has asked for it. We'll give it back to him with interest, rest assured. That was the Senior Manager of Hong Kong and Shanghai Bank not Tan Ah Fatt counting with bamboo beads in a Chinese bank. When Reggie says, Don't worry Mr Ezra, I don't worry. White is a colour you can trust.

That wasn't all Uncle Friam said. Four-foot-six, short-sighted Japs, blind as bats without their glasses were trying to fight six-foot-something Europeans. Rice balls and raw fish versus inch-thick steak. With sea on one side, jungle on the other, why should we worry? Japanese planes were like their toys, tanks were rice paper and fish glue and their soldiers marched in canvas shoes which any *orang utan* will tell you don't last a week in the jungle. Singapore was a Fortress and if that wasn't enough, Uncle Friam told the men around him, Britannia Ruled the Waves.

I nudged my father to mention the *Prince of Wales* and *Repulse*, the pride of the British fleet and the four destroyers and Uncle Friam said, Even he, meaning me, knows the Japs will shit in their pants coming face to face with the British Navy.

Come, my father said taking me by the shoulder, let's hear what others are saying.

We entered the synagogue where the second opinion was standing beside the *bimah* or half-sitting on armrests, speaking with hands, arms and fists.

Why didn't they switch off the lights? A small man with a scratchy voice wanted to know. Even a boy like him, he pointed at me, knows better. What is the first thing you would do in an air raid, he asked and before I could answer he said, switch off the lights, no? I nodded. There you are? And how old are you? I was about to say seven and a half when he said, Even you know what to do. Are they not getting bombed in London, day and night, so bad they call it *The* Blitz? Do they leave lights on in London? If they switch off for Germans why not for Japs?

Because Japs are short-sighted, Abe Shamash the short-sighted Hebrew teacher said, smiling at me through thick lenses.

Now's not the time to joke, said the small man. Let's stick to the point and my point is, if nobody knew where the switch box was, God help us. Seventeen planes came, lights blazing to show them where to go. Hammered the airfields,

Seletar, Tengah, Kallang, one, two, three, then Keppel Harbour, point blank, on target. On the way back the same seventeen, without a scratch, bombed the Naval Base also flooded with light. Direct hits. Hundreds dead if they tell us the truth.

Then what happens, Gahtan asked. Half way through they turn on the sirens. Why half way through? Because the ARP chief went to a midnight show and took the key with him. Is this how they are fighting Germany?

Outside they are saying the opposite, my father said. Friam says his bank manager put his arm on his shoulder and told him, Don't worry, the Japs asked for it, we'll give it back with interest, rest assured.

Have you seen for yourself? Raffles Place? Robinson's? Windows blown all over the street? Am I lying? Isn't my office round the corner in Market Street? Direct hit, bull's eye, in the heart of town!

Friam was right there, my father said. He said nothing about Robinson's.

Your brother-in-law? That was the scratchy voice again. Was he sober?

My father nodded.

If I know Ephraim Ezra, Gahtan said, he was drinking all night with the likes of them. Chin Chin. Bottoms Up. One more *stengah* for the road. These are those your brother-in-law mixes with. Drunks like him. Of course they'll say, Don't worry, we'll give it to them. Ask what they'll give and you'll hear another story. A kick up their own arses.

I looked at my father to see if that word was allowed in the House of God when Gahtan said, God forgive me. I think he was getting angry. His face was going red and he started coughing so my father patted him on the back till he stopped and cleared his throat. Have I not been saying this for months? Have we not seen soldiers in our streets? Why are they here? There is a war in Europe, or maybe you haven't heard.

I heard, my father said. What has that to do with us?

To do with us? Gahtan shook his stick in the air. You don't read the papers?

Okay, Gahtan, my father said. Calm down before you start coughing again and this time I won't hit so nicely. Sure I read, but I didn't go to school like you. Just tell me what's going on. I'm not so proud to ask when I don't know.

Sorry, Gahtan said. I'm not sure he was because he came right back and said, Listen also to the wireless.

I don't have one.

At a time like this?

Until I get one you tell me, my father said.

For one, Gahtan said striking the crook of his stick into his palm, Japan is fighting China. Since 1937. For two, striking his palm twice, Britain and America are interfering as if it's their business. Oil and steel embargos and a blockade so tight the Japs are choking.

So they bombed us at half-past four in the morning? Let them bomb America.

And what were they doing in Honolulu? Just flying past over Pearl Harbour?

Hah, my father said to me, that's where Honolulu is.

Which brings me to my next point, Gahtan's stick struck three times, Japan wants the whites out of Asia. British, French, Dutch, Americans. She'd also like to get her hands on Australia. Seventy million Japs are falling off their islands. Asia is her backyard and her market and that's the way to build an empire.

For four, the small man with the scratchy voice added, our local Chinese are sending money to help Kuo Min Tang in China to fight the Japs.

Thank you Howee, Gahtan said, I can manage for myself.

Where was I? Yes. For four, Chinese here are sending money to China to fight the Japs, and for five, his stick keeping time, to fight ... they need ... our tin ... our rubber ... our food ... and whatever else they can rob from us. Understand? Britain's hands are tied. Germany has her by the balls.

He didn't say, God forgive me, so maybe balls wasn't a bad word.

Is there more, my father asked. It's not that he didn't like Gahtan. He did, they were good friends, but he had a loud voice and wouldn't give others a chance to speak.

If you don't want to listen, go speak to Friam. He'll tell you what they've been telling us for years. The sun never sets on the British Empire, Rule Britannia, God save the King. But empires rise and empires fall. Now Japan sees her chance. What were the headlines today? **Japan Strikes Against Britain and U.S**. Britain and the United States. Follow?

Yes, my father said.

Good. Now go and tell your brother-in-law to stop drinking a couple of days, put his head under the tap and take his money out of the bank before the Japs do it for him.

The hazzan went up the *bimah*, thumped three times on the reading table and started praying. Men outside came in and I went with my father to our seats on the right with the hawkers, shopkeepers and small-timers while Uncle Friam and Gahtan went to the left.

My father wasn't praying. He had his finger in his book on the right page but his eyes and ears were roving.

Here they are saying hundreds dead, he said to me, and the papers said a few. Mainly Chinese they said, as if they count for nothing. A life is a life. How long before Jews start dying? Do bombs know how to tell who is a Jew, who isn't? Did we not see refugees here in this place, two, three years ago? Were they not running from Hitler? Japs are friends of

Germans, no? Will they invite Hitler to come and do the same to us?

Pa, you said you'd ask God what to do. Ask him now.

He closed his eyes and didn't say a word until the service ended.

When I closed my eyes, he said on our way home, I saw flames. Nebuchadnezzar the Babylonian Pharaoh was burning the Temple and Titus the Roman Pharaoh was doing it again. Both on the same day six hundred and fifty years, one to the next. He pulled my hand for me to look at him. Judgment Day is coming. *Tishah b'Av*, the ninth day of Av, the day we fast with tears in our eyes not for our sins but to remember those they slaughtered. He steered me round the corner into Princep Street. Mark my word, Hirohito the Japanese Pharaoh will come to our synagogue on that day, drag us out and slaughter us in the street.

14

Two days later the newspapers told us what to do. First was to get used to moving around in darkness. Blackout meant: NO LIGHTS VISIBLE AT NIGHT, not even a lit cigarette in the street. Air Raid Precautions wardens, with ARP helmets, were on patrol. If they saw a light they'd blow a whistle and shout: PUT OUT THAT LIGHT. If we didn't understand they'd shout: *TUTOP LAMPU*. If we didn't obey they'd cart us off as enemy agents. They had powers of arrest and some carried nightsticks. On the other hand if we were in the street in an air raid with nowhere to hide they'd take us to the nearest shelter.

Hah, my father said. So where is ours? Is there one near Princep Street? Supposing we are half way from synagogue? Does anybody know?

We had no curtains so my ma blocked off the windows of the boys' room at the back with sheets and that was the only room with 40-watts of light. To be sure not to be arrested as enemy agents my father removed the bulbs from rooms with windows. He didn't mind that too much and the other thing we had to do he actually liked. We had to stick strips of paper in a cross, corner to corner on small window panes with a second cross on larger ones to form a Union Jack which, in a manner of speaking, was to make us bold.

My father bought all the sticky tape he could get his hands on, sold out in two days and there was no more for love or money. When he ran out of glue he told customers to cut strips from newspaper, stick them with *congee* a kind of starch and pray to God. He made so much money I helped him empty his **KLIM** tin every day.

Pa, I said rolling 10-cent coins into 2-dollar tubes, is it okay to make money from war?

We didn't make the war, he said. Usual profit plus a little when things are short is fine, war or peace. That's called bizz-i-nezz and allowed and right and fair. When you're older think about it. For now come with me and we'll hide the money.

I'll count the bundles then we'll know how much we're hiding.

What did I tell you about counting money?

Count only when you give change or go to the post office.

10 upon 10.

Next day the newspapers said that if there was no air raid shelter close by, we should build one for ourselves, the best being with sandbags. Sandbags? Who in Princep Street has gunny bags? And sand? They think we are millionaires. It wasn't only my father. Everyone in the street was asking. Mr Pillai said he could arrange to supply sand from PWD stocks. It was not only in the civil interest but also civic duty, therefore perfectly legitimate so long as we paid for it and, to that end, he'd arrange transportation for free, but even his best efforts could not provide sturdy bags for the purpose, simply because they were not items on the regular departmental inventory.

So what are you saying, Mr Pillai, my father said, you can or you cannot?

Sand, yes, gunny bags, no.

Thank you, Mr Pillai.

Air raid shelters were not required by law and if we couldn't build one we should seek a place sufficiently enclosed, such as roadside monsoon drains, in an emergency.

There are no monsoon drains in Princep Street, my father said.

Drains? They are telling us to go into drains, my ma said. With rats?

We should be aware that everything was under control. The Civil Service was doing all in its power to protect citizens and public services were coping well with the present situation. It was most important not to panic.

Panic? Why panic? They didn't warn us what to expect, my father said. It's only our lives. See if they tell us what to do if we have no drains?

If you have a sub-stan-tial table, best if on the ground floor, cover the top with what-ever you can lay your hands on to pro-tect your-selves from falling de-bris.

I went next door. Please Mr Pillai, can you tell me what is de-bris?

De-briss? Can you spell it?

D-e-b-r-i-s.

Deb-*ree*, young Adam. English uses letters as its people wear wigs over perfectly good hair and ceremonial gowns over fine suits. In Tamil we do not waste letters. We speak so fast, rattling off one might say, it seems the word has more letters than there are. Now you mention it, it strikes me that in some way it reflects English wealth and Indian poverty.

What's deb-*ree*, Mr Pillai?

Yes indeed. That was your question. Fragments, broken pieces of something that has been destroyed. And remember, the s is silent though the fragments may not be.

Thank you, Mr Pillai.

We pushed our dining table against the sideboard to seal off that side, blocked the other side and one end with chairs stacked on their sides in two layers and left one end open to get in and out. Then we piled on reams of paper and boxes of envelopes. In two days night attacks became so regular we brought down mattresses and pillows and slept in our shelter, the whole family, air raid or not, we kids making the most of it, clinging together when we heard the siren, letting go only after the all-clear.

One night they must've been trying to hit Government House up beyond Mount Sophia where the swimming pool was. Bombs fell so close we kids hugged each other tight as bears to make the bangs go away. Judith told Joshua not to squeeze so hard he was making her want to piss. He said she wasn't allowed to say piss, if Ma heard she'd be in trouble. Jonah said if Judith wasn't to say piss why did he say piss and if Ma heard him he'd be in bigger trouble and my ma reached out between the chairs.

Who forgot to bring the pot?

Jonah told Joshua to stop saying piss and get the pot, it was his job. Joshua said, no way, he wasn't going in the dark, it was my job anyway and I said I only had to make sure doors and windows were locked and Judith said she couldn't wait, she pissed already. Joshua pushed her against Jonah, shouting, Sure thing, she pissed all over me. Jonah stood up, banged his head under the table, yelled that a plane had shot him to pieces and as he died he crashed onto me.

Stay where you are, my father said, and be quiet. When and only when we hear the all-clear, not a minute earlier, your mother will change the sheet and get new clothes. Judith started to cry and my ma said we shouldn't make a fuss, she was only a little girl and there was nothing wrong with a little girl's what she wouldn't say.

The next days, fortunately, air raids were light. Sirens sounded only as the planes, coming from airfields already captured in Malaya, were over us and by the time the few we still had got off the ground, the Japs had dumped their bombs and gone and Lim would come out of his shop next door half laughing, 19 planes come, 20 planes go. English join winners.

With little going on and blackouts, my father closed early

and went to synagogue where Gahtan's red face, big belly and knobbly walking stick seemed to be waiting for us.

So, he said, did you buy a wireless?

Do I know what to do with it?

Switch on and tune, he said. What else? You need shortwave to get BBC.

Switch on I know, my father said. Tune, shortwave and beebeecee the teachers in the school I never attended were too stupid to teach me.

Come on Judah. Turn the knob, listen and when you hear a voice speaking as if it owns the world, you have the BBC.

So you tell me the news.

You haven't heard? My father shook his head. Nothing? My father shook his head again. So where will I start? His cane thumped his palm. Thailand. Japs landed at Pattani and Songkhla same time as they woke us up at four in the morning, damn them. So now tell me, what did the Thais do?

Papers didn't say.

What they always do, Gahtan said. The Japs were welcomed by open Thais. My father looked at him. Open Thais, he said spreading his knees. No? Open thighs. Still no? If your boy wasn't here with big eyes I'd show you with fingers.

I understood. First time. That's not interesting to me.

Okay. So the Japs cross Thailand in tanks your brother-in-law said are made of rice paper, and which, by the way, we have none, not even rice-paper quality. Ours are busy keeping Mussolini and his German friend away from the Suez Canal. So. Half the Japs go straight, half turn left and down they go, both coasts of Malaya, in other words a pincer movement. His finger and thumb nipped the air and my father's hands clapped against his face. You're right, Gahtan said, but where are the British? What are they doing?

Chasing their own arses. He cleared his throat. God forgive me, he said and then, Hello, Howee.

The man with the scratchy voice had just come in. *Allah yistoor*, he said with a quiver. God help us, have you heard?

Kota Bahru has fallen, Gahtan said. That's old news.

Half way to Kuala Lumpur as if nobody wants to stop them, Howee said. That's not news. I'm asking if you know about the two ships.

Prince of Wales and *Repulse*, I said expecting Howee to say what Mr Pillai said about the great warships Britain sent to show us she is determined when Gahtan asked me in his loud voice, What have you heard?

The *Prince of Wales*, I said, is the biggest battleship in the world and the *Repulse* is a battle cruiser and with them the British people will not let us down. I felt proud especially since he let me answer and Howee never did.

Were, Howee said to me. They *were*. Now they *are* at the bottom of the South China Sea with more than a thousand sailors. *Allah yistoor*.

My father refused to believe it. Howee said he also refused at first. But if you leave lights on during an air attack you also send ships without air escort looking for Japs in the wrong place. When they can't find them they turn back, two capital ships, four destroyers, in broad daylight, in a battle zone knowing they will not to be spotted because Japs are squint. Right? I didn't answer. Then tell me what the Japs were doing meantime. I didn't answer. Pasting Australians and Indians all the way down the jungle and why? Because that's impossible our generals said. And why Indians?

Because Britain will never give up, Gahtan said with a laugh as red as his face. She'll fight to the last Indian soldier.

Is this true, my father asked and Howee said lying about good news is a joke but about bad news is a sin and God strike him dead if he didn't hear it with his own two ears on the wireless and, to crown it all, when did it happen? Two days, did we hear? Two *days* after we were bombed, to which Gahtan added, at four in the morning, damn them, and Howee asked who showed up after the Jap planes had gone if not the RAF?

Now I understand, Gahtan said hitting his leg with his stick. That's what Duff Cooper meant. I tuned in at the end of his speech. *Their loss makes us as unsafe as we were before they arrived,* he said. *In great days like these it is hardly honourable to be safe.* Like saying: I was dead before I became alive, now I'm going to die again, why worry?

My father didn't want to hear any more. His face went blank and white as the paper he sold. Let's go to our seats, he said to me but Howee held him back. What's the rush?

What more is there to say?

What we haven't been saying for years, Gahtan said. That the British got where they are because they did it first. Now others are learning and she's stuck in her old ways. Who's our governor, for goodness sake?

I thought he was asking me. Sir Shenton Thomas, I said.

A school teacher, Gahtan said. He used to teach boys like you to play cricket and also to read and write. That's how they select colonial officers. Cricket first, then reading and writing and a little arithmetic. Brains are helpful but not essential. Now, Gahtan said to me, did they tell you in school that our governor used to be a school teacher?

My teacher said he is a great man and lives in a big house and one day, if we behave properly, we will go and visit him.

Inshallah, Howee said. So, what would you do now if you were governor?

I thought this was another question he wouldn't let me answer, so I waited. He didn't say anything so it must've been a question.

I would, I said, I would …

For sure you would, Howee said. But him? He won't even arm the locals in case we start another Indian Mutiny.

Gahtan wasn't going to be left out of this. While little yellow men are chucking bombs we're filling sandbags and sticking paper on windows and our rulers are dancing to Dan Hopkins and his Orchestra at the Raffles and getting drunk at the Cricket Club.

Without a word, my father took my shoulder and we went to our seats.

When the service began his lips moved without a sound.

15

In the second half of December, after a couple of quiet days, we were bombed again. A dozen planes came over to tell us we weren't forgotten. Newspapers were censored but a grapevine spread about hundreds dying and trains bringing thousands of casualties and refugees from Malaya. It seemed that our population had doubled and we'd soon be out of food. Apparently we were retreating so fast the Japs were turning our guns around and firing them at us.

Not a single *ikan bilis* the size of my small finger anywhere to be seen, my ma said showing us her half-empty basket. No fish for love or money. Gone to Tokyo, the man said making jokes and no one is laughing. Fishermen can't catch because lanterns are banned at night, bombs are blowing them up in daytime and who wants to eat exploded fish?

Let this be a lesson, my father said to us. When you don't tell the truth people make up lies and lies become the truth, so when you hear the truth you think it's lies. Follow what am I saying? Let's hope they tell the truth from now on so we'll know how to behave if suddenly we see Japs in our streets with guns instead of barbers' scissors.

Then we heard about Penang. Planes, without resistance, bombed and gunned people in the streets for a week. On Wednesday, 17th December, our troops scooted in the dead of night taking all white civilians and leaving the locals to wake next morning at the mercy of the invaders.

Not true, my father said. Propaganda to frighten us.

I got it from the horse's mouth, Howee said walking up and down trying to calm himself. My agent in Penang. Runs my business and guards my stock. Gone. Confiscated. Are

Japs not looking for watch parts? Swiss parts to put in their fifty-cent watches? Last phone call before lines were cut. God strike me dead if I'm lying.

You don't know the half of it, Gahtan's thick voice backed Howee's scratchy voice outside the synagogue where men were sitting on benches and the porch steps waiting for the caretaker to open the doors. His uncle had been killed and while his wife went to find him, Gahtan told us how Yamashita was ramming British arses and Howee explained how the fat Jap with baggy pants used the roads until he met resistance then cut through the jungle on bicycles, bicycles would you believe, outflanked the whites, cut them off, closed the trap and wiped them out. Then Gahtan asked Howee to tell him why the two stone lions at British Military Headquarters in Fort Canning were sitting down. Howee said he wasn't an expert on riddles so Gahtan tapped his stick on the ground to give others a chance but nobody answered so he said, So you don't see they have no balls, but no one laughed.

On the way home my father told me Howee wasn't a ball-carrier like Uncle Friam who boasted how he got what he wanted with a little squeeze. Howee was self-made and didn't need to drink with the likes of those who thought he wasn't good enough to join their clubs. On the other hand Gahtan's money came from his father. He didn't need to prove himself. In short, Howee wasn't famous for loving the British and Gahtan was making it clear he felt the same, so with both saying Britain couldn't be trusted, what should he think?

Gahtan said to say *when* not *if*, I said. And Howee said we will know when they start bombing us day and night and machine-gunning our streets like they did to Penang. What should we do, Pa?

God will tell us.

Christmas 1941 came and went and by the second Sunday in January, Kuala Lumpur, 200 miles north, fell. We were bombed three or four times a day, mostly in daylight. Then, when we hardly saw our planes in the air, people said they'd gone to Java. With Holland gone, the Dutch had to stay and fight. Britain would join them in Java and abandon us like Penang.

For the time being military targets were being pounded and Princep Street was left alone. All the same we went in and out under the dining table making a game of who dared stay outside longest. My father's threats started with: If I have to say it one more time, going all the way to: If you're so brave, go stand in the street and see what the Japs will do to you, until my ma said, God forbid, this was not a laughing matter and dragged us in.

On Tuesday the 20th tactics changed. Houses were being hammered and the game became who could get under the table first. Then on Sunday Rafuli's son Manasseh, raced down Princep Street, barged into our shop shouting, Direct hit. My father says come quick, don't waste time.

Where? Who? Sit, my father said, catch your breath and slowly tell me.

My ma ran in from the kitchen with a glass of water. Drink before you say another word, grabbed my father's fan from his hand and fanned Manasseh.

Direct hit, he said still panting. Doshes, Oxley Road, all dead.

Calm down now and tell us slowly, my father said.

He already told us, my ma said and covered her face with the fan.

I must call others, Manasseh said and stood to leave but my father stopped him.

I will go. I need my shoes.

Direct hit, the boy said, one hand crashing down into the

other. Parrrrpppp. Direct. They cannot find the bodies.

No more, my ma said. Go home. Be quick. If the siren goes, run and hide. D'you hear me, run and hide, she called after him, and ran to the back to bring my father's shoes.

There was loud banging on the back-street door after sunset. It had been raining and we'd shut the shop. My father came in dripping, his face, even in the dark, looked as if he'd met the devil. Are you alright, my ma asked. He didn't answer. You're soaking. I'll bring clothes. Change before you get sick.

He walked into the dark storeroom, half closed the door and undressed. I stood outside. Pa, will you tell me what happened?

You don't need to know.

Did you find the bodies? He didn't answer. Together or pieces? He didn't answer. Did you bury them? He didn't answer. How did you know who was who?

God will know.

My ma came down with clothes, saw me behind the door, told me to brush my teeth and get under the dining table that minute.

My father said little the next two days. Schools were shut and children didn't need stationery. I was in my corner, he in his chair, hands in his lap, neither saying a word.

Call your mother, he said. If she says she's cooking, tell her I can smell.

I dragged my slippers to the back and returned. Ma says if you can smell cooking then you know she cannot come. Tell me what you want and I will tell her.

Tell her what I want I need to say to her and nobody else.

I returned and told him that if she left the food it would burn and he said to tell her to turn off the gas like she does when there's an air raid. If she can do it then she can do it now, do not argue, some things are more important than cooking. I said she told me to tell him she knew he would say that so I was to say if it was so important why didn't he go to the kitchen? Then, if he said he couldn't leave the shop, I was to say, were so many people rushing to buy paper and even so I knew how to manage it for five minutes.

Enough, he said. Tell your mother to come right now.

Yes, what is it? She was wiping a spoon with the kitchen cloth over her shoulder.

It's time to go, he said.

Where?

Anywhere. Leave the country. Until now I didn't know how bad it is. On Sunday I saw things I don't want my eyes to remember. Ships are taking people every day.

Ships are also bombed, no? Are we going from the frying pan into the fire?

Biha, he said, listen to me. I should have asked questions sooner but which questions I didn't know. Jews have left, gone to India, Australia, England.

He used to call my ma Biha when he didn't want an argument.

You're talking about rich Jews who are whitish and go where they please. Are they letting Chinese and Indians leave? Ask our neighbours and see what they say.

Biha, no. We cannot sit doing nothing.

Alright. Let's go. We'll all go to the harbour with our bags and get on any ship that takes us wherever it's going. Can you be sure they will?

Yes. But men are not allowed to leave. Women and children only.

You want me to take the children on the ship and leave you on the wharf? Is that why I married you? To leave and go? No. All or none.

Biha, they are close. We were talking in the cemetery. Shlomo, Kranji Shlomo I'm talking about. From his big bungalow with half a dozen servants he came to live in one room with his brother in Orchard Road because in the north he could hear guns, louder each day. This is how we find out what newspapers won't tell us so it's better not to repeat stories I heard, he dropped his voice to a whisper, about what they do to women. They are animals. What will I do if they do it to you?

That's your worry? I'll make myself in such a way they'll hate the sight and smell of me. Now can I finish cooking?

No. I want you to say now, this minute, that you will take the children and go and tomorrow I will ask until someone tells me what to do.

Alright, she said and turned to me. Call your brothers and your sister from upstairs. Tell them to come right this minute. I don't want to hear what else they are doing.

She stood us in a line, oldest to youngest, and told us our father was sending us away though up to now he didn't say where but tomorrow, maybe, he would know. Then we'd go to the harbour and sit on our bags until a ship came by and agreed to take us. We had to say goodbye on the wharf because men were not allowed to leave and he'd wave to us until we were gone. Pointing her spoon she asked each in turn who wanted to go.

Jonah said he didn't understand, Joshua asked could she say it again and Judith started to cry. I said I was staying to help Pa in the shop at which point my brothers realised something awful was happening and sobbed, then I cried, the siren wailed and my ma ran to the back to turn off the gas mains as we dashed in under the dining table.

16

As the monsoon gathered strength in the last days of January we heard new rumours. The Japs were closing in on Johore Bahru in the north. In Princep Street, in the south, we saw lots of people we'd never seen before looking for a place to live. Schools became refugee centres, hospitals were full with casualties and our left- and right-side neighbours met with my father on the 5-foot way once or twice every day.

They are breaking down our back door, Mr Pillai said. Royal Engineers are mining the Causeway in preparation. I ask you Mr Lim and Mr Messiah to imagine that. A previous generation, barely two decades ago, built that fine causeway, a symbol of progress and unity with our brothers in Malaya. Now we are taking steps to destroy it. Does that not break your heart? I will confess it does mine.

Bombing many times every day, Lim said. Bad sign. Now come time to finish us.

God will protect us, was all my father could say seeing as how he was going crazy about what to do next. Between raids he sat in his shop saying little and when he went to look up at heaven, I followed. On Thursday 29th we were in our usual places when the jade green Studebaker pulled up in front and Auntie Flora, in a stylish mauve dress, came out, her face nothing like her dress except, maybe, its colour.

Hah, it's good to see you in our house after so long, my father said. I wish times were better to say a proper welcome. All the same, you can be sure I'm happy to see you.

Thank you, she said and smiled without showing it. Jujube, please call your mother. I need to say something to your parents. Be quick, there's no time to spare.

Nice to see you, Flora, my ma said bouncing her rappa neckline to let out the heat. Is everything all right?

I don't know if it's good news or bad news but we're leaving.

Hah, my father said to my ma, Biha, I want you to listen carefully. Then to Auntie Flora he said, You are going with your daughters and Friam is staying, right? I want you to tell your sister so she will do the same.

Ephraim is going.

Women and children only. That's the law.

Ephraim is going.

If he can, I also can. We'll go, all together, in the same ship.

Ephraim is in danger. Auntie Flora was shaking now.

Sit, Flora. My ma said going into the dining room to bring a chair.

Can we go inside? You never know who's listening. Auntie Flora was already in the dining room looking for a chair.

My ma pulled away two from our shelter, gave one to Auntie Flora, sat in the other, I stood behind her and my father came to the bead curtain. Only Friam is in danger, he said, grabbing the beads to stop them chattering. Are the Japs looking to bomb only him?

Let Flora speak, my ma said.

There is a black list, Auntie Flora said searching in her handbag. Ephraim's business with Japan. She pulled out her nail file. Two years ago. He went to court but it's still not settled. She started working on her left nails. Reggie, his bank manager, phoned. Leave right away, he said. She stopped filing her nails. A ship is taking refugees. Saturday. He arranged a cabin, the last one, and a pass for Ephraim. Six of us in one small cabin. How we'll manage I don't want to think. At a time like this we must make sacrifices. She looked at her right nails then went to work on them. Ephraim has a price on his head.

How much, my father asked.

For the cabin?

For his head.

No. Judah. Please. Not now. I came for your help.

I was just wondering, my father said. How much someone must pay for my head so I also can take my family.

Yehuda. My ma stared hard at him and turned away.

What are you asking us to do? My father must have guessed because he let the beads go, crossed his arms and looked directly at her.

Live in our flat while we're away. Make yourselves at home. What's mine is yours.

And who will stay here? Someone will loot yours, he said, but not ours?

How can we, Flora? Everything we have is here, my ma said. Who will look after the shop? How will we live? Why not, she said and paused. I have an idea. Why not send your best things here? We'll make space. Send a lorry. You have time, no?

We're packed. Six suitcases standing at the door.

What's the name of the ship, I asked Auntie Flora.

Empress of Japan.

Empress of Japan? My father's voice rose as if to laugh then checked itself.

Two days later, Saturday, 31st January, not two months since it began, Malaya fell, the peninsula was in Japanese hands and our soldiers scrambled back to Singapore. Air raids kept us under the table and Auntie Flora's lorry did not come. It was the Sabbath but they were six and for sure more than six bags if he knew his sister-in-law, so my father went with them because it was the time to help and God would forgive him.

Auntie Flora was hysterical and had to be dragged out of her home. On the way to the harbour there was another raid. Halim drove like a madman with my father, the girls and baggage in the family car. My auntie, after my uncle threatened to break her neck, went in a taxi with more baggage and he took the remaining baggage in another taxi.

What will she do without baggage in her life? Let that be a lesson, my father said. Life is everything, baggage nothing. In and out we went, cars burning, people running. A bomb exploded in Keppel Road five minutes before we entered. Houses fell. People were running and screaming and trying to help others at one and the same time. It was late and dark without a single light. We found our way by the fires. When we reached the wharf the ship was gone. *Empress of Japan* was nowhere to be seen. An officer said, She's in the Roads, hurry. There's a good chance of another raid and she'll be off. He pointed to a big shadow, not far, with small shadows around. Nice man. Get a bum-boat, he said, and be quick.

Were dead people on the road, Pa?

Fires everywhere. Godowns and boats burning, fire engines and ambulances with sirens going and people like I don't want to see people in my life again. For sure many were dead. But Halim is not stupid like me. We had a car and two taxis full of people and full of baggage and a ship that's leaving any minute. He knows that when they go the car is his. So what does he do? Tells your uncle, Wait here, Tuan, runs and two minutes later he's back with a *twakow*. We loaded everything in half a minute. I took your uncle, auntie and your cousins, made a circle and prayed.

He had tears in his eyes. I'll get you water, I said.

Let me finish first. It was time to go. I said goodbye and blessed each one as they went into the boat and when it came to your uncle, last of all, he put his house keys in my hand and said to take anything I want. Sell it if you need money, he said. I was wrong. We'll not be back soon. I think he saw for the first time what I was seeing for the second time, but I must tell you this was a hundred times worse. We were driving through the middle of the bombing and I was seeing what someone can do to you when you close your eyes because you don't want to believe it will happen. The Japs are giving us the thrashing of our lives and we don't have saliva in our mouths enough to spit at them.

His lips were moving trying to say something. He closed his eyes.

Stop Pa, I said, I'll get you a drink.

As the *twakow* was leaving I shouted to them, he said handing me the empty glass. *Baruch atah adonai, elohanu malekh haolam*, God protect you and take you to safety. I didn't stop praying until their boat was a shadow with the other shadows. My father took my hands and drew me close. I'm telling you, he said, about the bad things people do to each other which I didn't want to tell you before. Only now do I realise, from what I saw, that your generation will be different from ours. What I saw in Bir Haroon is nothing compared to what I saw that night. A whole street without a house standing. We were innocent, we knew nothing. One day you will be a man and have others who depend on you. Keep your eyes and ears open at all times.

He squeezed my hands to help him say what he had to.

Never do what I did. Never speak how I spoke to your auntie. To leave your home and country where you were born is always difficult. When Jews were leaving Egypt to be free, were they happy? Their home of generations? Belongings and memories? Graves of their family? No. So Moshe Rabbenu told them to take their bread from the ovens without letting it rise. You understand what I'm saying? Bread needs time to rise and time they must not have to think. Did I want to go? Would I have left my home and my family? Some things to others mean a lot. Who am I to say they are wrong and I am right? At times like this, who can tell you how to feel, how to think? Only God. Remember this as a lesson because everything in life, no matter how bad, has a lesson to teach and for you to learn.

He told me this a week after they'd left by when we were being bombed so often we kids more or less lived under the table while our parents moved around when they could. Then my father said this was no way to live, people weren't rats to hide in holes, he'd come in only when explosions got close. We said we weren't rats either and came out. Get back, he yelled. Even a tiger, king of the jungle, hides his young when he goes looking for food.

17

He also said we should go to synagogue every morning, he, me and my brothers, in case we couldn't attend the evening service. Gahtan was always there, stick hooked on his arm, telling us what was going on and how somebody had hung a sign: THEY'LL NEVER GET US after a bomb smashed the Victoria Memorial clock. Let's see, he said. We're being bombed to smithereens and Sir Shenton still says Singapore is impregnable. Doesn't that sound like the captain telling passengers running to the lifeboats, We're fine, the *Titanic* is unsinkable? My father didn't ask him what he was talking about because, by now, he was saying all the Pharaohs had come out of their graves, God needed to hear our voices to know where we were so Gahtan should talk less and pray more.

Today, after the last Amen, we ran home. The siren was wailing so we crashed under the table as a bomb exploded close by. It rattled the house, shook plaster off the walls and dust from the ceiling. My father prayed extra loud and my ma tried to cover all four kids with her body even although she was smaller than Jonah. When the all-clear went we counted to sixty before crawling out in case the man in charge of sirens made a mistake.

Let's see if there's any damage, my father said. When the explosion is so loud you wonder what happened to people close by. In Bir Haroon we went into a hole under the floor which your grandfather covered with a bed and hid in a cupboard. If they didn't find us they couldn't kill us. If they found us we could beg or bargain or bribe. Here they kill from the sky. He looked up and down the street. Where did those pieces come from?

Shrapnel, Mr Messiah. Mr Pillai was also in the street inspecting his house. They stuff small metal balls into bombs to injure and kill.

Mumzerim.

Indeed. But our houses are lethal enough. Timber flies out like spears and millions of roof tiles become razor sharp fragments. Each raid takes a heavier toll. Saint Joseph's Institution and the Convent have been turned into makeshift hospitals. Even the splendid ballroom of the Raffles Hotel where our masters danced is crowded with the injured. White doctors, nurses and volunteers treat people as local as you and I. Now the end is near they have set aside principles of partiality.

What do you mean the end is near? Bombing will stop?

As soon as General Yamashita sees no further point to it. We are almost defenceless and every raid wreaks more destruction. Japan does not want to possess a ruined city.

For sure or more rumours?

Nothing is sure except our fate which, it seems, will be sealed in five days. February 11th is *Kigensetsu*, the most important day in Japan's calendar. Two thousand six hundred years ago, Jimmu took the throne and Yamashita wishes to present Singapore to Hirohito, a direct descendent. Imagine Mr Messiah, we are to be a gift to the Japanese Emperor.

Mumzerim.

They have us on the run, Mr Messiah, and running we are.

Someone said to you we are running? Who?

A man in his cups.

What kind of cups? Please Mr Pillai, if I don't understand how will I know what to do?

Alcohol, Mr Messiah. It loosens the tongue that would otherwise lie tight in a mouth.

A drunk man told you we are running and you believe him? Like my brother-in-law, always drunk, who said the British will never surrender until he changed his mind, took his family and ran. What does a drunkard have to say we need to hear?

Good afternoon Mr Lim, Mr Pillai said looking behind us.

Hullo Misser Pillai, hullo Misser Messer, our left-side neighbour said. Don't mind if I join? Chinese New Year next week. We fire crackers. Maybe bring good luck.

It may be too late for that, Mr Pillai said.

My father neither turned nor gave Lim his usual half-smile. So tell me please, he said to Mr Pillai, what the drunkard said we need to know.

The drunkard, as you call him, Mr Pillai said, is Richard Stuart McGregor. Our Chief Engineer, Granite McGregor to his friends, a man who goes out of his way to support local aspirations even as he shows solidarity with his own people. He arrived at work last Friday, as the saying goes, drunk as a piper on payday. The previous night he and his fellows smashed the store of alcohol at the Singapore Club. Next morning his private stock suffered similarly but not before having a few for breakfast.

By now he's very drunk, my father said.

Indeed. But at 10.30, more sober, he invited me into his office. Sit down P D, he said. You are a loyal officer and I want to tell you that I have let you down. I have let down all who worked with me these past five years. I have let down my house-boy Seng, my cook Choi, my amah Meng Lee and my syce Ibrahim. I have let down the people I lived among and came to like. We, the colonial administration who should have been more honourable, have let you down shamelessly. Our generals believed that defences declare weakness and are bad for morale. Attack is the best form of defence. Keep the enemy guessing, overcome him, prove British supremacy and there will always be an England.

Mr Pillai, who always spoke like as though his words queued waiting their turn, was still taking his time but the words were trembling as they came out.

We did not tell you what we knew, he continued, looking first at my father then Lim, then me. We did not trust you and we feared it would belittle us in your eyes. Now you need to know. Go home P D. Protect yourself and your family for what is to come and tell your friends and neighbours to do the same.

A drunk man said this to you? Hah. Sometimes a man needs to be drunk to speak the truth. Did he tell you what to do when the time comes?

No. But he did say that orders to destroy all alcohol had come from the highest level meaning, I presume, the governor. Japanese must be denied this should they be victorious.

So let them get drunk, my father said. They'll go to sleep and leave us alone.

Wrong, said Lim. Jap soldiers in Nanking get drunk, go crazy. Kill thousands of people, throw in river.

It seems, Mr Pillai said, they were well advised. What should we gather from this? Mr Messiah? Mr Lim?

What you think, Lim asked my father.

About unleavened bread I can tell you. About broken bottles I know nothing.

I don't need a prize, my father said. Just tell me so I also know.

Few were in synagogue on Wednesday. My brothers refused to get up after the night raids, the *shamash* hadn't come and Howee, standing in, read as fast as his lips would go. We could hear guns, ambulances and fire engines, refugees with bundles and carts were in the streets, drains were running with water from burst pipes, houses were burning and Gahtan was offering no prizes for guessing what the Japs would do next.

For two days, he said, Percival watches Yamashita shuttling trucks in broad daylight. I'm talking about a decorated British officer with more letters after his name than in front.

Can you go a little faster?

He's not a fool, Gahtan said. He prepares a reception: searchlights to turn night into day, best men and guns in the northeast, mines the beaches but no barbed wire. Why?

Because nobody knows where it is, I said.

It's in the store but it needs a chitty and nobody's there to sign. Next question, he said to me, did Percival think to check what Yamashita was carrying in his trucks?

No, I said. It was an easy guess.

Why bother? He knows Yamashita is taking soldiers to the northeast to launch his attack. As soon as they cross the Straits and come within range, lights go on, guns open up and the Japs wish they'd stayed home. Brilliant, don't you think?

So? My father glared at him.

Sunday night in total darkness Japs start crossing. Halfway. Then what happens?

Our guns start shooting, I said wanting him to hurry up and say Japs were blown to pieces, not one left alive, the Straits filled with floating bodies.

Our guns start shooting yes, but in the dark. The British have trouble with switches. In ten minutes, thousands of Japs pour across.

Hah.

The first principle of war, Gahtan said, is to know your enemy which everyone knows except Percival. In his eyes

Yamashita is an Asiatic hooligan not clever enough to drive empty trucks up and down to the northeast while his troops are gathering in the northwest. Even your son knows it's closer. Our lives depend on fools. Take my advice, stay home and pray. You cannot be sure you'll not see Japs in the street next time you come to synagogue.

How come you know so much, my father said. Newspapers told us nothing.

Not the radio either. Yamashita's headquarters are in the Sultan's Palace within range of our guns but, it seems, one of our generals promised his Royal Highness Ibrahim II his palace wouldn't be damaged. Did they tell us that? Did they tell us our governor told the whites to get on board anything that floats and go?

Mumzerim, my father said. We are surrounded by *mumzerim*.

My father half closed his shop all day and it was late afternoon when we stepped out to find Mr Pillai on the 5-foot way cleaning his Mahatma specs, shaking his head, telling Lim the whole island was under assault, appalling devastation, no nightmare could match the horror he'd seen not a mile away, the very fabric of our city was in peril.

Hah, my father said. Yesterday Yamashita was supposed to give us to his emperor, the monkey god of Japan.

A little behind schedule, Mr Pillai said, but their flag flies on Bukit Timah and they are closing in on our reservoirs.

No water, one week we die, Lim said, as an explosion sent up a cloud in the distance.

Black smoke, my father said. Oil. More Japanese bombs.

Unlikely, Mr Pillai said. Their soldiers are everywhere and bombing has ceased. That is Blakang Mati. Shell must be destroying its tanks. We are defeated.

Two explosions followed then a third as the sun was setting in the most beautiful red and orange I'd ever seen.

Next morning my ma shouted from the kitchen. I ran in as she was telling Judith to hold the bottle under the trickle from the tap. Both hands, she said. Don't spill a single drop. We filled three before the water ran out and the pipe sucked air. From now on, she said, anytime it rains rush with anything and catch water. Don't wait for me to tell you.

This was Friday 13th February 1942. It came to be known as Black Friday. There was no news from Gahtan and Howee and we did not see our left- and right-side neighbours. Hawkers hadn't come to our 5-foot way for days, shops were boarded, houses closed, not a soul in our street and gunfire was so loud we knew they were close.

My father called us boys out of the shelter and told my ma and sister to stay there and not let him see a single hair outside. With cap, shawl and prayer book he conducted the day's service in what remained of our dining room and read the whole of Psalm 6.

> LORD, don't be angry and rebuke me!
>   Don't punish me in your anger!
> I am worn out, O Lord; have pity on me!
>
> Give me strength; I am completely exhausted
>   and my whole being is deeply troubled.
> How long, O Lord, will you wait to help me?
>
> Come and save me, Lord;
>   in your mercy rescue me from death.
> In the world of the dead you are not remembered;
>   no one can praise you there.
>
> I am worn out with grief;
>   every night my bed is damp from my weeping;
>   my pillow is soaked with tears.
> I can hardly see;
>   my eyes are so swollen

from the weeping caused by my enemies.

Keep away from me, you evil people!
The Lord hears my weeping;
  he listens to my cry for help
  and will answer my prayer.

My enemies will know the bitter shame of defeat;
  in sudden confusion they will be driven away.

Then we too went into the shelter.

Our enemies knew nothing of sudden confusion. They had come from the war in China, trained to treat the enemy as if he'd killed their grandfather and the time had come for revenge. The bitter shame of defeat was ours.

Next day **The Straits Times** was a single sheet. At the top it said:

"Singapore Must Stand; It SHALL Stand" H.E. the Governor.

By now I was reading to my father without difficulty.

CITY'S NEW DEFENCE LINE
HEAVIER BOMBING AND SHELLING

We need them to tell us? Are we deaf and blind? What else?

> There was a tremendous surge of relief in London yesterday when a radio message gave the lie to the Axis reports of Japanese troops mopping up the Imperial forces in Singapore, and that the last phase had almost ended.

Hah. Maybe they should come and see for themselves. What else?

R.A.F keep it up.

AIRCRAFT of the Bomber Command attacked objectives at Mannheim on Wednesday night. Other aircraft carried out bombing attacks on Brest and Le Havre. Two of the planes are missing from these operations.

Where are these places, he asked. Are they in Singapore?

On Sunday, 15th February 1942, 70 days after it started, we surrendered.

The Occupation began next morning.

18

I was at my father's side when he pulled away the first plank of our shop front, peeped and slipped it back in again. Soldiers, he said. Two. Talking and smoking.

I want to see. Maybe they have different cigarette packets.

Cigarette packets? Rifles with bayonets. He swept me aside, slid the bolt and secured the lock. Go to the back and don't let me catch you with even one toe outside.

All day yesterday the skies were empty of what my ma called noises nobody needs and Princep Street was deserted. If we'd had a wireless a voice would have told us in Japanese what we'd worked out, and in English, Chinese, Malay and Tamil to stay home, there was a 24-hour curfew and anyone in the street would be shot. My father's – don't let me catch you with even one toe outside – said much the same.

I dragged a chair from the dining room to the back, put it against the outside wall we shared with the Pillais, climbed on but couldn't see over the top.

Come down, my ma said from the kitchen. What are you doing?

I want to talk to Mr Pillai. He will know about the Japanese soldiers.

My father marched into the kitchen. What did I tell you?

To go to the back and not let me catch you with even one toe outside. I just want to talk to Mr Pillai, I said as his head appeared over the wall.

Not a good morning, he said. How clever of you young Adam but you will need a ladder if you wish to talk over this wall. He reached down and patted my head. This may become our way to communicate if our new masters do not, in the foreseeable future, permit us sociable contact in the street.

My father came out to the cement patch when old man Lim's head appeared over his wall opposite. Bad day, he said. Japan win, England lose. Japs everywhere, China to Singapore. French no use, Dutch soon give up. Next Australia. You have food? He was talking downward to my father and across to Mr Pillai. If you need, ask me. I try.

Doh chay. My father thanked him and turned his eyes up to heaven to ask God if matters would get so bad he'd need to eat what Lim Ah Kow had to offer.

Indeed, Mr Pillai said. Food may become our principal problem but certainly not the only one. I thank you for your kind offer Mr Lim. We have a small provision at present for what I believe will be a long ordeal. By the way, Mr Lim, I wish you and your family *Kong Hee Fatt Choy* on the second day of your New Year. An inauspicious beginning to the energetic and warm-hearted year of the horse.

So sorry no *ang pow* this year, Lim said.

Our conquerors say they have come to free us from foreign rule, Mr Pillai said, and, as if to underscore their regard, our fair city is now called Syonan-to, which means Light of the South. Their declaration of friendship, though, does not seem so hollow when we consider how our late masters, resisting barely two weeks in a fortress, surrendered without so much as a nod in our direction. By the way, be sure to advance your clock ninety minutes. We are now set to Tokyo time.

Hah. How do you know this? I only see the empty street, my father said, two soldiers with rifles and I know it's better not to poke my nose in their bizz-i-nezz.

As a civil servant I made it my concern to keep abreast, and, wherever and whenever possible, a little ahead of events. More I will not say in these uncertain times. I confess though that I had misread a few. Brought up to believe Britain was almighty and trained to obey orders, my esteem for the British people was profound. Never once did I realise that below spit and polish there may be rotting leather. I apologise Mr Messiah. I may have given you false hope that memorable night of the first raid.

My father looked at him then at me, raised his eyebrows, shrugged and said nothing.

So, I also ask you, time to time, okay, Lim said. I'm not sure if our left-side neighbour really understood our right-side neighbour. Be careful or get trouble, he added.

Mr Lim and Mr Messiah, you too young Adam, in such times we must be more than neighbours. We must bind as if brothers in which vein I advise you, with especial regard to your children as I have cautioned my own, which brought my ma out from under the zinc awning where she was smearing condensed milk on thick bread for our breakfast, to bow whenever you pass a Japanese soldier. If you do not the penalty is wholly in his judgement. Many soldiers come from the lowest stratum of humanity with demeanour commensurate.

Did you hear, my ma said to me. I nodded. You have to bow, she said. I jumped off the chair and bowed. Did he bow correctly, Mr Pillai, she asked.

I will instruct you as my former Japanese colleagues, with whom I worked in happier times, demonstrated. Place your hands just above your knees. I did and looked up to check I was doing it right. No, never look at their eyes. Look down, pause, count to five then rise, slowly. I did and he said, Full praise. If the soldier is walking past you, wait until he has gone. If you are walking past him do so with head and eyes lowered.

I did everything he said but didn't know if I was walking past a Japanese soldier or he was walking past me so I decided my ma would be the soldier and I was walking past her when she said, Call the others. They need to learn.

Now? My head was bowed, my eyes down when Mr Pillai continued, And before you venture out, he said and thinking he was speaking to me, I stayed where I was, when my ma said, Go, but I was afraid to look at her because he was saying, I would advise you ... so I said, Wait Ma, I want to hear Mr Pillai's advice and she said, I will tell you when you come back. So all I heard was ... Dhoby Ghaut in the vicinity of Cathay Cinema ... three heads on poles ... former owners, allegedly, caught looting.

Ma, I said, can I tie your longest knife to the broomstick? We were having breakfast on the stairs, balancing plates of bread with condensed milk on our laps.

Don't touch my knives, she said.

I told her I was teaching them how to bow and what I did wasn't hundred per cent. Bowing is different if the soldier is standing and you are walking from if he is marching and you are standing. To teach them properly I needed to be a Japanese soldier with a gun and bayonet, so could I tie her longest knife to the broomstick, otherwise how could I do it correctly? If they don't learn, it won't be my fault, so don't blame me.

Jonah wanted to know why he couldn't be the soldier, he was oldest. I explained for the third time that he couldn't learn how to bow if he was the soldier because soldiers don't bow. Only people walking in Syonan-to have to bow. Joshua said, Sure thing, and Judith said she didn't know where Syonan-to was and anyway, it was a stupid game.

I asked my ma to tell them for the last and final time, what Mr Pillai said. Also his advice not to walk in Dhoby Ghaut. They should pay attention and listen to me or they could be beaten by a Japanese soldier from lowest humanity and if they bowed really badly they'd get their heads cut off and stuck on a pole, all three of them, allegedly.

God forbid. God forbid. God forbid. If she ever heard me say that again she'd wash my mouth with what she wouldn't say at a time like this when we were all on edge and why couldn't I just show them how to put their hands on their knees and count to five like I did it before? It would be better to keep our minds on nicer things when Jonah butted in saying it was my fault for not calling him right away and if he couldn't be the soldier he didn't want to play which left Joshua. He said he'd do what Jonah told him, and anyway, I was making it up, there was no such place as Syonan-to so I could go take a flying jump, by which time my ma was going crazy trying to shut us up, this had to stop, nobody needed to be a soldier, it wasn't a game, just watch how Adam bows, do it three times and God will protect us. And do it quickly. There was no reason to be eating on the stairs, human beings sit at a proper table which we hadn't done for how long she didn't want to think, we weren't going to be bombed again, let's clear away our air raid shelter and get our lives back again.

My father came in and said that everything was in the hands of God and only He knew if we would or would not be bombed, so how could she be so sure?

My ma said there was no need to tell her. She knew only God knew, but meantime could she please tidy up, get back the dining table and put the chairs where they belonged? She didn't know what would happen or when it would happen, only good would happen, please God, to which he added, Amen, but in the meantime, why do we need to live like refugees in our own home? Many hands make light work. In ten minutes we'll have a dining room again, whatever happens.

In the early afternoon we heard noises in the street. I ran up to my parents' room, opened the shutters and peeped out when my father came in. What are you doing?

There are people in the street, Pa. What's happening?

What's happening is that you and your nose are staying inside.

I put our shop ladder against the wall. Mr Pillai, what's going on outside?

It appears the curfew is over, young Adam. I'll find out and duly report when I return.

You would have been impressed, young Adam, he duly reported. Never have I seen so many tanks with soldiers marching alongside. It was a victory parade. Behind the tanks, trucks with more soldiers, officers in cars, Japanese flags everywhere and men shouting, *Banzai, Banzai,* which means, Long Life, or Hurrah, cheering their achievements.

Where were they going, I asked as the whole family came out to our cement patch.

I followed them to the Padang and lost myself in the crowd already gathered there. Then what do you think I saw? Our soldiers lined up, several deep, along the route, all made to bow as the victorious Japanese army marched onto the Padang, the very ground Britain laid out to parade her imperial might. It even seemed to me that our majestic Law Courts and Municipal Building, flanked at each end by graceful whites-only clubs, were also paying homage. What do you think of that Mr Messiah?

Let's see what happens.

The monsoon rains had taken a break and the sun was baking the streets as if the devils couldn't stand the heat in hell, opened the oven doors and blew in our direction. To play it safe my father hadn't opened the shop since surrender. One afternoon we were gasping for air and he, who'd said street windows, no matter what, must stay closed, pulled the shutters fully open. A minute later we heard a commotion.

Two soldiers were dragging Ng out from **Long Yuan Chinese Restaurant**, his hands tied behind. A truck stood across the road with a dozen Chinese men tied together and below us an old woman was holding back Ng's wife, thrashing about like she'd run amok. She broke free, ran out shrieking and pulled her husband away. A Jap jumped off the truck, swung his rifle butt into her belly and she crumpled in a heap.

As my ma tried to drag us away, close the shutters and cover our eyes all at the same time, we heard the woman scream and saw the bayonet go into her again and again. Ng puffed his chest, shouted something that sounded heroic and spat in a soldier's face.

That was the first time I heard a rifle fire.

The soldiers kicked the bodies, saw signs of life, plunged their bayonets in several more times, jumped into the truck and drove away.

My ma, pale and shaking, herded us downstairs to the kitchen. She shovelled sugar and salt into a jug, filled it with water, stirred frantically, poured it into four glasses, told us to drink and went to sit in the dining room on the floor, her head on her knees, her arms around her legs, rocking back and forward, back and forward.

I was still drinking when I heard my father wailing upstairs. He was at the window, closed now, beating his head and breast with his hands. I jumped up and grabbed his arms but couldn't stop him. Tears rolled down his cheeks and he was saying words, so choked, I couldn't make them out. I begged him to stop and when he didn't, I broke down, and there we were, the two of us, holding on to each other, crying until everyone came upstairs.

It was the twenty-first day of the Occupation and the war had come to our street.

19

Next day my father told us to sit at the dining table which we never did all together unless we were eating, that's to say Friday nights and High Holidays. This being Monday morning Joshua wanted to know why and Jonah said that when there is war people must practise sitting without eating. My ma said, God forbid and my father put on a serious face.

He told us that when we were woken at half-past four in the morning he should've realised, from that moment, our lives had changed. But, he said, blaming himself, himself alone, totally, he wasn't thinking. From now on everything had to be different.

Jonah said, Isn't that what I said, and Joshua was about to say something when my father raised his hand. To do anything, he said, you must do it properly which is why I'm explaining how things happen to make your life go one way or another. There are three ways. First, those which happen under your control for example, you take a job and work for someone all your life or you open a shop and be your own boss. It's in your hands. You choose what you want to do. If things go wrong you have only yourself to blame.

Is that why you opened a shop, Papa, Jonah asked.

Is that why you're blaming yourself now, Joshua said.

Never mind, my father said, let's go to the second way which is in the hands of God like for example you are born a boy or a girl and remain one or the other all your life. The third is what happens not only to you but to everybody at one and the same time like for example disease that spreads and you catch it, or war.

Yehuda, my ma said half rising, why don't you talk to the

children while I clean the house? Things must change in wartime but not everything.

Biha, he said. He was calling her Biha more than ever. Biha, what I'm saying is also for you because even when I go out, rules are rules. Sit please. What I want to say is, after what happened to me in Al Basrah, anyone would think I should know that anything, no matter how small, can grow so big so quickly and change your whole life.

Tell us an Al Basrah story, Papa, Joshua said, about the donkey who spoke Arabic ...

From today, nobody, I say it again, nobody goes out from this house except me, and even me, only to synagogue and to buy food. That's Rule Number 1.

Since when do you go to market? That was my ma.

Since today, he said, and part of Rule Number 1. I don't want you in the street with soldiers who don't know how to respect a woman. Your children need a mother so stay at home with them. Rule Number 2: Children play only at the back or upstairs.

Why? We said it together.

Rule Number 3. Back lane door remains locked, always, front windows upstairs also, just shutters halfway in the afternoon when we need air and not before next Monday when seven days are over and you all know why.

Rule Number 4. Very important. When I lived in Al Basrah, did I speak English? No. Did I see English people? No. When I came here what people did I see?

Jonah said, *orang puteh*, Joshua said, *orang melayu*, Judith said, *orang cheena*, and I said, So you had to learn English, is that what you're saying, Pa?

Right. So now I'm asking, what must we learn?

Jonah said Japanese, I asked who would teach us, my father pointed at the wall and my ma wanted to know if there were any more rules.

Rule Number 5. He stopped to think with his fingers up. Hah, the shop. I have to open the shop or how will we live? Tomorrow, but not so early, children are not going to school and only a few planks not to show all the stock to the street. Other shops are doing the same. Why invite trouble even though people are looking for food not paper?

Pa, I said, all Lim's food has gone. Signboard too. Like there never was a shop.

You are right. Yes. Good. Your eyes are open. I understand. Totally. We must do the same. Why put temptation in people's eyes?

We helped move half the stuff out of the shop stacking all we could under the dining table but the tablecloth wasn't big enough to hide it. My ma said she'd sew together two old bed sheets first thing tomorrow, and my father sent me to ask if Mr Pillai was home.

I called as I climbed our ladder now permanently against the back wall and he came out in a *lunghi* and bare on top as if this was how he was now he wasn't Deputy Chief Clerk, Public Works Department (Planning).

Good morning young Adam, he said. I hope you did not witness yesterday's outrage. I didn't answer. Alas. Now we know what we can expect. We must buttress ourselves.

I didn't know what buttress meant but didn't ask because my father was pulling on my pants telling me to ask if he could speak Japanese and would he teach us.

Mr Pillai climbed up his ladder and when he saw my father and all us kids looking up at him he said, Good morning to all of you. A sight to erase from memory. Sadly Mr Ng was a marked man branded with tattoos of Japan's enemies. With regard to your enquiry, I will say a smattering, enough to know what not to say.

I wanted to say, Please Mr Pillai, is a smattering something not to say to Japanese but my father got me down and was up two rungs asking if he could teach us, thank you, and how do you say, Good morning?

You know Mr Messiah, I wonder now if Japanese greet each other in the morning. I am uncertain and, not wishing to lead you astray, will teach you a friendlier, more casual address. You could say, *Konnichiwa*.

Konnichiwa, my father said to us. Now repeat, *Konnichiwa*.

Konnichiwa, Konnichiwa, Konnichiwa, Konnichiwa.

Good. What does it mean?

Hello.

Hello, Hello, Hello, Hello.

You can also say *Hajimemashita*, Mr Pillai said scratching the hairs on his chest. It means How do you do?

Haji, haji ... No. *Konnichiwa* is enough, he said to Mr Pillai then to us, Say it again.

Konnichiwa, we said and bowed to each other.

You see, my father said to Mr Pillai, children learn fast. How about, Thank you?

Here we encounter a problem. Japanese thank in several ways. A. When you wish to thank someone for a service already rendered, you say, *Arigato gozaimashita*. B. A more general Thank you, not necessarily for something already done, possibly still ongoing, you might say *Arigato gozaimasu*, and C. A more straightforward Thank you, when no specific deed or time is intended, you can say, simply, *Arigato*. I hope that is not too confusing.

While Mr Pillai was explaining to my father, two steps up the ladder, knees jammed against the rungs for balance, Jonah said he heard my ma calling, Joshua did the bunk and Judith ran after them.

So if I say, *Arigato*, my father said, am I saying the right word? Understand what I'm saying? After yesterday I mean.

I would say so, Mr Messiah. You will not be specific but you will not be wrong.

Now all of you repeat after me, *Arigato*.

Arigato, I said.

My father looked down. Where did they go?

I shrugged. I hadn't heard my ma calling.

Very early next morning there was loud banging on the shop front. We got out of bed and held onto each other, asking what was happening as the banging and shouting got louder. Stay here, my father said, all of you.

That was impossible. As soon as we heard him say *Konnichiwa* we crept downstairs, stood in a row behind him, bowed and said *Konnichiwa*.

The sergeant saluted and handed my father, still bowing, a sheet of paper.

He shook his head. No Ni'hong'goh, he said turning his hands over and over, no Ni'hong'goh, he said, bowed again and stayed bowed.

The sergeant, cropped hair, puffy eyes, skimpy moustache, face that might fracture if it smiled, growled and one of his men shoved his bayonet inches from my terrified father and shouted, *Temae aho da* pointing at the shop front. When he didn't move, two soldiers grabbed his arms, dragged him and banged his head against the boards. My ma screamed and a bayonet appeared at her belly. She threw her hands out by her side and walked backwards to get us kids out of the shop into the dining room. With trembling eyes and a finger across her lips, she whispered not to move or make a sound and went to the kitchen.

The sergeant, scowling with his eyebrows, barked at one of the Chinese men to explain the document. My father bowed and said, *Arigato gozaimashita, Arigato gozaimasu, Arigato*, and with the help of the Chinese removed all the front planks.

My ma returned with drinks. The sergeant refused but the others drank with his permission. While the locals were rushing in and out emptying the shop, a plump soldier with a fixed grin came into the dining room, saw what we'd stacked under the table, sucked in his breath and shouted, *Ah so desu ka*.

The sergeant marched in, opened cupboards, looked under the stairs, searched the back of the house and went upstairs. He was there a while before we heard the Smith's alarm go off and ring all the way down the stairs. He scribbled something on the paper he'd given my father explaining with his hands that he'd added the clock to the list.

My father bowed. *Arigato*, he said, *kus'umuk*. He bowed again. *Kus'umuk*.

They removed the entire stock but before leaving, the plump soldier, not much taller than Jonah, gave Judith a sketch pad and a box of crayons, tickled her nose, said Coocoo, Coocoo and got her so scared, she peed in her pants and we all bowed.

The soldiers bowed, my parents bowed three times, my father said, *Arigato, Arigato, Arigato*, we kids in the back room bowed to each other three times, *Arigato, Arigato, Arigato* and they left but we didn't hear the truck drive away.

Get your father a glass of water, my ma said to no one in particular as they were closing up the shop. We ran to the kitchen, each filled a glass and brought it to him. He drank a mouthful from each with a sad smile and shaking hands. My ma looked around the empty shop, sighed and rocked her head. We're still alive thank God, she said, took the glasses to the kitchen and washed them giving those the Japs used a second scrub, made up a jug of her salt-and-sugar cure-all and watched that we drank a full glass each.

Light filtered between the planks into the shop, picked

clean except what they didn't want and threw on the floor. My father pulled down the **KLIM** tin, removed the money, dropped in the sergeant's paper and hoisted the tin to the ceiling.

Papa, Jonah said, they took your alarm clock. How will we know the time?

We don't need to know the time in Tokyo. When God, blessed be His name, made the world, did He need Tokyo time to tell Him what to do? When the sun sets it's evening and when it rises it's morning.

What did you put in the **KLIM** tin, Joshua asked.

A receipt, my father said. From His Majesty, the Monkey God of Japan. My ma glared at him. Now listen to me, all of you, he said, never say Monkey God. Are you listening?

But why, I asked, do they need so much paper?

To write letters to their mothers when all their sons die.

Yehuda, no more, she said and gathered us around her. Come children, let's tidy up before cockroaches come out from their hiding holes. Yudit, go bring the Flit pump. We'll sweep a little then see what we find for breakfast.

My father said it was his fault, he should've woken early as usual, my ma blamed herself for not sewing the sheets there and then, a stitch in time would have saved some of what we had, then she stopped dusting and said, You know, I think God was helping us.

My father stopped feeling for stuff on the higher shelves. You are right, Biha, he said. If they thought we were hiding our goods, would they leave us alive?

I looked at the old whitewash behind the empty shelves and unfaded bits of floor and said, Yoohoo ... listen ... Yoohoo, the room echoed Yoohoo and we kids were still laughing when we heard our left-side neighbours shouting. We ran upstairs, opened the shutters and saw Lim and his two oldest sons, hands tied behind, being pushed onto the truck beside my father's lost property.

They didn't find his goods, my father said.

God keep them alive, my ma said and went downstairs to check our food stock.

Rice, half a gunny, lentils, two, two and a half *kattis*. Sugar, salt, oil, one month. Half a salt fish. One basket onions already sprouting, half basket potatoes with eyes, chillies, limes. Let's see what's in the store room. Three, six, nine, eleven Chap Ayam Pilchards in Tomato Sauce. Condensed milk, two, four, six, ten. **KLIM**, two big tins. Pickles four bottles, jam three. I'll make them last. No fresh vegetables.

My father sat a while in his chair in the empty shop. The few dollars he'd salvaged from the **KLIM** tin and tubes of coins hidden around the house wouldn't keep us long. He stood up abruptly, put on his shoes, walked to the back door and said, I'm going, without the Biha that didn't want an argument.

Where?

Your sister's house.

Why?

When he didn't answer she told him to be careful and back before dark. This wasn't the day she wanted to be alone with the children and worrying.

20

It was an hour before sunset. We were lying on the cement patch drawing the plump soldier with what he'd given Judith and things we found after they ransacked the shop, my ma's word, looted was my father's. She was sitting on the kitchen stool by the back door cleaning rice, the best she could get with so many stones and *kutus* one would think they swept it from the floor when we heard, Biha, from the lane behind.

My father carried a case and Auntie Sally, big smile, hair flat and pinned down in her it's-getting-so-hot-these-days-I-can't-stand-it style, had a stuffed gunny bag.

Joshua and Jonah rushed out, she dropped her bag and they did a hugging dance in the lane. Then Judith and I had our turn because Auntie Sally hadn't come to Friday night dinner since bombs started falling from the skies and what would she do getting stranded between the devil and deep blue sea if the siren went in pitch darkness?

Going to Auntie Flora's house in the morning and returning with Auntie Sally in the evening, a case, a gunny bag and calling Biha, Biha, told my ma all she needed to know. Use Yudit's bed tonight, she said. She'll sleep with me. Tomorrow we'll see what's best. Now the shop is empty we have lots of room.

Auntie Sally started to say, No, I'll be fine on the floor, why go to all the bother, but my ma went into the kitchen to wash three cups of rice same time as telling Judith to take Auntie Sally upstairs and find a place to put her things. While the rice was boiling, she chopped two of the sprouting onions and a long red chilli to make *nasi goreng*. Three or four eggs would give it more taste, she said, but where will we find them, at which point my father brought the pilchard she'd left for him so she cut it up and mixed it in with the rice.

After we'd eaten Judith showed my father her drawing of the soldier who'd looted his shop and he tried to smile but it didn't come out right. He told her to leave it on the table, he'd look at it later and took something long and thin out of his pocket.

That's all they left of your sister's house, he told my ma, carefully unwrapping the paper. If they knew what it was they'd have taken it also.

Jews fix a *mezuzah* to their doorpost to tell people, in a way, where to find them at rounding up time. Being Auntie Flora's, it was gold plated with tiny diamonds in the ש.

Flora's house was ransacked? *Simha'lekh*. Who did it?

Neighbours knew nothing, heard nothing, saw nothing. Two-ton piano and furniture you need a dozen men to carry and nobody saw nothing, heard nothing, knew nothing and I want to tell you, I found the door locked and in one piece.

Who else had a key?

Friam told me to take anything I want but all they left was the dust on the floor.

So Flora was right, my ma said. In my heart of hearts I wanted to say yes, we'll stay in her house but how to save both? Now both are empty.

Auntie Sally said it was horrible even to imagine soldiers in the house. Bad enough seeing them in the street like pigs with spectacles and was going on about their bandy legs like walking on a pair of dhobi tongs when my ma said, No more, please, before the children say these things, so Auntie Sally said, Who wants to play five stones, and went upstairs.

I stayed to ask my father what he'd seen in the streets, and he said, I cannot sit and do nothing. We have another mouth to feed.

Feeding seven is the same as feeding six, my ma said. A

few more grains of rice and an extra cup of water in the soup. Sally's no problem.

With those in the street I don't want her gallivanting, my father said.

My ma looked at him wanting to ask how we were going to live and he looked at her saying he didn't know. There was a long silence after which he said, Please God tell me what to do before we starve and went upstairs to wind his clock and find it too was gone.

The three Lims did not return that night.

God must have answered my father. The moment he finished praying next morning he looked down, paced the cement patch end to end, side to side, counting on his fingers and, without making coffee reduced from four to one a day without sugar, took me to

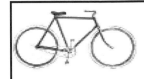

Solly's Cycles

SALES AND REPAIRS

44 Short Street

Solly Shirazee whose family came from Shiraz in Persia was sitting outside his shop, smoking. Uncle Solly, who wasn't a real uncle, was my father's friend but not a synagogue friend. I only saw him there on High Holidays when all Jews go just in case God had His eye on them and, when the time came, asked awkward questions. On those days he took my cheeks between his knuckles and pinched. I got prepared but he didn't do it that day.

When?

Two days ago, Solly said.

Hah, one day before me. Did they give you a receipt from the Emperor of Japan?

Too bloody rough to wipe my arse, Solly said signalling with one hand behind his ear, pointing the other into the empty shop.

Be sure to keep it, my father said when we were sitting inside. When the British come back, I'm going to wave mine in front of them. Your fortress fell on its face. Now pay me.

Not me, Solly said stubbing his cigarette butt on an empty shelf and dropping it into his pocket. Japs came down the peninsula on bicycles and now they're confiscating them from under our arses in case the British return for what they left behind. They'll call me a collaborator and hang me for supplying military transportation to the enemy.

Both men were laughing, not loud, telling each other the world had gone mad. If an army on bicycles beats one in armoured cars, then they had to start learning as if they'd just been born. Solly took off his glasses, breathed on the lenses and polished them with his singlet. If I blame the British for anything, he said, it is that they didn't trust us. Like a fool I went to Fort Canning and volunteered. Teach me to fire a gun, I said to an officer, and I'll shoot a few Japs for you. I'm truly sorry, he said in an accent like broken glass, but I could join the ARP. I took the helmet, the whistle, the nightstick and came home.

Did you arrest anyone, I asked.

You're Joe, he said.

Adam.

Okay Adam, tell me the date Singapore surrendered.

15th February 1942.

Remember it, he said. Something changed that day. What, I cannot say now but you will talk about it when you're a man. Now Judah, I'm sure you didn't come to buy a bicycle. What can I do for you?

I need a hammer, heavy, and anything you can lend me to break cement.

Don't tell me, Solly said, you're digging a tunnel to Australia. Don't waste your time. They've bombed Darwin. Once they have Port Moresby Australia's as good as theirs. They'll be there before you, millions of them. Take my advice and make yourself comfortable. This is going to be a long war.

How long?

Who knows? Germany's bombing the shit out of Britain and Churchill's changing his generals in North Africa faster than his cigars. But, and right now it's only a small but, there is a ray of hope. When God made Hitler ...

God didn't make Hitler, my father said.

... like he made you and me, he also made Hitler. Not only did he make him a Jew-killer for only God knows what reason, he also made him mad. Three days after the Japs bombed us and Pearl Harbour, Hitler declared war on America. If you want to know what mad is, that is mad. All the same it's going to take time, years for all I know.

Do you have a wireless, Uncle Solly?

If I tell you, he said straightening his smile, you will have information our conquerors want. Can I be sure you won't betray me when they pull out your fingernails, one by one?

Solly, my father said, don't frighten him.

If you and I have to be babies again, Solly said, he has to grow five years for every year of his life. Judah, be prepared. This is not going to be easy. The British may have looked down on the colour of our skin and wouldn't rub shoulders with us, but they played cricket on the Padang. When you play cricket you have rules. Japs don't play cricket *and* they have no respect for life.

What are you saying? We surrendered. Isn't that enough?

You're not listening Judah. This is war. Not a cricket

match where winners and losers go back to the clubhouse, drink and tell jokes. Japs are brought up according to *bushido* and jokes are not in the training manual. Their intentions are clear. Whites were assembled on the Padang and men, women and children were marched off to Changi, miles in the sun, no food, no water. Right now something is going on we don't talk about. Chinese are being rounded up. Thousands are disappearing. There are rumours.

We need more rumours?

That's all they can be. But they don't go away. They call it *Sook Ching* in Chinese. It means Purification by Elimination. A kind of cleaning-up operation. As Hitler is clearing Jews out of Europe, Japs want to get rid of the Chinese. Now remember, he said pointing his finger at me, the less you know the better your health and your fingernails. So I'll not ask your father why he wants to break cement. The workshop's at the back. Take anything you want and bring it back when you finish.

He put on his specs, went out to sit on his bench, lit a stub and read the one-page final edition of **The Straits Times**.

The patch was eight or nine yards long, five or six broad and open to the sky. Within a week my father had smashed the cement to the earth beneath, kids, my ma and auntie dumping the broken pieces in the back lane. Then he turned over the earth with Solly's *changkol*, dug shallow trenches and told them to be careful bringing it. My ma folded three hankies in triangles, dripped eucalyptus oil and they tied them over their noses. She pulled her rappa halfway up her legs, hitched it at her waist with a ribbon, told us to get into the house and don't let her catch us opening a window anywhere.

Jonah peeped, shut the window and said they were in our new garden, spreading piss and shit from the bucket. Joshua said it wasn't fair, they were having all the fun, ran down and we followed. My ma yelled but we were in there with bare feet, stamping around, taking turns to vomit and in ten minutes we'd had enough. My ma stripped us – boys first – scrubbed until our flesh glowed and we were in tears, sent us in, and worked on Judith.

My father went to Thekka Market next morning and bought any fruit and vegetables he found with seeds including a small papaya. With a delicate touch I never knew he had, he broke up the soil between his fingers, put three papaya seeds into two holes in the back corner and dripped a little water. Soon you will see what God does with them, he said.

There is a saying in the tropics: put a walking stick into the ground and two weeks after the first rain it sprouts leaves. He left the two strongest shoots and in six months we had tall palms with long yellow papayas. Each time he twisted off one he looked up and praised God. See, he said, from tiny seeds God keeps us alive and inside the seed there is everything it needs to make the tree, totally and it's the same with human beings. I asked where humans keep their seeds and he said that was a lesson for later.

Soon the plot was crowded with all the vegetables we could cram: onions, tomatoes, garlic, cucumbers, *bamya, shwanda, labu, pak choy, kai lan, kangkong, ubi kayu* and two papaya palms. He added clay pots, wooden crates and empty tins, anything to hold earth and grow food, called it our Garden of Eden and put us kids and Auntie Sally in charge of different parts. Whoever kept it tidiest and produced the best vegetables would get, he scratched his head and my ma said a big hug and kiss, what else did we need?

From now on Rule Number 6 was no Jeyes in the bucket. My ma spread it around the back and added Rule Number 7

– keep the dining room window shut at all times and close the door anytime you step in or out or God help us. In time she exchanged two big baskets of vegetables for a cock and hen. I was to gather the eggs, look after the chicks and tell her when they were big enough to slaughter. Okay, I said, and told myself they'd always need to be bigger. I called the cock Abraham and asked God to make him father of a nation of chickens. The hen was Sarah his wife.

My father explained that she could lay without Abraham interfering with her, but her eggs wouldn't turn into chicks unless he was there to make sure but again wouldn't tell me how. I asked my ma and she said, Can't you see I'm busy? I said, Can't you wash and speak at the same time? She said, Go ask your father. I did, I said, but he won't tell me until I'm older. That'll do for now, she said and I said, Maybe when I'm older I won't want to know, I'll have different questions, and she said, Fine.

A couple of days later I saw Abraham droop a wing, circle Sarah, grab her neck with his beak and jump on her back. I asked my ma what they were doing. Fighting, she said. So I shouted and shooed him off and she said, Leave them alone. To be healthy chickens need to fight now and again. I think all that fighting must have made Abraham feel special because he started crowing in the morning and my father said it was fine, that's what cocks are supposed to do but why didn't he wait until 5.45?

Then my ma added Rules, 8, 9 and 10 to do with keeping clean and healthy, making do and doing without, knowing when to stop and leave some for others, sharing with big hearts which was the only way to survive at a time when even what we took for granted was no longer granted. That was fine with my father but when she proposed Rule 11, to do with starting the shop again, a place for people to exchange stuff they didn't need for what they did, he said,

No. For one, we don't need Japs looting, for two, exchanging is not bizz-i-nezz and for three, if Ten Commandments are enough for God, His name be praised, why do you need eleven?

21

It must have been November or December 1942 when Simon came to our house. He was starting a school for boys, would I join? Who's the teacher? I am. But you aren't a teacher. You don't have to be to teach, he said. I have heaps of books all the way to Standard 7. I'll read the previous day what I want to teach and before I could answer, he asked my father.

Sure, my father said. Pity. I have no more a shop to supply your school or we could do a little bizz-i-nezz. Special discount. So, Simon, how much you charge per month?

It's free.

In that case can his brothers come also?

They are older than I. They'll know more than I do.

About that, my father said, you don't need to worry.

I would like to start with Adam. When I think I can handle more students, his brothers will be welcome, he said to my father, and to me, we start at 9am prompt. I look forward to our first lesson tomorrow.

He talked to me with our eyes at the same height and always in contact, no one trying to outsmart the other, and explained as many times as I needed.

When you grow up, I said, you should be a teacher.

We are all teachers, he said. Read and you have something to teach. There are so many books. I looked at the piles around his room, his windowsill, poking out from under his bed, thick as gravestones. I'll need twenty lives to read those we already have and in that time how many more will be written? Knowledge is endless, Adam, thank goodness.

Like me he was born and bred in the thickest part of the *mahallah* yet nothing like us. He told me, without my father's rigmarole that needed reminding to get back to where he was, that our fathers came from where civilisation was born then died, abruptly.

Simon, I said, if you put your sayings in a book, you'll be famous, and he said, What if I change my mind? That gave me a problem. On one hand my father filled my ears which, in a manner of speaking, bracketed my thoughts. All his life he read a single book with moving lips and loving mumble in a language he half understood. On the other there was Simon saying what couldn't be more opposite than the other end of a tunnel and often I couldn't see where it was going. Once, after my father told me a Bible story with a lesson in it for life, you understand, I said to Simon, I'm proud to be a Jew, aren't you?

Of a birth without choice or part in? Would you, if born Confucian or Catholic?

Judaism is a gift from God, I said repeating what I'd been told. We are His People chosen to show others the proper way to live. We gave the world the Ten Commandments.

If you were Hindu what would you say about the compassionate and merciful Vishnu, the all-pervading protector of the world and restorer of moral order holding in each of his four hands an emblem of his divinity?

My father never mentioned Vishnu so I said, I'm not Hindu so that's not an argument.

There is no argument, he said and put his arm on my shoulders.

What I liked most was that he had no problem having a Jew in class called Messiah and didn't make me stand to answer questions. He taught me for two hours three times a week, Reading, Spelling and Arithmetic before going on to Grammar and Constructing Good English Sentences, including parsing, conjugation and declension which I think he invented because no schoolteacher ever taught them. As soon as you are ready, he said, I will teach you Algebra. That trains you to think logically.

Mister Pillai stopped being my hero. Now I wished I could think and speak like Simon and began to wonder if he was a genius. Nice to have one for a friend but, for the time being, it was okay also to listen to my father. I was learning fine but I think he tried too soon with Algebra. Why do we need to find the value of X if X is unknown? That's exactly why, he said, it is its own reason. When I still didn't understand, he tried Geometry, step-brother to Trigonometry which solves problems in three dimensions, he said, isn't that exciting? I asked him what dimensions were, so he taught me ratios and proportions.

One day, going home from a lesson, head full of percentages, I wondered how he could be so clever not only to understand but also make me understand. What I'm saying is, after explaining that *centum* was the Latin word for 100 and *per* meant part of, it wasn't difficult to figure out that 15 per cent meant 15 parts of 100, like: How many per cent is 22 of 200? 11, I said, that's easy. So he said, Imagine you were running your father's shop and wanted to know percentage profit, buying and selling. I don't think he can, I said. If I said, What's per cent, Pa? he'd say, foreign money. That got Simon laughing. Sons should always know more than fathers, he said, or how will we progress, and got me to work out the percentage profit if I bought 10 pads of paper for $2 and sold them for $2.30 which I had to do in two steps, profit, 30 cents, then percentage. When I said 15 per cent, he said, how about if I sold each of the 10 pads at a higher price than the previous one because I had fewer left to sell.

Anyone who can do that, I said, would be the richest man in the world.

The procedure is the same for ten pads as it is for one. First calculate profit on each, then total profit, then percentage based on total original cost price. As I was doing the subtraction then addition followed by division and multiplication, he said, You see, you've just done all four arithmetical processes, and when I got it right first time, I swear I did, I said, excited as hell, I'm not stupid then, am I?

There's no such thing as a stupid student, he said, only stupid teachers.

For homework he gave me 5 sums about my father's bizz-i-nezz which I thought I'd teach him while I was at it and I had to make grammatical sentences with words like honourable, beget, withdraw, appoint, comprehend, acceptable, and so on which came from my reading exercise, that's to say two paragraphs in one of his gravestone books.

Meantime we'd got used to seeing Japanese soldiers in one-size-fits-all khaki uniforms and cloth caps, rifle slung from a shoulder, seldom smiling. Two patrolled Princep Street from the corner of Bras Basah Road to Bukit Timah Road then back again on the opposite side. I'd wait until they were well past before stepping out or if they were standing nearby, take another route but couldn't avoid the one at the bottom of Wilkie Road on my way to Simon so I slowed down and bowed. Once, still bowing, he put his hand through my hair and said, Ainu. Thinking Ainu meant he was going to cut off my head I turned to stone. Instead he laughed and patted my curls. Mr Pillai explained that Ainu lived in the north of Japan. They were taller with long curly hair like mine. The next time I went up Wilkie Road I said Ainu to the soldier, he said Ainu to me, I smiled, he laughed and we became friends.

Whites were in Changi Prison and Eurasians, meaning one European parent usually the father, soon followed.

Those who ran hospitals, public services and so on got armbands and did their old jobs and, for a while, priests were allowed to go around freely. The Japs printed new money, people returned to work, *toti*-men emptied our honey buckets, garbage was collected and life slowly returned to halfway okay if you ignored rationing, what didn't work and what you couldn't get.

Without knowing who you could trust, people said little. No one else had been killed in our street or taken away but we knew it hadn't stopped. The YMCA in Stamford Road, half a mile away, was Kempeitai headquarters supposed to be military police but more like secret police working with local spies. Few taken there for interrogation came out alive. People knew what was going on, heard the screams and avoided that stretch of road.

The three Lims hadn't returned. Lim Ah Pat, a younger son, time to time would climb up his ladder to chat with us. Day Japs raided, he said, they bring hooded man. Hundred per cent informer. No words. Pointing finger. Nothing to do now. One day.

Being so many, they had to find work and when Ah Pat whispered that if we needed anything just let him know, we knew he was in the black market. My father was friendlier now that their cooking smells no longer bothered him.

Mr Pillai got back his old job. Up on his ladder he told me how he'd discovered, after careful study, his mother tongue, namely Tamil, had similar grammatical parts of speech, structure and syntax as Ni'hong'goh. Hence, he said, substituting the word of one language for that of the other, I can speak Ni'hong'goh. Moreover, I am pleased to say, my two sons, already multi-lingual, are gainfully employed as interpreters.

He rose a step and leaned over the wall. We wear this, he said twirling an armband. White and red stripes represent

Japan's emblem and the words mean Civilian Enemy. What do you make of that, young Adam? They purport to have liberated us then give us work if we concede we are enemies. We are paid in new currency which sports a branch of bananas and a promise, in *English*, from the Japanese Government to pay the bearer on demand.

Hah, my father said coming to join us.

No different from Britain's promise, wouldn't you say, Mr Messiah? But no serial number hence no telling how much they print. Clever, wouldn't you agree?

My father agreed.

All this plus Simon's homework were going through my head when I reached our back door and saw splashes of fresh blood. My father's! In synagogue he still called Hirohito, the Monkey God of Japan. I knocked, not loud. I was trembling. My ma came out singing,

> *Animal crackers in my soup*
> *Monkeys and rabbits loop the loop*
> *Gosh oh gee do I have fun*
> *Swallowing animals one by one.*

I hadn't heard her sing since the war began. How could she sing, smile and swing a soup spoon with my father's blood all over the door? Then I smelled Friday smells and saw Sarah sitting on my ma's stool, head half buried in feathers, eyes three-quarters shut. I called but she wouldn't come. I offered her a handful of chopped leftovers from the feed box and got the other chickens clucking but she didn't even lift her head.

My ma had disappeared so I asked Judith where Abraham was. She shrugged and ran into the house. I lifted the cover of a bubbling pot on the stove. It had soup to the brim.

Another had my ma's Friday-night-special and there, between onions, potatoes, cinnamon sticks and cloves, Abraham lay in pieces.

Who did this?

Silman came, Jonah said, and Ma asked him to cut a chicken.

I screamed. She was upstairs, back to me, pretending to make up a bed already made. This is not acceptable, I said, hands on hips. If you wanted to be in charge, why did you appoint me? It's not honourable.

Sorry. My ma turned. I should've asked. But you were with Simon. How long is it since we had a proper dinner? I don't remember how chicken tastes.

Abraham wasn't a chicken. He was Sarah's husband. Just look at her now. You'll see. She'll not lay another egg as long as she lives. Oh God, I thought, she'll be in next Friday's pot. I withdraw that, I said, I'll talk to her. But how will she beget more chicks without him?

There are other males.

They're her sons, I said raising my voice and my finger.

My ma's smile broadened. She turned away, carried on pretending, picked up the pillow, gave it a thump, put it down at the wrong end of the bed. It'll be fine, she said to the pillow as she moved it to where it belonged. You're too young to understand.

That's what old people always say. I comprehend everything Simon tells me. That's why he's the best teacher in the world because he says there is no such thing as a stupid student, only stupid teachers.

My ma turned. She wasn't smiling. No, Adam, she said gently, tilting her head, nobody is stupid. There is a time for everything and now is not the time. She put her hands out calling me to her. I felt myself softening but Abraham had been murdered. The least I could do, if I wasn't going to mourn for him, was to be angry for seven days starting today. I stomped out of the room and went down to talk things over with Sarah.

I refused soup at dinner because I could see bits of Abraham's skin floating about and when my ma put the whole of his neck onto my father's plate, I threw a fit. My brothers were waiting. Jonah said, Cock-a-doodle-do, Joshua went, Boobooboo and laughed till he choked. Stop it, I shouted. See, Pa, they're doing it on purpose. Tell them to stop.

He sent them to the empty shop but they came straight out again saying their soup was getting cold and if I didn't want mine could they have it?

My father finished nibbling Abraham's neck and cleared his throat.

First, he said, I want to thank your mother for such good soup which God gave us to enjoy. Auntie Sally agreed and the others clapped. I sat with my hands in my lap staring at the wall. We haven't eaten proper Friday night food so long, he said, I was forgetting what it means to be a Jew. Second, I want to explain to my third son who I carried on my lap, eight days old when he became a Jew. When God, may his name be praised, made the world He brought all the beasts of the field and birds of the air to stand in front of Adam, which is also my third son's extra name which only he got in the whole family which I won't talk about now, so he should be proud. God told Adam to give names to the animals, horses, cows, pigeons, ducks which are the names we use to this day.

But Pa, I said. I called him Abraham.

The first Adam called it a chicken and a chicken is a chicken. Calling a chicken Isaac or Jacob or Moshe Rabbenu, God forbid anyone should give a chicken the name of the greatest man who ever lived, you should know it's still a chicken and people are more important than chickens. God brought animals and birds *to* Adam, not the other way round, understand what I'm saying? He looked at me. I didn't nod. Never mind, he said, I have more to say. Whether it is better to be born a man or a woman I will not talk about with women in the room. But when it comes to chickens I can tell you it's better to be a hen than a cock. Hens lay eggs, cocks are needed only to make sure eggs turn into chickens and God, who is eternal, arranged it in such a way that one cock can keep an eye on five, six, seven chickens, so the other four, five, six can be eaten. You understand?

Jonah said, I think so, Joshua said, Me too, Judith banged her spoon in her empty bowl and said, I want more Abraham soup. Auntie Sally went to fill Judith's bowl and my ma brought in the main course. She served my father the breast, asked which piece I wanted, I hadn't had soup and must be hungry, would I like a leg and a thigh?

Onions and potatoes, I said, and only those not touching Abraham and the cinnamon stick if no one else wants it. I couldn't see what her spoon was doing inside the pot, but she was saying, No, not that one, that one's not touching, here I've found two more, but I knew she was pretending which she did a lot.

When I came down next morning Sarah was off the stool, scratching for food. In a couple of minutes one of her sons drooped his wing, circled her and I didn't stay to watch.

We stayed healthy, skinny but never starving, mainly because of my ma's care, my father's worry and Auntie Sally playing with us. She taught us card tricks and games like 21 and rummy. We played so often with the same packs I could recognise cards by crinkles and knew what others were holding. It wasn't cheating. It was what my father called: keeping your eyes open when others are shut, a lesson to learn for life.

On Monday 5th April 1943 Gahtan went up the *bimah* in synagogue, interrupted the evening service, placed both hands on his walking stick, clamped the other end between his shoes and told us how, before dawn that morning, soldiers rounded up a hundred Jews, gave them twenty minutes to fill a case and grab a mattress. So why, he fixed his eyes on Howee, why, all of a sudden, are they putting Jews in jail?

Why not? First Europeans then Eurasians now us.

Think, Howee. Gahtan rocked on his stick. Japs want Europeans out of their corner of the world but know nothing about anti-Semitism. Religion means nothing to them. They haven't interfered with churches or synagogues or temples. So why are they jailing us who do as we are told, no one more dangerous than an office clerk or a cloth merchant?

I give up, Howee said.

Germany, Italy, Japan, Tripartite Pact, September 1940. Nazis want the Japs to do in Asia what they are doing in Europe.

Hah, my father said. Like I said. German Pharaoh tells Japanese Pharaoh what to do.

So what are you saying? Howee said. They're going to kill us?

One hundred Jews are in jail, Gahtan said, not a concentration camp, for now.

That evening we prayed, twice as long and thrice as loud, for God to hear and listen. I suspect He did, partially, because we remained free until Sunday 25th March 1945.

22

In the few minutes they gave us, my father climbed our ladder and begged our right-side neighbours, please stay in our house, vegetables, fruit, chickens, take anything you want, totally, please, immediately, one, two of you, sleep in our beds, no mattresses, sorry, don't leave or we'll lose everything. The Pillai girls said their father and brothers were at work, so sorry. You come, my father said, please, now, up the ladder, don't let them see you or God knows what they'll do, don't be afraid, you won't fall, I'll hold.

Padmal giggled. Saris aren't made for climbing ladders, she said and told her sister Parul, Hold on, don't let go, tossed off her slippers, climbed and tried with another giggle to swing her sari over the wall onto our ladder. My father, eyes down, felt her skirt brush his arm, told me to take over and left. Hold, Adam, she shrieked, and don't look up.

You're so silly Padmal, Parul giggled over the wall. It's not possible to look up a sari.

I said goodbye to our chickens, helped Padmal down, then Parul who said be quick, their mother was fetching rice rations and their grandparents were alone. My ma came out carrying two bulging gunny bags.

Thank you girls, she said. God bless you. Hide upstairs. Soon as we go, close up and be sure to lock with the bolt, top and bottom. Tell your father Changi Jail. He'll know what to do. God will bless your family and find good husbands for you and why are you still here, Adam? Get your bag before they get impatient and God forbid, who knows?

When all were down with mattresses and gunny bags, my ma stuffed our pockets with small packs of tea and coffee, salt and sugar, bread and dried fish and anything eatable. My ma told me to tuck my shirt into my pants and be sure not to knock them or bend down. She'd make an omelette, she said and went to pluck two red chillies from the garden.

My father put on his kippah, we covered our heads with a hand and repeated after him, Hear O Israel, the Lord is our God, the Lord is One, all the way to Blessed be the Name of His glorious kingdom for ever and ever, in Hebrew, when a soldier burst in flashing his bayonet, saw us praying and stood back respectfully. My father, wanting to show a pagan the dignity of Jewish prayers, went on reciting the next two parts slowly, making us repeat every word and when he finished we all said a loud Amen.

Nan-nin no, the soldier asked.

Nana, my father said showing seven fingers. The soldier checked his list, slung his rifle, stepped into the street and I slid into the dining room. Coast is clear, I said to the girls hiding at the back. See you soon, I hope.

Simon, who'd been picked up earlier with his parents and sister and another Wilkie Road family, helped us onto the open truck. Lessons continue, he said. You have made me confident and if the whole community is being corralled, we'll have a bigger class. My brothers asked if they could join. Simon said he'd designed a short test to which Jonah said, it was okay, if he could come he'd let him know and Joshua said, me too.

We went from Jewish house to Jewish house in the *mahallah*. A soldier jumped out, looked for the *mezuzah* on the doorpost, hammered with his rifle butt and half an hour later another family came on board. It was well after noon when we picked up our last passengers, Howee and his family, halfway up Selegie Road. The truck was full, sun high and hot and our two water bottles empty. We thought we'd soon be moving toward the sea and breeze when the truck turned up Bukit Timah Road.

Where are we going, Simon's father asked. Isn't it to Changi Jail?

They moved Jews to Sime Road last May, Howee said. Former British Army Base. New huts. He sounded cheerful. Whites had to walk, we're going by truck. That's something, no? Do as they tell you and all will be well.

My father, who'd not said a word until then, hoisted himself on my shoulder to see where we were when we swung sharply into Adam Road and I felt liquid seeping into my pants. We were entering a road with my name, greener than anywhere I'd been before with tall *lallang*, giant trees and bamboo a mile high and I wasn't going to tell my ma our dinner was destroyed.

We turned into Sime Road then into the camp where our driver and guards jumped out and vanished without a word. Two trucks were already there crowded with veteran prisoners looking for family. It seemed crazy that they should be rejoicing to see each other surrounded by barbed wire and guardhouses but all the tears were happy. So many had arrived together we didn't know who to speak to, what to do or where to go.

Is this where they're putting us? Huts? With attap roofs? Where insects make nests? No doors? No windows? What's to stop rats and wild animals eating us alive?

Biha, my father said, Biha, don't start worrying before we know. Saying Biha twice meant my ma was showing signs that this was not a place she wanted her family to be, why did we have to leave a house to come here and live like what she couldn't bring herself to say, was this the way to treat people? What did we do so wrong they had to disturb our lives? It will be alright, he said patting her hand. God is with us.

Solly Shirazee caught sight of us and came through the crowd under a battered straw hat, a sunny smile across his tanned face. Ho, he said to my father and doffed his hat with a short bow to my ma and Auntie Sally. Have you finished your tunnel? I was sure you'd popped out in Australia and making a mint selling pencils to Aborigines.

Is this a place to joke, Solly?

Will it get better if I don't? Promise me that, Judah and I swear I'll never joke again. No seriously. Wouldn't they let you in? We have Australians on the other side of the hill. I'll lodge an official complaint about their Whites-Only Policy. No colour-bar here. All sun-burned. No high-class and low-class either, only coolie-class. No expats and locals. We're all rats in the same shithole, excuse my Spanish, ladies.

Hello Uncle Solly, I said pulling on his arm. Do you remember me?

You're Joseph. No, Adam. Have you been smashing eggs?

What happened? My ma turned me around. Let me see. My goodness. Did I not say be careful? They gave us twenty minutes. Could I boil them, pack and be ready in twenty minutes? That's not the way to treat people. What a waste. Four eggs. Laid this morning.

Four eggs! Solly said. That's a meal for thirty. If you wish we'll take your son to the kitchen, boil him, squeeze out the eggs and crush the shells for calcium. And that's not a joke. Okay, down to business. Today I'm Billeting Officer. Yesterday Latrine Inspector. Tomorrow, who knows? How many are you?

Seven, my father said touching each of us on the head.

Males over 10 in the Men's huts, everyone else in the Women's. Lights, the few we have, go off at 8 and it's wise not to be outside your hut. Our Nipponese boys are pretty tame, but time and again one may have a cup of saké too many. By the way we don't call them Japs here. In a couple of days you'll know all you need to know. Now kiss and say goodbye until Sunday when you see each other in the orchard for half an hour, hold hands and show off how well your diet is going.

No, Solly, please. My ma was pale. We cannot be separated. Who will look after them? Are there no family houses? Just a small one. No fuss, I swear to you Solly. Please.

Family houses? Solly looked up, scratched his head and brought his hands together. For you Sabiha, I know just the one. But not just yet. That's Phase 17 when we build the swimming pool and casino with à la carte restaurant. Now we do as they tell us and they leave us alone. You'll not see much of them, except Field Marshall Shimura, D.K.A.F.E, 1st Class. He's in charge of our camp. He looked at each of us boys in turn and said, Watch out for him and his whip. Otherwise we run things. So. He pointed over a low rise. Boys with Judah there, girls, pointing in the opposite direction, there. Find a hut that isn't full, speak to the secretary, lay your mattresses, keep your *barang* close, you never know, and when you hear the gong that's dinner.

Is the food kasher? My father would rather have starved.

You doubt it? The Chief Rabbi of the British Empire dines with us every Friday. What's wrong with you, Judah? There's nothing to eat within a mile of camp that walks. It's a good day when a couple of *ikan bilis* float on your *congee*. Your contract with God is safe, believe me, his eyes twinkled, unless, but not often, a snail loses its way and ends up in the *buboh*. By the way, Solly said as he walked off to another family, don't dress for dinner.

I took my rolled mattress under my arm, picked up my bag and moved off with my father and brothers when my ma grabbed the back of my shirt. You're ten until I say you are eleven. Don't argue. And nobody is saying goodbye because nobody is going away. Yehuda, look after the boys,

boys, look after your father. If anything happens to any of you, you are all responsible so don't say I didn't tell you. Come Sally, take Yudit's hand. Adam, come with me and take off your clothes right away. I'll ask where to wash them. Four eggs. What a waste. And two red chillies.

My ma found a broom, swept an area much bigger than we were allotted and we laid our mattresses edge to edge leaving no gaps to roll onto the cement floor. She took one side, Auntie Sally the other, Judith and me between.

We were a hundred women and children in a long hut living with mosquitoes you knew were there when they bit. After sunset the jungle got very noisy. Insects cheeped, frogs croaked, monkeys hooted and now and again soldiers laughed. I didn't sleep much. Solly carried me naked and screaming and dropped me into a giant cooking pot. When I was boiled and bloated Auntie Sally scraped the eggs off my legs with a bayonet and gave them to my ma who was slicing two red chillies to make it do for thirty people and how much tastier would it be if she had a drop of soya sauce so no one would say camp food was shit and I knew I was dreaming because my ma never said shit.

Auntie Sally shook me. Poor boy, you had a fright. Pissing in bed is okee-dokee, she said loud enough for a hundred women and children to hear and tell it to the whole camp in the morning when I'd not done that since I was six.

Next day trucks delivered the remaining Jews, none more bewildered than the old synagogue regulars with sad eyes and long beards picked up as they came out after the morning service. They stayed together as if still praying, each asking another what to do, all shrugging and looking to heaven for a sign.

Solly said we'd have no roll calls so long as we didn't upset the Nips which included not trying to escape, listening to the radio, sending messages to the enemy, planning an uprising or enraging Captain Shimura DKAFE – Doesn't Know Arse From Elbow – 1st Class. We had to keep the camp clean and grow food and anyone over 10 who didn't work didn't eat. There was a hospital with many doctors and a dispensary with few medicines. Anyone who volunteered to cook as a way to eat on the sly should know that guards watched and kitchen workers were weighed once a month. Stealing food meant a good thrashing.

Religion was our own affair and we didn't have to work on the Sabbath. They know God is watching, my father said our first Sunday together but neither he nor anyone else knew why the whole community had been interned and nobody dared ask.

After a week Simon started his school. Four boys had passed his test and with me lessons got going in the shade of a hut. He was teaching us about words spelt the same way but different in sound and meaning, like entrance and en-trance, minute and min-ute and while we were cracking our heads for others, Captain Shimura in brown boots, white gloves, revolver, sword and jockey whip appeared. He walked so quietly nobody ever heard him coming. We jumped up and bowed.

Study. Very good.

Hai, Simon said with another bow.

Engrish ressons, he said, striking his left glove with his whip. For me.

Hai. Simon bowed a third time.

Come office, his finger looped to say tomorrow, Engrish ressons, and five fingers stood up twice to tell the time.

Hai, wakarimashita. Simon bowed and Shimura marched off.

Are you going to teach him? That was me still bowing as I sat and the others joined in about making him pay. Kayloo said bananas, Ikey One wanted sweets for the sugar his mother said we needed, Ikey Two asked for condensed milk he hadn't tasted for who knows how long and Hayoo said one of the pomelos, big as Shitimura's head, his brother Benjy had to carry, yesterday, a whole basket to his office.

I'll exchange mine for Ni'hong'goh lessons, Simon said.

Over the next five or six weeks, Shimura came by and repeated bits of what Simon had taught him, grinning at the end of each. The quick brown fox jumps over the razy dog, To be or not to be, that is the question. The class stood in a row bowing and saying in chorus, O-*tsukaresama deshita* which Simon said meant well done and Shimura's tiny eyes lit up. Simon's Ni'hong'goh was improving and he shared Japanese sweets and biscuits with us.

All seemed well until, as we were finishing a class, Latifa, Auntie Sally's friend who lived in the same hut as Simon's mother and sister, came running, grabbed his hand and took him away. Next day Ikey One asked Simon if he would teach Shitimura after what he did and Simon said, Today we'll learn Voice. It comes in two forms, Active and Passive. Ikey Two said, you shouldn't, and the two Ikeys said they'd interfere with the lesson. Simon said, When we empower others, we enslave ourselves – both parts of the sentence are in the active voice. We can change them to passive in this way: When others are empowered by us, we are enslaved. You will notice that though both active and passive forms have the same meaning, the active voice shows the subject taking the action.

Kayloo said, That's not what happened, the others started arguing about what they'd do in his place and Simon got uneasy so I chased them off and when I got back he was on the bank behind the hut, his head on his knees, his body quaking. Shimura had turned his back on him when he went to his office that morning. Ressons hereby terminated.

Auntie Sally said if I promised not to tell him I knew,

she'd tell me the true story. Jacob Sefardi wasn't well and being separated from his wife she couldn't look after him. So the Hut Secretary gave him his job to work less in the sun. He was writing his Hut Report when Shitimura, the worst kind of excuse-me, walked in. When Jacob heard him it was too late to bow. Shitimura kicked and beat him leaving him unconscious until the men found him with two ribs broken. I didn't have to keep my promise. The whole camp knew.

23

Nips have a pecking order, Solly said as we were preparing a treasure hunt which he called:

3rd Grand Treasure Hunt for Young Enemies of the Rising Sun in Residence at Sime Road Internment Camp.

Interned with the first batch of Jews in April 1943 he knew how to get on with our guards. He'd bow three times and ask, *Ogenki desuka*, how are you? in their rough kind of voice, they'd say, *Ogenki desuka*, and he'd go on, *Watashi wa genki desu, arigato*, I'm fine thanks. Once or twice I'd see him with his arm around a soldier, walking and chatting in Japanese, while they were on duty. What's more, he was the only person who dared to say, *Chotto matte kudasai*, just a moment please, when a Nip called him, and, believe it or not, they waited. He got on so well with everyone the Nips appointed him Welfare Officer, or so he claimed, and allowed him to move freely around the whole camp with the smile he always had as if all this was a crazy dream he'd wake up from and find it never happened.

When you've survived the Double Tenth, he said to me as we were stripping ribs from coconut leaves to make brooms, you quickly learn to kowtow and know how far you can go.

That was October 10th 1943, the day all prisoners in Changi Jail were brought into the main yard and fifty, including two women, went to Kempeitai headquarters. The rest stayed in the sun without food or water all day while the prison was searched for hidden radios. Even torturing the fifty, many of whom died, they found none. So they stopped all food and Red Cross parcels. What nobody knew then was that commandos had sunk seven ships in Singapore harbour and the Nips thought prisoners were sending messages.

It was like Yom Kippur every day for months, Solly said, without the prayers and the good things to eat afterwards. What would I give for a cheese *sumbusuk* right now, he said and I said, date *babas* like my ma made and agar agar with coconut on top and he and I carried on driving each other crazy, until he said, Enough or we'll both go mad, and I said, Just one more, please, rose syrup with **KLIM** milk and *biji selasi* with ice from the coffee shop to put in it.

When they decided we had no radios, Solly said, life went back from deadly to bloody awful. But as the saying goes, he said with a wink, there's no smoke without a fire. By the middle of last year there were rumours. Our Nips, nothing like the fellows we had in the early days when they thought they ruled the world, became friendlier and life in camp no worse than outside.

I liked him a lot and I think he liked me too. Anytime I wasn't growing vegetables I'd follow him around which means I got to see much of the camp and other prisoners and also my father and brothers, taking news back and forth between them and my ma. But he never took me into the POW camp.

He didn't have children and while he was locked up his wife Nellie went round collecting food to send to prisoners for the festivals. My ma gave her baskets of vegetables and, taking my father's word for it that God created the world for people not chickens, totally, I didn't complain when she got a chicken or two. She was a tallish woman with a thick long plait down her back, loaded with smiles and happiest with children around her.

When survivors started returning from the Burma Railway, Changi Jail got crowded, civilian prisoners were sent to Sime Road which is when we were rounded up. So Nellie and Solly started Scouting groups, teaching us first aid, how to tie knots and make fires without matches. We collected cane and bamboo, coconut fronds and tall *lallang*, to weave mats, make baskets and rope. Once a month we displayed our work, had a treasure hunt – two ripe coconuts – and ended with a sing-along.

What's a pecking order, Uncle Solly?

Did you never see your chickens pecking each other?

Sure, I said and told him how cocks would lower a wing and jump on the backs of hens and bite their necks and my ma said that was the way they got strong.

If that's what you were told, he said, I'll say no more. A pecking order is the class system of chickens. Senior chickens peck junior chickens to say we're in charge and don't you forget it. Juniors don't mind. They know one day the seniors will get their throats slit and they'll do the pecking. The British used to peck us, now the Nips, short, on the yellow side and without cut-glass accents, peck them and us.

He made me laugh a lot and when he used those words my ma said I wasn't supposed to, he'd raise his eyebrows as if to say, hurry up and learn them. And his stories weren't like my father's with a lesson for life. Nor did he ask questions to test me or count each point or ask which number he was on. He was a kind of Mr Pillai with lower class words.

Nips train soldiers brutally to make them cold-blooded, he said. Soon after surrender, Yamashita beheaded two of his soldiers caught looting. Remember, he said looking into my eyes, this is between us.

I swear, Uncle Solly.

Senior officers slap junior officers, junior officers rupture sergeants' arses, sergeants kick corporals in their privates, so what do privates do? God help you if you happen to pass one with swollen goolies. Privates are worse than shit. And that only goes for Nips. Koreans and Formosans don't even rise to the rank of shit. They may all look alike but these fellows have darker skin from standing longer in the sun. Now, let's get on with what we're doing.

Uncle Solly helped me get over not having my father with me every day. Come to think of it, except that we lived in crowded huts, were always hungry, often sick and guarded by armed men who might get drunk and run amok, this wasn't a bad time for the hundreds of European, Eurasian and Jewish kids. I'd never seen white children in Princep Street and now I was playing with them. They'd been in camp longer, were thinner and not so high and mighty seeing as how we were all coolie class.

We bathed without soap and brushed our teeth with a finger sometimes dipped in ash. An egg cost $5 and if you could afford one, you hid and ate it slowly, licked the plate clean and powdered the shell to sprinkle on your *congee*. I never got to eat one and my ma never mentioned the four I destroyed but anytime I saw an egg $20 jumped into my head. Some days we got a little rice boiled with the *kutus* which I put around the edge of my tin plate. My record was 27 weevils until Solly said to think of them as tiny chickens which was okay so long as I didn't feel them on my tongue.

The black market smuggled in palm sugar and oil from nearby *kampongs* and cans from anywhere in exchange for jewellery and Straits dollars, banana money being worthless by then. As we had neither, Jonah trained us to pick up anything that looked useful short of stealing. That too, maybe. Rusty nails, pieces of wire, string, anything that could be traded for food until our eyes never left the ground.

Medicines were impossible. Our doctors concocted cures

from rubber seeds, weeds and bark and made a thin brown tonic from rust, palm sugar and water. It was always a good day when Nips got sick. They trusted our doctors more than theirs, operations too, and our so-called dispensary got the over-ordered supplies.

The lavatory was a deep hole with a plank across and you weren't always alone. By the time I got used to sharing, it didn't matter because I was doing well if I went twice a week. Everyday my ma asked, I shook my head and she said, I have to do something. When Judith started saying she too hadn't my ma asked Uncle Solly if he could get his hands on a little castor oil. Don't worry, he said. Having constipation is better than having diarrhoea which is better than having dysentery, and having any of them means you're still alive. So be thankful and look on the brighter side of life.

Why can't you be serious, Solly?

I am, he said and showed her his hat which had more holes than straw. Every month I poke a new hole to cool my head not to get brain disease. If only bodies were straw hats.

A couple of people might die each week but it didn't seem to bother me. Okay, I didn't know them but when I went with the crowd to the cemetery I never once saw anyone cry. I asked Solly if he could tell me why God wasn't doing something about it. I believe in God, he said, because it's easier than not to. Most of all it's easiest when the sun goes down and I'm alone in the dark. Now don't go telling your father. So I asked Simon and he said, we forgive god his trespasses calling them our trials, which I also didn't mention to my father. He liked Simon. Learn what you can from him, he said, so long as you keep some of your mind for yourself, understand what I'm saying?

I did understand and it began in camp, the kind of place you would feel naked and afraid even when you had clothes on and there were enough good people to make you bold.

Eleven wasn't too young to ask myself what he meant by keeping some of my mind for myself so I wondered if it included not believing everything he said only because he was my father and was that also a lesson for life?

24

There were new rumours – by mid-May Germany had surrendered, by the end of the month America was at Japan's throat, by early June British POWs, marching to work in Singapore Harbour, saw a German submarine at the wharf. The captain told his men to fall in and salute the POWs which made the Nips mad but told us the first rumour was true. Then we heard that commandos were sinking Japanese ships in the harbour, Chinese guerrillas were killing them in Malaya and MacArthur had returned to the Philippines.

When nothing changed we thought it was propaganda, hopes of liberation to keep us going while our miserable diet and open latrines added beriberi and pellagra to diarrhoea, dysentery and the constant fear of malaria.

My father went down with jaundice. Jonah had sores and Joshua was losing his hair. If my ma hadn't made Judith and me wash our hands and face every ten minutes and wear our only pair of shoes all day even though they were cramping our toes, we would've caught all the diseases looking for bodies. Apart from two beestings and legs cut by razor-sharp *lallang*, I was fine. Ikey One wasn't so lucky. Unable to hold it he went into the *lallang* and got circumcised a second time. Uncle Solly and I put up signs wherever we saw *lallang*:

> KEEP YOUR FEET OFF THE GRASS
> AND HANDS OFF YOUR FLIES

Then guards were getting edgy and Shimura made more inspections, demanded more work and used his whip more freely even on his men.

In mid-June the camp commandant Onoda announced that Jewish internees, women and children included, would get bigger rice rations if they worked on a tunnel. I joined in for the extra rice. Jonah's sores were worse and Joshua looked like a balding old man. The three of us formed a ring around my father whose body was yellow and eyes bloodshot, to make it look as if he too was digging and with guards among us we spoke Arabic.

It's their escape route to Japan, Solly said.

Another joke about tunnels, my father said.

This is no time to joke, Howee said putting down his *changkol*. Since when in my life did I do this kind of work? My back's broken in three places. Be serious.

Keep working, Howee, Solly said slantwise.

So what will they do? Cut my rice ration back to what it was? Two spoons less? If they're losing the war, they need my goodwill.

It's not over yet, Gahtan said, his walking stick now a wheelbarrow. They won't surrender like the British, a hundred and thirty thousand pairs of arms in the air. They'll fight street by street until not a Nip remains alive.

So why the tunnel? Howee dropped his clay into Gahtan's barrow.

Don't spread it around, Solly said. It's for us when the time comes.

Which time when it comes? That was Howee.

First Allied assault and they'll pack us in as hostages, Solly said.

I said it before and I'll say it again. Gahtan picked up his barrow and moved off. Nips don't surrender. They fight to the last man, them or us.

So? Howee raised his *changkol*, crashed it into the clay, pushed forward and levered. They'll bargain with our lives and what if the British don't agree?

Use your imagination.

We finished the tunnel, built gates at the entrance and returned to the vegetable plot in the first week of August. I was no longer ten but nobody cared and my ma said my father had enough on his hands so I didn't argue. Apart from rice rations reduced to what they were our lives didn't change. We saw no planes and there were no reports of invasion. Rumours of liberation were dying and with them our hopes. Food was very short, more people were in hospital and there was fear of diphtheria and typhus.

Then the Nips eased a little, worked us less, gave us more time with families but no extra rations. I saw my father more. He wasn't a big man, now he was small and shrunken. He hardly spoke and when he did, it wasn't much above a whisper. I couldn't imagine what I'd do if he died. Would I treat it as just another death, go to the cemetery and not shed a tear? That wasn't a good thought.

Pa, I said taking his hand, you haven't told me a story since we came to camp.

Which story do you want?

Why you had to leave Bir Haroon to save your life.

Now I wonder, he said. Did I do the right thing? Did I save my life only to bring my family to a place like this? How will I save your lives?

It'll be okay, Pa. People are saying it won't be long.

People say more then they know. What were they saying when it started? Did one not say the opposite of the other? Even newspapers told us lies. Let that be a lesson for you. In the end you have only yourself and God whose name is blessed.

This wasn't the time to tell him I wasn't so sure about God anymore.

Though we'd never seen the POWs we knew they were in huts beyond the hill. With more rumours about the war coming to an end we guessed they had radios and when I saw Solly smiling more than usual each time he returned from them, I asked.

Show me your fingernails, he said. A little chewed but if I were you I'd keep them.

Monday, 19th August 1945 started like an ordinary day. After breakfast of a bowl of hot water and congee to which my ma added, for my sister and me, a pinch of salt and the last grains of sugar she turned out from the corners of the packet, we went to work in the vegetable plot. It was hot and even at the start of the day I was tired.

When Solly came by he wasn't smiling. A Korean soldier, he said, told me yesterday, *Ooki sugiru, ooki sugiru.* Too big, too big, bomb too big. Now Onoda's assembling the POWs for a special announcement. I need to find out. If anyone asks say I'm in the shithouse.

He wasn't gone a minute when an outburst of hooting and whistling and laughing and cheering from the direction of the POW camp was so loud we heard it half a mile away. We threw our *changkols* and ran to the orchard and when the guards didn't stop us we knew it was true. I grabbed my sister and ran looking for my father and brothers and we went wild, hugging and jumping, yelling and screaming when, for the first time, I saw the POWs from the camp over the hill. They'd cut the wire and were coming through like ghosts, a few in uniform, most in rags, many in loincloths, some hobbling with homemade crutches, all smiling like skulls on bodies that might break. Then, suddenly, they burst out, skeletons hopping and skipping in bright sunshine, teasing the Nips for cigarettes.

The war had ended four days earlier. The POWs had two radios – one in the leg of a bed the other in a broom handle – which they listened to with stethoscopes. The Emperor told his people that the war situation had developed not necessarily to Japan's advantage. Moreover, the enemy had begun to employ a new and most cruel bomb, the power of which to do damage was, indeed, incalculable, taking the toll of many innocent lives. Should we continue to fight, he said, not only will it result in an ultimate collapse and obliteration of the Japanese nation, but also it will lead to the total extinction of human civilization.

Fine words, my father said. He doesn't think to say who started it at half-past four in the morning. Two bombs? Someone should remind him how many he dropped on us.

Damn them, Howee said. They took four days to tell us, four more days to eat congee.

Has anyone seen our liberators? I still see Japs with guns, Gahtan said. Is it a hoax?

We were not liberated, Solly said. The Japs surrendered. There is a difference.

The Japs – we were calling them Japs again – stayed in control three more weeks but we never saw Shimura again. It was rumoured he'd committed hari kiri. Onoda gave us extra rice and left us to run the camp. We found a store filled with Red Cross supplies and a few medicines the Japs hadn't taken. Even so what there was, was marvellous.

My ma begged the camp doctors to treat Jonah's sores. All they could do was paint his hands and face with mercurochrome. We called him Geronimo, the only Red Indian name we knew. The sores subsided but the doctors couldn't help Joshua. One said, Don't worry, madam. My ma who'd never been called madam in her life looked up to see if he was talking to someone else. It's not as bad as it looks, he said. Medicines are on their way. Meantime we'll shave his head.

No way, Joshua shouted.

But laddie, that may encourage the other follicles to wake up and sprout.

He didn't know what follicles were but that they'd wake up and sprout excited him.

A few days later a couple of planes dropped food, medicines and leaflets telling us to stay in camp. Until the British returned the Japs had been ordered to assist us.

Now remember, my ma said, your stomach's forgotten about proper food. Take it slow and don't be greedy. That wasn't easy. My brothers challenged each other to see who could finish a can of condensed milk first. Judith and I spread butter on each other's tongues, shovelled on jam and swallowed and I still remember what a tin of Kraft cheese did to me.

My father did well. It's not the food, he said, it's being free. A sick dog running in the street is always happier than a healthy dog in a cage.

On Wednesday 5th September those with homes to go to were free to leave. I went with my father to see Solly who'd set up as Transportation Officer in Shimura's office. He wore khaki shorts, bush jacket, US sergeant's hat and rubber slippers. He blew on his glasses, wiped them, put a stem on one ear, pulled a rubber band over the other and went to his wall with pictures of US Army trucks. Which of these beauties would you like?

We are seven, my father said, all thin, and seven mattresses. You choose.

Solly went to the window, his fingers in his mouth, whistled and the only vehicle he had, a battered Japanese truck missing mudguards, rolled up. Just a second, he said taking me by the shoulder. Do you remember the question I asked you in my shop three and a half years ago?

What was the day Singapore surrendered and I said 15th February 1942.

Right, he said. I didn't know it then but I know it now. Remember it. Remember also that we didn't see British soldiers coming over the hill to set us free. Remember and tell your children that the15th day of February 1942 was the day the sun set on the British Empire. It's going to rain, he said to my father. Take this tarpaulin and *Allah wi'akum*.

25

So gratified am I to see the Messiah family safely home. Mr Pillai came out to the 5-foot way to greet us in his out-of-work striped *lunghi* and white *kurta*. The rain had stopped, the sun was out and steam rose off the damp streets. A little worse for wear, he said, but intact nonetheless. I regret some in our street have not been so fortunate but refrain from taking a count. To do so may weaken resolve and there is much to do to reverse what undeserved animosity has brought upon us. A bold spirit in a loyal breast always triumphs and that we must do, triumph, would you not agree Mr Messiah?

Thank God, my father said taking both Mr Pillai's hands, though which part of his welcome he was thanking God for is uncertain. You also I must thank for guarding our house. Many are still in camp with nowhere to go because others have taken their houses. God, whose name is blessed, knows what you have done for us. He will bless you and your family with happiness and good health and long life, Amen.

Amen, my ma echoed as she slid down off the truck.

I have made a list of all we have taken from your garden and traded from among your chickens. Alas, I am in no position to reimburse you at this time. You can see all around, the value of the Japan's promise which, foolishly, I trusted. He pointed up and down the street and in the drain. All my sons and I have earned and saved is worthless.

Waahh. Jonah stopped offloading mattresses. Come on, he said stuffing his pockets, filling Judith's pouch skirt and wedging Japanese notes under her arms when Joshua saw someone heaping a pile of notes on the 5-foot way to set alight. No, he shouted and ran.

Stop, my ma said. How many times have I told you? No rubbish from the street.

It's not rubbish, it's money, Jonah and Judith said in turn as Joshua returned hugging hundreds of notes. New, he said. Brand new money.

Come to our house, Mr Pillai said to him, whenever you wish and take ours, crisp as the day they came off the press. You will help me close a sorry chapter in our lives. I have been summoned to my old job, he said to my father, and look forward to my first salary in good Straits currency with the head of King George VI, not a branch of bananas.

Ogenki desuka? I asked him how he was.

Watashi wa genki desu, arigato. Atanawa? He was fine, he said, how was I?

Watashi wa genki desu, arigato, I said. *Saikin dou desuka?* What's new?

Kawari nai desu, he said. Nothing much.

Mata atode aimashon, I said. See you later.

Sayonara, he said, put his hands on my shoulders and laughed out loud. I wish you well, he said to all of us and returned to his house.

At the doorpost my father touched the *mezuzah*, kissed his fingers, *mezuzah* again, touched his eyelids, kissed again and made each of us do the same. He entered the house, my ma behind then me. The others went with Mr Pillai and Auntie Sally went to see the Lims. In the dining room, my ma laid her palms on the table, closed her eyes and swayed.

What's wrong, Ma?

All the way in the lorry, she said, I was asking myself what kind of home will we come back to. Did they ransack again? Did they give the house to others? I'm thanking God for bringing us home alive and giving us neighbours who not only protected our house but kept it spotless. Come Adam. Let's see what we find in the garden. Now we're eating again it's lunchtime. She went to the kitchen. Children, Yehuda, Sally, come. Thank God, thank God, thank God. I have food to give you.

There were two small loaves of bread under a food cover, a jar of coconut jam, tea leaves, coffee powder, sugar, salt, a slightly rusty can of condensed milk, bowl of eggs and half a bottle of cooking oil on the kitchen table.

I climbed the ladder and called to Mr Pillai.

Young Adam, he said smiling at me. Our late oppressors may still be in our streets, but their authority has been countervailed. We have no need for ladders.

After more than two years with Simon, Mr Pillai's big words didn't bother me. I didn't know what *countervailed* meant but could guess. My ma wants to thank you, I said.

You are a good man, my ma said taking my place on the ladder. God will bless you with good son-in-laws and daughter-in-laws and grandchildren, many, please God, Amen.

God's ears must have prickled with the number of times my parents called upon him.

It is small recompense, Mrs Messiah, for what we have taken from your garden and livestock. The eggs at any rate are from your hens, bountiful producers as they are.

How did you know we'd be back today, my ma asked.

We put food out each morning and took it away in the evening. Bread is scarce but available and our Ah Pat, a very resourceful young man, knows where to get it.

Ho, a voice and one leg came over our left-side neighbour's wall. Ah Pat popped his head over the wall and gave a broad smile. Good to see you, he said. How was jail?

My brothers and sister ran in clutching wads of money, the four remaining chickens flew up squawking and my father came in. Thank God, he said to Ah Pat. How about you?

Ah Pat's smile faded. Fadder, brudder, cousin-brudder, not back. Must be died.

Allah ir hamu, my father said. God will protect you.

Hooded man also died. Ah Pat showed a new smile. How to say? He looked across at Mr Pillai who'd also come up his ladder.

I presume you mean, revenge is sweet.

So sweet, Ah Pat said. We fix him, first not to talk, then not to breathe. Okay, from now I take no vegetable, no fruits. Your chickens no like me. They see my leg and they hide. Partners, huh Mr Pillai? We make money, we live. Many tanks for you.

Unable to obtain your prior agreement, Mr Pillai said to my father, I gave Ah Pat permission to take produce and the occasional chicken to barter on the black market for those commodities it would have been difficult to be without.

Take, my parents said together. Anytime you want, my ma added.

After some months of getting by, my ma said it was fine for the war, that was the best we had, it kept us alive, thank God, we were lucky, so many had it worse, but now things must return to how they were, otherwise how would we know the difference? Make sure to leave the papayas, she said. Never kill a tree bearing fruit or someone close will die.

We reduced the vegetable garden slowly. Then the chickens, distant descendants of Abraham and Sarah and those born while I was away and didn't know by name, left us, one each Friday. The cement patch returned bit by bit, we boys doing the work, my father supervising. He hadn't fully recovered, felt feverish especially in the evenings, always tired no matter how little he did and his skin, wrinkling like noodles in the sun.

Auntie Sally stayed with us until her friend Latifa came in a blue blouse, red skirt and green hat, straight from camp without losing a minute with such good news. Solly was still there distributing clothes and food from the Red Cross and she'd helped herself to a few things for Auntie Sally, skin-and-bone size, where was she, did I know?

They threw their arms around each other then, catching her breath and wiping her tears, Latifa said the Kasbah in Waterloo Street was open again. They could have their old rooms if they wanted but don't delay or they'll be gone with the wind so I'm saying, like Scarlet O'Hara, Great balls of fire, go pack your things. Auntie Sally said, Frankly, my dear, I don't give a damn, which got them screaming with laughter.

She kissed the whole family, told me I was the only person who pissed on her, but not to worry, she still loved me more than anyone in the whole wide world except my father, mother, sister and brothers and Latifa of course so I wasn't to let it go to my head. Now give me a kiss, she said, and don't be stingy.

Next day I got on a chair to pick the ripe papayas, toppled and brought down both palms. Quick, my ma said, dig out the roots and fill the hole as if they were never there.

Markets had food, shops goods to sell and the streets were working again. On the other hand American bombs had destroyed many Japanese cities, Hiroshima and Nagasaki were dead, the country was starving and thousands of Japanese soldiers who could not be sent home were put to work clearing up the mess they'd made.

When a gang came to clear our drains Ah Pat enticed the Chinese guard into their reopened shop with coffee and cake while two brothers ran out the back with bamboo sticks and beat the hell out of the soldiers. I was watching from a window.

How you say, he called up.

Revenge is sweet.

Okay.

In January schools started. Missing four years of school meant senior boys had hairy faces. I'd passed Primary 1 and, four years counting as two, should've gone to Standard 2. But Simon's coaching in English and Arithmetic, the only subjects tested, sent me to 3A, A for better students. Our textbooks came from Britain which means we didn't have any that first year and had to copy off the board into exercise books keeping my father busy.

He took his receipt from the Monkey God of Japan to the Custodian of Enemy Property but didn't say: Your fortress fell on its face, now pay me. He was very polite even with the fifth clerk he was sent to see. What's going on, he said. Newspapers say the government is claiming from the Japs for what we lost. I lost everything including my alarm clock. Look. The soldier wrote it here. See? The Chinese clerk smiled a small smile. If you wish, he said, I will add One Alarm Clock to the government claim.

My father went off with his receipt to Solly who'd restarted his cycle business in a half a shop in Middle Road after a Chinese family moved into his place while they were in camp. Sorry, I can't help you, he said as we walked in. My tunnelling tools went with my shop.

You also got one of these, my father said.

I softened it and wiped my arse. My father stared at him without a word. That's not what you want to hear, Solly said. Okay, you went to see the Custodian of Enemy Property after I told you not to. My father nodded. They sent you to their storeroom in Havelock Road. My father nodded. If you could identify anything and were prepared to swear it was yours, you could have it. My father nodded. You didn't find any of your old stock, so you showed them the receipt and they smiled.

Five of them smiled, one after the other.

Did the war teach you nothing? Don't you remember what happened to Abe Mansoor? No. You weren't with us in Changi. Like a fool he went and asked the commandant if the Japs would give him back the textiles they took from his warehouse. He couldn't sit for a week and didn't stand for a month.

But the Japs are gone.

The British are no different, just more subtle. They walk you to the door and say: Don't worry, Mr Messiah, leave it with us. We'll get back to you.

So what does the Custodian's office do if they don't get our property back?

Sure they do. But not for us. White is back in fashion. White banks, white trading companies, white mines, white plantations. Go home Judah. Keep your mouth shut as you did in the war and be grateful your children are no longer hungry.

My father mumbled in Arabic a kind of curse but not his worst. Let's go.

Adam, Solly said, what did I tell you the day you left Sime Road?

15th February 1942 was the day the sun set on the British Empire.

That is what I said. But nobody has the balls to tell them and I plan to keep mine.

Two years later, going on 13, I got to Standard 5. Joshua, 15, had failed again and the Principal sent him home with a polite letter. He found a job as a trainee salesman in a store in Raffles Place. Jonah, 17 and shaving daily, made it to 5B, saw me in 5A, took the hint, said, No point, in a deep voice, and went to work at the Head Post Office in Fullerton Building. They left the house together, came home together and together helped my father from their salaries. Judith was in school and I brought home exam reports my father pinned up and proudly pointed out to customers.

26

Dong Yong Jeng – Chinese for Always Upstanding Dong which made him wonder what his parents were thinking when they named him – and I sat at adjacent desks from 3A to 6A after which the Reverend Dr D D Desai D D, decided Jewish boys weren't adequate material for the A class, all except Simon who could argue him to a standstill any day of the week and did so outside the chapel one Friday morning on the matter of idolatry in Judeo-Christian polytheism until the dark brown face of the D D turned bright orange. The first two Ds were Desmond and Dudley – names Simon said converts pick up from tombstones before getting baptised – the last two were Doctor of Divinity.

He sent me to 7B. I protested but got nowhere with a Vice Principal in a white robe and ended up a marked student. He said Jews didn't have to attend chapel but looked to see who was missing while his fingers played with a bulky cross lying on his belly.

I was 16 and so was Dong, a rich man's son with private tutors and top of the class, while I stayed a quarter way down. He called me Madam, I called him Ding Dong and being good friends we didn't mind which, in a way, is saying that of all the wrongs the Reverend Doctor committed against me, separating us the next three years was the wickedest.

Religious Knowledge, that's to say Gospel according to Saint Mark on Tuesdays, Acts of the Apostles, Thursdays and as the first period ended each of those days I shrank into my chair, bowels complained, pulse speeded, dreading the moment Mr Low, the Maths teacher, did a little dance at the door to get the chalk off his leather shoes and the Divine

Doctor came in looking at me as if the sight of a Jew gave him heartburn, as if I was the only unbeliever in his class, as if he had to put me on trial for my people.

Chapter 7. You. Verse 51. Let me hear you bleat.

I stood. *You stiff-necked people with uncircumcised hearts and ears! You are like your fathers: You always resist the Holy Spirit! Was there ever a prophet your fathers did not persecute? They even killed those who predicted the coming of the Righteous One.*

What does stiff-necked mean?

A neck that's stiff, sir. You can't move it.

How erudite. Stiff equals can't move. Q E D. Take note, if you please, we have here a scholar who gives me back what I give him, for which, nonetheless, I am thankful. Unlike his tribe, he doesn't withhold the usurer's portion. He looked out the window, his signal for the class to laugh, but only Francis Owen, chapel organist and class ball-carrier-in-chief, did so, just as Jwee Howe, class idiot, stuck his ruler up my back parting and hissed, *Jawdi.* I jerked, my desk screeched along the floor and the reverend's eyes rested on me. I was dead. He laid his hands on his belly and wove his fingers where his cross would sleep in chapel next morning. Who has a worthier definition?

Francis Owen raised his hand.

You may answer sitting, Desmond Dudley said. A body is standing in your behalf.

Stubborn, sir.

Simple and apt, but I am looking for a meaning closer to that intended by Saint Luke thought to have authored the Acts. Would you not also say, haughty thereby unable to accept what is plain to see?

Yes sir, Francis said standing, unable to address so divine a doctor sitting down.

Arrogance too, Francis, and love of self more than love of God?

Oh yes, sir.

A stubborn, haughty people who love themselves more than God. You may sit.

I sat.

Did I say you could sit?

I stood and Francis Owen, chapel organist, sat.

Uncircumcised hearts and ears. What do you think that means?

I don't know, sir.

I don't suppose you do. Anyone?

Francis Owen's ball-carrying organ-playing hand half rose, half lingered, half returned to his lap and the doctor sucked his teeth. Deuteronomy 10, 16: *Circumcise therefore the foreskin of your heart.* Does that not suggest removing an obstacle, a covering, to allow the Good Word to enter? Isn't that what circumcision does? What covering does it remove?

Cock, muttered Jwee Howe behind me. Say cock.

You. Stand up. What is your name?

Jwee Howe, sir.

Well then, Jwee Howe, tell the class what it covers? He didn't answer. I heard what you said and I want you to tell the class. Truth please and shame the devil.

Cock, sir.

Not even Owen who played the chapel organ with ball-carrying hands dared to laugh.

Gutter word. Penis, from the Latin root, *pendere*, to hang. Words like pendulum, appendage, suspension, similarly pay homage to Latin. Ah Latin! Without Rome and Latin would we have the Gospels? Ponder that. And English would be a wretched jabber without prefixes and suffixes. But that is not what circumcision removes or the whole race of Jews would long have disappeared. Reflect upon that too. Circumcision removes the foreskin thereby uncovering the glans. I do not presume to take Saint Luke to task, but he might better have inverted this passage: uncircumcised ears and hearts, first to hear, then to accept. Then a poor fish like you would understand more readily. Are you still standing?

We sat.

Not you.

I stood.

You are circumcised I presume, uniquely in this class. I said nothing. Well?

Yes, sir.

On the eighth day as was our Lord. This would have been an enigma of the highest order had it been for any reason other than that God his Father chose to place His only begotten Son in the most troubled part of the Roman Empire. Remember boys, it was Rome that, in time, would spread the faith. Therefore Jesus' circumcision was merely an outcome of locating His son among men, not, I repeat not, because Jesus was a Jew. Being God's son he would not have been a Jew because God isn't a Jew. Do you accept that?

Yes, sir.

Could I have said No? I'm not Simon with a tongue to match his brain and right now I didn't care whether God was a Jew or not, I just wanted to sit. I tried.

Do you find it difficult to stand?

No, sir.

Then stand until I tell you to sit. What is your name?

Adam, sir.

A weak man who couldn't obey the simplest of God's wishes and allowed a woman to manipulate his judgment. A poor fish if ever there was one. Do you have another name to attest to knowing who your father is?

Yes, sir, I said aloud to cover the tittering of that bastard Owen who wanted the whole class to know he understood the other bastard's crack.

Well?

Messiah, sir.

The reverend doctor's eyes opened as if I'd said something blasphemous.

Lord help us, he said and I prepared myself for crucifixion. I prefer the image of the weak man, he said, his tone much like the Roman soldier's when he picked up the first nail and told Jesus it wasn't going to hurt. You would be hard put to save your own soul, he said looking for the other two nails. I presume your father is also a Messiah.

Yes, sir.

Have you brothers?

Two, sir.

Four Messiahs. In one family. Remarkable.

It was my last year but one and next year the Divine Doctor would be class master teaching History and Geography over and above Religious Knowledge, three ways to make me stand from the moment he entered until he left. What's a fellow supposed to do when he knows someone's going to kill him, how and when? What could I do but boil on the trolleybus all the way home? Even as I got off I was planning what I'd do to him before I died.

I crossed Ladies Green, kicked a swing, banged an empty see-saw, marched past the crowd of hawkers and, as I stepped onto our 5-foot way fuming, my father saw me. Thank you, he said to a customer touching everything, buying nothing, come again not too soon, and to me, What happened to you, without changing tone.

Jews are a stiff-necked people, I said.

So?

What d'you mean, so?

Am kesheh-auref, he said picking up his Chumash. God

said so Himself. Wait till I find it. I put down my schoolbag and wiped my face on my sleeve. Read where my finger is.

And the Lord said to Moses, I have seen this people, and behold, it is a stiff-necked people; now therefore let me alone, that my wrath may burn hot against them and I may consume them.

God wanted to destroy his own people?

His privilege. But He didn't or where would we be? You don't understand? What were we doing that got Him so angry? Worshipping a golden calf, no? Breaking a commandment.

Moses had come down the mountain two minutes, I said. He smashed the tablets. How could they be breaking a commandment they didn't even know?

5 upon 10. 10 upon 10 if you said Jews should know better after all God did for them. What I am telling you now is the real lesson to learn. Did Moshe Rabbenu say, Okay, consume us, we deserve it? No. He faced God face to face. You've just rescued us, he said, after sending ten plagues to *buzzle*, he said, sifting his fingers for the English word.

Irritate.

Right. Don't you think you'll be a laughing stock with Pharaoh if you kill us now?

Moses said laughing stock to God?

Not exactly. But you see what I'm saying? So now God is listening, is Moshe Rabbenu going to stop? No. He rubs it in. Don't forget what you promised Abraham, Isaac and Jacob, he says. So God thinks about it and repents. *Ve-yinahem Adonai.* Hear what I'm saying? Tell me which other people can argue with God who created the universe and make Him repent? Only Jews. Now tell me why you came home with a face that wants to kill someone.

I told him what Doctor Desai said about Jesus being the son of God and the messiah sent to save the world but Jews rejected him because we are a stiff-necked people and how he made fun of our family name in front of the class and I had to stand the whole period ...

So which you want me to answer first? I shrugged. All together then. Close your ears from these people. *Wahad takhil elakh* ... his fingers sifted again.

One is worse than the other.

That's what I said. To have a son you need a wife. Who is God's wife?

Virgin Mary.

A woman has a name like Virgin?

No. She was a virgin.

Hah. You're sixteen, no? You know about these things? I nodded. I don't need to explain? I shook my head. Good. You called your teacher Doctor. He's a real doctor?

Doctor of divinity.

Which part of the body is divinity?

Not the body, Pa. Divinity is the study of God.

People make a living studying this? *Adonai ehad*. God is one. What else is there to say or more to study? What will they find out we don't know? I shrugged. In that case I understand. The doctor's head is in a place, I won't mention. So. Hebrew has two words: *alma* means young woman, nothing about what she did or didn't do with a man, know what I'm saying? *Betulah* means virgin which is to say no man has interfered with her, totally.

I see.

Sure you see. But I think your doctor doesn't know Hebrew or he's mixing what Isaiah said about the messiah being born from *alma* and he thinks she's *betulah*. Don't tomorrow go and tell him. People like him can be, what shall I say? I want you to finish school not like your brothers who couldn't find the door to Standard 6. So what was I saying, yes, God doesn't need a son. A man needs a son for when he's old. God doesn't get old and when the time comes to save the world, He doesn't need help. In the second place, gods or their sons don't come out from a woman. More I won't say except to say people say things and give Jews a bad name, so what am I saying?

I think you've said enough.

No. What I'm saying is, as a Jew you have a special place and if you have to suffer, don't complain. Maybe it's all part of God's plan and we'll never know what the plan is until the world comes to an end. Now go outside. He pointed his fly-swatter at the drain beside the 5-foot way. Turn round seven times and spit each time, then come back here.

As I was doing my seventh turn and seventh spit, my ma walked through the shop asking if there was a piece of breeze she could stand in front of. The air at the back was as thick as last week's macaroni soup and what's wrong with you, why are you spitting?

Pa told me.

She looked at my father.

No need to talk about it, he said.

I teach the children not to spit in the street and there's no need to talk about it?

I'm teaching him what my father taught me and when the time comes, he will teach his sons, please God. That's the way to learn and to teach.

Did your father give you a reason?

To get rid of bad influences. Seven times and bad influences are gone, totally.

Your father didn't say spitting spreads disease? There are posters everywhere because people are dying of TB like flies and they cannot stop it because of people like you. My ma shook her hand at him. Maybe they didn't have TB in Basra?

TB yes, posters no. Turning and spitting gets rid of bad influences which ruin your life and that's final. Come, he said, put his hand on my head and mumbled, *Baruch Atah*

Adonai … may God bless you as He blessed Abraham and Isaac and Jacob who carried forth the life of our people. Now maybe your mother, who knows all about what spreads disease from posters but nothing about how to get rid of bad influences, will give you her special salt-and-sugar medicine which is supposed to do what she won't say. Then I need to tell you about my life for you to know and understand what it means to be a Jew living with other people in the way a father teaches his son and a son learns from his father.

This seems a good time to stitch in another school story which played a part in later life though I didn't know then. Thomas Evans was a big fellow, square head, blond hair, blue eyes, sergeant-major moustache, a voice like two trombones and nothing like the Divine Doctor. He survived the Burma Railway to teach English to boys who couldn't stop their conjugations interfering with their declensions. We called him Tommy KaTongkat because of the limp he got from a dose of beriberi in the jungle.

Everyone should have a passion for the stuff of the spirit, he said and when he recited,

> *Half a league, half a league, half a league onward*
> *Into the valley of death rode the six hundred,*

in his grand imperial voice it was plain to see why Britain ruled the world. When he picked me to read, it was with a smile not a sneer like D D and it wasn't until halfway through my final year that I discovered why. Time to time, when God smote the Divine Doctor in the throat with laryngitis or the other end with diarrhoea, Tommy took Friday chapel, getting students to play Pharisees while he, Jesus, argued with them. Once, after chapel, he called me aside, stood me in the sun and walked around examining my face from all angles.

I don't think the Great Masters ever used a Jew to model Christ, he said. Hence the mawkish look in his eyes. Except Rembrandt, of course, who lived among the Sephardic Jews of Amsterdam. He ran his finger down my profile. I think he'd have looked more like you. Coils of black hair, longer, stalwart nose, shrewd hook, dark searching eyes. I think Jesus smiled a lot and had a sense of humour, don't you?

Yes Sir. Stands to reason, Sir.

Which reason in particular?

The one you gave, sir, he lived among Sephardi Jews. In Amsterdam. In Holland. I knew where Amsterdam was and wanted him to know I knew.

Hhhmm. It was a long hhhmmmmmmmm. I don't think you have the faintest idea.

Yes sir, I mean no, I don't know what you mean, sir.

But you should. I think your people would have needed a sense of humour to have lasted thus far. What do you think kept me alive, eh? Malnutrition and malaria weren't our biggest killers. Nor our captors' contempt for us. It was despair. We had a Joke-telling Club. We gave them numbers, told them one to a hundred then retold them backwards and laughed even after they ceased to be funny. Do you understand?

Yes Sir. A Joke-telling Club was a good idea. What could I say? My classmates were at their desks and here was I sweating in the sun while the whitest teacher in school was telling me, a *mahallah* boy, how he cheated death in the jungle. I felt like the poor fish the D D said I was, standing at semi-attention in short pants, ants crawling up my legs while a teacher, semi-priest and amateur painter rolled into one was deciding if I looked like Jesus.

I fidgeted, killed ants going up my legs with my shoes but

that didn't stop him. He did another walk around. You're a little old, he said. Thank God. How would I tell my father I was a model for Jesus? Twelve. Jesus Contending with the Elders in Jerusalem. But then you would have been in an Internment Camp and I was a slave building a jungle railway. A year before your Bar mitzvah. Jesus didn't have one. You know that of course. Like hell I did. That didn't come for many centuries. How many would you say since your obligations were formalised in a ceremony? Five, ten?

Maybe sir, yes, five or ten.

Yet we believe that Jesus practised as Jews do today. We never quite understand each other, do we? Well it was a thought, idle, but apt with a name like yours. Now hurry along Messiah or you'll be late for class.

27

After a glass of my ma's salt-and-sugar medicine, my father told me to sit, it was a long story, he wanted to tell it start to finish, to know it wasn't just a story but one to help me in life when he wasn't there to guide me. I said he shouldn't think that, he'd have a long life, to which he said, please God but all the same coming home as I did with anger in my eyes reminded him of how he lived in Al Basrah among people with camel shit in their heads and if he wasn't careful, before he knew it, would he also think like them? Then where would he be if he didn't know *aleph* from *bet*, if I knew what he was saying?

I was born in a place with two streets, he said. Thirty, forty houses, dried mud in rows. If everyone, men, women, children came to the market, we were three, four hundred, totally. Goats more than people. Jews called it Beir Aaron because Aaron dug the well and found water where they lived since before Arabs became Muslims. To change from one to the other they made our stories their stories because we have the same father, Abraham. What I'm saying is, Haroon is how Arabs call Aaron, brother of Moshe Rabbenu who they call Nabi Musa but changing Aaron to Haroon and Moshe to Musa doesn't mean they belong to them. Like when you marry, your wife changes her name to your name and you think she belongs to you until one day she tells you. Or like the Japanese did to us.

Syonan-to?

Right. As if changing the name made Singapore theirs forever. Not even four years and thousands died just to change a name. One hour with a fresh donkey, Bir Haroon to Al Basrah, that's to say in Mesopotamia where Turks were in the days I was there.

What year, Pa? I thought I'd try again.

Did we have calendars? We saw something: lambs born dead, she-goats dried up or the Basha threw out one wife to take another because these people can have only four at one and the same time and he needed a new flavour. I was born the year the well dried and people started to see things at the bottom not from this world. Women fetching water fainted and pregnant ones wouldn't go near. The whole village fasted three days and nights and the well filled again with sweet water. On that day I was born.

It was hot in my corner so I undid my shirt buttons and took off my shoes.

As I was saying, we lived in a house, bricks of dried mud like we made in Egypt when we were slaves. Eight, ten houses in a row to stop each other falling down, always looking out for Turkish police with long sticks whose job was to push Jews to the dark side of the street so our shadows didn't fall on Muslims. We were *dhimmi*, I explained to you, no?

Non-Muslims, I said. Jews and Christians.

No Christians in Bir Haroon. God help you if you didn't pass them on the left-hand side which is to say the side of the devil. Ottomans and Arabs. Both not famous for loving Jews. Opposite the same, eight, ten houses, a street between, understand?

You said thirty, forty houses and two streets.

Hah. Right. One street between, he divided the shop to show two sides of the street. One, like Princep Street, coming to the village going to the next. Houses? Yes. Here and there. Hah, when it rained Jews weren't allowed in the two streets because rain from our bodies would dirty the feet of the Muslims as if they were not also in mud. I'm first of six, three boys, three girls, exactly. Auntie Sally you know, others who knows? My father makes cheese. When I'm not milking sheep and goats or helping to make the best cheese not only in Al Basrah but all Mesopotamia, north south, east west, I'm studying Torah, ten, twelve boys in a poky *heder*, no window, the *melamed* teaching us to read and sing the same thing by heart. Or I'm in the street, Jews and Arabs, friendly those days, you understand, not totally, but enough to play and talk and visit when we didn't see Turks. Sometimes all together at a wedding. That's all. As I said, Abraham had two sons, Ishak and Ishmael, half-brothers. Jews from Ishak, Arabs from Ishmael so we can be friendly. Up to a point.

In another house lives Zahidah, Arab girl, eyes like a ewe's, hair long and straight as a horse's tail. She's number one five-stone champion. With small hands she catches stones any order, eyes closed, one hand behind her back. So good, people take bets. Do I win? Even once? One day she challenges me, alone, behind my house. We're playing, she's winning and suddenly her eyes open. I turn. Who do I see as I'm holding her hands begging her to teach me? Abu Sayeed the barber. His face black as the devil's arse.

It was okay, I was a man and such words were allowed.

The barber starts yelling. Not me, I tell him. We played tricks, me and other boys, hiding his scissors to make him mad and now he's accusing me. Stones still in her hands, he grabs Zahidah. If I catch you with her again, he shouts, *W'Allah*, I'll kill you. Am I afraid of him? He's an Arab, not a Turk. So I say, I didn't take your scissors, I swear, don't get so mad. A blow from him sends the left side of my face to the right side and he drags her to his house. Did I know? He's fifty-plus and he made her his wife two days ago. Six years old. He could be her grandfather. Are these people? Even animals wait for the season and the smell. Am I going to risk my life with the likes of him?

My father paused, brought his hands together in his lap and looked at me.

Did God make me a fool? Am I going to play with his new wife? But where's his shop? In the street facing our door. Chair with one lame leg, piece of mirror, scissors and razors in a box, cross-leg table, prayer mat rolled on one side. Can I avoid him? Don't I know he's watching me? But I know he prays five times a day. Soon as he opens his mat, goes on his knees, head down, arse up, I run from my house like a fart from a horse.

My father swiped all around with his swatter without a fly in sight, laid it down and flipped it over as if turning the page to start the next chapter.

Zahidah? Nowhere. Sometimes I spy her looking between his railings at the back with a face that wants to come and play. Once or twice she's in the veranda teaching Abu Sayeed to play five-stones, his other three wives watching. Can you imagine? Morning he plays five-stones with a girl of six, night-time ... better not to think. On the other hand, maybe God should have changed Number 5: *Honour your father and your mother that your days may be long*, could also say: *and honour your children*. Moshe Rabbenu should have mentioned it when he went up to fetch the new tablets.

Didn't you tell your father?

Not him, not my mother, not nobody. Did I want trouble? But when trouble wants you, it knows where you're hiding. In our street, opposite side, also lived Khalid, Mohammad ibn Khalid, the *habaz*, with an oven in the floor of his house to bake *roti shtambul* for Turkish soldiers. My father's good friend. Nice man. Always with sweets or dates for us. Don't I remember? He used to say, Take if you find. We searched his *gelabieh*. Nothing. Off comes his turban and they are sitting on his head. Next time we search his turban they're in his pocket. His smile could brighten the sun.

This wasn't another of his Arabian Nights stories about *dhimmis* and *djinnis*, *bashas* and beggars, peddlers and thieves, sages and fools. I knew Abu Sayeed, Barber of Basrah, but not Zahidah, his six-year-old wife. My father was getting edgy and shifted in his chair.

Okay, he said after a while, Khalid and my father, your grandfather, in the market, side by side, one sells bread the other cheese. Arab and Jew like brothers. Khalid comes to our house, passes the barber shop just as Abu Sayeed is bowing down to pray. This is my chance to run out but as he bends, Abu Sayeed lets out a fart you could hear from seven streets and we had only two. Would I say a word as I'm running? But trouble finds me and a *djinni* shouts from my mouth, Abu Sayeed, you farted in Mohammad's face. He jumps, comes for me, scissors in his hand. Do I stand there waiting for him? Into the house, bolt the door, piss running down my legs. From the back, I hear him yelling. Allah hasn't made the hole for you to hide. My father stops making cheese, my mother screams, brothers and sisters go under the bed and before your grandfather can ask what's going on, the scissors enter his arm.

He was talking with difficulty, had a lump in his throat, asked me for a glass of water, took his Good Morning towel from the hook by his chair and wiped the sweat running down his face and arms. The story was no longer start to finish. He repeated himself, stopped to remember his life at home – father slogging day and night to feed his family, mother slaving to bring them up clean and healthy and, as if there wasn't enough to do to stay alive, there was the constant worry a Jew would offend a Turk and the whole community made to pay for it. A good day was when you came home without being insulted twice. Then he'd ask me where he was and take up the story again.

Mohammad the baker took Abu Sayeed the barber by his hands looked into his eyes and told him he should finish his prayers. It wasn't right to stop halfway. Jewish boys weren't worth spitting on. He'd make sure the boy's father gave him a thrashing until no part of his body wasn't bleeding. He swore on his mother's grave that from that day no Jew would interfere with the barber, his shop or his four wives. He was blessed to have one like Zahidah, young enough to look after him in the years to come. Arm in arm they walked out of my grandfather's house and crossed the road. Meanwhile Aleeza, the midwife from next door, pulled out the scissors and told my grandfather that if he didn't want to find his son in the street with scissors in his throat he should lose no time and send him away.

It was time for another drink so I got one before he asked for it.

Where was I?

You had to leave home.

Hah. Right. Your grandfather said to me, Sit and keep your mouth shut. Nobody needs a son who doesn't know not to interfere with people praying. Respect, understand? Even if a man is praying to a piece of donkey shit, leave him till he finishes. It's his donkey and his god. Didn't we do the same until God had a word with Abraham? Idols, not donkey shit but what's the difference? That's how my father taught me and I am teaching you, understand what I'm saying?

He put down his fly-swatter to stop his hands shaking.

By now Khalid is sitting with us on the floor. It's time to talk, he says. My brothers and sisters come out from under the bed and I tell the whole story. Mohammad saves me. I am not to blame. Abu Sayeed is crazy. He already killed two people in blood revenge.

He killed two people, I said, and he's not in jail?

Did we have laws? *Baksheesh* was the law. Whatever the *qadi* said was the law. If two Muslims fought in court and one had to pay a fine, he could make a Jew pay for him. We were *dhimmi*. Everything we had was theirs even our women if they wanted. So now Aleeza's making a sling for your grandfather's arm. Hah, she says, her brother Nissim, years back, went to India. There he found a wife, took her and her dowry and went to live in another place. Where, she wasn't sure, but there was a letter in her house.

Two weeks later my grandmother dressed my father in a blue gelabieh, money sewn into the hem, put a red tarbush on his head, gave him bread and *zahtah*, cheese, halawa, quince jam and two bottles of olive oil in bags tied at his waist or slung from his shoulders, and a basket of dried dates, figs and apricots. With tears and prayers my grandparents sent their son as a deck passenger on SS *Zanzibar* to Aleeza's brother who lived in a place whose name was written on a letter in her house next door.

After a month without bathing, food and money gone, he got off the ship, a bumboat took him to Telok Ayer Basin where he saw bullock carts and rickshaws, Chinese coolies, Indian stevedores, Malay hawkers and white men in linen suits and topees but no Nissim. Terrified and in tears, he clung onto anyone who'd listen, pointed at where he thought the *Zanzibar* was and begged in Arabic to get back on board and take his chances with Abu Sayeed the Barber of Basra when he heard, Yehuda, Yehuda.

How old were you, Pa?

Ten? Maybe.

I always thought you were much older. I thought you were … never mind.

That he'd left Iraq to save his life was true but not what I'd glued together from bits he'd told me over the years about Turks with razor eyes, smoking hashish and beating up Jews till he said, Enough is enough. Nothing I could've imagined would have him playing five stones with a girl of six. There was a Nissim in the *mahallah* but he'd died before I was born and I wasn't going to follow a trail that might show me a different father. Nor did I ask him why, finally, he told me the whole story, start to finish. I found out next evening.

28

I returned unusually late from school. He'd shut the shop and was at the bathroom mirror dabbing Bay Rum on his fresh face.

Hah, you're back. Good. Where are your brothers? Don't they know today is Friday?

On the way to synagogue he said he wasn't feeling good, why was he always so tired? I told him to see a doctor and he said health was in God's hands, by which time we were climbing the stairs into His house where he always felt fine so it wasn't until we turned the corner into Bras Basah Road on the way home that he said, There are things I must tell you, things a father must tell his son.

I know Pa, I said, my brothers told me.

Those things mothers tell daughters to protect them from men and fathers don't need to tell sons. I need to tell you about more important things, how to live the way God wants.

Okay, Pa, what are you saying?

I'm saying that the Bible has everything we need for life but to know what it says, the way God wants us to understand, you must feel, feel is what I'm saying, feel what the words mean? So I have to add a few things to help you. Soon you will be looking for girls. That's the way which is fine but what I'm saying is if you're not careful you mix up fun, think it's love and it turns out to be the wrong one. Each with his own kind is what I'm saying, how God made us. Do you see a dog with a cat? What will come if a horse mounts a cow? So what am I saying? I'm saying that as long as I'm alive I'll be here to give advice.

You'll live to see your grandchildren, Pa.

Please God. I know you will do the right thing and since we still have the feeling of synagogue in us, keep what I'm saying in your heart and your head will tell you what to do. Your life is your life so I'll not ask you to promise me not to do the wrong thing.

He was drying like seaweed left on the beach by the tide. At first our doctor said he was rundown and prescribed vitamins, pep pills and tonics, bottle after bottle which didn't do an ounce of good. Saying our doctor sounds like we had one. Andrew Cheow ran the VD Clinic at the corner of Short Street. My ma took us to see him only when she and her friends couldn't come up with a cure or forgot what their mothers did to bring down fever, ease stomach ache and treat illnesses we get just growing up.

He was a kind young man fresh from College, qualified in venereal diseases but not a proper doctor. He put a thermometer in our mouths and listened to our breathing free-of-charge if we entered the clinic by the back door after closing time. We got free medicines from a cabinet I wasn't allowed to touch or anywhere else especially not the bed where day-time patients left God knows what brand of germs, so keep your hands in your pockets.

Apart from salt-and-sugar water which wasn't medicine, she might give us barley boiled with rock sugar taken by the gallon to flush the fever out, so drink up and don't make a fuss. If that didn't work she took us to see Dr Andrew calling him Doctor to give him respect and herself confidence. Last of all she got my father, with kippah and shawl, to pray while we drank the medicine but he'd do it only when our bodies were burning and not bother God when we could manage by ourselves.

My father came home after his third visit and said he wasn't going again. Dr Andrew told him he needed rest.

How much more could he rest sitting in his shop all day? To rest more would tire him out. When he couldn't carry his body around, his eyes red smudges, my ma told him to stay in bed and did her best running up and down between shop, house and him, scraping dollars for tonics, keeping us in food with a family meal every Friday night when we boys helped him down so he'd feel no change in his life.

My brothers brought regular income, I was 17 in my final year and it seemed as if God was on my side. The D D had taken over the A class and Tommy KaTongkat was our form master. He wasn't the sort to have favourites but I think he liked me and didn't make me stand through his lessons. In short, my father wouldn't let me quit school and though my sister had taken it upon herself to do so, she was too young to run the shop.

After Dr Andrew shut his clinic one evening he came over to see how my father was, took one look and said, This will not do, you must go to hospital. No dice, my father said in Arabic which isn't so polite. He knew his days weren't many and chose to leave matters in God's hands. I think he just wanted to die in his own bed.

Two evenings later he visited again. Mr Messiah, he said taking my father's hands in his. I am too old to be your son, but in Chinese reckoning you're not too young to be my father so I will tell you as a son that you don't look good.

So tell me, my new son, and I'll do what you say all except live in a hospital.

I will take you to see Dr Sinnadorai. He's a specialist at the General Hospital.

He sat with my ma in the dining room and spoke in a whisper. Tests were positive.

What does that mean, Doctor Andrew?

Cancer, Mrs Messiah. The marrow in his bones has stopped producing blood cells. His body isn't functioning and it's too late. Tonight I will bring pain killers. Give him one when it becomes unbearable. Make him comfortable and let him pass away in peace.

In those days people shaped their lips to say cancer. It was shameful, as if God was destroying you for a life of wickedness. Auntie Sally came to sit with him and tell stories about how Basra was after he left and my ma made it seem like business as usual. She smartened him, propped him with pillows from around the house and put a bowl of hot water by his bed with a few drops of Eau de Cologne ready for when his friends arrived on Saturday from synagogue. They were much the same age now I'd reckoned he was in his late forties, Shooli Deborah's grey beard giving him five years more. Even so they looked ancient, as if someone had shaken the Bible and out fell a bunch of old Jews.

My father recited the prayer for wearing the shawl, Shooli draped it over his shoulders, stood back and swore he looked as rosy as an Australian apple. They went through the day's reading, slowing down for him, then Shooli and Ezra would start a discussion which went well until Silman said something and they turned on him, all except my father who smiled a half kindly, half didn't-you-learn-anything-in-thirty-years sort of smile.

My brothers and I were with them that last Saturday making seven so my ma brought three more Jews from our streets to make a *minyan*, the quorum Jews need before God will take the time to listen. I think she knew. We stood around his narrow bed, all praying until when we got to the *Shema*, Hear O Israel, the Lord is our God, the Lord is One, Silman started blubbering and Shooli and Ezra shoved him with their elbows. For sure my father heard but kept his eyes on his book until we finished.

My ma and sister brought a tray with rose syrup, the new arrivals wished my father well and left. As my ma was clearing away the empty glasses she whispered to Shooli to hurry up and do whatever they did after the service in synagogue.

It's a wonder, he said, how Noah could build such a big ark. Three hundred cubits, he said waving a finger in the air. Do you know how far that goes?

Ezra paced the floor to the back and returned. Longer than this house, he said.

For sure, Shooli said. Can you fit two of every kind of animal inside this house?

Don't forget, Silman said, the ark had three storeys. Who of us lives in such a house we can say how big is a three-storey house?

No one could imagine what he'd do with another storey but even so fitting two of every type of animal including elephants, big as American cars and seven pairs of those Jews are allowed to eat. By the way, where did Noah put the pigs?

Kavanah, my father said in a feeble voice.

I think he was telling us we'd just been praying, our thoughts should be meaningful but thinking he was about to give an account of himself to the Almighty, they stood, closed their eyes and fell silent. My father's face became a smile that seemed to say, Have I been so foolish all these years? Will I find wiser men to talk to where I'm going?

Judah, do you want us to pray to God for you, Silman said and opened his eyes.

Are you guarding the door? Do I need you to ask if I can enter? All my life I spoke direct with God whose name is blessed. What has changed?

29

Wednesdays ran into an afternoon session at school. I got home after 4, found the shop shut and entered from the back lane. Wash your hands and face, my ma said, and drink this, handing me a glass of her miracle water, not the usual greeting that came plain from the tap. I drank half and put the glass in the sink.

Where's Judith?

Gone to fetch Auntie Sally, she said, her eyes still and quiet. Please help me bring your father down the stairs.

His eyes were closed, his face calm. I can do it, I said.

I laid him on the dining room floor, where my ma had cleared a space, pointed his feet toward the door. He was small and shrunken and for all his praise, piety and devotion, God should have given him a kinder departure. As the only son present I put my hand over his eyes as if to close them then tied a handkerchief under his chin with the knot at his head. I straightened his arms by his body, opened his hands to face upward, removed his wedding ring and gave it to my ma. She put it on her middle finger beside hers, shook open a clean white sheet, laid it over his body and went round the house emptying water from basins and buckets and the half glass I hadn't drunk. I fetched a candle from the sideboard, lit it, dripped wax onto the stone floor near his head and stood it in the pool.

Adam, we mustn't lose time. Tell people and ask the men to come.

I went to Silman in Short Street. Before I'd said a word, he raised his eyes and hands to heaven asking God to forgive him for any wrong he'd done or said to my father, put his arms around me, his head on my shoulder and sobbed. I didn't tell him I was happy not to have to see my father cringe into a tight ball trying to force the pain into one spot in his body so he could bear it, that I wanted to share his pain but God made sure we couldn't.

I need help.

Not another word, he said squeezing tears from his eyes. I'll see to everything.

When I got home my ma had covered the mirrors, surrounded his body with a ridge of turmeric powder to keep off crawling insects and lit coils to chase off flies. I pulled a chair and sat beside her in silence.

Fifteen minutes later the first men arrived and in an hour the house was full. My brothers returned, saw people across the 5-foot way and in the road and burst out crying. That got my sister howling and when I went to put my arms around her and tell her to go upstairs before my ma started, my ma broke down and so did Auntie Sally.

The vigil started when my brothers, sister, Auntie Sally and I, all blood relatives, sat on the floor. My ma didn't have to but she did. She got between Jonah and me and in this way we passed the night, lost in thought or talking quietly. The men sang psalms while the women fed us and kept us awake with my father's strong black coffee.

They sang Psalm 23, his favourite, and my ma asked them to sing it again, seven times, because that was how he felt about God, whose name was blessed, and what else did a man need, totally? And when they sang the last line the seventh time,

and I will dwell in the house of the Lord for ever,

my ma sniffed, my brothers and sister wiped their eyes, Auntie Sally cried and choked and Silman, Shooli and Ezra blew their noses with whatever came from their pockets.

In the morning my father was shaved, his body washed and wrapped in a white shroud, doused with rose water and placed in a wooden bier, a simple version of the ancient Ark of the Covenant. His three sons and five of his many friends lifted it onto their shoulders, left the house and stopped on the road outside the shop.

Silman led, and as we were reciting the 49th Psalm:

> *Hear this, all you people; give ear, all you inhabitants of the world:*
> *Both low and high, rich and poor, together.*
> *My mouth shall speak of wisdom; and the meditation of my heart shall be of understanding …*

our left-side neighbours Lim Ah Pat and two of his brothers came out to the 5-foot way holding lighted joss-sticks and as we moved off

> *I will incline mine ear to a parable: I will open my mystery upon the harp.*
> *Wherefore should I fear in the days of evil, when the iniquity of my heels shall compass me about?*

our right-side neighbour Mr Pillai, on the 5-foot way with his family, said something aloud in Tamil that sounded like a prayer and all along the row, people came out of their homes and shops and lined the street as my father went on his way to Thomson Road Cemetery three miles away. His friends followed in procession and with the heat and long walk making the bier feel heavier each time we slipped under to carry it, we changed places often which was okay because everyone wanted a chance.

More men were waiting at the gates to take the bier from us down the long entrance lane then stop before the first graves where Jonah and Joshua took the front rails. I took one at the back and Solly the other. Shooli, Howee and Rafuli slipped in between us as Gahtan hooked his cane on his arm, eased himself into the remaining space saying, Please don't walk too fast.

Silman, already in the open grave, laid my father on the bare earth, Jonah went down, Silman pulled aside the shroud, Jonah sprinkled Jerusalem earth on my father's face and Silman brought the shroud together, then Joshua and I pulled them out.

The sun was scorching and we had to hurry. As Jonah dropped three spadefuls of earth Silman praised God for His compassion and asked Him to forgive my father his sins. Joshua sent in the next three then I, three more and, with all his friends there, the pit quickly filled by which time Silman was asking my father to forgive us any disrespect or harm we may have done him in his lifetime.

Then all fell silent. Jonah, Joshua and I said the Kaddish, the Aramaic mourner's hymn praising God, praying for peace from heaven and life upon us with the congregation joining in with blessings and amens. We placed pebbles on the mound and Silman pushed a peg into the ground. 11/7/51.

We washed our hands without drying them and started back home.

Only as I walked out of the cemetery beside my ma did I realise he was gone.

At home, we settled down to begin the seven days and seven nights we'd eat and sleep and live on the floor. Silman held the left side of Jonah's shirt and was about to cut it with scissors when my ma said, Not his collar, I can't mend it. Cut his pocket and I'll stitch another one. We're not millionaires.

Silman cut the top of Jonah's heart pocket and as Jonah

ripped it he said, Blessed art Thou our God, Ruler of the Universe, the True Judge.

Joshua was next and when it was my turn, I didn't need scissors. Judith had no pocket on her dress.

Where do you want me to cut?

Where it won't show when I mend it, my ma said. You have three daughters. Don't you know how much dresses cost these days? Find one with a left-hand pocket, she said as Judith left the room, the green one with the hem hanging down I've been telling you to fix but you're always too busy.

Auntie Sally's dress had two large patch pockets below the waist.

It must be near your heart, Silman said.

My heart has gone with her brother, she said.

Silman cut the left pocket and sniffed and wiped his eyes and whoever was with us in that crowded room sniffed and wept and wiped their eyes and as I sat on the floor, my head fell forward onto my folded knees and it all came out.

30

Things must change, I said the first time we were alone on the last night of mourning. I didn't know what must change or how and when no one said anything I let it go. Anyway, it wasn't right to discuss the future, seeing as how our present was living on the floor trying to come to terms with the past. I suppose I just needed to say what I hadn't out of respect all the years I sat watching my father do what he thought he knew best. The shop brought little money and even adding what my brothers shared from their salaries it only kept us going with nothing for the just-in-case that never sends greetings before showing up.

Next morning my ma and sister fixed up the house they hadn't cleaned for a week and Auntie Sally wanted to know if we were still having Friday night dinners and could she come now her brother was gone? The only difference, my ma said, was that Jonah, being head of the family, would sit in his father's seat. She was always welcome, not just Friday, did she need to ask? So she kissed my ma and said, Okee-dokee, cheerio lovely children. Whatever happens, I will love you just as I do now until I die, another of her lines from *Gone with the Wind* and turned to Tefaha who'd missed her so much she came to escort her back to the Kasbah. It's Thursday, Auntie Sally said, shopping day, don't you know and Tefaha said, Great balls of fire, I can't think about that right now. If I do, I'll go crazy, and they walked away without laughing.

The next night was our first Friday meal with Jonah at the head of the table, my ma on his right with Joshua. I sat opposite with my sister, Auntie Sally at the end. Stand everyone, Jonah said, totally. He blessed the wine and passed the silver cup along then the bread, tore it in hunks, dipped each in salt and threw it around the table as my father had, saying it was the manna God spread across the desert to feed the Israelites, totally.

We need cash, I said after my ma had doled out our dinner.

Pa said not to talk bizz-i-nezz on Shabbat, Jonah said. Totally.

Out of respect for Pa now he's gone, Joshua said.

I have a simple plan, I said.

Tell us tomorrow night when Shabbat is over, Jonah said forking a potato.

Can I speak now, Ma?

My ma looked at Jonah with the potato in his mouth and nodded.

The shop is stuffed with dead stock, I said. For the next two weeks we'll sell it at half price, what remains at quarter and so on until it's all gone then discount good stock twenty per cent. Meantime we buy nothing.

Joshua said we'd lose money, Jonah said they were Pa's things not ours, totally. I told him that was Pa's word, he wasn't Pa, please stop using it and my ma said I was right. Even if we lost money we'd have enough for rent and food, we can't eat paper and pencils.

When it's all gone, I said, we'll buy new stock on 90 days credit. Tomorrow and Sunday we'll make HALF PRICE SALE posters and stick them on the pillars outside.

Jonah said, It's a sin to make posters on Shabbat, totally, and Joshua said, What would Papa say if he knew? Judith said she used to draw on Shabbat when Papa wasn't watching, what was so wrong with that? God had more important things to do than spy on her and since her hands didn't get paralysed, God wasn't angry, was He?

She'd never said so much all at once before.

That's what she and I did Saturday and Sunday. I got her to bind three 3-cent pencils with a rubber band and mark them at 10 cents and when her smile said she understood, I told her to do the same with other small items. She put together two pencils, sharpener and rubber, added two cents and we stacked them at the front of the shop ready for reopening.

On Monday my brothers returned to work and my ma ran the shop with Judith. If I swore not to tell, she said, she'd tell me the real truth about why she left school which was only partly to give Ma a hand, poor thing. Miss Cheong her English teacher was a crab, Miss Liow her Art teacher a spider, Miss Ong her History teacher an octopus with nothing to say she needed to know. Her best friend Katie said, confidential and all, clever girls don't find husbands, just look at the teachers, spinsters with arms and legs. Standard 5 was more than a girl needs and that's where she was, thank you very much. And I, short of 18, went that Monday morning to my last year at school.

When I returned home Judith was singing

> *Yes, it's a good day for singin' a song,*
> *And it's a good day for movin' along;*

making a mess of Peggy Lee's American accent, my ma humming in tune, more or less. They'd emptied the **KLIM** tin twice. Judith and I rolled coins in 5-dollar tubes and folded notes into $10 bundles. We put tubes and bundles in $100 envelopes and hid them.

I ruled an exercise book in columns: DATE, RECEIPTS, PAYMENTS and showed her how to carry totals to the next page and asked my ma to please search the house for unsold stock under tables, over cupboards, anywhere my father stuffed it. By the time we'd sold everything the discount was 90%. The shop had never been so empty since the day it was raided, but now we had a shop, not a junk store, and all it took was three months.

I took the first five envelopes to Selegie Road Post Office to open an account.

One Messiah, the clerk said, is a blessing. Two must be a misunderstanding.

What do you mean?

We have another account by that name.

Which Messiah?

Sorry, not permitted to divulge.

I asked my ma and she said, Jews, only us. Not Jews, who knows? I went back and showed the clerk my father's Certificate of Death. Is the account in this name?

Sorry, not at liberty to divulge, he smiled and pointed at the ceiling. First get authority from higher up.

Where are your stairs?

Not up the stairs dear fellow. Further up where angels live also known as Fullerton Building. Someday, when I become an angel, I also will work beside sea breezes.

It took many weeks and a lawyer to discover my father had been depositing money before the war. Then I remembered: Don't count money unless giving change or going to the Post Office. After the soldiers had left he ran his hand along the upper shelves. He must have been looking for something. I also recalled Solly saying white was back in fashion and we'd get no compensation. The war, it seemed, had taught Europeans nothing. Indonesia threw out the Dutch, Indo-China the French. Guerrillas were ambushing planters and miners and destroying British property in Malaya and anti-white riots had started in our streets. Locals were caught and hanged and my father, never one to look for trouble, must have said, *Kaparah*, let it be, thank God we survived.

A little over a thousand dollars went into my ma's new

account which kept us going and now I could negotiate better prices for cash.

In December I sat the Cambridge School Certificate Examination without Simon's help. He was in England studying something or other. I got Grade 1 all the same because Ding Dong's tutors had past papers and how many questions can examiners think up? I wrote answers to enough for a sporting chance, learned them by heart, poured them out as fast as my pen would go and my ma said, Bravo. Now you must choose a profession.

What?

Any. Then people will look up to you.

I said I could do something with the shop and she said did I want to end up like my father searching in the **KLIM** tin for her to go to market? The shop didn't need more brains than she and Judith could bundle between them. This was Princep Street. The shop could stay open 25 hours a day, 8 days a week, sell everything at half price and how much would we make? If I told her what to do there'd always be food on the table, what more did we need? A profession would make me a man and I wondered if I suddenly had a new mother.

A school with a Careers Master in those days would be like a cat with a bark. The big world outside was someone else's problem and whether it was colonial policy or not, we were a nation of clerks and hawkers. Jonah was still a clerk and Joshua sat cross-legged on a mat in Arab Street hawking cloth, singing songs from Malay movies, winking at customers, and few women left without brown paper parcels under their arms. For someone who said little more than, Sure thing, he came home a bowl of smiles with clinking pockets.

My father had told me that we are only what God makes us. It was 1952 and my ma had spoken. So I thought I'd give

Him a prod. I stepped out of the shop, turned right and walked, street by street, stopped when I was a pool of sweat, returned, had a drink, cooled off, then went out again turning left. No shop within walking distance sold sweets or cheap jewellery. I bargained as my father taught me and soon the shop flashed with colour which brought new customers. A month before Chinese New Year, Hari Raya, Deepavali and Christmas we sold greeting cards. Jews didn't send cards.

I put a permanent SALE sign across the front and we sold more in a week than my father did in a month. My ma asked customers their names and remembered them. Elsie, you look so good today why not try these hairclips? Nice. Now the matching bracelet. My, like a movie star. Don't you think so, Judith? Tell the truth, beautiful no?

After Judith saw *A Date with Judy* she permed her hair to look like Jane Powell, demanded we call her Judy and didn't give a hoot when my ma said Yehudit meant little Jewish girl, her first after three boys.

What's up with you, I said, that's not the way to speak.

I speak any way I want and do my hair how I want and be what I want. Pa was okay for sons to make them like him but I'm not growing up in a rappa like Ma. I'll be a modern miss, wait and see.

Then I changed our lights to 75 watts and bought a second-hand till which delighted my ma each time the bell rang, drawer shot out and money went in. She pulled down the **KLIM** tin for the last time, cut the string and turned it into a waste bin. I had a telephone installed which got everyone excited including our left- and-right-side neighbours and a table fan my ma sat in front of to shut her eyes for a few minutes in the afternoon. I took her to C-Rite, the Chinese optician in Bencoolen Street and she stopped squinting.

Without making it seem I was getting my father out of our lives, more in a memories-are-sweet-but-life-can't-stop kind of way, I told the street we were under new management by changing our shop front to door, low wall and glass instead of fifty Meranti planks which the carpenter took in part payment. Most of all I got a real kick from twiddling the knobs of the Phillips Bakelite radio running back and forth across the shortwave listening to the hiss and crackle and strange beep, beep sounds from far away.

Between the N and D of LONDON, I found the BBC Overseas Service and a woman with a perfumed voice spoke to me. Hello my darlings, she said, sit back now, or if your limbs are up to it, move aside the furniture and dance for thirty uninterrupted minutes to the sweetest music this side of heaven. It's Guy Lombardo and His Royal Canadians with something old, something new and something, maybe, just for you. So I pushed away the table and chairs and slid in slippers around a small patch of floor and though my steps were nonsense they made me feel good enough to want to learn.

That was just the start. I went to see Fred Astaire and Ginger Rodgers in *Top Hat* twice and *Shall We Dance* four times, first alone then with Judy, then her and my ma who'd never been to the movies in her life. She said she didn't enjoy watching people dancing up and down steps as if that's the way to behave. What I didn't tell her, or anyone else, was that I was taking dancing lessons twice a week though not up and down stairs.

When things are going well you know you can be brave so I said, Ma, trying not to say it in the way she'd know I had something to say she wouldn't like and when she looked at me through her spectacles in the way she did, I knew it hadn't worked. All the same I said, Ma, I think we should open the shop on Saturday.

No.

But Ma, it's the busiest day of the week.

Your father wouldn't like it.

Let's hope he doesn't find out.

It's a sin.

God won't mind, I said. Considering what He's done for us so far and, being a Jew Himself, He'd like to see us do better.

On the first Saturday she refused to come into the shop, leaving it to Judy and me. The next Saturday she served customers but wouldn't handle money. That lasted a couple more Saturdays before the bell going and the drawer jumping out were too much to resist.

Three weeks later I said, Ma.

No, she said.

I want you to start wearing dresses.

Not even your father said such a thing to me. What kind of son are you? You want your mother to walk in the streets showing her legs? What d'you think I am?

Only three other women wear rappas and they're old grandmothers.

You know something Adam, a person who finds out his father left money nobody knew about and sells dead stock and finds new ways to make people come to our shop, can get the idea he can do no wrong. That can go to his head until he thinks he's in charge. But such a person should remember who he is and keep his place.

The first time she came into the shop in a dress she complained about wind up her legs. I asked Judy if wind went up her legs and she said, Ma doesn't wear drawers loud enough for the street to hear. I returned from the dining room when voices had died down, took ten dollars from the till and gave them to my ma. You'll find a shop in Middle Road.

31

Eight months after finishing school, a year after my father died, I decided it was time to see to myself. I looked under Dong and found my old school friend. Had his surname been Lim or Tan or Chan, I'd have been calling all week. He was off to Cambridge, early September, I must attend his farewell party, when could we meet and what was I doing these days?

Thinking to do accountancy, I said.

University?

Can't afford it.

Do it by correspondence, get articled, earn while you learn.

I told him not to go so fast, please explain and he said he'd call back in ten minutes. When he hadn't for half an hour, I called. He asked how long I'd had a phone, said I was a prick not to know I didn't get into the directory until the next publication and did I have paper and pen? A shop full, I said. I was to see his father in two days, third floor, Meyer Chambers, Raffles Place, 11 o'clock, don't be late and he rang off before I could thank him which I knew was intentional.

I got there, centre of town, at 10.00, a 5-cent bus ride from home but where I'd never been. My ma had ironed knife-edges into my dark blue best drill trousers, starched my only shirt with long sleeves and as I looked into John Little's window to check my hair was okay, I saw a row of neckties, checks, stripes, circles, patterns weaving in and out and heard Uncle Friam saying to Raab the Jewish tailor from Romania: Ties, half a dozen, striped, different colours. Stripes cost $8 all the way to $25, that's to say equivalent to my ma selling 250 to 770 pencils. I counted my money. $6.25 in crumpled notes and coins.

I looked at the cheapest – $5.50. 172 pencils. For a tie? And not striped. I must be crazy. In Middle Road I could buy a shirt and trousers and leave with change, I swear. No way. The 5.50 tie had red I's going one way, white I's the other. It would leave me 75 cents. The white I's were more silver-grey and stood out a little. Nice. There are better things to do with $5.50. You wouldn't dare go into such a shop in the first place. In the second place, who would serve someone with only $6.25 in his pocket? I took a final check to be sure I looked okay and there was my reflection looking at me with the 5.50 necktie hanging exactly in the right place from my starched collar.

Can I help you, sir?

The Sikh *jaga* at the entrance – white uniform, black beard, silver JL medallion on a red turban – had been watching. He'd called me Sir.

It's okay, I said and moved off when I heard myself saying, There's a tie in the window.

Please step this way, Sir and speak to that lady. He nodded toward a Chinese girl in high heels and slinky *cheongsam*. She will be happy to help you.

I combed my hair, straightened my ma's creases in the dressing room mirror, smiled at the *jaga* who raised his eyebrows to say I looked good, walked to Battery Road, up the steps to Meyer Chambers, took the lift to the third floor, marched into the reception of Dong and Partners at 10.45 and at 11 exactly, was admitted into Ding Dong's father's office.

To say it was an interview would be exaggeration.

I said, Good morning sir. Thank you … and he said, Sit.

The phone rang. His secretary came to sit by his desk and picked up the phone. She said, Mr Dong's office, listened, covered the mouthpiece, Mr Chua of United Holdings, says it's urgent, and handed him the phone.

It's always urgent with that man, he said and took the phone. Well? … … That's not correct. Our position hasn't changed … … No, that's not what we agreed. Three million, eight hundred and seventy-six thousand and not one cent more or we'll withdraw the offer. He put down the phone.

I looked at the window wondering if he was talking dollars when he said, Well young man? Sir, I said, Yong Jeng told me … and he said, Yes of course. You're his school friend. Accountancy, is it? Fine. Alice, get me Bernie Siow, he said to her and to me he said, He'll be at his desk, praying, and into the phone he said, Siow, I'm sending a young man to see you … what's that? … he'll tell you when he arrives … what's that? … ask him yourself. Regards to Nancy.

Alice took the phone, listened and wrote something on a fresh page of her pad.

Was there anything else, he asked and as I opened my mouth he said, Yes, Jeng told me. Alice, get me Wilson, School of Accountancy, took the cover off his Chinese mug, sipped green tea twice, put down the mug, covered it and said to me, Slow old codger, well past his time but gets there eventually. You'll have no trouble with him. If you do come see me. Wilson? You old rascal … what's that? … too long at the eighteenth hole? Hahaha. What's that? … … no, I'll tell nobody, scout's honour. Listen here Wilson, I'm sending a young man to see you. He'll tell you his name and anything else you need to know. Be nice to him. What's that? … … Yes. Jeng's farewell. You'll be there? Barbara too? … … Good.

Alice took the phone, listened and again wrote in her pad.

Wilson got so drunk, Mr Dong said to me, he pissed in his pants.

A second phone rang. Mr Dong's office. She listened and handed him the phone, Mr Chua of United Holdings, she said and put down the first phone.

Well? Agreed? Fine. There are papers to sign. Speak to Chua. What's that? ... No, not you. Would I be telling you to speak to yourself? ... Maybe I would. My Chua, in my office, for God's sake ... what's that? ... speak to Alice, she'll transfer you. Alice tore the sheet off her pad, gave it to me with one hand and took the phone with the other.

I got up and stood at a corner of his one-and-a-half acre desk waiting to be dismissed, hoping maybe to shake his hand and thank him, kiss his shoes, bow all the way to the door of his gigantic office filled with priceless vases, Ming, Ching, Ding, ivory gods, jade horses, golden Buddha, not to mention paintings and scrolls ceiling to floor, when he said to his secretary, Where was I?

In the sum of, she read from her pad and rattled off a number with at least seven digits. He continued dictating and she carried on writing in her pad as if I wasn't there.

This man with close cropped spiky hair, tinted rimless spectacles, gold Rolex Oyster, diamond pin in a $25 black and gold striped necktie who'd never seen me before and didn't say please to anybody, got me, with two phone calls, while I sat at attention in his office in my $5.50 tie, a job and admittance to night school in an instant as if time never happened. Eventually, when he noticed I was still at his desk he said, Is there something else?

I want to thank you, Sir, I said, for every ...

Thank me by being a credit to yourself.

I will, sir, I said, I promise you that, and he said, Good luck, to me and to Alice, Where was I? and she said, The parties of the second part, and I said, Thank you Sir, thank you very much, I will always remember this, and thank you too Miss Alice, and she half looked up from her pad and gave me a smile and I left walking backwards.

32

There was more to accountancy than the simple and compound interest sums we did in school but not so much as to give me reason to go on about it, except to say it wasn't long before I learned that accounts can be made to say more or less than they mean. I also discovered how to make money using other people's money and, more important, how to make money without using money at all. That's not to say it came from Wilson or his night-school teachers who stuck to textbooks and marked our exercises accordingly.

If truth be told, the Jew in me listened, said nothing even when disagreeing, okay with both points of view at the same time because, opposite though they may be, both can be right. As my father used to say, only Jews can see what even God, whose name is blessed, has missed, understand what I'm saying? Above all else I knew I was on the road to the place I wanted to go, and though never top of the class – Chinese are the most competitive students in the world – I planned to be successful.

I worked and studied hard while bits of the Empire were falling off like coconuts from a dying palm and by 1957, when I sat the final exams, Singapore had a kind of let's-see-if-you-can-manage-by-yourselves local government with limited power. I didn't get worked up about it except to take notice that money was moving from the old colonial companies run by whites on 3-year contracts and paid-for home leave into Chinese hands and that was where I placed my bets.

Old Man Siow – he wasn't, but when you're short of 23 anyone over 50, balding and thickening voice is old – was a decent God-fearing Methodist Christian. He may have loved God as much as, but I doubt was as good friends with Him as my father. Bernard Siow believed he and his life belonged to God who could do as He wished with him. My father said God expects Jews to stand on their own two feet. We may be in His hands but He wasn't going to play with us like toys. We had free will so if things went wrong it was our fault, totally, no point looking up and saying: Why are you doing this to me?

Siow had a framed photo of his wife and kids on his desk which I decided I'd also have when my turn came, an abacus with ivory beads as old as the Ark and a New Testament, as worn as my father's Chumash, from which he read a passage before starting the day. His church believed there was a bond between them and us, sharing roots in biblical revelation, and having a Jew in his office brought him closer to Jesus to which I said to myself I'll do nothing to change your mind Bernard, I swear.

When I passed with a respectable all-round score I went and printed cards:

> J Adam Messiah ACCA UK
>
> 47 Princep St   Tele: 665516

the UK for people to know I wasn't a locally qualified sub-standard accountant for hire at cut rates. I needn't have. Messiah, he said, not the usual Adam so I thought it was another prayer session and put on my sincere face, these are for you, handing me two small boxes, which told me my right foot was on the first rung of the ladder. I'm moving you to the Market Street office, he said. You'll have your own room, two assistants and have to handle clients directly on your own. You don't speak Cantonese and some of them don't speak English so you'd better learn how to deal with them.

I'm okay, I said, I speak Malay and I've lived among Chinese all my life.

I've been Chinese all my life and I'm still learning. From today you can call me Bernard, he said, and from tomorrow you will spend half an hour each morning with me, in this office, learning to be a nominal Chinaman.

He called me over soon after his Bible reading and taught me by way of stories, much like my father explained life to me. When he started in the thirties colour bar was solid as concrete. The white old-boy network did its deals in the Masonic Lodge in Coleman Street. Locals called it *Rumah Hantu* – Ghost House – and they couldn't join.

So I searched Boat Quay for clients, he said. All Chinamen to the whitlows on their toenails doing business in pyjamas so you never knew who was boss, who was coolie. They did accounts on an abacus, carried profits in their heads and didn't need me, you see?

Like my father's **KLIM** tin, I said.

That's yellow. Chinese prefer red tins for good luck. Notice how people only remember profits, never losses? That's why they don't employ us. I was getting nowhere, he said, until one day I walked into a rice dealer's shop. An oldish man in baggy drawers and torn singlet puffed a cigarette like an *Ah pian* enjoying a smoke between loading gunny bags. But the fingers of his other hand were flying over an abacus. He didn't look up, just jerked his head for me to wait while he added the same number several times. Obviously, I said to myself, this man can't multiply on an abacus. What would you do, Adam, if you were trying for his business?

I don't know how to use an abacus but if I did I'd teach him how to multiply.

Big mistake. Chinese consider age more worthy than money. You, being younger, he'd lose face and you'd lose a potential client. I praised his speed on the abacus and asked if he'd teach me. As I was pretending to be learning I moved the beads to multiply the same numbers he'd been adding fifteen times. You're doing it wrong, he said, stopped, banged the table, cursed himself for being a fool, told me to sit, have a coffee, gave me a cigarette and asked me to teach him. I netted my first client. He introduced me to his friends and in two years I was keeping accounts for half of Boat Quay and a quarter of the warehouses along Singapore River. Adam, he said, behave like a Chinaman A-S-A-P. If not I'll expect you to net a few Jews.

To get my left foot on the second rung I had to take him seriously. Eating Chinese food the first time was tough. Pig, my father said, can't you see? When it wasn't in lumps, I told myself it wasn't there, swallowed without chewing, hoping God didn't notice. If I woke next morning then it must be okay. My father was wrong. God cursed the serpent, not the pig.

All in all I was doing better than okay. Siow was good to me. He paid me ten per cent above going rate to tell me my value. But doing well is only half as good as showing it. So I converted our shop into a private limited company and printed another set of cards:

J Adam Messiah ACCA UK
Chairman
Messiah Stationers Pte Ltd
47 Princep St   Tele: 665516

I bought a company car, second-hand Ford Popular, SP 297, a black coffin on wheels but all the same my pride and joy. My ma and sister received salaries just below taxable rate and I charged everything permitted tax-wise to the company. We engaged a part-time servant to help with housework – office cleaner in the books – and my ma was in the seventh heaven no longer making ends meet because they were overlapping. When there was cash to spare she helped Auntie Sally who came now and then to work in the shop becoming great pals with my sister, all of which made me feel worthwhile.

33

Jonah worked his way up the establishment, a notch a year, and was now Acting Assistant Chief Clerk in the Water Department of the City Council. He was walking out with Ramah Jacob who was on the verge of changing her name to Jacobson to sound high-class but they got married and she reckoned Messiah unusual enough for people to notice.

I called her Drama Ramah behind the back she said killed her sitting at a typewriter in a girl pool where she'd fish a Collins Pocket Dictionary from her handbag when no one was looking, close her eyes and mumble, abnegate, renounce, give up, abnegate, renounce, give up, as many times as it took to sink, determined to be private secretary to a boss who knew her true worth, with a room to herself, never mind how small, instead of waiting like a dummy until someone said, Take a letter. So unbecoming, don't you think, to a woman's innermost ego, especially after spending three weeks and all that money on a DALE CARNEGIE course on HOW TO WIN FRIENDS AND INFLUENCE PEOPLE and did I think she could write DC after her name like my ACCA? Okay, maybe not so highly-strung but she did have a way of rubbing me the wrong way in a manner of speaking.

Joshua too was doing fine with a stall in Rochore Road Market, selling sarongs, saris and batiks. He had two bank accounts, two cheque books, two signatures and told me to stop studying and find out about girls, the real way to enjoy life, sure thing. How Yona Deborah – my father's friend Shooli's daughter – did that for him, I never asked. She was a mouse who lived in a shoe and I think he married her because her name was the female version of my brother Jonah's, his best pal, and they were very happy.

Our bedroom was now all mine. I gave some of our furniture to Auntie Sally, bought new stuff including a shop display refrigerator and charged the lot to the company. All of which is to say that while Pluto was doing me favours Venus was also making her presence felt stirring up those places that make you itch so you either scratch or go mad.

When I shook Ding Dong's hand, five years earlier, I thought it was goodbye forever, he'd come back a lawyer, join his father and get into a crowd too far above my station. But not a week after returning from Cambridge he came from his mansion in Leonie Hill to the jumble of cobblers, hawkers and stray dogs on our 5-foot way to loaf, haunt dancehalls and go anywhere there were girls, he said, hoping to find a couple or more to replace the plump pink English girls who queued outside his flat just to nibble his Chinese noodle, or so he said. It was fun for sure but not what I was looking for. I said virginity is a match to light a fire and not burn itself out. He said I was daft. Matches were to burn just to see them burst into flame and his two boxes were full of matches dying to catch fire.

Maybe he was right. Maybe I mislaid part of my life and now I'm wondering if, maybe, it was my father again, telling me to be careful, not to mix fun with love and it turned out to be the wrong girl. So I stopped fooling around and settled into a let's-wait-for-something-to-happen-without-making-it-happen until one Saturday afternoon, hot, sweaty and thirsty, I slipped into Luna Café where a bunch of *mahala* boys and girls were having a Pepsi.

They spread out and I sat facing Maisie, pretty, frisky eyes, tempting lips, encouraging cleavage and not walking out with anyone so far as I knew, in other words ripe for plucking. With knees close and once or twice touching, I felt Venus slide onto my lap. So I went along with the How're things? What's happening? and other airy talk, biding time until we were leaving and found a way to say, Will you be here next Saturday, thinking she'd answer with her eyes like it was some kind of code but she said, Every Saturday and you're welcome to join us. I should've let it go but as they were taking leave I got close enough to say, I meant just you and me, we could meet here then go somewhere else. Okay, she said. Two o'clock, I said. Fine, she said and went off with the others.

I reached the café with time to spare and, as I might've guessed, she arrived, chaperon attached. I put on my casual face – between pleased-as-punch and no-point-complaining – said a special hello to Rebecca and, dumping my plans in the back row of the cinema, said, Where'd you two lovely girls like to go and when they had no suggestions, I said, My car's round the corner, let's drive to the Esplanade and think of something there which didn't help so I took them down to Market Street, showed them where I worked, walked along the river where I said most of my clients had offices, talked about what I did, how the world was changing, how we lived in Sime Road Camp, believe it or not in the same hut, and so on with a couple of coffees between and as the sun was setting they said they had to go home. I dropped Rebecca first and driving off with Maisie told her I wanted to take her out alone, I'd pick her up at her house and be back before dark, I promise.

Not even now, she said. Drop me before my house, please, or my father will kill me.

Oh, I said, does that mean ...

No, she said, we'll meet same place then Rebecca will go her own way.

I stopped a hundred yards before her house, said, I'll see you next week and sneaked a squeeze of her hand which she pretended not to notice.

Did I know her brother had followed, saw us meet and Rebecca take off? Did I know he saw us enter Cathay cinema? Did I know he stationed himself across the road when the movie came out and saw us holding hands? All I knew was what I heard about the grilling of Rebecca, her confession and the hammering her mother gave her and the roasting of Maisie with what her father said and did which I prefer not to have on my conscience. Then, two days later, home from work, my ma told me to sit, she was bringing me a cup of tea.

Why didn't you tell me, she said, like your brothers?

I'm not my brothers, I said. And what did they tell you?

That they were approaching girls.

What does approaching girls mean?

Your father's gone so they spoke to me and I went to speak to their parents.

Why? Don't Jonah and Joshua have the … I said guts seeing as how it was my ma.

You mustn't think wrong of them, she said. They respect the old ways.

I wasn't approaching Maisie, Ma. I just wanted to get to know her, see how it went. There aren't more than half a dozen girls in the community, I said, leaving out the ripe for plucking bit. She's pretty and has more in her head than my sisters-in-law. I enjoyed myself enough to want to see her again and that's all that happened.

To you maybe. Her father came today asking your intentions.

Tell him I intend to make a lot of money. I don't have a target, but when I reach it, I might think about marrying.

I don't need to, she said. I already told him times have changed, we don't control our children anymore and he said, until they are married he controls his children and if my other sons knew how to do things the right way what makes you so special?

No, I said, no chaperons, no contracts and no dowries.

Drink your tea, she said, then tell me what you'll do when it's Judy's turn. Won't you want to know who he is before she walks with him? I'm sure your brothers will.

I'll leave it to you and them and their wives. Ramah will surely have her say.

What the hell, I told myself, from now on it'll be in a crowd or not at all. So I took courses in banking and taxation, anything to keep Venus off my lap when one afternoon at that time when even the sun sweats, I went to stand in front of our table fan. It was busy cooling my ma and sister so I went into the street to catch any breeze on offer when up comes Ding Dong in his gleaming white sports Mercedes with tinted glass.

As his window slid down giving me a gush of air conditioning, he said through Raybans, Social & Tea Dance, Nurses Home KK Hospital, tomorrow, 4 o'clock, and, as the glass rose added, fetch you five-to, be ready and skidded off leaving me in a blast of well-to-do exhaust fumes. Fine, I thought, dance a little, drink a little, flirt a little with flat-chested Chinese girls, get home in a pool of sweat, have a shower and go to bed.

It didn't turn out like that.

34

Madam, I'm Adam. That's what I said to her minutes after Ding Dong and I entered and I caught sight of a blaze of curly red hair in the far corner of the hall amongst straight black Chinese hair, left him at the door and made a beeline. It made her laugh and filled her hazel eyes with whatever it is that makes a fellow go weak in his legs.

Can I have the pleasure, I said with my wise-guy face, and in no time we were gliding over the empty dance floor until other couples took courage, followed suit and when the waltz ended I asked her name. Being parched from the thrill of dancing with a girl the likes of whom I'd never seen before, I led her to the refreshment table still holding her hand and when she didn't take it away, told myself she's beautiful Adam watch out.

What would you like, I asked. She shook her head and smiled and her dimples caught the light and she said something so softly I didn't hear in the noise of who knows how many nurses and doctors and guests trying to have a good time in a crowded hall.

Juice or squash?

Penelope, she said a little louder.

Sorry. I thought you said pineapple. What's penelope?

My name, she said taking her eyes from mine so I'd not notice she was laughing.

Penelope, I said as if tasting it. I've never heard that name. Did your parents give it to you? I couldn't have been more an idiot if I tried, I swear.

You're funny, she said.

Penelope, Penelope, Penelope, I said and squeezed her hand and, stuck for something to say, reached for a Red

Lion and said, You don't mind if I do, and put the bottle in my mouth with the bloody cap still on as if I was going out of my way to look a fool.

She bit her lip and turned away and unwilling as I was to let her hand go, I got the drinks nurse to open it please and took a gulp, holding the bottle to my lips for a long slow swallow telling myself, be calm or she'll think you've fallen out of a tree, never met a girl before and why doesn't the gramophone nurse hurry up and play another 78, when, as if God had taken pity on me, the speakers sang out,

Tum, ^{tum,} tum, tum,

the first four beats of *La Cumparsita,* and I knew my time had come.

Down went the Red Lion and without even walking to the dance floor where a few couples were standing but afraid to risk a tango, I swept her into my arms and we swished over the talcum powder, bodies meshed as if they'd been looking for each other, her yin with my yang, whichever way they go.

Our legs moved like scissors with timing and tempo, two halves of a whole, one with the other, the only couple on the floor, everyone watching as our fused bodies swept and swayed like tall rice in a ripening paddy. You can't get closer on the dance floor than a tango, bodies wedged, my leg between hers, hers clutching mine and her rosy chiffon dress whirling and whooshing around until all eyes were on us as I made those thrilling swirls, curling her around me, twirling and bending, sweeping over the floor.

We were spinning tum, tum, tum, another swirl, tum,

tiara pum pum pum pum, another twirl, ta rara rararah, deep, daring bends, and seeing a real live dancer the likes of whom

I suspect had never before appeared at their Annual Social & Tea Dance Evening, the music-minding nurse, probably still on page 1 of Steve Conway's Book of Ballroom Dancing for Beginners, flipped over the record and *Blue Tango* floated down from the speakers and that, as the saying goes, was that.

The floor belonged to us. Edmundo Ros and his jumpy *Wedding Samba* followed by rumba, cha-cha-cha, then the mambo when we pressed our palms together and locked fingers, I slid along, twisted around her, turned side-on, then she swung her skirt, rocked her hips, looked into my eyes and I tried to work out what was happening to me.

Without a break Victor Sylvester's silver strings played old and new waltzes, foxtrots, quicksteps and every ballroom style of those happy days when dancing was polish and style and I never put a foot wrong in pointed red patent leather shoes, white slacks, black shirt and white silk tie with double Windsor, curls dancing on my forehead in rhythm with my feet flitting over the floor.

By now we were panting, she sipping, I gulping a Green Spot in between telling her I was born in this very hospital which should come as no surprise and she said it wasn't, everyone told her the same, this being the biggest maternity hospital in South-East Asia but what she really wanted to know was, Where did you learn to dance?

So I told her about Guy Lombardo on the radio and Fred Astaire at the cinema but nothing about Amy Ho, a taxi-dancer at Great World Cabaret who gave me private lessons on her night off until one night I turned up earlier than expected and discovered she could be hired for other pass-times. You're pretty good yourself, I said when a tall white lady wearing a senior sort of cap came by and Penelope pulled her hand away from mine.

Young man, the lady said, thank you for livening the

party. So I put on my princely face when she added, Rudolf Valentino danced the very same tango in *The Four Horsemen of the Apocalypse* at our local in Liverpool when I was a girl, a little before your time. Today I've seen him in the flesh.

My tongue stuck to the roof of my mouth trying to say something cleverer than Thank you, when Penelope said, Please don't swell his head, Matron or it'll be too heavy to dance, and we all laughed just as someone shouted, Conga! Conga time!

Enjoy yourselves, the Matron said and stepped aside.

Bodies formed bits of lines going yah-ta-ta-hey, I got behind Penelope, others joined behind me and as she led the dance I ran my fingers in her pomegranate hair, down to her shoulders, then slid them to her waist and her hips and a little lower and in and out and around the room we went, yah-ta-ta-hey, louder and louder, until the whole place was moving one-two-three-kick, music ripping the evening air, feet thumping one-two-three-click, bodies swinging, one-two-three-flick, spinning the hall around.

At 8 o'clock the party was supposed to shut down, guests tie shoe laces, tuck shirts in and leave but there was such uproar the Matron announced an extension to 8.30, not a minute later mind, she said, her nurses had to prepare for the night shift.

At 8.25 lights dimmed and Jim Reeves sang *I Can't Stop Loving You*, the last waltz in those serene days when you put your cheek against a girl's and for three minutes roamed in heaven with her close against me and I said will you and she didn't hear so I drew her closer feeling her breasts against me the scent of her hair telling me I had never come so close to anyone before and asked again will you my heart going like it didn't know how to handle something so new and she said yes I will and I asked her again so I could hear her say yes I will and she said yes I will yes and I said when and she said call me tomorrow so I said please can't you tell me now and she said that was when she'd know her roster so I took her hand and pressed it close against my lips kissing it because I longed to kiss her mouth so I said parting is such sweet sorrow a line from a book called *Sweet Things to Say to Someone You Love* which made her blush and she turned and ran away just as the lights came on and flooded the hall.

She went out the door and disappeared and I went to look for Ding Dong.

35

I want to speak to Penelope, please … Yes, she's a nurse … Surname? Sorry, I don't know … Sorry, I don't know which ward … Sorry, I don't know if she's on duty … She's a trainee, does that help? … Please, I need to speak to her urgently … You can't find a needle in a haystack if you don't know who the needle is … Okay, I'll try the Nurses Home … Thanks.

All the numbers under KK Hospital chased each other down the wires to the exchange until a soft sweet voice said, Hello, this is Penelope. I grabbed my chair and sat down.

Hello, I said. Remember me? My God! What was wrong with me?

You mean the fellow with red shoes, she said with a small giggle and when I didn't answer she said, Are you the tall, dark, handsome guy who was showing off all evening, and laughed that laugh of hers that seemed to roll inside her throat.

Yes, I mean no. I wasn't showing off. Was I showing off? Never mind. I want to see you. How about this evening?

Sorry, she said, I'm on middle shift all week. Sunday's okay.

Sunday? I knew I'd shouted when all heads in the office turned. A whole week, I whispered, I could die. I'll fetch you. She said to tell her where and she'd meet me.

I shaved with a new blade, splashed Old Spice, face, body, hair, handkerchief and socks, puffed my waves, sparkled my best leather shoes, put on a long-sleeve orange shirt, matching bowtie and brand new brown polyester slacks then took them off or what would I say if she had something to say about my red shoes? White shirt, black trousers, no tie but I couldn't resist a new leather belt with pewter buckle.

I parked behind the Cathay half an hour early, picked up the $3 tickets I thought would impress her, 6.30 show, back row and stood in the lobby out of sight assuming she'd get off the bus outside Tiong Hoa Hotel directly in my line of vision and waited, I'll admit, my heart halfway up my throat.

6.25, five minutes to curtain up, hopes sinking with the sun, when, what did I see if not her red hair bobbing along Bras Basah Road, a totally unexpected direction which didn't register being so overjoyed. I watched her cross the road, graceful as moonlight, white cotton blouse with long sleeves, brown skirt dancing below her knees and as I stepped down two at a time, she saw me and a magical smile broke over her face.

With arms open like when I asked for our first dance, I greeted her as the second bell rang. Hello, I said, it's so good to see you, I said, scooped her up the stairs, got to our seats, pulled hers down for her, put a packet of mixed salted nuts in her hand and said, Penelope a week was too much to bear. I may look alive, I said unbuttoning my cuff, but actually I'm dead. Feel.

She dropped the nuts into her lap and took my pulse looking at the watch she wasn't wearing. Goodness, she said with a twinkle in her voice, I'm out with a corpse, just as the festoon curtains stopped changing colour, opened, lights faded and we smiled at each other in the dark. I took her hand and squeezed it until I plucked up the courage to kiss her fingers one by one and she didn't pull her hand away and it felt so good, I swear.

A Matter of Life and Death with David Niven and Kim Hunter was an okay movie with a view of the British idea of heaven, neat and empty with dead famous people walking up broad stairs saying, How do you do? others walking down saying, How do you do? We were having a laugh, not much, when a piece of nut stuck in her throat making her cough. As she fetched her hanky from between her breasts out came a chain dangling a golden man pinned to a cross and tiny as he was and dark as it was, he had my father's face.

Ignore it, I told myself, it's an accident. No it's not. If I hadn't given her the nuts she wouldn't have choked. If I'd given her my handkerchief she wouldn't have pulled hers, her cross wouldn't have jumped out and I wouldn't have seen my father. And how about the movie? *A Matter of Life and Death*? And it all happened just as the judge, maybe God himself, was telling David Niven to tell the truth, the whole truth and nothing but the truth.

All that and it's an accident?

A little something, Penelope, I said opening the car door for her. Sundae? Coffee? Or would you prefer the Satay Club? Your wish is my command.

I'd love to, she said, but I'm still under probation.

If that's an illness, I said, a Knickerbocker Glory, three scoops, chocolate sauce, crushed nuts, no, no more nuts, jelly babies and pineapple chunks will cure it.

Very funny, she said biting the side of her lip with a slantwise look. It means Matron needs to know.

You don't need her permission to go out, do you?

My father let me leave home if Matron promised to keep an eye on me.

And what's wrong with going for something after a show?

I said I was going to church.

Oho. Is that why you came down Bras Basah Road? Which one, I asked, as if the man on the cross hadn't already told me.

Good Shepherd.

Okay, I said to myself, she's Catholic and that's fine for now, no point jumping to conclusions when you don't know what they are or where to jump, so I let her in, slid into my seat and said, What did you mean your father let you leave home? Where's home?

Penang.

Pearl of the Orient, I said, like you are, and when she didn't say thank you or smile at my compliment or maybe she didn't think it was, I asked, so why did you leave?

Bigger hospital and better training. My parents wouldn't have let me go otherwise.

I pulled out of the car park and only when I turned into Dhoby Ghaut did I use the classic line I was saving. Why wouldn't they? Don't you have sisters as beautiful as you?

No.

Not as beautiful as you?

No sisters, silly. And no brothers.

Sending an only child to the City of Sin, I said. My my.

It's not, is it?

Only the first three letters. Quite tame really unless you're looking for it. Are you?

Funny fellow, she said and looked away.

Cathay to KK Hospital was five minutes on those dark old roads in my bone-shaker but I stretched it to twenty, trying without prying, tactful as a toothpick and she wasn't telling. I headed for Serangoon Road where it was easy to lose my way and have to double back. So, I tried a new line, when did you start?

Three weeks ago.

Aha, I said. Would you like a tour of Sin City? I'm the best guide in town, it's free and I'll pick you up. Where d'you live, I asked as if I wasn't halfway there.

The Nurses Home.

Oho. Your father made sure to keep you safe. No worries, I said, I'll fetch you and take you back before midnight when my car becomes a pumpkin and I turn into a mouse.

And my clothes don't turn to rags, she said and gave me a little shove. But outside the gates, please. I don't think you should come to the Nurses Home, not yet.

My God. Not yet means okay later, later means okay. Okay means now's the time, never mind her parents, is she legally old enough to make up her own mind?

Almost twenty, she said.

Aha. She doesn't want me to think she's a teenager. Okay, next question.

My mother has someone in mind.

And your father?

He wants me to finish my studies first.

And you? We were close to the Nurses Home so I accelerated.

You've missed it, she said.

I want an answer.

What's the question?

And you?

Adam. It was the first time she'd said my name. Last Sunday afternoon we danced, this Sunday afternoon I choked and felt so silly.

Next Sunday afternoon then, I said. If I promise not to give you nuts.

I really must get back, Adam. Matron will be pacing up and down.

I started a 3-point turn which took seven in that old Ford halfway up Kampong Java Road in dim light all the while telling myself, no more shadow boxing, get to the point and with my eyes dead ahead I said, I'm a Jew.

I know.

Does it make a difference to you?

Should it?

But you're Catholic, I said, aren't you?

Does that make a difference, she said. To you?

Well then, I said. Next Sunday afternoon.

I'm on duty next four Sundays but Tuesday I'm off.

In my excitement I pressed the accelerator so hard we jerked back, I braked and we shot forward, the engine stalled and I felt a bloody fool. You mean week after next, I said.

No, she said, day after tomorrow.

Straight from work, I said starting up again. Five o'clock plus a bit for getting here. I'll think of somewhere nice. Can I fetch you this time?

Outside the gates and please hurry or Matron will be asking questions.

I switched on the light, turned as far as I could in that straitjacket car and in its dim yellow light saw her hazel eyes looking at me and I didn't know what to do with mine so I took her hands without kissing them and said, Tuesday, and she said, Tuesday, took her hands from mine, smiled, opened the door and walked away and though I knew she'd not have pushed me away, like a fool, I didn't go after her.

Outside the gates I watched her enter the porch and disappear. When a light came on, third from the end on the first floor, I started the engine and drove away.

36

Her roster guided my life four weeks at a time. Whenever she wasn't on duty and I wasn't working we were out together, eating at hawker stalls or a steak at the Pavilion Restaurant which I didn't much care for but wanted it known I could handle fork and knife just as well as chopsticks. Movies, dancing at the Raffles Saturday night, Adelphi Palm Court Sunday afternoon or Seaview Hotel midweek or anywhere something was going on.

Then for a string of Tuesdays she worked the morning shift. I set off early for work to grab the parking spot right by the entrance to Clifford Pier and, when I finished, sprinted more than walked to where she was waiting in the shade under the porch looking bright and beautiful. She gave me a smile the size of forever, we got into the car, I squeezed her hand, took it to my lips, threatened to tell Matron I'd kill myself all over her office if she didn't give us more time together, started up and went where the wind took us, usually to the grassy bank up Mount Faber to look out to sea until the sun took its leave, darkness stretched over the deep, the spirit of God hovered over the waters and I was drenched with love and, though plain to see, I never told her. In this manner we spent those perfumed Tuesdays walking, sitting, talking among crowds of bougainvillea, shy hibiscus, cannas in clumps like soldiers with red and yellow and orange helmets and white gardenias smelling like women of the night until the only light came from the moon and stars.

One Tuesday afternoon she called to say her ward was a nurse short. I told her Tuesday was mine, they could go find someone else. She couldn't let Sister Lau down and anyway she promised her a whole extra day off so I said make sure she does.

I took the next Monday off, fetched her, raced to the Botanical Gardens before the sun got spiteful, stopped at the gates to buy two packets of peanuts by which time she was skipping up the path with me running after her, shouting, Watch out for the monkeys.

Don't fuss, she said taking a packet from me. Penang's full of monkeys.

In that place, like other red coloured patches on the globe, God used green English fingers to remodel His third day of creation which my father said was the most beautiful day of all when God told the earth to bring forth vegetation and that was where Penelope and I held hands, talked and laughed as we wandered among those splendid trees and she danced around them and showed me what I'd never seen before.

Just read that, Adam, she said, pointing at a plaque between the buttress roots of a kapok tree. It's come from Brazil, the other side of the world, but looks like it's always lived here. Everything everywhere, she said slipping her slender fingers into mine, is God telling us He loves us and given it all to you and me.

Before I could tell her what a wonderful thought that was she bounded off searching for monkeys in the trees. There's one, she called, and over there, a baby clinging to its mum. Aren't they sweet? Two big eyes in a ball of fur, she said and walked towards them holding out a peanut. Don't get too close, I called but not soon enough for her to see a troublemaker swinging down from high in the treetops, run at her and grab the peanut right out of her hand. She screamed, the packet flew up in the air bringing a gang of rowdy monkeys out of the trees and she crashed into my arms.

I don't think you'll do that again, I said kissing her ear.

She put her hand in my pocket, pulled out the other packet, flung the peanuts as far as she could and stuffed the crumpled paper all the way back down.

You must think I'm a coward, she said.

I think you're adorable, I said and we walked up the hill among the orchids, my arm around her waist. Don't you think orchids are conceited, I said, the way they stick their tongues out at you? Angels put them in the lobby to heaven to humiliate people waiting to know if they get to go in or take the lift down.

Where d'you think you'll be sent?

I can make a good case for myself, I said. But heaven must be as dull as the first movie we saw. Bored people saying, How do you do, going up and down marble stairs.

All I remember is coughing.

I have an idea, I said and paused. It was a long pause. Let's do something, you and I, something so really bad, we'll both be sent to hell.

Like what?

On second thoughts, I said, anything you do will always be good in the eyes of God.

I'm not Miss Goody-Two-Shoes, she said, and anyway I'm hungry.

All our roads lead to the sea and that's where we were, under a tree alone on Changi beach, holding hands, looking at each other, talking without words, watching the sun set the sky alight as it sank. Come Penelope, I said helping her to her feet, let's go up to the Point and watch the moon come up. She dusted her Bermudas and I rubbed the sand off the back of her legs and she tidied her cotton blouse and pulled down the sleeves as a light wind came up. We were walking, my arm round her, when of its own accord it pulled her against my body and I kissed her full on her mouth, my hands running wherever they dared and she slid her arms up gripping my shoulders and if we kissed any more we'd have bled to death.

Penelope, I love you, I said and her laugh gushed and her head fell back so I said it again, Penelope, I love you, and then I said, I love you, Penelope, in all the world, I love you, and brought her gently down onto her knees enclosing her until we were lying on the sand, my body demanding the promised land right there under God's great dome. No, I said to myself, sat up, ran a hand through my hair then over my face and covered my mouth to stop what I wanted to say because she was lying there looking at me and I had to say something so I said, When are you back on duty?

Tomorrow afternoon, she said without taking her eyes away from me.

What about Matron?

I told her I was visiting family friends, I'd be back late.

Penelope, I said and not knowing what else to say, said Penelope, and again, Penelope.

She got up, pulled me to my feet and, in dim light, we left the beach to find ourselves inside a half-built house. Rubble burst under us like crackers in the stillness as we climbed the stairs, she ahead of me, my knees scared and my hands uneasy. The house had no roof and the moon, between rafters, gave little light. We stumbled in the shadows and found a room swept clean, tiles heaped in a corner ready for laying. She came into my arms and as we kissed I unbuttoned her blouse, she my shirt, button by button, piece by piece, until, when only the last remained, we hesitated.

Penelope, I said, Adam, she said and we were naked.

Your hands are cold, she said with a tiny laugh.

I'm not sure I'm alive, I said and then, my God, she

touched me and the flesh of my belly tightened driving all the breath out of me and I pulled her against me and if that was the last moment of my life it would have been enough. I erupted, quake after quake after quake. She kissed my shoulder, kissed my chest and nuzzled close into my neck. It's alright, she said. You'll be fine. I opened my mouth to speak but she covered it with her hand. Say anything, she said, but don't say sorry.

I bit my lip.

I'll wait, she said and I went, a little ashamed, to lay my shirt and trousers on the floor, spreading the sleeves and legs like a spent man. When I turned she was laying her cross on her clothes. I dropped my Star of David side by side, picked her up and put her down with no part of her body touching the floor.

It made me love you more, she said and as I covered her body with mine she tensed, her head turned aside, her arms rose up my back and her fingers dug into my flesh.

There was a long silence.

Penelope, will you be all right?

Yes, she said chewing my ear. I'm in my safe period.

How safe?

Didn't you see my eyes? They always shine the day after.

37

When your life swerves suddenly as if the earth has tilted you have to stop and think. It was gone midnight, Judy asleep, my ma in bed, the house dark except for the light over the stairs she left on and stayed awake until it went off to know I was safely home. I switched off the stair light to tell her she could go to sleep, crept into the shop, switched on the light, sat at the desk, pulled out a sheet of paper, ruled a line down the middle, wrote *PRO* in blue one side, *CON* on the other in red.

Under *PRO* I wrote bold, black capitals:
LOVE
WANT
emptying my desires to the bottom of the sheet.

Under *CON* were my father's two R's:
RACE
RELIGION
to which he added that Jews are the only people on earth who are both, one and the other, one and the same time, together, totally. Chinese can be Buddhist, Christian, Muslim, what they like, but a Jew is a Jew, born, live, die, which boiled down to a single CON.

I crossed out ~~*RACE*~~ and ~~*RELIGION*~~, and wrote:
JEW

It's funny though. When I asked Simon, What is a Jew? he said, Only Jews don't know the answer. Ask a gentile and he'll soon tell you. Be serious, I said. I am, he said and launched into what he called clashing couplets – doctrinal exclusiveness, prejudicial inversion, fictional rationality, speculative ethnicity and so on until I said, Okay, I don't know what you're talking about.

So I read what I'd written, twice, got up, walked about, returned and sat. No way could I balance one side against the other like a Statement of Assets and Liabilities which I always finish, both sides, with exactly the same total in the bottom line and a satisfied grin.

I took another sheet, picked a fountain pen from Judy's cigarette tin and wrote:

My darling Penelope,
I'm writing this letter to tell you

when my ma, quiet as the night, shuffled into the shop.

It's gone three Adam. What's wrong?

Nothing, Ma. I folded the sheets and slid them into my pocket.

I can see something, she said narrowing her eyes. You're not what you were yesterday. Why don't you tell me? God gave children mothers for when their fathers are gone.

Give me time, Ma, I said. You'll be first to know, I promise.

Before I set out late Sunday afternoon I stood in the centre of my room and looked around a full five minutes, then I spent two more checking for anything lying on my bed, under it, sitting on the floor, hanging from the ceiling or clinging to the walls that would, the moment I left, follow me out. To be sure I shut the window and closed my door as I walked out.

Fine, I said to myself, went down, said, Goodbye to my ma and sister shutting the shop. I'll not be late tonight.

I parked outside the synagogue and, bold as a bottle of brandy, strode off to the Cathedral of the Good Shepherd, running my fingers over my shirt buttons to check my Star of David wasn't showing, got to Queens Street and, as I reached the church, slowed, walked right past the open gate and away.

Coward. I turned around, marched back, swung through the gate, up three steps, put my hand into my pocket for my kippah only to see the men bareheaded and sat at the back near the open doors for the first time in a house of prayer not Jewish.

The church was decked with flowers, very nice, three-quarters full with people mainly in the front, men and women together, facing a large crucifix high up on the end wall which caught my eye because right behind were thirteen bright sunbeams that seemed, in the dim light, to make the cross float in mid-air.

Synagogues are usually full of light. Men sit downstairs, women upstairs, the Rabbi and his henchmen in the middle so that nobody gives his back to the Ark where the Torah scrolls are kept. What did I see here? Priests and altar boys coming and going on and off a platform, facing Jesus up on the cross their backs to the congregation.

I chalked up: Sameness No.1.

Okay, men and women sitting together was Difference No.1, but not being a bad idea I cancelled it in my head. I couldn't follow much because the priest wasn't speaking English. Also not a problem. We pray in Hebrew and though we read it, most of us don't understand it at which point I noticed something I hadn't expected. The priest wore a cap and a kind of shawl, narrower than ours, but what the hell, it'll pass.

Samenesses 2, 3 and 4.

There was a sort of ledge behind the bench in front with books and another below I thought must be a footrest and thought, how kind. So I opened a book to look like I too was one of the crowd, noticed every page divided vertically, one side Latin the other English like ours – Hebrew and English. Sameness 5 and also I could now follow the service.

The sun was going down giving Jesus on the cross a saintly look when a gentle breeze shook the palms outside and the meagre light seemed to make him breathe. A murmur rippled through the people and even I felt something stir inside me. Then the priest tinkled a small bell and people started going down on their knees on what I'd thought was a footrest. What should I do? I half moved half my body so I'd not look like I was sitting but wasn't kneeling either and hoped I'd got away with it while all eyes were shut praying, after which an organ started up, people stood and the priest sang the first words and the whole hall in one large voice echoed through the grand old building,

> *Holy, holy, holy, Lord God of Hosts*
> *Heaven and Earth are full of Thy Glory*
> *Hosanna in the Highest.*

Okay, we also sing and say Hosanna, more like Hoshana. Another sameness.

When the singing was done, people sat again and three priests stationed themselves behind the table. My book was open so I started to read: *May the body of Christ bring us to everlasting life and May the blood of Christ bring us to everlasting life* and I recalled the Last Supper when Jesus blessed the *matza* and the wine and the Divine Doctor made me stand and explain the Passover ceremony and for once he said, Thank you, that was enlightening and told me I could sit and didn't call me a poor fish.

Then the priest drank the wine and another two popped biscuits into open mouths in the front row. Okay, I thought, bread and wine, same thing done differently until I heard him calling it *the blood* and *the body of Christ* and now he was drinking it and putting the round thing in his mouth which means ... OH MY GOD.

With all eyes focused on the front I slipped out. And there, all along Queens Street, mocking me, was everything I'd locked up in my room and all it took was twenty minutes. I started crossing to get away and who did I see turning into Queens Street if not Silman, the man who laid my father in his grave? Had he seen me shoot out of the Cathedral? I turned to give him my back and bent to tie my laces which were fine, hoping he'd go by.

Hello Adam, he said, why were you coming out from that place?

Doing research, I said. Love versus Duty.

Like a football match? Who's winning?

It's a draw, I said and he said to give his love to my family.

I ordered a coffee, took an oily Chinese sponge cake from under a mosquito net and sat at the back in Luna Café. I ate the cake, downed the coffee, asked for another with extra condensed milk and one more cake. If I was going to have heartburn, it better be good.

I peeled off the wrapper, laid it on top of the previous one and ate the cake in two bites. No way would I convert. That extra spoon of condensed milk was overdoing it. I ordered a black coffee and a third cake. Penelope would have to.

Another coffee and another cake. The waiter piled the saucers, folded the wrappers, put them on the top and took away the cups. Not easy, but not impossible. My ma would teach her. The heartburn was becoming painful. How would I ask her? Belching made it worse. What would she say? I called the waiter. Okay, why does either? Why can't both live as neither, nor? I could. The waiter counted saucers and wrappers. Would she?

I paid and rubbed my chest all the way home.

Ma, I said two days later, I met a girl and she wants to meet you.

That's nice. When?

Sunday.

She counted on her fingers. Four days. Fine. Who is she?

You don't know her.

Not from the *mahallah*?

Elsewhere.

And where did you meet her, may I ask?

At a dance.

Am I not entitled to proper answers? When a son brings a girl to see his mother he usually says how beautiful she is, how intelligent, how special or she already knows her because her son's been walking with her for months. Am I not right? How shall I greet her? Nice dinner, something special? Or tea and sandwiches and maybe a nice cake from Polar Café? I can bring out the new tea set and make proper tea with paper napkins. I don't want to look empty-handed.

You didn't make a fuss for my brothers.

I need to make a fuss for *mahallah* girls? I played in the streets with their mothers. You said your friend is from elsewhere. I don't want her to think we're *orang kampong* who don't know how to behave. So what's her name?

She'll tell you.

Even that you won't tell me? Okay, can I ask another question? I didn't reply. Do you love her?

Yes.

Do you want to marry her?

Don't know.

Is that why you were sitting till the early hours? I didn't reply. Is there something I should know? I didn't reply. Something you don't want to tell me?

I want you to meet her as I met her the first time.

Should the others meet her also?

280

No. Certainly not Drama Ramah.

Your sister? Shall I send her off somewhere?

Judy's okay.

Ma, I said, this is Penelope.

What's your name? My ma brought her ear close.

Penelope.

It's a beautiful name, my ma said, but I don't think I can say it to sound right.

You can call me Penny, Mrs Messiah.

That's easier. Like penny for your thoughts? In school, Sister Solace taught us to say, I need to spend a penny when we wanted to go to the lavatory.

Ma.

That's what we learnt in school, she said to Penelope. Did I say something wrong?

No, Mrs Messiah. Penelope took my ma's hands. Take no notice of him.

It's not as though he has to teach me manners, my ma said. I went to Convent of the Holy Infant Jesus where teachers were nuns and very strict. If you weren't sitting with your back straight as a rod they came from behind and hit you with a ruler.

I too went to a convent school, Penelope said.

See, my ma said to me. You know nothing. Penny and me went to the same school.

I went to school in Penang.

Penang, my ma said with a sparkle. So that's why he wouldn't tell me. Lovely place. I've never been. This son of mine, she said and turned her back on me. Come dear, we'll sit inside and I'll turn on the fan which Adam bought after his father died. We'll have tea and I'll show you what else he bought to make my life more enjoyable.

Judy came in wobbling a laden tray. Please Ma make space before I drop everything. She put down the tray, looked at Penelope, turned to me and said, Why have you been hiding her from us? If I had a boyfriend so good looking I'd show him to the world. Maybe you don't think you're good enough. By the way, she said to Penelope, my name is Judy.

Hello Judy, I'm Penny, and from then on Judy didn't take her eyes off Penelope or stop asking her questions or telling her about herself, talking even as she blew to cool the top of her tea until my ma said to her, You're not the only one here. Let us also say a few words now and again and anyway the teapot is empty. Put a few more leaves this time. Also please bring more milk from the fridge and Penny, I want you to remind me to show you the fridge Adam bought for me so I don't have to go to market every day.

Penelope looked at me as if to say, you're such a goody-two-shoes, then turned away and said to my ma, The sandwiches are lovely, Mrs Messiah, and Judy said, I made them all by myself with my own hands and Ma made me cut off the crusts because it seems it's not polite as if someone with false teeth was coming, at which point my ma said, Why are you still here? It's time to cut the cake. Penny you have the cherry before Adam takes it.

You can have it, Penelope said to me and put her hand on mine and I said nothing because nobody was talking to me and she said, Don't look so sad.

So I mumbled something when Judy returned with a full pot and filled all the cups.

They carried on talking to each other and laughing and Judy asked Penelope to stand and do a twirl. Her dress was so simple but so lovely with a gathered shirt, pink with thin black stripes cut on the cross meeting exactly in line and a broad black belt being so slim she could wear it, where did she have it made?

My mother sews all my dresses, Penelope said and Judy said she wished she had a mother who could sew like that and my ma said so did she, but what could she do, her mother wasn't good at anything except cooking and cleaning and looking after her children. We should all be happy with the mother God gave us because that was the way things were.

I didn't mean that, Judy said, but all the same it's a beautiful dress. It shows off your beautiful figure, she said to Penelope, such a lovely dress. Don't you think so, Ma?

My ma said, Yes, and Penelope said, Thank you, and I looked at my watch and said we'd have to leave to make the 6.30 show, if nobody minded I'd go and get dressed.

Nobody said they did or didn't and I left while Judy was asking what Penny thought about the new bob style girls were doing with their hair, the name was enough to put her off, she wasn't a boy, why should she look like one?

At the top of the stairs, dressed and combed and smelling of Old Spice, I could see Ramah standing, looking down at Penelope, sizing her up, asking questions more than talking to her and Jonah, sitting with a cup of tea, eating cake. I came down and looked hard at my ma. She turned her hands in her lap, looked up at the ceiling with the slightest shrug and half-closed her eyes. I looked at Judy and she looked away.

How nice to see you, I said. Both of you.

Jonah said, Me too, his mouth full of cake. Ramah, in maternity dress she'd started wearing the moment she knew she was pregnant for the world to know she was fertile, said, As I was saying, Adam, we decided spontaneously to go to the Rex you see, before my time comes and we can't go out with a baby in the house. So I said, seeing as it's early Jonah, why don't we make a surprise visit?

I'm sure you did, I said, and it seems you've met.

Yes, she said, and why didn't you tell us about Penny? She says she's a nurse at the KK and I said to her wouldn't it be nice if perchance I end up in her ward in three months, didn't I say that, Jonah? She stroked her belly and Jonah, the shoe to his shoehorn wife with two opinions to make up for the none he had, stopped chewing and echoed in his temple-gong voice, Yes, it's true what she said, why didn't you tell us?

Right then, I said. Come on Penelope or we'll be late.

Going already, Drama Ramah said. We've only just arrived.

It was a spontaneous, surprise visit, you said. Had I known you were coming …

Where are you going?

Cinema.

But it's too early, she said. That's why we're here which is what I said the moment we arrived and again to you, so why don't you sit down a minute? Jonah move a bit, make room for your brother who tells us nothing.

I'd like to get good seats, I said covering my shirt pocket so they didn't show, and I haven't got the tickets. Thanks for tea, Ma, I said. You too Judy, especially the sandwiches without crust, I added with a smile to answer her you-ungrateful-dog look.

My ma was alone. Before you say anything, she said as I walked in, I didn't invite them. Judy, by accident, told Ramah about making sandwiches and you can guess the rest.

I took off my shoes and socks and we sat in silence for a while before my ma said, She isn't Jewish. Pity. She'll make a good wife for a lucky man. Then she turned to face my father's photograph on the wall. Maybe now you have something you want to tell me.

I don't know where to start.

At the beginning as your father used to say.

Let's say it was a Friday and Pa took me to synagogue.

Your father went to synagogue every Friday of his life. Even when it was difficult to walk he somehow managed until to come down the stairs would have killed him. So? I didn't answer. Adam, look at me and tell me why you won't say what's in your heart.

My head's the problem.

You want to marry her? I didn't answer. Talk to me as if you are talking to your father.

I don't know what I would have said to him but I know what he'd have said to me.

He would go out of his mind, she said. He would give you reasons from one to a hundred why you mustn't and if you said anything, he'd say, Let me finish first. I'm not your father. Our parents arranged our lives and we did as we were told. It was bad because we had no choice but it was good because we believed they were doing what was best for us and sometimes love came with the years. Nowadays love comes first. You must do what your heart tells you and your head will follow.

Is that what you'd do?

I'm not twenty years old in this kind of world. I can't think the way you think. But if you're asking how I feel, I'll tell you I'm not happy but it won't break my heart. Sure I want my grandchildren same as me and if their mother isn't Jewish they aren't Jewish. But like they say, time heals all wounds. I will learn to love them.

That doesn't make it easier, I said looking directly at her.

Will it be easier if I lie? I didn't answer. Will she convert? She leant forward. Others have. Do we not see them in synagogue wearing a Magen David twice the size of ours to prove they are Jews?

I will not ask her.

I'll speak to her if you wish. Woman to woman, make her understand. But Catholics are like us, they don't change.

38

Does food from such big kitchens taste better, my ma asked, turning an old LIFE magazine toward Judy. So many drawers and cupboards and a cooker the size of a yellow cab?

Let's see, Judy said when Ramah walked in through the open door leading Jonah, Joshua and his wife Yona, on an urgent matter and without exchanging greetings, she elbowed her husband, Go on, Jonah, you have something to say.

Thumbs in his pockets, cigarette twitching at his lips, he tried to tell me, before the words jammed upstream, that Ramah was saying and Joshua was thinking and Yona and Papa, yes that's right also Papa, what'll he say if he knew, have you thought?

Please sit, I said, all of you, but Jonah, trying again, said, No, really, they are asking, when Ramah, still standing, pushed him into a chair. Against my better judgement, she said, slicing the air. I said so, didn't I? First I want to tell you, her rhinestone spectacles swerved to glare at me, it's not a matter of religion, before going on to God's testimony, lifeblood of the nation, abnegation of heritage, by which time, I swear, the rhinestones were blaming me, personally, for the six million.

Is that the urgent matter?

Not yet, the rhinestones replied and went on to tell me about the sacrifices our people made to remain a nation why was I trying to end it with mixed-blood children. If Jewish girls were good enough for my brothers who the hell was I, which got me about to speak when up went her hand about five thousand years of history dissipating, am I not right?

Joshua said, Sure thing, and because Ramah was staring at him so hard, he added to Jonah, What d'you say? She has a point, no? and Jonah took a long draw on his cigarette.

Can I say something, I said but Ramah held out both hands. Let me finish, she said. It was clear to all four of us yesterday ...

Joshua and Yona weren't here, I said.

That's irrelevant. You being youngest should follow your brothers' examples and do nothing to ruin your life.

Thank you. I think I can look after myself.

You see, she said to the others, I always said he was ungrateful. I wasn't getting drawn into this. You see, she said, silence is consent. And I may as well tell you, if you think she's beautiful, she isn't. There are girls in our community ten times more beautiful.

This, I could not resist.

Us for a start, her finger wagging back and forward between Yona and herself, then, as an afterthought, pointing at Judy, when my ma got up saying she'd fetch a jug of ice water. We should all calm down and Ramah should sit and not get excited in her condition, let's leave things in the hands of God.

Be your own man, I said to myself. Nobody's going to get you down, especially not when your body's remembering the night in the empty house. After a tempest, currents settle back into old channels until winds whip them up and right now a storm was gathering.

I went to look for the house that possessed our virginities, found it built and locked with a Sikh *jaga* on his charpoy across the door. The owners weren't moving in until the *Tong Shu* day for good luck but if I wanted a look-see he had a key. I asked if there were other houses under construction and he said he was guarding two. People were having parties and leaving rubber skins.

There were few hotels in those days, fewer for that purpose, but when a body bangs its head against a wall, a fellow can't sit still. I made another list.

<u>Danger</u>: Penelope will be recognised.
<u>Solution</u>: Dark glasses and scarf to hide her red hair.
<u>Danger</u>: Do they change sheets after each customer?
<u>Solution</u>: Kraft paper.
<u>Danger</u>: Safe period?
<u>Solution</u>: Mackintosh. Check the rain stays in.

Minimum one hour, said the girl in the small Strand Hotel in Bencoolen Street. My beret and dark glasses hadn't fooled her. Extra per hour. Pay before stay. How long?

What's usual?

Two hours … Fine, I said … because men want to look like heroes but if it's your first time … I was about to say I did this twice a week … three hours safer in case of misfiring.

Do I need to book?

NO SWEAT – ROOM TO LET, she said. Come when you have the urge.

I paid for two hours in the name of Abu Sayeed, the Barber of Basra who threatened my father's life and without whom none of this would have happened, took the key, fetched Penelope in her disguise, hurried down a long corridor, dived into the room, locked the door, jammed the chair under the handle, drew the curtains and switched on the light.

We were trembling.

There was a double bed, side table with drawer half open, bin and washbasin, no bathroom. In the drawer I found a small square foil pack *With the Compliments of Strand Hotel*, shut the drawer and searched the walls and ceiling for peepholes. The bed sheet wasn't warm thank God, but crumpled and the pillow had a dent. I threw it onto the chair, pulled the sheet tight, laid the Kraft paper, doubled over, switched off the light and ticked off the checklist in my head.

You okay, I said.

I'm always fine with you.

Then kiss me and let me know how fine you really are.

Even if, like me, she was on edge with sneaking and ill at ease not just with the grubby room but having to come to a place like this, she didn't show it. She kissed me and I kissed her until we were naked, standing and looking at each other with wet, dreamy eyes.

My God how that Kraft paper crackled.

I was climbing to the first plateau when Penelope started giggling.

What's the matter, I said slipping off the edge.

That paper of yours.

It'll soften soon and stop complaining.

I think it's laughing, she said.

None of my preparations, D & S list, beret, scarf, dark glasses and false name had imagined comical paper. I laughed.

This won't do, I said and moved about on the bed slowly and gently trying to find a tempo to suit the paper. Okay, I said to myself, it doesn't laugh when I don't rush and started up again, travelling smoothly with the paper singing in tune. Nothing to stop me now, I thought and raced ahead when suddenly, as if it had a critical speed, the song turned into a cackle. The harder I tried the louder it got until that was all we heard. She giggled, I laughed, admitted defeat, rolled off and lay beside her. I have to get it right, I said. Maybe third time lucky.

She turned on her side and looked at me with a mischievous grin. Let's forget about the paper, she said and climbed over me. I promise I won't laugh.

39

A couple of days later we watched Leslie Howard scramble up to Moira Shearer's balcony,

> *for stony walls cannot hold love out*
> *and what love can do, I too will do,*

which sent sparks off the black and white screen. Okay, it was Romeo and Juliet and not what I could say to Penelope but wouldn't it be a miracle if I did?

Did my brothers court their wives? Ramah would've done the talking. And Joshua? Maybe he sang Malay songs and said, Sure thing. Simon had poems for every occasion tucked into the corners of his crowded room but he was a million miles away. That's it! Thinking of him recalled his father getting beaten up in camp which reminded me of the other war casualty, Thomas Evans, my English teacher.

I drove up the hill and there he was outside the Principal's office feeding crumbs to sparrows all over him, head, shoulders and pecking in his hands. I stopped, opened the door and back came my old fears of talking to teachers. Would he think me crazy? I was about to turn round and go down the hill when the school bell rang and boys ejected from everywhere. I stayed in the car until they thinned out, saw him in my rear view mirror limping towards me and got out.

Sir, I'm Adam Messiah. I put out my hand.

A name not easily forgotten. He shook my hand and I swear I heard my bones crack. Then he started looking at me the way he did those years ago and before I knew it my chin was between his finger and thumb turning my head to view my profile. Hmmmm, he said and let my face go. Have you come to see someone?

You sir.

What can I do for you, Messiah?

I'm in love, sir. Those very words, I swear. He crossed his arms. Words, sir, I said to stop his eyes telling me I was mad. I need words.

How singular. Old boys come to me, time and again, but never for words.

You attended an Old Boys' Annual Dinner. I spoke fast hoping he'd forget how the conversation started. Next day, in class, you told us that none of them had anything to say. So you gave us a lesson on How to Make Small Talk. In five minutes, you said, you can tell if you want to meet the person you're talking to again, become acquaintances, friends, or lovers. I should have paid more attention.

It seems you did. I assume you want to get beyond acquaintances and friends.

Yes sir.

I wonder how the Ministry of Education would respond if I suggested adding that to the National School Curriculum. Ostrich heads. Never mind. Which play did you do?

Macbeth.

That's all we do, Macbeth, Julius Caesar, Hamlet. Troubled men. Nothing for life. Romeo and Juliet would be better suited but the powers that be, to this day, think it is more than young men's loins can withstand. Thus prudence leaves it off the syllabus. I take it it's a girl you are in love with. One never knows these days.

A very beautiful girl, sir.

Nothing woos a woman like poetry, except, possibly, a diamond ring, he said and marched me to his house.

At the door a short fat Chinese lady greeted him. Why so late, Thomas?

This is Messiah, he said, a former student with a rare predicament. Won't be a minute, Chicken. Come along, he said as I followed him, that's my wife, Annie, and pulled out a book, slim thank God, *Love Poems, Spencer to Tennyson.* That should do. I'd like it back when you've won your beloved's heart.

Thank you sir, I said and about to take off when his vice of a hand gripped my arm.

It's good to be in love, he said.

Yes sir. Except I don't know what to say and how to say it.

You don't need a book for that. Tell her what you feel. Not small talk. That's for people who don't expect to meet again. In conversation we trade feelings. Is she Jewish?

No.

Shouldn't matter. Jesus was in love and I don't mean with humanity. Whatever we put out about him, he was human and would've found it in his heart to love a woman. Implicit in God's mandate to go forth and multiply, don't you think? Is she light skinned?

Darker than me. Why do you ask, sir?

Jesus in Love. I would paint it. Watercolour. No. Charcoal. It will be splendid. Jesus looking lovingly at a woman. Her hair?

Red, sir.

Not colour, texture.

Thicker and curlier than mine.

He took two steps back. There, on that couch. Jesus sitting this side, she, the other side, facing him and looking into the distance behind. Would you consider it?

Must I grow a beard?

No. Jesus got his in imitation of a Roman god. What's her name?

Penelope.

Wife of Odysseus. A loyal woman who waited twenty years and would have waited all her life for the man she loved to return. Would you?

Wait twenty years, sir?

Consider posing, and when I didn't answer immediately, he added, clad of course. We could do it here, in this room, hang a few drapes. Annie is good with that. She helps me see my finished work before I start. Chinese art, in one form or another, goes back at least seven millennia. They have a keen eye for form. Their compositions possess a harmony that strives less to convey reality than to impart awareness of inner life and wholeness.

He was about to move furniture around when Annie came in from the kitchen. Hully up Thomas, food alleady cole.

Sorry, Chicken, I'll be right there.

I dashed out, said goodbye, thank you very much, I'll be back soon, and bolted.

One drove me mad. It had no misspellings like those in school that got us wondering why they taught such stuff when most of us couldn't spell proper English. I learned it by heart, said it to my mirror trying to be as stylish as Evans in his well-brought-up accent and was still saying it when I picked her up at Clifford Pier and took her to our tree on Changi beach. She sat on the sand and pulled her skirt close around her and I kneeled by her side, took her hands, looked into her eyes and, too nervous to smile, said:

> *Drink to me only with thine eyes,*
> *And I will pledge with mine*

and she never took her eyes off me as if the words were mine until, when I got to the end,

> *Since when it grows, and smells, I swear,*
> *Not of itself but thee!*

she pulled me into her arms and smothered me with more kisses than all the kisses we'd ever kissed, her hands clutching my hair in bunches and there I was, in the middle of it all, blessing Tommy Evans after which she made me say it again.

No, she said, on your knees and look deep into my eyes.

Drink to me only…

Slowly. I want to hear every word.

Drink to me only…

Hug me so I can feel you.

Drink to me only…

until, when to kiss any more would mean to consume each other, we leaned against our tree, faced the rising sea, looked at the low large moon and she said, Who are you, Adam?

A Jew from Canaan.

What are you doing in my life?

The same I hope as you're doing in mine, I said and turned onto my knees to face her. Now tell me Miss Penelope Robinson, who are you?

A girl from Penang.

And how did she come into my life?

You asked her to dance and held her so close she felt something she'd never felt before. Now she must stop loving you or she'll never be able to let you go.

I could've said a thousand things but hadn't learned a poem about eternal love so I tried to trade my feelings and still the words didn't come until eventually I said, I will love you forever, and she said, Forever's a long time, and I said, That's how long I will love you.

Thomas Evans, my old schoolteacher, wants to do a painting of us, I said as she scooped the cherry off my ice cream and her eyebrows slanted to say, Why? so I told her how I told him she was very beautiful and he thought I looked like Jesus and while she was switching her empty Peach Melba for my untouched Knickerbocker Glory, her eyebrows demanded, What else? You're always telling half stories tell me this one from the beginning.

We were at the Cold Storage Creameries, the only air-conditioned café in those days, and I told her about how he waylaid me in school wanting to paint Jesus Contending with the Elders all the way to my recent visit leaving out borrowing the book. Neither of us talked religion after our first date and with my father never far from my elbow and a sister-in-law the likes of Drama Ramah, I wasn't going to mention it until I had to talk or die.

I tried to explain it was only a painting of Jesus and a woman which got her asking which woman which got me tongue-tied about which Mary, since there were three and all the while her spoon was reminding me it was a sin to tell a lie. Thomas Evans is solid Christian, I told her, top to toe, lay minister, time to time in the cathedral, the big one with bells you hear all over town from the white steeple not far from one you go to yourself once a week. If he does all that he wouldn't be blaspheming, I said, would he?

If it's not Mary Magdalene, she said finishing off my ice cream, it's fine.

You made me go through hell and swear on my life and you had no objections?

She dabbed the sweat off my face, smiled and dropped her spoon into my empty glass.

The following Sunday I parked by the school bell and as we walked to the bungalow I said, Now remember, he calls his wife Chicken. Don't even smile.

I knocked on the door.

Good afternoon, Mrs Evans. I'd like you to meet Penelope. Penelope, this is Mrs Evans.

I'm pleased to meet you Mrs ... Penelope turned to me shaping her lips into Ch.

Evans, I said. I swear for the angel I thought she was, she gave the devil room and board in a place behind her eyes which sharpened each time he was about to pounce.

Thank you for having us over, Mrs Evans, she said and gave her a bunch of daisies.

Tank you. So solly, Tommy taking shower. Come si dow I'll get dlinks. Tommy has Chinese tea this time of day.

That'll be fine, I said.

Me too, Penelope said, poking her tongue at me.

Mrs Evans went to the kitchen and I stood wondering how my old English teacher got himself married to someone who barely spoke his language. Everything in the room was Chinese. Had he also become one? Penelope was looking at his watercolours and called me over when a bolt slipped and in he came in a towel, bare on top, hair dripping, singing,

> *I looked over Jordan, and what did I see*
> *Coming for to carry me home ...*

in a bass down to the floor.

Oh, he said and stopped. Whoever designed this house didn't live in it.

I wasn't sure if it was polite to shake hands with someone half naked and barefoot, so I said, This is Penelope, sir.

She turned around at the paintings and he stared hard.

No, he said, you were the temptress. I never cared for blaming the serpent.

He disappeared through one door as his wife came in through another with a tray. Penelope helped her serve while I tried a bit of chitchat to keep things going until he returned in shorts, singlet and flip-flops, hair, eyebrows and moustache combed.

Chicken, he said after his wife took away the cushions and put the finishing touches to the curtains, you've done it again, a perfect composition. It breathes the end of paradise and the beginning of life on earth. Penelope, take your tea and sit there. Look into the far distance knowing what you have done but do not regret. Adam, sit here. Look at Penelope, your eyes telling her that what she'd done was human and right.

I don't understand, sir, I said and went to sit where he pointed.

We are not doing Jesus in Love. You are Adam as Penelope assuredly is Eve, the young lovers who have to cope with the earth God, in His infinite wisdom, gave them. Bewildered by expulsion, they sit outside a shelter Adam has built. They have stopped blaming each other and Adam, having found his courage, has placed it squarely on God.

He moved fast limping around, clipping paper to his easel, wetting it and while it dried under the fan, mixed colours talking all the while. It was not an apple, he said. The only apple in the Old Testament is in a Song of Solomon. More likely a painter found an apple with rosy cheeks, put it in Eve's hand and filled his picture with all things bright and beautiful, all creatures great and small and we believed him. I have overruled myself. Watercolour will take a little longer, he said turning on one light, switching off another and loading a brush. Let us paint.

He talked much as he did in school, unravelling thoughts more than teaching, hoping bits would sink into our heads. Had he been born with a Chinese hand, he said, he'd have painted in the Chinese manner, submitting everything to patterns of nature, suggesting, never imitating, so that even their calligraphy is sublime, didn't I think so?

Yes sir, I said turning to look at him.

Speak without moving, he said. If that is too difficult do

not answer. My questions are rhetorical. As a former student you are bound to agree with anything I say no matter how facile. Do you know anything about Chinese art?

No sir.

Good. You didn't turn your head. They don't paint nudes, violence, martyrdom or death. It would be revealing to assemble in one place all the art in the world on the crucified Christ just to discover how much space it takes. Town and village crucifixes, church and personal effigies, paraphernalia hallowed or otherwise divine, would jostle for every square inch of this island. Paintings would cover every billboard leaving a multitude unhung.

By now he was painting, changing brushes, squeezing tubes, looking at us around and over his easel, two brushes tight between his fingers holding the palette, one locked between his teeth and one he used as if splashing paint on a wall. He dropped the brush from his teeth into a pot of water. Chinese art, he said, is noble and inspiring. Portraits show viewers the character of good men and bad men as models and cautions. A man on a cross would be either, neither or both.

His wife came in with a pot of tea, filled his cup and left.

If Jesus had been Chinese, would we have had Christianity? What do you think, Messiah? Chicken, he called, I need a fresh bowl of water, please. Then Jews would not have been persecuted and who would dare take it out on the Chinese? If they urinate into the sea, all at once, they'll drown the British Isles. A tiny smile crept into Penelope's eyes and curled the edges of her lips when he suddenly exploded. No, he said, this is wrong. Love is happy. Hopeless love more so. Adam and Eve, Rama and Sita, any number of Greeks and Romans, Pyramus and Thisbe, Romeo and Juliet. So I ask you Penelope, you too Adam, please look at each other and disregard whatever befell you before. I want to capture a moment of bliss. Eve, drape your hair over your right shoulder and give me your barest profile. Your eyes must say it all. Adam, raise your rebellious Semitic nose an inch.

Penelope turned to face me and in her eyes I saw a yearning for forbidden fruit, I swear, apple or not. But I'd raised my nose too high so he turned my head down and to the side where I could see the painting in a mirror behind him when his wife came in with a bowl of clean water. Thank you, he said washing out his brushes. Who are the great lovers of Chinese literature?

Many love stollies, she said, few lovers. Chinese care more about life and filling stomach than falling in love.

Who are China's great heroes, then?

Gods and monkeys, she said. Not men.

That puts an end to that, he said.

You changed positions, Tommy, she said. Harmony out of balance. She rolled a pot of bamboo beside me and placed a pair of mandarin ducks between Penelope's feet and mine. Ducks mean loyalty, husband and wife. Good omen for lovers.

Thank you, he said. No one, so far as I am aware, has painted a bamboo backdrop to Paradise. In Chinese art it suggests the scholarly spirit, bendable by circumstance, never broken. For us it will signify love forfeited by decree yet holding fast.

Chinese tea has a flushing effect. As we were returning to our places I said, Sir, I was telling Penelope that you are a lay preacher in Saint Andrews Cathedral.

Was, he said. My clarifications, I called them, dissensions they called them, infra dig either way, caused my departure which I did with those who would listen. Let us paint.

I must have started something. Picking up his brush, he went on about meeting in homes or the open air, no different from the Early Christians. His sermon that morning was about conversion, he said holding up a brush with yellow paint. Could we imagine Spanish priests in the jungle telling Indians that once upon a time a Jew lived in a Roman colony called Judea, a place they'd never heard of, who was crucified so that they, the Indians, would have eternal life? How would they have responded, he wanted to know, before they were cooked at a stake to resolve their disbelief? Then reeking of burnt flesh, dusting ashes off their cassocks, the priests would count the souls they'd saved and proceed to dinner.

What would you say, Messiah, he asked painting long up and down sweeps and in the mirror I saw bamboo growing behind my head.

I frowned to make out I was thinking when, thank God, he carried on. Now I ask you, is conversion to save souls or gain congregants?

Was this another question? He was looking at me then the painting then me again so I said, Well … Sir … and he said, I would not suggest it to anyone. Not even my dear wife. Annie remains Buddhist. If she cannot accept a different doctrine, how will a few drops of water persuade her? What do you think Messiah?

This time he stopped and in the mirror I saw his brush waiting. He was looking hard at me. I was back in school and he was demanding an answer.

I don't understand sir, I started to say but he wasn't going to wait. Belief is not to understand, he said, it is to feel. The cognitive brain will certainly reject it. It is acceptable only in that place where emotions stir, love and joy and gladness and gratitude for life on earth sprout and thrive.

That, I think, is how he taught us in school at a time after the war, when textbooks were scarce. He made up his lessons from his experiences, what he did, whom he spoke to the day before of even on his way to class.

To call myself Christian, he said, classifies me. I cease to be individual. To follow the precepts obliges me to love Christianity, even its inconsistencies. I love Christ not as the Son of God, which he couldn't have been without Joseph being cuckold, God lecher and Mary wanton to be stoned to death as contemporary law prescribed, but as a man, the man of the Gospels.

I shifted my eyes to look at Penelope. Her face gave away nothing.

I love good men. And women of course. I love my wife for her tolerance and kindness. She is more patient with me than I am with myself. Who do you love, Penelope?

My parents.

Who else?

Jesus.

Man or god?

I didn't know there was a difference, Mr Evans.

Then you must persevere in that belief. Consummatum est, he said and dropped his brushes into the water pot. Penelope shook as if a shiver had gone through her, turned and looked at him. You may rise and stretch, he said.

The painting was nothing I could have imagined. Only someone like Tommy the Teacher would stop, quarrel with himself and break the rules. Adam and Eve, with our faces and their clothes, were telling each other they'd done nothing wrong.

I have enough to finish it, he said. Then it will be framed. I will hang it there.

He pointed at a space on the wall facing the entrance door. I think he liked it too.

See, Annie said, Tommy painted ducks hiding in bamboo, heads outside. Good sign.

Did he offend you, I said as we turned down into Upper Serangoon Road.

No, she said. It wasn't a one word No as if she didn't want to talk about it. It was a soft No, a gentle No. A No that said, No, I wasn't offended, why would you think that? He's not the kind of man to give offence. It's the way he speaks.

You seemed startled when he said something in Latin.

Consummatum est?

That's the one.

The last words Jesus said on the cross.

Did that upset you?

No. It was the same kind of No, silky and quiet to say she was still thinking about it.

What does it mean?

It is finished.

What is finished?

The painting, silly.

40

Was it a sign? I know what my father would've said but what would Simon say if I told him about Tommy Evans, who also taught him in school, saying consummatum est? But where was he if not piling one degree upon another as if philosophy answers all our questions? I wasn't thinking about that the next day as I took her to the train station to visit her parents in Penang for Christmas. I gave her a bumper pack of Stanley Assorted Stamps seeing as how her father was a collector and an embroidery set for her mother with a little speech about a gift from someone so in love with their daughter he'll go mad these seven days without her. As she stepped onto the train I gave her a small box and when she got to her seat by the window and opened it, the joy in her face, seeing the black pearl earrings and matching pendant, carried me through the week. But it was not only empty, it crept like a month going uphill on crutches until I stood at the station again for the train bringing her back to me carefree as a kite in a breeze, full of happy tales about parents and neighbours treating her like visiting royalty, everyone crying when she left.

Then New Year's Eve, she, me, my sister and a table of good friends celebrated at the Seaview Hotel dancing under the dome and I got a little drunk after which babies started appearing from the first day of the new year. For children to be born in the Year of the Dog, the most agreeable animal in the Chinese zodiac before the lazy boring Pig came along in February, couples had to plan well ahead and I suppose this was the tail end of the rush. Penelope was doing one-and-a-half shifts, days in a row, catching up on sleep, attending tutorials and what else that kept us apart until I was planning to march on the hospital when she called. Sister Lau, her guardian angel, had taken pity on her. She had Friday off. Let's meet after mass, 5.30, she said and I said, Thank you God.

I parked outside the synagogue, dived in to say a quick prayer for my father, washed hands and face to freshen up, walked to the Cathedral and stood across the road at 5.30 exactly. By six she hadn't come out. Most worshippers had left but as a few were chatting outside I thought she might be inside talking. I crossed to where I could see past the hibiscus bushes and through the open doors. She wasn't there. No worry, I told myself, she'll soon be out, you'll kiss her hand, crack a joke and laugh all the way to Food of the Orient Special at the Cockpit Hotel. The sun was taking its leave and the Cathedral, one of the earliest buildings on the island, looked like a benevolent old man blessing the natives.

I looked at my watch. 6.20. She's doing a combined Mass-Confession, making peace with God and easing her conscience in one visit. This may be sin-cleansing season like our Yom Kippur to bring our sin-gauges back to zero. Maybe there's a long queue. Oh God! The empty house. The hotel. Working ourselves up in the cinema, the car, on the beach.

No way. Father d'Souza was a nice young man, soft voice, very shy, she said, and she went to confession only because she promised her father and when I asked if she had a cut-off point, what not to tell, she told me to mind my own business. No really, I said, does it make a difference that I'm a Jew? and she said, I didn't promise my father I wouldn't fall in love with a Jew. Okay, I said, so how d'you cancel your sins? and she said she had to say six Hail Marys and not to do it again. Teach me how to say Hail Mary, I said, and I'll say three. If I share the crime I should share the punishment. She screwed up her nose, glared at me and walked away.

It was 6.30. The Cathedral was dark, grounds empty, stars turning off in batches, moon a sliver and clouding over, breeze brisk and me getting anxious. Maybe she wasn't inside and I was waiting on the 5-foot way like a chump. Maybe they changed her duty and she called but I was out all afternoon. Maybe I mistook the day. Maybe a hundred maybes that may be when we tell ourselves nothing's wrong and something inside is breaking down the doors to say, Stand by for bad news, so when it doesn't come, we breathe again.

Then I thought I'd venture in. Then I thought if there was a problem my presence might make it worse. Then I thought, just wait. I put my hands in my pockets, walked up and down and five minutes later she appeared clutching two parcels and my heart did a dance. I went through the gate, up the gravel path and, even in the dimness, could see moist points in her eyes. They were very still as if she hadn't seen me.

What's the matter, I said. She didn't reply, just kept walking in a terrible hurry to get away. You look miserable, I said getting up beside her. What's d'Souza said?

It wasn't d'Souza. Where's the car?

Synagogue.

She started to cross. I took her arm and steered her between honking cars.

Who was it, I asked when we reached the other side. She started running so I ran, opened the car door for her, got in and rolled down the windows.

Father Rozario.

Who's he? She wasn't looking at me. Penelope. Who's Rozario?

He knows me.

So does d'Souza.

Not the same way.

Well? She said nothing. Penelope, please. I took her hand.

He was from Penang, a family friend, her father's schoolmate. He visited when she was home for Christmas. Arrived last night on church business found d'Souza sick and stood in for him. Her eyes were beautiful but troubled and very sad. She was trembling. I squeezed her hands. Maybe you don't want to talk about it, I said.

The curtain was slightly open, his light was on and as she got on her knees she saw him. He thought she'd received her father's letter and had come to collect the presents her parents' sent her. She said she'd come to confess and with all the talking and confusion she told him about me. She bit her lip and closed her eyes sending two tears down her cheeks.

That's okay, I said, you tell Father d'Souza.

Father Rozario isn't Father d'Souza.

Okay, I said, he's a family friend. So what? She was silent. Did you say something you don't say to d'Souza?

No.

So where's the problem? She didn't reply. Okay, I said, you said something you didn't intend and went past your cut-off point.

No. He said it was fine if I loved you in the name of the Lord so I asked for absolution.

That's it then, you're done, right?

He said he knew I wouldn't do anything to disturb the repose of my soul and I'd always use my conscience to guide me so I told him about you.

What about me? She said nothing. For God's sake, what did you say about me?

That you're a Jew. She pulled her hands from mine and covered her mouth.

So what? D'Souza knows that.

He went off to bring her presents leaving her alone a long while, on purpose for sure, then told her how special her parents were, how much they loved her and how could she honour her duty to God if she married someone not Catholic? She had a duty to look into her soul. Was she doing the right thing? Was she not making difficulties for herself and for me, he said. As if he cared. The kind of questions that get under your skin till you don't know where to put your face and, now I think of it, no different from what my father used to do. Crafty swine. Him, not my father. Even so I couldn't see why she was so upset until it suddenly hit me.

Why didn't you tell them? Penelope?

I'm sorry, Adam. She was crying. I've done something terrible.

I reached out to put my arms around her when sharp cracks hit the car and not a moment later, as the Good Book says, the voice of the trumpet was exceeding loud.

Shema Yisrael. I said the first words that come to the lips of a frightened Jew, Hear O Israel, the Lord is God, the Lord is one and Penelope crossed herself.

Lightning lit the skies, thunder boomed, cars stopped and drains overflowed. This was the grandmother of all monsoons. I switched on the light. She was terrified.

God seemed to have a great sense of timing. It wasn't coincidence: D'Souza falls ill the first day in the year Penelope goes to confession, Rozario turns up and her father's letter is still in the post. Any moment now a bolt would strike my car, outside the synagogue at the start of the Sabbath, Penelope would be fine and I'd burn to a frazzle. I laughed.

What's so funny, she said.

I pulled her into my arms. I love you, I said wiping tear stains off her face. Your parents are good people. They'll understand when you tell them. They were young and in love. They'll forgive you. We aren't Romeo and Juliet. On the other hand, the priest was on their side. It'll be all right, Penelope, I promise. See? Even the rain's clearing. If I can get out from between these two bloody cars we'll be at the Cockpit by 7.30.

Please take me back, she said in a broken voice, her eyes wet and half closed.

We reached the entrance to the hospital and crept into the lane leading to the Home shrouded in silence.

Don't park, she said.

I stopped inside the porch, leaned across to open the door and she slipped out.

When will I see you, Penelope?

I'll call.

Don't keep me too long. Please. Let me call. I'll come for you. Tomorrow. Tonight. In an hour. We'll drive to the beach. The sea air will do you good. Me too. Please.

I need to be alone.

I got out and gave her the parcels. Our lips touched, she went up the stairs and I parked among the trees where I could see her standing in her dark room looking for me. I came out of the car, she closed the curtains and her lights came on. It started raining again. I put my hands round my mouth to call her then slipped them into my pockets and went to sit in the car hoping she'd look through the curtains, see me and come down.

Oh my God. What did she do with my presents for her parents? And the black pearls?

The light behind her curtains vanished and I drove away.

41

Sometimes I can't understand myself. For a start I could've phoned even although she said not to. I could've told her for the millionth time I loved her. For a whole week I did nothing. Friday afternoon the phone rang. I answered in a dry business voice. Adam, she whispered with a smile, I want to see you. Right now, I said, I'm on my way, but she said, No, she was on duty, off at one tomorrow, she'd meet me, tell her where. Adelphi, I said, three o'clock, I'll save a table. She said she may be a little late and I said I'd wait forever. Then she said she had something to tell me, it wouldn't take long. Take as long as you like, I said, my life belongs to you, trying to keep her talking, but no, she was on the ward and had to go.

Expectation keeps the earth turning. I sat there telling myself I was right not to call, she needed time to think, she'd cleared her conscience and overcome her guilt, even told herself she couldn't live without me. Rozario lost. I won. Her parents wanted to meet me. How long does that take? Adam, I wrote to my parents and they want to meet you. Four seconds. It's like biting on an aching tooth to remind yourself it still hurts.

I dropped a file into my briefcase as if the call was urgent business, mumbled to Dolly our telephonist, I won't be back, knowing full well she'd listened in and she winked.

Saturday came and the sun was scorching, not even a powder-puff cloud. My shirt stuck to my back and my trousers hugged my legs. I parked under the neem trees in Coleman Street, crossed, dived into Adelphi Air-conditioned

Hygienic Gents Hairdressers and fell asleep in his chair.

The Adelphi was half-brother to Raffles Hotel where Charlie Chaplin, Noel Coward and Somerset Maugham had slept and where the Singapore Sling was born at its famous Long Bar, both hotels holding on gracefully to dying colonial days. The Adelphi Tea Rooms were flanked with open windows and starched waiters. Low tables dressed in Irish linen, origami napkins, EPNS cutlery, hotel emblem on the crockery, all set for afternoon tea, a dollar cheaper than Raffles, in long lounging chairs under slow-turning ceiling fans.

I eased into a chair at the only table for two in the corner and watched the entrance as the place filled with locals now that the whites were fading into the background. I wasn't going to anticipate anything so I let my mind go blank when, beaming in a sunhat, she came through the door in a sleeveless bright yellow dress with long yellow ribbon sash.

I went to meet her, opened my mouth to say how lovely she looked, choked and coughed so much she had to pat my back and I had to hurry back to our table not to feel like a jellyfish left on the beach by the tide. She blew me a kiss as she sat and I told myself I'd coughed up all the bad influences and my world had come right again.

Are you okay, she said then smiled a different kind of smile and I said to myself, Consummatum est. She's made peace with herself and there's no place for you in it.

You haven't heard a word I've said, she said.

Sorry. What did you say?

There's someone trying to attract your attention. She leaned her head toward a table halfway down the long room.

That's Old Man Siow, I said, with his wife and grandchildren.

I waved and smiled and he beckoned, pointing at two empty chairs at his table.

We have to sit with them, Adam, she said.

But you have something to say to me.

It can wait, she said picking up her purse and hat. I took my case, told the waiter to please bring our tea to another table with lemon slices for Penelope and as I introduced her, out came that smile of hers like sea spray bursting in sunshine. You're wrong, I told myself, it isn't finished.

Adam, Mrs Siow said, where have you been hiding this lovely girl? You never bring her to office parties. Are you afraid someone will steal her?

Sorry, I said. Penelope's a nurse and always on duty at the wrong time.

Which hospital?

Kandang Kerbau, Penelope said.

I know the chiefs of all the hospitals, Mrs Siow said. One way or another they benefit from our charity work. Listen to me, Adam, next time be sure to tell me and I'll get the whole day off for you Penelope.

Penelope thanked her saying how much she'd love to come and we sat there chatting and chewing sandwiches while the lounge brimmed with talk, laughter frothing at the top with the orchestra setting the tone for the afternoon. The Siow children tapped their feet enjoying the music when *La Cumparsita* brought Penelope to the edge of her chair.

Do you mind, she said to the Siows.

Please, Mrs Siow said. Bernie and I used to dance to this very piece when we were young. It'll bring good memories.

Penelope pulled me up. I took her in my arms, slid my leg between hers, brought her close and said, Now tell me.

I love you, she said.

And?

I will always love you.

Penelope, I said, digging my fingers into her back, why are you being cruel?

You always hurt the one you love, she sang in my ear. The one you shouldn't hurt at all.

I'm not, she said. I'm only trying to ease the pain.

Yours or mine?

Ours, she said and kissed my cheek.

The orchestra had packed and people were leaving. I looked at my watch, put on my honest face and said, I'm sorry but we're going to the movies.

Mrs Siow took Penelope's hand. Now remember, call me anytime you want a day off. Adam knows how to get me. Enjoy yourselves while you're young.

Penelope told me to meet her at the door and went toward the Ladies but didn't get that far. She stopped at the Florist and came back with a vanity case. I took it from her and as we crossed the road, shook it trying to work out the soft sounds.

I didn't see you come in with the case, I said putting it on the back seat.

I came earlier and left it with Consuela.

I reversed out. What's in it?

Are we going to the movies?

I stopped at the lights. Where would you like to go?

I want you.

The lights changed. I got into gear and turned into North Bridge Road.

We'll go to Changi.

That's not where I want you.

Not the Strand Hotel, I said, in disguise. Is that what the case is for? She didn't reply. And tomorrow? Are you on duty?

No.

We'll cross the Causeway, then. No one knows us there.

With evening traffic not yet in the streets we had a clear run and were far up Bukit Timah Road when I saw a small roadside shop and pulled over.

I've packed a spare toothbrush, she said.

Prevention is better than cure, I said.

I have that too. We're giving them to women after their second child.

We were in the *ulus* beyond municipal limits, street lights far behind, moon nowhere to be seen, stars too shy to shine and I was heading for the Causeway to spend the night with her and hadn't made a list.

Adam, she said. This must be our last.

I braked. The car screeched, swerved, struck the verge and stalled. I cut the lights and all went black around us. I said it sounded like a death sentence. She said I shouldn't take it like that. I said it was that damned priest. Until eight days ago everything was fine and would go on until we found a way which we had to, being too much in love not to, please don't let it be the last.

I started the engine and drove off.

I'll have to live last week all over again, she said. And you didn't call. All week.

I did. Many times. Each time I dialled I hung up before it rang. I didn't wish to, I said, I didn't wish to do what I don't know what I didn't wish to do.

That made it worse, she said. I thought you didn't care.

Impossible.

That's what it is, she said. Impossible. Father Rozario's right. I have a duty to others. Love is magical but life is more than that.

I'll marry you then, I said. She was silent. Penelope, answer me.

What was the question?

You're right, I said and pulled the car into a siding. I got out, walked round, opened her door, got on one knee on the road, took her hand and said, Miss Penelope Robinson, I love you. Will you marry me? It was neither a giggle nor a laugh. Please, I said. She smiled. You're not making sense, Miss Robinson.

You're so sweet and so silly. You're asking me to marry you for me, not for yourself. How will I say yes?

Okay then, I said, I'll show you it's for me.

I got into the car and drove away. If I kept going, I thought, we'd take the morning ferry to Penang. I'd talk to her parents and they'd understand.

Miss Penelope Robinson, I said, I love you, I want you and I need you. Will you marry me for me and only me?

She took a long deep breath. Would you convert?

My father would turn in his grave, I said. You could. Only men are circumcised.

Wouldn't your father turn in his grave?

I want to think it wasn't me but the Ford that crossed the Causeway, turned left, followed the coast, braved the hill to the Straits View Hotel and rolled to a stop by the porch instead of carrying on all the way to Penang. With Chinese New Year a week away and people gearing up, the grounds were awake with light and the hotel glowed like a bonfire.

I won't be long, I said, entered the crowded lobby tight with cigarette smoke and people intent on fun at any cost. Finding a room was as likely as meeting a Chinaman with blue eyes. I was about to leave when I spied a small reception tucked into the corner.

I need a double room for the night, I said to the young Malay over the racket.

Saturday night, sir, his friendly face replied. Booked up.

I put on a helpless face and told him my wife was

pregnant. We were on our way to Cameron Highlands before the baby arrived. We'd started late because my boss, a very wicked man, sure to go to hell when he died, made me clear my desk before leaving the office. His eyes told me I was getting through so I went on about our bags at the door when who should show up if not good friends? No option. We had to sit for tea and chat and, cut a long story short, we had a booking at Malacca Rest House but it was too far with my wife in her final month. She needed a bath and a bed and what would I do if the baby came in the car on the way? Would he please check his register again?

Well, there was a small room, not in the main hotel he was sorry to say, an old section left over from gone-by days, round the back.

I grabbed his hand to thank him even as he was telling me it wasn't up to par and, out of respect, had to mention there was no bath, only shower, while the WC, he was obliged to bring to my attention. I said fine, signed the register Mr and Mrs J J Judah, took the key, paid and left as he was wishing us a good holiday, Sir, especially for your wife and a happy childbirth. I dived into the phone booth to tell my ma not to wait up, dashed out as veranda lights came on at a short block behind the hotel.

The room, as he said, wasn't up to par. Cement floor with leftover lino in the centre. I put our cases on a table covered with cigarette scars and rings from sweating glasses. The bed had a thin kapok mattress on wooden planks, pillows overstuffed and hard. I opened front and back windows and set the table fan at maximum to clear the smell of damp.

Penelope came out and I went into the bathroom. We had a sunken toilet bowl, a roll of paper on a stool and the luxury of a flush. The shower rose was rusty, two Good Morning towels and a bigger one on nails by the washbasin. Back in the room I sat in a rickety chair and watched Penelope unpack her few things onto the bed, her back to me.

Let's go eat, I said. We haven't had a decent meal today. On second thoughts, I added, you'll have to stuff a pillow under your skirt. She turned and glared at me. I needed to sound desperate so I said you were pregnant. Final month. She didn't smile. They were full. I had to make up something or we'd be looking all night.

She walked over to the fan, turned it down and shut the front windows.

I don't want to go to the restaurant, she said.

She seemed lost in thought. Was it because we'd crossed into Malaya, closer to home than she'd ever been with me?

I'll get something, I said and made for the door. What d'you fancy?

Sandwiches and coffee. And two oranges.

Keep the door latched, I said. If anyone comes knocking, you're Mrs Judah.

Not Mrs Messiah?

I used my father's name. Jews do that. The first son takes his father's first name as his surname, I said, opening the door. I'm not the first son but I did it anyway and I think I'm talking too much so I'll just go and get some food before I say something stupid.

The tray was loaded so I kicked against the door. She was fresh and fragrant in a rose pink kimono barely halfway down her thighs. Sorry, they have no oranges, I said laying the tray on the table which I pulled away from the wall then wiped clean with a serviette, set the crockery and cutlery in the middle of the long sides, facing each other, taking my time and never did her eyes leave me.

My, she said when I finished, so neat. Everything so exactly in place.

Tidiness is next to godliness, I said, took off my shoes, pushed in my socks and laid them under the bed. Chitchat, at a time like this, can make a guy nervous so I went for a shower, came back and sat opposite her at the table, a wet towel over my lap, hoping she'd say something. She didn't. I bit into a sandwich. She took one and munched slowly.

Eventually, before I turned to stone, I said, Why are we here?

Because I didn't fancy the beach, she said.

You know what I mean.

Is it wrong to want you?

I've not seen you a whole week. For God's sake, Penelope, tell me. Did you go back to the cathedral? Did Rozario have another go? Did you write home? You saw me from your window, didn't you? Then your lights went out.

Only to make you go away. I couldn't bear to see you waiting in the rain.

Then what happened?

I went to sleep.

You don't want to tell me?

I will.

42

A cock, crowing like he ruled the world, woke us, naked, before dawn. I sprang out of bed, picked her up and we stood under the cool morning shower. The towel had dried in the night and I wiped her until it wouldn't take any more water then blew her body dry. We splashed powder over each other, dressed in yesterday's clothes, put our stuff in the car, spread the damp hotel towel over the back seat to dry, left the key in the door and went westward until we hit the coast and turned north toward Malacca.

This was unspoiled Malaya. Narrow roads winding through jungle overhung with a timeless peace nobody should disturb. Once we'd left what nature had planted we got into rubber and oil palm estates where trees in diagonals swing into perpendiculars the moment you turn your head to look. The early light made everything seem like an old watercolour and I hoped the sun would take its time. I took her hand, squeezed it and put it against my cheek and she rubbed my day-old beard, giggling as if to say now I know what you're like when you're not smelling of Old Spice.

We were well out of town and my Ford which usually had a seizure when it saw a hill climbed without complaint, turned a tight curve where the road widened then fell sharply to the sea on the left with the sky empty for a million miles to the horizon. I tooted the *Tiger Rag* and Penelope tapped it on her lap. I blew her a kiss, freewheeled downhill and pulled up. She took off her shoes, pushed them into my pockets and we ran to the water's edge.

I picked her up in my arms and said, I'll drop you in if you don't tell me.

I've already told you, she said. I love you.

Now tell me the rest from the moment you left me.

She said she couldn't talk up in the air so I carried her back, got a mat from the boot to sit in the shade of the car and that's where she told me all the things I should've asked long before. How much she loved her parents, how they cherished her, promises broken and anxieties now about consequences later. She told me about her father, how he took her, as a child, everywhere he went, talked to her endlessly and instilled in her everything she knew about her faith as if it was life itself. If she'd been born a boy he would've wanted him to be a priest. He cried, she said, when she left home to study nursing.

It was getting hot. I took off my shirt, rolled up my trousers, put her hat on her head and asked how she'd tell them? Would she write?

I wouldn't know how to write such a letter, she said. I'm going back.

When?

Tomorrow.

No, Penelope. Please. I'll help you write the letter. I swear.

Only for three days.

Why three days? What will you tell them you can't put in a letter?

Oh nothing much but better to say it than write about this boy she met at a dance in the Nurses Home and went out with just for the company. Nice chap, really. Full of fun. Me and my love wrapped up in nice chap, really. And how about the devil incarnate, had she seen Rozario? He'd told her to confess everything first to God to receive absolution, then everything again to her parents as an act of love.

Does everything mean everything?

My mother would die, she said.

Oh God. Her daughter ravished by a Jew.

And your father?

I think he loves me enough to forgive me, she said. I'll tell them everything I told Father Rozario which wasn't much and I don't have to tell God because he knows.

Miss Penelope Robinson, I said taking her face in my hands, when God made you He knew what He was doing. I kissed her forehead, kissed her nose and kissed her cheeks. You will see me when you come back, I said, not making it sound like a question.

What d'you think?

Of course. I want to see you, same as always.

It can't be. We can't be doing what we did last night.

Platonic from now on? I don't think I was taking her seriously enough and when she didn't answer, I said, In the first place Plato wasn't a Jew. Second place he preferred boys. Third place, I can't promise anything.

The wind changed, the light breeze off the water died away, all around was quiet and there was I telling myself that without the Devil's Deputy interfering we'd have found a way. I sighed. Whether from shame for the trouble I'd brought her or pity for myself or some of both I don't know but it made her grab my hair, turn my head and kiss me hard on the lips.

Women are tougher than men, I said and she kissed me again with all her mouth.

The sun was on the way to blistering, the sea dazzling and the shadow from the car no longer cool. I put my sunspecs over her eyes and we drove away with the windows down, catching the wind on our damp faces, the car chugging along the middle of the road, happy to be moving again.

How many times did we do it last night?

I wasn't counting, she said.

With all that loving and eating and drinking and loving again it must've been one, two, three, four, five, give me your other hand. If I have to stop I'll go mad.

You'll find another girl.

Impossible, I said. I love you enough to know I can never love so much again.

How much is that? In feet and inches? Or is it yards?

Don't tease.

Yes, she said, yes, and threw her arms around me and chewed my ear and the car zigzagged across the road so I edged and stopped and there, in the middle of the jungle, we were rousing each other, steering wheel and gear stick interfering and I was swearing so much she covered my mouth with her hand and I bit her fingers till she started laughing.

What're we going to do, she said when I gave her back her ribs.

You weren't serious about being our last.

My promise begins tomorrow, she said.

Let's go back. The room's ours till noon and the key's in the door.

The beach.

Where we were just now? In the sea, you mean?

On the beach.

I did a quick three-point, went looking for that parcel of beach, found a more secluded spot to squeeze into, laid the mat and the hotel towel and when I reversed out she was dropping her cross on the sand.

With my hand I indicated the bed I'd made but she pointed at where she stood and my Star of David fell in a heap over her cross.

43

I was talking a lot unsure if it was okay seeing as how I'd used up the forbidden fruit skins last night the way we'd been going but didn't mention it thinking she knew best how her body worked and when she said I was talking too much, we'd not had breakfast and she was parched, I pulled up at the first *kampong*.

I found a boy, offered him twice the going rate for a couple of coconuts each. He went off behind a hut and returned talking to a monkey perched on his shoulder.

Monkeys can count, I said just as the monkey looked down from a palm heavy with fruit as if to say, how many? The boy pulled on a long string, a coconut crashed then three more and the monkey scurried down to get his handful of peanuts.

There you are, I said, he told him *empat kelapa* and that's how many we got.

The boy was hacking them for us when she said, Now say *empat kelapa* and send the monkey up without the string and see what he does.

If you don't want the last coconut, I said, I'll have it.

Don't change the subject, she said. I know you better than that.

Which she did of course giving me tit for tat all the way to Malacca. I was talking the kind of nonsense people talk trying to hide their feelings, laughing when nothing's really funny until we entered the city and drove past the quaint old red buildings and churches. She said to park and we'd walk up to Saint John's Fort where she'd show me why the Portuguese, Dutch and British fought for years over Malacca.

We got to the top and as I looked out over the Straits for the first time in my life I said that in school I learned a lot about the history and geography of England but nothing about Malacca. How come a Penang girl knew so much? She said she was president of the History Society in school doing field research in the day with campfires and sing-alongs at night having great fun so I told her this was not the time to leave me when I was just getting to know her but she'd already taken off to an old cemetery beyond the Fort.

Saint Francis Xavier is buried in Malacca, she said when I caught up. Well kind of buried in St Paul's in the town but that's not what I want to show you. She pulled me along to a blackened old stone tilting so far it too seemed to want to die. The words were faint, covered in mould and I could just make out 1857 and below it PENELOPE ROBINSON aged 29, ROBERT aged 7, MARY aged 5, ARTHUR aged 4 months, each with a date in April and at the bottom, YOU ARE ALL I POSSESSED.

Isn't that sad, she said, all dead within a few days from a disease they knew nothing about. She half turned and must have seen tears starting in my eyes. Oh Adam, she said, that's just how I felt the first time I saw it. You're so sweet.

Is that ... I mean ...

I don't think so. I think I'm descended from James Robinson from Glasgow, an aide to Captain Francis Light, who leased Penang in 1786, from the Sultan of Kedah.

For sure?

No. But I found his grave in Northam Road Cemetery in Penang, close to Light's grave. Both died in 1794. James was only 31.

Did he have red hair?

He was Scottish.

Does your father have red hair?

Black as yours and his father too.

If it was James Robinson who left his calling card, I said, it has resurfaced after a century and a half. Isn't that unusual? How come you never told me?

You never asked.

I did. I asked where you got your red hair and you said, I hate you and bit my ear, I swear. We were on the beach …

… and you recited your poem and drove me mad …

… which is what you're doing to me right now Miss Penelope Robinson, President of the History Society. If it was the done thing in a cemetery …

… sure it is. Don't the spirits come up looking for love? I would. Wouldn't you?

How long have I known you? Nine months? Why have I never seen this side of you? Don't answer, I said. I think I know. Just show me what you'll do when you're a spirit.

You'll have to catch me first.

I'm hungry, I said.

Me too, she said. The Rest House has the best fish and chips anyone's ever eaten with green peas and tomato sauce. Our school had to fix it for us in the days locals weren't allowed in. We were looking into how colonisers and immigrants changed our food and the manager said his biggest problem was trying to make tropical fish taste like cod. I asked him why and he said he couldn't imagine but he gave us lunch for free.

It was big and busy, set in a garden near the town centre, one of a string of Rest Houses like watering holes for British District Officers, planters, miners, their wives and children. We sat at the far end of the open veranda and no sooner had our meal arrived than Penelope picked up the large wedge of lemon lying on her fish, took mine, and pressed them in quick succession between her teeth, puckered her face and closed her eyes.

An elderly Chinese lady at the next table smiled across and said, Funny how you do that. Our daughter Dewdrop does exactly what you just did. That's not her name but we've called her Dewdrop since the day she came to brighten our lives, isn't that so Pauly? She's the older one. We have twin daughters, don't you see, and two sons, but they're not twins. Can't see a piece of lemon without sucking it dry.

Oh yes, said her husband, as sure as the day is long and God loves little children. And what about Baby? Which by the by also isn't her name. Will you tell or will I?

Go on, his happy wife said, you tell.

He told us that Baby wouldn't get within a mile of anything sour, the strangest thing since they were twins, identical to the lobes of their ears and brought up at the same table. He could see Penelope had a passion for lemons and she said anything citrus which got him on to telling us that the first oranges came from China but now they came from Australia which is where they'd been just last year, hadn't they, the missus and him? P and O to Sydney, first class now Asians were allowed to rub shoulders with former masters. The world was changing he kept telling the missus, the young getting on a silver plate what they had to fight for, wasn't that the truth? Now his children had homes and cars, blessed with nine grandchildren and looking forward to the great-grand generation. Our Father which art in heaven, he said looking first at Penelope then at me, blessed be Thy name.

His missus called him The Orient Express, once he started he didn't stop, but all the same he was right, it was a fine country, land of opportunity. If they were younger they'd live there too, so big and so empty people needed binoculars to spy on neighbours. They'll welcome you with open arms, she said to us. And you're so pretty, isn't she Pauly?

Penelope's long eyelashes came together and I said, She is. She's the beautiful queen of my heart.

Isn't that the truth Pauly, the beautiful queen of his heart? Don't tell me, she said, I can see it. You're so much in love you must be. Don't you see Pauly, they're newlyweds.

Penelope's left hand slipped under the table.

Plain as the day is long and God loves little children, Pauly said draining the last of his Tiger Beer. The missus can spot young lovers seven leagues away. Honeymoon is it?

I smiled a commanding smile and Penelope looked away.

Next year will be our fiftieth. Golden as every year was golden. Don't you see, the lady said jangling a wrist full of bracelets. We're still in love after forty-nine years.

Fifty-two, Pauly said, counting the three I secretly courted you, too afraid to show my black face around your father's house.

Didn't approve, the missus whispered. Marry a Tamil and you'll have black bastards for children. Excuse my French, she said shielding her mouth with a plump jewelled hand. Telling me all the while to keep out of the sun, don't you see? I'm Chinese yellow like he was, Hainanese to his hind legs and he wanted Snow White for his daughter.

Each child is a different shade of brown, Pauly said, except the twins of course. They're sun-baked peas in a pod and who cares? We're all blood red beneath.

Take my advice, the woman said leaning over, resting her hand on our table and looking straight at Penelope, have lots of children. They bring joy. I would've had a dozen if it pleased God. Is he intelligent? Penelope nodded. The lady looked at me. Certainly no fool if he found you.

Penelope shyly took her fork in her right hand and picked at her food.

How thoughtless of us. We shouldn't be disturbing their meal.

Sorry, I didn't mean to, Penelope said and put down her fork.

Come Sweetness Itself, the old man said rising and taking his missus by her arm. We have waylaid these young people long enough. He extended his hand and winked at me. Proctor, Paul Proctor, formerly general practitioner, presently happily retired.

I stood. He was a small man with a professional handshake.

You must be visitors, he said. If you're here again drive past the airport, first left, laterite road. Can't miss it. Large as life itself and pink as candy floss. If we're not home the bearer will look after you till we return. And who have we had the pleasure of talking to, he asked, a huge smile lighting his face.

Jacobson, I replied, my hand still in his, Adam Jacobson and this is my wife Eva.

Adam and Eva, he said to his wife. Did you hear that Sweetness Itself, Adam and Eva? This marriage certainly was made in heaven.

Penelope dabbed her lips with her napkin.

After saying wonderful things about Penelope, some whispered by Sweetness Itself in her ear, they left, she with a walking stick in one hand hanging onto her husband with the other, he repeating at every table on the way out, Adam and Eva, can you beat that?

Why did you say that?

That you're my wife?

The Eva bit, but that too.

Because that's what I want.

Why don't you ask me, then? And Eva?

Can you imagine the next letter to their children?

They're nice people, she said. You didn't have to.

I didn't, I said. With all my heart I didn't. They're happy

and want to spread it. Now he can tell his friends, As sure as the day is long and God loves little children, I've met Adam and Eve. He'll wink and Sweetness Itself will laugh and all her bangles will rejoice. It's a gift, don't you know?

I hate you, J Adam Messiah.

At about three in the afternoon, when the earth can soak no more heat from the sun and starts giving it back, we turned homeward and only then did the penny well and truly drop.

Penelope, I said, it's going to hurt. It's hurting already. Can we keep it going a while, a few weeks, a month, give me a little time. Talk to your parents. Tell them about me, that I'm a decent fellow. I mean they can't hold against me an accident of birth.

She was silent for what seemed too long. I don't know if they've ever met a Jew, she said, then another long pause. How will they know, except what they've been told? I looked at her trying to make out if she meant all the things Jews are supposed to be when she said, All they know is that on the Day of Judgement Catholics will be saved and everyone else damned. That's what they were told, what they believe and that's what my father told me every time he came home from confession.

Do you believe that?

He's my father and I respect him. So would you if your father were alive.

I saw my father fanning himself. Did you ever see a horse mounting a cow?

But if he meets me, I said, if they meet me, they'll know it's a lie. I have as much right to heaven as they do. Come on Penelope, these aren't the dark ages. People don't think like that anymore. You don't.

I met you and don't remember anything before that.

Okay, I said, Okay. I thought she was letting her mind run ahead. Her parents might take it in good grace not suspecting their daughter had committed the unthinkable. Within three days I could work out a plan. All I needed was for her to call me when she returned. Please, I said, call me the moment you get back. Will you do that?

I'll call you, Adam.

Shall I call you?

In Penang? We don't have a phone.

Penelope, I turned to face her, look in my eyes and tell me you are coming back.

I have two more years to qualify. I have to come back.

The sun was far over in the west. We'd driven many miles in silence before I stopped in the porch of the Nurses Home. I got out and gave her her bag. She'd taken off her yellow sash and dropped it on the back seat. I reached in to give it to her, changed my mind and slipped it into my pocket. I did not say goodbye. When she'd gone up the stairs, I raced round and waited for her to come to her window.

She kissed her palm and blew the kiss to me.

44

On the fourth day I called the Nurses Home. She hadn't returned. I called twice, each of the next three days. Nobody could tell me where she was. Each of those days I wrote her a letter and in the last I asked her to marry me. Our approach to God may be along different paths but He will guide us and see us through. Priests are fools. They know nothing about love. Their heads are in the clouds looking for God but they'll never find Him because, knowing them for what they are, He hides. Marry me, I said, and we'll show them. I put each in an envelope, addressed it to Lorong Pasir, Penang, stuck the stamps, and put them in my wardrobe under my pyjamas. What would her parents say if letters arrived every day? And the postman? And the neighbours seeing him at their door? I'd give them to her when she returned, one each week. With two years to go time was on my side. I'd woo her like no woman has ever been wooed. How could she resist me?

Only once, on Saturday night, did I go out with Manasseh whose father circumcised me. We called him Manners but not because he had them. He lived in Niven Road with a family so large, his mother still breeding when his married sister started, they took a roll call before locking up for the night. He was going crazy in a house of talking bodies with babies everywhere you had to check before you sat. His sister Seemah was pregnant again, her husband Silas carrying on as if he owned the bloody place, please, would I take him for a spin before he went mad.

One thing led to the next and we ended up at the Satay Club in Beach Road. As we were crossing to the stalls, Hayoo the Horn shouted, Come, sit, kicked two stools as he pushed two dripping satay sticks into his mouth and rummaged in the satay man's box for a cucumber. He spat the tip between his shoes, shoved the rest into the hot sauce and crammed half of it into his mouth. Lucky you came now, he said chewing. Ten minutes and you'll be looking at naked sticks.

Flossie who was ashamed to say how long she'd been walking with him, his older brother Benjy who spoke so little people said he made up for the Horn and a girl I knew of rather than knew, pushed their stools into a bigger circle. I said a general hello and, as Manners was already sitting, sat on the stool next to her. Oh hello, I said, strange to see you here. I didn't think you were a member of the Club.

Her parents named her Hadassah, Hebrew for Esther. Apparently she didn't like either and when she discovered that Queen Esther got her name from the Persian word for star, she called herself Stella. That lasted until she changed it to Estelle. For all I knew she'd changed it again and I wasn't going to risk the wrong one.

Well, yes, she said pretending she wasn't there. I don't but Hughie, her name for the Horn, was over at our home and you know how persuasive he can be. Weren't you, she asked him, her look saying she wouldn't be seen dead in a place like this and he'd better back her up or God help him.

Yeh, yeh, he said licking gravy off his chin.

He works for my father now we've expanded, she said half turning to me.

Oh, I said.

Yes, she said with some pride. Paid a fortune in key money. Hughie knows the details.

Hayoo dragged three bare satay sticks out of his mouth and lined them up. X-otica, X-travaganza, X-celsior. All named by Ella. Bought out the Tin-Pan Man, lock, stock and barrel, sold the stock cheap, emptied the barrel and kept the lock. He laughed a spicy laugh and arranged his brimming belly more comfortably in his lap. I tell tourists, if they want cheaper go next door, but it's junk. Half stay and buy from me, the other half buy from her father and vice versa and all the money goes into the saucepot.

Don't you think that's terrible, she said to me with a lipstick-coated smile.

It's business, I said. Ella.

The satay-man picked a handful of fresh sticks off his grill, set them down for us and Ella took one. Can't be more than eighteen, I thought, and still trying to work out how to organize her new bumps. After her fourth satay in my presence, she dipped the fifth into the sauce, our eyes collided, No I can't, she said and gave it to the Horn.

Manners shifted on his stool and cleared his throat preparing to speak either about his family or the Party taking over from the British, who at least had a sense of humour, he said, but Chinamen never tell jokes and who dared poke fun at our new leaders. The Horn said he'd heard it all before, dunked three sticks into the sauce, gave one to Manners, told him to eat up and shut up, we were doing fine. If one or six people who couldn't keep their mouths shut got picked up at four in the morning and locked up without charge, it was their choice. The British did the same and we were using the laws they gave us. So long as tourists kept coming and spending money we shouldn't complain.

Manners returned the uneaten satay to the Horn. It wasn't right to tie students to railings, he said, and turn hoses on them when all they wanted was their grievances heard.

Grievances? The Horn shouted. Did we have grievances in school? Whites are out, Chinese are in and nothing else has changed. Get used to it, he said, plunged Manners' satay into the sauce, swallowed and belched.

Oh Hughie, you are so rude, my neighbour said and turned to me. My father says it doesn't matter who governs so long as they don't interfere with business. Chinese are the Jews of the East and money makes the decisions. She tapped my hand. What do you think?

My father used to say respect your rulers whoever they are, never find fault and pray for them once a week.

How wise he was, she said.

As for myself, I said, this is the only place I know. I've lived here all my life and I'd like it to continue being good for my children.

That's so sincere, she said.

When the satay-man started counting the empty sticks, the Horn gave him twenty dollars, told him not to count, he didn't wish to know how many he'd eaten, stood up, belched and farted. Manners said if he'd known he was going to meet the Horn, he'd have stayed home where there were plenty of both. Ella walked away, Flossie wandered off asking herself why she was still with such a *kachra* and Benjy said nothing.

It was nice bumping into you like this, Ella said as we walked away.

Likewise, I said and now she was standing she looked more plump than fat. Fifteen, no twenty pounds she wouldn't miss would make her not bad at all. Pretty too. Please give my regards to your parents, I said, and she put out her hand. I shook it, grabbed Manners, said an all-in-one Goodnight, dropped him home and returned to mine.

I was just in the door when my ma told me that Simon's father had died. It was sudden. He was resting on his couch, sat up, called to his wife, Sarah, and barely had she reached him, collapsed and died in her arms.

Oh God, I said, Simon's not here.

Just returned. His father must have waited for him.

I went right over intending to sit with them but the house was empty. Simon said he'd been home a week but hadn't had time to catch up after seven years away. His mother wished to be alone, the funeral was at 11 but he'd appreciate it if I came earlier.

I was dressed and ready to leave next morning, Sunday, when the phone rang. Penelope. Where are you? Of course I'll fetch you but I'm going to Simon's father's funeral. Will you come? You don't have to wear black. A scarf over your head. I'll fetch you. Ten minutes.

We stood to one side of the large crowd at the Thomsom Road Cemetery, the row behind my father's grave. She wore a dark blue dress and scarf, looking glorious even as tears rolled down her cheeks when Simon went into the grave to perform the last rite.

45

The Coconut Grove was crowded. We sat on the terrace in the shade of a trumpet tree in full bloom. I put my hands in my lap and looked at her in silence.

I told my parents about you, she said across the table. That you're Jewish and we'd been going out for a few months but it was over.

You were just saying that, right? You didn't mean it?

I didn't tell them any more, Adam. My father said how happy he was to see me home, it was a big bonus to be back so soon after Christmas but if that was all I had to tell them I could just as well have written, he'd have understood. My mother was darning his socks and didn't say a word. I thought everything was fine, they didn't think I'd done anything wrong and they trusted me enough to believe me. Her eyes were misting. I practised on the train. It was awful. She swallowed hard. I practised telling lies. I reached across the table and stroked her hands lying beside her cutlery. It was easier than I thought. Next morning, as if I'd come for a holiday, I was helping my mother in the kitchen when I heard my father talking on the veranda. It was Father Rozario.

He's been following you.

No Adam. He'd just returned to Penang.

To check on you.

He was visiting old Noni Farmer three doors away. She'd had a second stroke. He didn't know I was home and that's the truth. My mother went to say hello and I followed. He said how nice it was to see me and when was I returning to Singapore?

The waiter brought our meal, I thanked him and he left.

My mother asked him to stay, tiffin would be ready soon. He said he had a busy afternoon and his bus was due soon. My father accompanied him down the lane. Father Rozario wouldn't have told him anything.

There are ways to say something without saying it, I said.

He wouldn't break his oath. When my father returned he asked me to sit with him on the veranda. Penelope lowered her eyes. She fiddled with her cutlery. A finger went up and down, wiping away the sweat on her glass. Oh Adam, she said, I love my father. He's such a good man. He started talking the way he used to when I was little and sat on his knee. He told me how much he trusted me and knew I'd never do anything to blemish the joy and sanctity of my faith or extinguish the light of God's love. That's how he spoke when he had something special to say. She sipped her drink. He had tears in his eyes. He said there was nothing he wanted more in the world than my happiness. If I wished, I could return to finish my studies, he'd not say another word, but friendships always start innocently.

Who said that?

My father.

Saying every friendship starts innocently, doesn't break an oath.

He said I had to think ahead, she said.

You didn't answer me, Penelope. It was Rozario, wasn't it?

I just want to remember what my father said. He asked if I was sure I wouldn't fall in love, if I'd thought about the consequences, for both of us, you and me. How would your family feel?

What did you say?

It wasn't a question. He wasn't upset and he wasn't angry. More people were involved than just us.

Matthew Robinson must really have been a good man

who loved his daughter and yet, right then, I hated him. I picked up my fork and played with my food. Penelope hadn't touched hers. Even her lemons lay unharmed.

After tiffin my mother asked me to walk with her on the beach. She didn't say much but, when there was nobody in sight, she stopped. There must be something you haven't told us, she said. What are you hiding? She held my arms so tight I thought she'd never let me go. Nothing, I said. Pa believes me, why don't you? Look into my eyes, she said, tell me you are hiding nothing and I too will believe you.

Penelope picked up her lemon juice, trembling as she put it to her lips, put down the empty glass and covered her mouth with her napkin.

There was a long silence.

I lied, she said, her voice a whisper. I answered every question with a lie. Adam, I lied to both my parents. I had lied to my father and then I lied to my mother. I looked at her and told her I didn't love you. I said nothing happened between us, you never touched me and I didn't care if I never saw you again ...

No, Penelope, don't say any more.

I cannot do that again.

You won't have to, I said. Believe me, we'll find a way, I swear to you.

I'm going to finish my course in Penang.

No. Heads turned and I knew I'd shouted. I reached across and held her wrists. You can't do that. Please Penelope.

What else can I do?

Stay. Finish your course here. You need to. You'll never get the same training in Penang. I'll keep away. I swear.

How do I know I can?

I'll make sure you do, I said. Call me and I'll not answer the phone.

I know where you live, she said.

I'll lock the doors. And the windows. I'll tell you to go away. I'll do something. Penelope, please. I'll find a way.

And until you find a way?

Please don't leave me, I said. We'll work it out, I swear.

Before tonight?

Tonight? I must've shouted again. Why tonight?

My train's at ten.

I was still holding her wrists. She turned her hands around to hold mine. She said nothing, just looked at me, her eyes filled with pity, not for me or for herself but for all that had happened. And now, right now, even as I'm stitching in this story of my life, I know what was in her face that I should've seen but didn't, not then. If I'd given her my last letter, every word of which had come from a head that at last accepted there was no other way, she would've stayed. But it wasn't with me. Saying it across a table of cold food wouldn't have been the same. Such moments come when due and never come again.

Will you take me to the station?

I think I nodded. I left enough money on the table and we left.

At the station we stood a while looking at each other. She wiped my damp cheeks then she wiped hers. I stayed on the platform until the last carriage was out of sight, the train not even a speck in the darkness, its rumble dead. She did not look out of the window.

We had met at a dance in a maternity hospital and parted nine months later after a funeral. Have I missed something?

46

Four weeks later Hayoo the Horn was having his over-crowded, over-catered, very noisy, flood-lit engagement party at his parents' home in Bencoolen Street. Flossie, rumours went, had told him to choose between marrying her and the walking ticket he'd get the next time he took her back to her father's house after another night gorging, belching and farting at one or other hawker stall. My money was on a long engagement.

He'd rounded up half the community and anyone passing, annexed the 5-foot way with a barricade of flowerpots, balloons, bunting and loud music, and was drunk, insisting that everyone must be happy and no one can be unless he makes a lot of noise.

There were five help-yourself drums filled with ice and beer, none more than ten steps away. The night was hot, the bodies, the 200-watt bulbs and I was past tipsy. A three-piece band played in the corner of a room piled with furniture along the walls but nobody was dancing. I was outside on the front steps above the crowd in the street with a bottle in my hand when someone tapped my shoulder.

A little bird told me you're a great tango dancer.

Oh hello, Esther, I said, I mean …

Ella.

Ella, right, I said. I hadn't seen her when I arrived. I put down the bottle, took her hand and backed up into the house. I'll show you what my legs can do, I said and asked the band to play a tango, but not *La Cumparsita*.

Why not?

Beyond my ability, I said.

But the rhythm's the same. Isn't it?

Not exactly, I said, when the band played *Tango por Dos*.

My right hand searched around her waist for a place to grip, I held her a few inches away and did fancy steps on the spot trying to get her to follow my footwork and she was doing fine when the Horn appeared.

Aaahhhh, he bellowed, move aside everybody. Make way for the Tango Tornado.

What the hell, I thought as people came to watch, gave it a go and danced as best as my fuzzy head would let me.

You're not bad, I said over the applause three minutes later, considering.

Considering what?

Considering we've never danced together before.

We could make a good team, she said as I walked her away from the floor in case the accordionist started another tango. I was sweating so heavily my brain must have been floating in alcohol. I need some air, I said, walking out ahead of her. She followed me down the stairs and, as we got to the street, I vaguely remember hearing myself say, Lose weight and I'll marry you. For all I know I may have been talking to two women at the same time. She crossed her arms to shield her body from my eyes. I'm sorry, I said, trying to laugh it off, reached out to reassure her but she turned and walked away into the crowd.

That must be the worst thing I've said to anyone in my life and I wasn't sure I wouldn't make it worse apologising with so much company. I looked for the Horn and Flossie and, finding neither, walked home without saying goodbye.

Next morning I remembered everything. Okay, I said to myself, she must've known I was drunk. She'll soon forget. Call her now and you'll stir things up.

Five months later the phone rang at home. Is that you Adam? It's my birthday next week. I'm having a few friends over, will you come?

How old will you be?

Twenty-one.

Twenty-one, I said. How can I say no? At that point I still didn't know who she was and between guessing which 21-year-old's invitation I'd just accepted and trying to get her to tell me without asking, I recognised her voice.

The grass verges on both sides of Cairnhill Road were lined with cars and I couldn't park. I gave my keys and a dollar to one of the syces at the gate and walked up the drive, also crammed with large cars, to a house with a long veranda overflowing with people. This wasn't the *mahallah*. In terms of class, she was well inside the middle while I was only creeping into the outer fringes. Even so this was grander than anything I'd expected. I was halfway up when a slim girl in a three-quarter length, lilac lace dress waved and ran down the steps. Her black hair was short and permed and she gave me a smile just as jolly.

Hello Adam.

Ella?

She laughed. I did what you said, she said.

What did I say?

Lose weight and I'll marry you.

My God. I'm sorry. I was very drunk. I'm not like that, I swear. Will you forgive me?

I forgive you, she said taking my hand. I had to do it and you gave me a reason.

You said a few friends, I said halfway up the stairs. There must be a couple of hundred.

Welcome, her father said at the top. Welcome to our home. He cleared his throat. First time but not last. Now you know we are here, come often, always welcome.

Thank you, Mr Hardoun.

I think you know all of us, he, his single eyebrow and masterful moustache said. Anyone you don't know, tell me and I will introduce, personal. Come, tell me.

Oh wow! his daughter said opening my present, a book called Tango I'd bought on the way there. How lovely. Dad you can introduce Adam later. I can't wait. D'you mind, she said to me, even before I get you a drink?

She handed the book to her father, led me to a large room decorated as if New Year's Eve had come early, changed the LP in the radiogram, as big as our sideboard, turned up the volume and the room throbbed with *Tango por Dos*. The floor emptied, people stood in a circle and her mother said to her father, I was right, no?

One hundred per cent, *Habibiti. Ush'ismah*, he said, turning to his wife to remind him.

Letti, she said.

Letti? Now her name is Letti? Since when?

Since two weeks, she said and smiled like a watermelon wedge.

All eyes were on us. I slipped a knee between hers, held her new body firmly and as we danced I told myself, Remember. She's Letti now.

The party was lavish, birthday cake enormous, food from Raffles Hotel served by an army of crisp waiters. Her mother made sure my plate was always full and to be sure I wasn't a stranger in their home invited me to dinner the following Friday, she would not take no for an answer and kissed me on the cheek.

Nobody left before midnight.

I expected another big affair where I could hide in the crowd with an excuse to leave early. The dining table was stylish, china, crystal and silver, laid for six. I told Mrs Hardoun how nice it was and she said it was a simple Friday dinner like always, nothing special. When prayers were done, we talked and we ate and we talked some more, all directed at me after which Letti took me to her orchid nursery behind the house and told me they were around with the dinosaurs. They'd found orchid pollen on the wings of a bee embedded in amber a hundred million years ago, wasn't that exciting?

Okay, I said to myself, be polite, go along with it and told her I knew nothing about orchids but they always made me turn and look again because, somehow, they looked like insects pretending to be flowers. That was the strangest thing to say, she said as though she didn't agree, then she said maybe I was right and led me by the arm to a spray growing from a coconut husk. That's a ... ... she said, reeling off a long Latin name, and now you mention it, it does look like a scorpion with a long deadly tail.

See, I said, now you'll never see them the same way.

Thanks to you.

Her parents, younger brother and live-in unmarried Auntie Simha had moved to the veranda when we returned and we talked some more with coffee and sweetmeats, home-made from ancient Arab recipes, Auntie Simha told me, like only she knew.

My father and mother, may they rest in peace, were dead five, six years. Letti's father Isaac got straight to the point faster than my father did. I was eight, nine. My brother Harun five years more. Two children between, boy and girl, also died, poor and sick as it was in those days. Like dogs we lived in the street begging and stealing. My policy is: beg yes, steal yes, borrow no, unless you can pay back.

Dad, Letti said, that's not a nice thing to say.

I'm telling the truth, he said. Thanks to God, no begging, no borrowing, no stealing since years. Now let me go on.

What was I saying? Yes, one day my brother and me enter an office to beg or to steal whichever comes first. Do I know? Maybe he's a Basha. All were fat, red fez, stinking cheroot. If not cheroot, *nargila*, you know, or *shisha*, the glass one with hashish on the coal, drinking coffee, black and sweet like the devil's tongue.

My father also smoked a hubbly-bubbly, I said, if a friend brought one over.

Right, he said. Hubbly-bubbly. Never smoked once in my life. There are better things to do than burn money. A map is on the Basha's wall. My brother Harun, always brave, asks what kind of picture has so many red patches? Red like your fez, Effendi, he says. Map of the world, the Basha answers like he's a professor, each colour a country. *Ya'Allah*, my brother says, all belonging to Turkey. What a great nation we are. *Ya'Allah*, you hear? My signal. The Basha starts explaining to my brother. First War I'm talking about. England is slicing pieces of Turkey, putting them in her pocket and I'm also putting what I find that fits in my pockets. What did I steal? What to exchange for food. One day at a time. But what I want to tell you, that day, in the Basha's office, a map on the wall with red patches is the day my life changed. We are sitting, Harun and I, eating bread and onions from what I stole and he is thinking.

This is a long story, his wife said, holding out a bowl of stuffed dates.

I took a couple, not knowing if taking would offend one, not taking offend the other.

Where was I, he asked creasing his long eyebrow at her. Yes. Harun is thinking and before I know it, I'm hiding with him inside a ship, God knows where, so small one only can lie down at a time. On the side, not the back. By turns we sleep. Do we know where the ship is going? Like they say, port luck. One thing my brother knows for sure, the flag is red, white, blue with crosses this way and that way. After two days, hot, when I say hot I mean hot like a desert is hot and all around, iron and we are not talking so nobody hears and we have no more food and no water. But now we feel the ship is moving and we can show ourselves. First they beat us then they drag us to the captain. But God is with us that day. Good man. Took pity. Gave us food, where to sleep and made us work till we reached. Those days there were no passports. From the steamer we looked for the synagogue. Three months more it's forty years. Now you know my story. I'm telling you so you know where all this comes from. Not begging, not stealing, not borrowing. Hard work.

You don't need to tell him, Dad, Letti said. Adam works very hard, don't you?

You don't have to tell me, he said to her. Harun my brother, God bless his memory, used to say, a star sheds light even as it is rising.

That was nice. I was shedding light even as I was rising. Friday dinner, prayers, the head of the house listened to even though he'd told the story a dozen times. A pleasant evening all round and I left with a box of Auntie Simha's sweetmeats for my ma and sister.

47

It wasn't a long courtship. She listened to all I said as if it mattered, laughed at my jokes, took my stories seriously and never once gave me that sidelong glance to put me in my place. There was no curl in her lips to pamper me, no mischief behind her eyes to tease me, no slant in her brows to dare me and never once did she bite my ear. Her maiden aunt told me that from the day I first came to their house Letti had blossomed from a bud into a flower full of morning dew and that her brother-in-law kept saying, Harun, God rest his soul, was right – a star sheds light even as it is rising.

While I was at work, Letti visited our shop once or twice or thrice with gifts for my ma and sister and Auntie Sally. The families met and dined in each other's homes. Drama Ramah embraced her and never missed a chance to tell me how good a catch Letti was.

We went out often and had fun. Our friends were from the community, most of them married and I too would raise a family with nothing to explain to children who might wonder if they were fish or fowl. No doubt, no conflict, no fraying at the edges and in the end, we would prosper simply by doing what we'd always done. And most of all, her father wasted no time. She was twenty-one. In a dwindling community he'd have an unmarriable daughter on his hands. Her party may have been crowded but the men were married, her father's friends and age, or not Jewish. Her dowry included a new house on Katong beach, jewellery and three camphorwood chests with the trousseau her mother had been putting together since her daughter was six. I would receive fifty thousand dollars, no strings attached.

When I told him I didn't need the money his eyebrow rose.

Jews don't like working for others, he said. You're twenty-five, no? Five years I give you. By thirty you will be your own boss. That's when you use the money. Meantime I'll show you how to make money while you sleep.

He was darker skinned and didn't look anything like my father. They would have been much the same age with the same Arabic voices that knew all the answers. Both told stories but his came from the streets and the marketplace about getting out of your rags and never once did he mention the Bible. Don't ask God for anything, he said, get it yourself. God has so many children by the time He finds what you want it's out of fashion. Never be satisfied with what you have, always look for better. A contented man becomes lazy and when everybody is lazy, the world goes to sleep.

The wedding, of course, was to his account and he threw in a honeymoon in Bangkok. If I preferred Hong Kong or Manila, I just had to say so, but not Bali, it was a shithole.

Start to finish, it took less time than a dignified period to mourn a loss, too quick to make a Pro and Con list and I sleepwalked into the next part of my life.

My ma, sister and Auntie Sally had new dresses. Their nails were manicured and hair set for the first time in their lives. My brothers and their wives looked smart. I wore white sharkskin with a massive creamy white orchid from Letti's collection in my buttonhole. Her bouquet, also orchids, was flown in from the Himalayas. I asked Simon to be my best man but he said he didn't own a tie and for once I understood. I asked the Horn and he said, What took you so long?

After I smashed the wine cup under my shoe to a roar of Mazal Tov from the packed synagogue, Ramah, who'd wheedled herself under the canopy as Matron of Honour, kissed me on both cheeks. You've done the right thing, she said. Your father would be proud.

The reception was at the Raffles. My bride was radiant and we danced a stylish *Tango por Dos*, now our song. I had taught her and even with her layered bridal gown we swept and swayed effortlessly. My father-in-law got drunk, we clapped to an Arabic beat and he danced with a bottle balanced on his head. A grand dinner followed at Cairnhill Road but my wife and I left early to board the late flight to Bangkok.

I hooked up her seat belt then mine and picked a couple of confetti from her hair. She seemed a little anxious. I squeezed her hand and asked if she was afraid of flying. She shrugged. Our courtship wasn't only short it was without discovery. Letti was pretty and bright but she didn't smoulder below the surface for me to stoke a blaze. When I attempted a little exploration, she reminded me we weren't married. But now? Was she afraid? Are Jewish virgins extra virgins? Had her mother told her nothing?

I was full of praise for her family. A grand wedding, I said, and now this luxurious air-conditioned Dusit Thani Hotel with a baby elephant to greet us at one in the morning. I made silly jokes and did everything I could to get her to smile. In the lift I again asked what was wrong and again she shrugged.

In our suite I saw what looked like terror, nothing I would have imagined from a bride on her wedding night. I took her in my arms. She stiffened. I told her not to worry. If it was too soon and she wasn't ready, she could choose her own time. She said it was alright, it may as well be now and went into the bathroom.

Then I had a strange thought. I had presumed her virginity. Maybe she wasn't. Jewish men expect their wives to be virgins on their wedding night. I suppose I did too. What if she were damaged goods and didn't want to be found out? Oh God. She was away a long time and I must have fallen asleep because I was aware of her only when she slipped into bed under the sheets. The lights were off. I moved toward her. She was naked. She'd said it may as well be now so I primed my pumps. She lay like a fallen statue. I whispered softly that God had designed us such that I had to lie between her legs. She went rigid.

I didn't sleep much that night.

Next day, at breakfast in our bridal suite, bright and breezy as I could, I moved the bowl of orchids aside, took her hand across the table and said she shouldn't be upset. It had all been too much, she wasn't ready, we hadn't had enough time to get to know each other. I blamed myself. I'd been thoughtless, please forgive me. Her pale smile said she'd heard the words but didn't tell me what they meant to her.

What else could I do? I'd married her, hadn't I? Our romance, if that is what it was, had been pleasant and polite, painstaking too, but too damp to take light. Now she bore my name I reckoned I should be kind.

We got through the day touring temples and silk markets and that night, in our room, it occurred to me that though we'd touched each other the night before, I by intention she by accident, it was in the dark. As if to break the ice I asked her to let me see her body, tempted to add, you let me see yours and I'll let you see mine. What the hell, this wasn't how it happened on a cement floor in an unfinished house.

No, she said, not yet.

Well, I said already down to my underwear but not aroused, would you like to look at me, you might not be so afraid. For all I knew she'd never seen a male body above the age of six, certainly not on parade.

I'm not afraid, she said.

What is it then? Is there something I can do to help you?

It was slow and painful. Her answers, if she gave them, took so long I thought she hadn't heard and repeated myself.

I'm not deaf, she said.

In that case, I said, I may as well get some sleep.

I showered with the door open then she did so with the door locked. I was in bed in pyjamas when she came out in a long nightgown. The lights were on.

How do I know you're all right? She wasn't looking at me.

What do you mean, all right? Didn't you feel how all right I am?

That's not what I mean, she said. I'm sure you're all right in that department. Haven't you been playing havoc all this while with what's-her-name?

Is that what's bothering you? I sat up and didn't wait for the answer I wouldn't get. You knew about her. It was no secret. Why did you marry me?

Going out is one thing, doing disgusting things before marriage is another.

Okay, I said. One more time. Why did you marry me?

I only found out after all the arrangements were made. I'd upset my parents and end up like Auntie Simha. People will say jilting runs in the family.

Auntie Simha was jilted because he didn't turn up. I did. I'd have been the jilted party.

Same thing.

Anything I said would have sounded hollow. So I thought I'd explain to her the facts of life as I saw them. It's not doing disgusting things, I said. Did your mother not tell you? It's called making love. Love, love, love. The way God intended. He explained it to Adam who told it to Seth who taught it to Enoch.

I don't need a Bible lesson.

It's not a Bible lesson. I'm telling you what it's called: LOVE, L ... O ... V ... E.

Call it what you wish.

Making love, I said again, louder. It was okay. The suite was large with many walls. Making love. Something you could learn to your benefit. I was digging myself in deep. Everything I said sounded more and more like rejoicing over a past love when all I was trying to say was that she and I could benefit from a little intimacy.

Not till I'm sure.

For God's sake, I said. Sure of what?

That you're all right.

Please, I said, please tell me what you mean by all right?

That you're not sick. Not diseased.

I could have said a million things. You don't get diseased making love with an angel. In heaven all things are perfect. Body and soul suffer no corruption. I said, Oh.

A friend saw you, she said. At a VD Clinic. The one in Short Street.

V ... D ... Clinic ... in ... Short ... Street. I strung out the words trying to make sense of it. My God! That was years ago, I said. Bad cough, high fever. Or with my father. Nothing venereal. We were poor. Doctor Cheow gave us free medicine. Who the hell is this mischief maker? She didn't answer. You don't believe me, do you? You've put two and two together and come up with twenty-two. Tell me who this friend is and we'll settle it when we're back.

I had a second shower to cool down, went to sleep and stayed on my side of the bed. I could've given her father back his money, told him it was intact as was his daughter then told the rabbi the marriage had not been consummated and had it annulled. Instead I saw the doctor she chose. She read his certificate in silence, folded, and returned it to me.

I spent the next two weeks ignoring the body lying a little more exposed beside me until my flesh overcame my spirit. What the hell, even mosquitoes can't keep off each other. But the gates of heaven did not open and I visited her side of the bed only when the trickle became a stream and reminded me of my marital rights.

Okay. The stories I've been stitching together are beginning to tell me what went wrong but not why. I'll try a couple more to see if she meant half of what she said or was she covering up something or showing me her real self, now she had me?

This isn't pleasant. I shouldn't have started.

48

After two years and a lot of effort, mine, we became chummy but were childless and both families were asking questions. Drama Ramah called to say she needed to see me soonest humanly possible, could she come to my office for a tête-à-tête?

It isn't nice to talk about these things to a man in front of his wife, she said leaning confidentially across my desk half an hour into what turned out to be a monologue.

Have you spoken about this to Letti?

Didn't she tell you? I shook my head. In that case don't tell her I came. Let it be our little secret. In the first place it isn't my business. I'm only trying to help.

I was half-amused, half-baffled, wholly unprepared. As far as she could see, Letti had good child-bearing hips and should be fine, why didn't I have a check-up, if I knew what she meant, to find out if I was good for a woman, like my brothers. I could take her word for it that she and Yona really had to take care, if I knew what she meant. My brothers only needed to sneeze and they'd be pregnant twice a year. Five between them and one on the way, God bless them all. I told her I came from the same good stock and she said, with a faint smile, even a good batch can have a faulty product, if I knew what she meant. There was no shame, heavyweight wrestlers could be like that.

I thanked her for taking the time and making the effort to come all the way into town to tell me. It showed how much she cared. She brushed aside my thanks, then, as her hand came to rest against her heart, she added we were family and what are family for if not to help each other? I offered to take her to lunch but she had to rush home to her children.

That was the second time I needed a doctor's certificate. For good measure, and so the blame didn't shift to her, Letti got one too. Praise the Lord, we were both able to go forth and multiply. I put it down to my arriving at her station after her train had left.

I'll leave out stories of the next few years not to rub it in except to say, like it or not, I used my father's donkey driver's quota which is all a man needs to scratch his itch. As Venus went into the backseat Pluto took the wheel. The money Isaac Hardoun gave me to marry his daughter went into the Stock Market. He was either a wizard or knew an insider. I'd get a call before trading began. His brother Harun, God bless his memory, had spoken to him in a dream. I bought long or sold short and was soon floating in liquid assets. All the while Letti was talking to her orchids.

So. What does a fellow do when his doctor certifies he's fine and he knows something is wrong? He goes to see Rashidah. She was large and Lebanese, spoke Arabic, Malay and half a dozen English words, and read coffee cups. Marriage, birth, health, wealth including illness and death, God forbid, but only if you asked and no one did.

What the hell. People swore by her. She might give me a peep into the future, hoping more than believing, she'd tell me something beyond What the Stars Foretell which I read every day knowing full well what they told me applied to anyone, any age, any star sign, anywhere in the world.

You came alone, she said in better-class Arabic than I learned from my father. Your wife is looking for orchids?

A coffee cup told you that?

Have I seen yours? Jewish women come to me and talk, no?

What else do you know?

We will see, she said and blessed me. Come, while the feeling is strong. Are you ready? I nodded. This is your first time so I must explain. Your cup will show everything, good and bad. So tell me what you want to hear. Only good?

Everything.

Next thing I must tell you. What I do is not allowed. I am not *kaafir*. I respect my religion. But if God gave me this it must be for a reason. She raised her palms and looked towards the open window as my father did whenever he thanked God for His little mercies. So I do not charge. If you are happy, give what you want. Go in peace also if you give me nothing. Okay?

I smiled.

She got up, pulled her skirt out of her rear cleavage, waddled off and returned with a smell of strong coffee. Drink, she said, and leave a little. No sugar. Sweet coffee makes different pictures. It was very bitter. More, she said, until your lips feel powder.

She covered the cup with the saucer, flipped it, circled a palm three times over it, said a prayer and let it stand while telling me about clients in high places. When the coffee had done its work, she looked into the cup and said her six English words, No worry, all fine, good luck. A cup like yours, she said in Arabic, I've never seen. Be careful. Evil eyes everywhere. God protect you.

Show me.

There, there, there, she pointed, and here. Everyone wants to eat you. But God is watching. Then she rocked her head and opened her eyes like a pearly oyster, Adam, Adam, Adam, she said and paused. It was a very long pause.

What's the problem?

Problem? Why problem? No problem. You have your own business? I shook my head. See this? Cloudy. Your past. Her hand pushed it out through the open window. Now you are here. Empty. An opening. Your way is clear. Luck is sitting outside your door. Don't let it wait. In the morning open your door, put the luck in your bag, take it to your office and make it work for you.

To do what?

To say goodbye. I told you, a cup like yours I have never seen.

Rashidah, I said, how can you see all this in a tiny cup?

Don't ask. Only hear what I say. If you don't do what I tell you, don't come and tell me afterwards. If you do it, come and give me what your heart tells you.

Okay. But that's not why I came. What else do you see?

What do you want me to tell you?

Children.

One. The one you have.

I don't have a child.

Then it's coming, she said pointing at a smudge.

Boy or girl?

I must look for a *shindool* in coffee powder? I see one. Boy or girl is up to God.

When?

Look at me, she said, her eyes bright with mischief. I read coffee cups. You've been married years, no? I nodded. If you don't know how to make babies, take lessons.

Fine, I said. When I have a child, I will give you anything you want.

Ticket to Beirut, she said even before I finished. Go and return. God will give you a child and I will see my family after twenty years. What else you want to know?

Tell me.

She twirled the cup. Health? No worry. Wealth? From heaven. Home? Fine. Friends? Don't ask how many. You will live … she paused, it's okay, good health all the days of your life.

I patted her hand. Rashidah, we agreed. Everything, good and bad.

Her lusty Arabian eyes had a stare so disarming I had to believe she was telling the whole truth. Good health all the days of your life, she repeated and wiped the cup clean. How many people are so lucky? I gave her a large note. Too much, she said.

It's a down payment. I'll be back with more when the time comes.

I returned home chirpy and eager to see my wife. I told her nothing of my visit but believing she'd give me the child I longed for made me affectionate.

Letti, I said, let's go away.

AGM, she said. In two weeks, don't you know?

After that.

Buying season. Sabah, Sarawak, Brunei.

Okay, I said, let's holiday in Sabah and/or Sarawak and/or Brunei. I'll go with you or meet you anywhere on the route. Your choice.

I'm looking for new hybrids and need to be alone.

You can't be doing that all day and all night, I said.

Of course I didn't go. But such matters don't need a holiday. Until she left for Sabah, Sarawak and Brunei, I doubled my quota and again when she returned a month later.

By now the British had packed their privilege, politics and Union Jacks and gone. We were trading with the world and a little boom was on its way. In short, there was more money around for people like me to count and, if I wanted a slice, I had to work on the other part of my coffee cup. I didn't make a Pro-and-Con list because there were no Cons. I went to see old man Siow at his home the following Sunday.

I'm surprised you didn't come sooner, he said.

I feel my time has come.

Well, what shall I say? None of my children wanted to join me and take over.

These days you can't tell them what to do, I said as if I knew. Why don't you sell me the company? I'm sure we can reach an agreement. A percentage of turnover for the next ten years, shall we say? Rashidah's assurance made me bold.

What will happen if one of my grandchildren decides to join later?

There will always be a place. It's fine with me. We'll put it into the agreement.

Agreements are made between parties that don't trust each other, he said looking at me over his half-moons. They start searching for loopholes before the ink is dry. If both intend to keep their word why do they need an agreement? A handshake will do. Not even that. Chinese *hsin* will do. Deeds match words. But three of my grandchildren are Siows. Will you not change the company name? I did not answer. So I must carry on until one of them decides. Keeping family name alive is important to us Chinese.

I wanted to say, Jews too, but I could see he wanted to talk, which we did for a couple of hours. When I got up to leave, I said, Let's do the *hsin* thing and not shake hands.

He laughed. We've become used to western ways, he said taking my hand in both his.

In six weeks, with his blessing and in accordance with our unwritten agreement, he helped me set up, find offices and advised my office team and all his clients in my portfolio to go with me. Eighteen years before, Roger's father introduced me to his friend Bernard Siow and now he was making me my own boss. They were from the school where worth was not measured in money. My many younger Chinese friends measured it in dollars, simple and accurate, and so I didn't have to be Chinese. Earning more in a year than my father did in his whole life may not have got him saying, *Shabash*, 10 upon 10, but it gave me another card:

J Adam Messiah
Public Accountants and Auditors,
32 Battery Rd   Singapore
Tele: 982312-4

Then my wife declared the house her father gave her was too far from friends and too small for orchids. She'd seen a round house in a magazine and that was what she wanted.

Why a round house?

It's perfectly balanced, don't you know? Basic feng shui, she said as if I was the only person in the world who didn't know. I bought a book.

Angles and sharp corners interrupt the stream of positive energy. Curves and circles promote good feeling. A round house eliminates friction in relationships, maximises the flow of the life force and improves vigour and good fortune which must make Eskimos the happiest people on earth. There was more. Feng Shui was a potent tool for conception. My head had to point northwest. A square house, the book said, could mean placing the bed in an awkward position. Or, I thought, moving it just before and spoiling the surprise. All I had to do in a round house with a round bed was find northwest once with a compass, mark it with a dot on the wall, and she'd never know what I was up to.

What the hell, I said, give it a go. I bought an old house in a half acre, pulled it down and built a large round one. We sat on round chairs around a round dining table, the sofa and easy chairs were round, she had round rugs specially woven in Kashmir, I made sure my head pointed northwest once a week on our round bed and my friends got tired of the joke about my life going in circles.

Her friend, the president of the Singapore Orchid Society designed what she liked to call My Orchidarium, also round. It was so large her plants only half filled it giving her the reason for another Southeast Asian tour this time to breed a hybrid for herself. The petals of an orchid, like a five-pointed star, were too much to ignore so she became Astrid and while she was at it, returned to her maiden name with a twist. The new hybrid would be called – *Vanda Miss Astrid Ardent*. I wasn't looking for an argument and didn't tell her that Astrid has nothing to do with stars.

There was no new hybrid. Despite her doctor's certificate I don't think she could breed anything. Round house, feng shui, head pointing northwest did nothing and it wasn't me. My doctor said I could repopulate the earth single-handed. My brothers and I could fill the world with Messiahs which brings me to the last story to stitch before I go crazy wondering why I'm trying to find out what I did I shouldn't have done or didn't do I should've done, which is to say that by now she was an orchid expert and started researching a book she wanted to write. It gave her the excuse, if she needed one, to take off on another orchid trip then another and another. Each time she returned she was best friends with me and I came to look upon those times as God-sent even although I'd given up facing northwest.

She called the book **For the Love of Orchids** and when I saw the first proofs and the stunning photographs I told her to print a limited coffee-table edition, 1000 numbered copies, sign every one, sell them at $500 each and give the proceeds to charity. She threw a party in our round house, invited her orchid friends and I, my clients with money. I knew everyone and was mixing happily when a young Chinese woman arrived, unescorted and, apparently, no stranger to many guests. She was lovely, tall, slender, well put together and nicely turned out. I was intrigued.

Astrid, I said to my wife, aren't you going to introduce me to this lovely lady?

She's Adele, my wife said and went off to greet others.

Hello, Adele, I said, are you an orchid person too?

Sort of, she said.

What sort of sort of?

I'm a trader.

Why haven't we met before? I think I know all my wife's orchid friends.

Orchids are a big world, she said. You can't meet everybody.

Oh, I thought it was small and closely knit. Experts and enthusiasts. I must be wrong. Where do you buy your orchids?

All over the world.

You have agents then, searching rain forests, I said. Like the shamelessly beautiful ones Astrid photographed. You'll see them in her book. The very best, I think, came from a trip to Sabah and Sarawak.

I know, Adele said, I was with her.

Oh, I said, just as the society president clapped his hands and called for silence.

The finest book you'll ever see about orchids is now on sale here and nowhere else, he said. There are no discounts for multi-purchases so please form an orderly queue. And, oh yes, he added, everyone will be happy to know that the manuscript and photographs, all original and bound in finest hand-crafted leather from the *wayang kulit* masters of Surakarta, will be put up for auction later in the evening.

I looked for Adele but she was gone.

Every copy sold that night and the manuscript went for $5000. I told my wife she could be proud. It was a fine work of art. She kissed me on the lips, which was nice.

49

The last story can't be about selling books so I'll skip the in-between about how my father-in-law was calling me twice a day. His dead brother Harun, God bless his memory, whose territory now also covered Australia, Hong Kong and Thailand, had so much to say I had to leave my accountancy business to my partners just to keep up with Pluto. Venus, by the way, had taken her leave.

When I got home one evening I found a Chinese Chow asleep on our bed.

Leticia, my wife said, get down. Leticia? A dog called Leticia? One of her discarded names? I looked at her for an explanation and she said, Don't you think she's beautiful?

Okay, a lot more was said before I got to the point of asking, Why female? They breed. They are more loving and give without expecting in return, she said.

Not so, I said. Males are more affectionate, saying it as if I really knew, going on about females coming for attention when they need it and moving off when they've had enough at which point she stopped stroking the dog and glared at me. No, I said, I'm not talking about people. Just dogs. And bitches. A female dog isn't called a bitch for nothing.

That was a mistake.

Then Leticia got pregnant without Astrid's permission. The neighbour's poodle was prime suspect. It was a mongrel and Leticia, the Chinese Chow, produced a litter of the ugliest pups ever seen. Astrid got rid of them and, to prevent another impregnation when she wasn't looking, bandaged Leticia's hindquarters when she came into season.

That won't keep off randy dogs, I said. Get her fixed like you should've done to yourself then we'd both know why.

That was another mistake.

I reached out to take her in my arms and say I was sorry but she stepped away.

That's not what I did, she said.

What do you mean?

Nothing.

Not nothing, I said, what did you mean? She didn't reply. If that's not what you did, what did you do? She looked away. You did, didn't you? She started for the door. When?

She spun round.

I never wanted children. It's fine for you. You have the pleasure without the pain.

You never told me.

You never asked.

Why would I? All women want children. I took it you did too.

Like everything you do. What makes you think I would have your children?

My God, oh my God, I howled and bolted from the room.

A couple of days later she was photographing in the orchidarium for her Society magazine. I gently took away her camera and placed it on the shiny white round cast-iron table with matching round chairs, took her by the hand and sat her down.

If you'd asked I'd have told you, she said, but you assumed I wanted what you wanted.

Before we were married, you mean?

That would have been a good time.

But I thought …

Sure you did. All men do. They think all a woman wants is children. I don't. Do you know what it does to the body?

My mother had them all. Hysterectomy, prolapse of this, that, the other and almost died giving birth to my brother, in and out of hospital for a year.

Doesn't mean it will happen to you, I said.

Even as we were talking and I thought I had her attention, her eyes were roving from orchid spray to orchid spray. She got up, moved two pots, gave the one behind a half turn so the flowers stuck their long mottled tongues out at me, picked up her camera, focused, clicked, replaced the pots and moved two more onto the table at my elbow.

To write any more means reliving it. I'll say only that as she was moving pots I saw in her everything I hated but also something I had to admire. She was her father's daughter. She needed nobody. I was made in my father's image. Without people I am nothing.

Don't you want something to love, I said.

Everything I love and want from life is right here.

I am here too, I said. Do you love me? Her camera clicked. She changed angle and clicked again. I can't be an orchid, I muttered and left.

Years before she'd blamed Penelope. Two days earlier it was me. She could've been lying both times. How she did it was easy. Our population had to be controlled before people fell off the island. Posters everywhere said: **Two Is Enough**. The mackintoshes Penelope brought with her that last time came courtesy of this campaign after which sterilisation also came with compliments. She needed my permission but Astrid, or whoever she was then, knew her way around and had the money to do it without.

When was also easy. I was often away on business and she was hunting orchids. Her surgeon must've been a magician and if I was inconvenient she knew how to say no. I wasn't going to dig in the dirt so I let it go. Then, out of the blue, I saw Rashidah pointing at a smudge in the coffee cup. Oh God! She'd also had an abortion.

I couldn't prove anything, nor cite orchids as co-respondent. Then, as if in passing, she told me she'd bought into Adele's WORLD ORCHID TRADERS PTE LTD. To combine our expertise, she said. Two heads are better than one, aren't they? We'll expand and from now on I'll escort her wherever there are orchids.

This was not something to make a Pro and Con list about so I bundled together everything she did not tell me and blocked them from my mind.

50

In a full page with pictures, **The Straits Times** reported Simon's appointment as Professor of Philosophy and Ethics at The University of Singapore.

Tell him the messiah has arrived, I said to his secretary.

He came out to greet me even before she put down her phone, took me by the arm and led me into his office as crammed with books as his old bedroom used to be. His desk was heaped and when I rolled out the visitor's chair it too was piled with books.

You should build shelves across the window like you did at home, I said.

He reached for his pad and scribbled: shelves v sunlight [?]

I congratulated him on his appointment, talked about my lessons with him during the war, the school he ran in camp and congratulated him again. I couldn't congratulate him a third time nor could I hold back something eating me up inside out because I hadn't told anyone. I said I had no proof only speculation and doctors' certificates.

Fearful concatenation of circumstances, he said.

What does that mean?

An old American legal case expanded the boundaries of guilt by circumstance. A thought in flight, he said. Ignore it. He looked at me then at his hands, turned them over a couple of times as if examining his nails then looked at me again. Cognitive dissonance.

I looked hard at him.

Simultaneously holding two contradictory beliefs. To reconcile the differences you resort to a change in behaviour to preserve the stability of your world, he said, rooted around his desk and pulled out a book.

No, I said. Not another tombstone book. Just tell me, slowly and simply.

Our brain, allowing us to think beyond experience, permits contradictions. But the cognitive process, preferring logic, tries to reduce disparity. It modifies or ultimately rejects one belief in an attempt to maintain the other.

For example.

A cult leader tells his followers a cosmic collision is about to end the world. They must prepare to enter the afterlife with grace. When they cannot find evidence of an approaching body large enough to destroy the earth, he says God spoke only to him. All assemble but the appointed time passes without cataclysm. He says the message was flawed. The manner was wrong but the time of death, correct. All commit suicide.

I looked at him again without a word.

Rationalising a bad choice, he said.

I see that. But what has it to do with me?

I leave that to you.

Come on, Simon.

Your father would have told you the creation myth but I don't suppose he mentioned the other woman in Adam's life, Lilith. Lilit in Hebrew. She appears once in the Bible. Isaiah refers to her as a screech owl in a passage predicting God's day of vengeance when all is turned to desolation. She appears in paint and sculpture and has different names in Akkadian, Sumerian, Mesopotamian, Greek and Roman texts.

You're not making this up?

As a baby you would have worn an amulet to keep her and her retinue away until you were circumcised and made your pact with God. There must have been one in your home.

My ma pinned it on me if I sneezed. I don't know what

she did when more than one of us was sick at the same time. We weren't pinned together.

There is also a tradition among western Jews to leave a boy's hair uncut until he is three or four to divert Lilith's attention. Not unlike Chinese who pierce boys' ears with rings to confuse the devil. He pulled the Chumash off a shelf. How's your Hebrew?

I read it.

I'll read the translation. Genesis I, 27: *in the image of God created He male and female*. Then II, 7: *the Lord formed man in the dust of the ground*, but it is not until II, 21 that God puts Adam to sleep and forms woman from his rib. This time the woman is named – Hawa, mother of all living. We call her Eve.

Are you saying God created them twice?

Which gave the rabbis a problem.

Okay Simon you've got my attention. Who the hell is Lilith if she's not in the Bible?

Genesis Rabba, he said, the expanded Genesis, a learned interpretation without the authority of revelation. He must've had a map in his head which took him to the right shelf for the book and an index, also in his head, which found the passage and, not a minute later, he read, *After God created Adam and saw him alone, He created a woman for him, from the earth and called her Lilit. Adam and Lilit immediately began to quarrel. She said, I will not lie below you, and he said, I will not lie beneath you, but only on top.*

Missionary position, I said.

It gets better, he said without looking up. *Then Adam said, For you are fit only to be in the bottom position, while I am to be the superior one*, to which Lilit responded, *We were both created from the earth, so we are equal*. Adam would have none of it and when Lilit saw she was getting nowhere, she flew away. He closed the book. When Eve becomes Adam's wife, Simon said, Lilit, insanely jealous, turns herself into a serpent, tempts Eve with a fruit from the Tree of Knowledge and brings about the downfall of mankind. Being created together, Lilit would have known the tree was anathema. She is demonised. A woman who will not have children from a man. Would you like to read Genesis Rabba?

I've heard enough.

There was a knock on the door and his secretary poked her head in.

Simon, she said, is there anything you need before I leave?

My God, I said, it's five. I've been here two hours. Time to leave.

Don't unless you have to, Simon said to me as he waved goodnight to his secretary. There's nothing worse than marking papers and assigning a grade you wish the student deserved but can't fail him just because he hasn't understood.

So, I said, that makes Lilith the first woman to demand equal rights.

Which rabbis would have found too radical. In Hebrew *ba'al* means husband, owner and master. *Isha* is woman and wife. The language supports the relegation. But no. I think Lilit and Hawa are the rebellious and congenial sides of woman. Strange though, don't you think, that women sit in the floor above men in synagogue?

The lies our fathers told us, I murmured, more than said.

Lies only if they were intentional. Our fathers believed what they told us. We can choose not to.

Is that what I did wrong?

Cognitive dissonance, he said with a smile.

Fortunately my wife, whatever her Akkadian, Sumerian, Mesopotamian, Greek, Roman or Persian name was at the time, was not at home or in her orchid sanctuary. I showered, went to bed and when she returned much later, pretended to be asleep.

Next morning I told my secretary to cancel my appointments and not to put callers through. I reached into the back of my drawer and pulled out the sandalwood box where I kept Penelope's yellow sash, the one she wore the day we went to Malacca. Bernard Siow had a family photograph on his desk, I would have this. I took up my leaky Waterman pen, the one my father gave me for getting full marks in an exam which I did only once, filled it with ink and started to write:

My mother, God bless her, conceived me on a Saturday in September 1933, at night.

Penelope Robinson
Lorong Pasir
Penang.

20 March 1982

Dear Professor Sefardi

Adam came to our home. I was at work and did not return until the next morning. He gave a parcel to my mother. It was a manuscript. He mentions you in it which is why I am writing to you at the University. She is old and doesn't hear well. She remembered only a little of what he said. A storm is coming and I have to go. I'll be back in a few days. Please ask your daughter to forgive me. Then he left. It is a pity. If he had stayed a little longer he would have met his son. His name is Seth. He looks like his father. My father suggested the name. They were good friends.

Two days before Adam came the manager of my bank wrote to me. A new account had been opened in my name. The deposit was very large. He wanted to know what I knew about it. Seth said we should look for his father. We were trying to find him when I read it in the newspapers. There was a lot about him and the inquest and how the Piper crashed into a hill in the storm. I don't know what to do. If you can advise me I will come to Singapore. Maybe Seth too to meet his father's family.

Yours very sincerely
Penelope Robinson.

Moshe Elias was born and lived half his life within the Jewish community of Singapore; he spent the other half in India, Scotland, England and Israel. After many years designing ships, teaching English, building kitchens and working as sous chef, he settled down to write fiction. As a wandering Jew he found much happiness wherever he lived and presently resides contentedly in the UK.

The Messiahs of Princep Street is his first novel.

PRINTED AND BOUND BY:

Copytech (UK) Limited trading as Printondemand-worldwide,
9 Culley Court, Bakewell Road, Orton Southgate. Peterborough,
PE2 6XD, United Kingdom.